The Forest
~ a tale of old magic ~

By
Julia Blake

Copyright © Julia Blake 2018
All rights reserved

This is a work of fiction. All characters and events in this publication, other than those in the public domain, are either a product of the author's imagination or are used in a fictitious manner. Any resemblance to actual persons, living or dead, or actual events is purely coincidental.

No part of this publication may be reproduced, distributed or transmitted in any form or by any means, without the written permission of the author, except in the case of brief quotations embodied in critical reviews and certain other non-commercial uses permitted by copyright law. For permission requests contact the author.

www.juliablakeauthor.co.uk

ISBN 9781726727938

Suffolk Libraries	
DON	02/19

~ *Dedication* ~

To Mandy, Ruth and Becky
who never stopped believing in
The Forest
Thank you for persuading me
to carry on believing

To Danielle
Thank you for your excitement and
absolute conviction that this
book simply had to be published

~ *Acknowledgements* ~

As Winnifred Blunt and the other matriarchs of Wykenwode often remark "it takes a village to raise a child". Well, in this case it certainly took a team to publish a book, and credit must go to so many people.

Firstly, a massive thank you to my editor, Danielle Vinson. Who tirelessly worked to make this book the best it could possibly be, who checked and double checked every comma, semi colon and hyphen. You are a star. Without you, The Forest wouldn't be half the book it is.

Then there is my trio of diligent and eagle-eyed beta readers K.M. Allan, Amelia Oz and Ruth Miranda. Thank you my lovelies, for picking through all my words, finding the bad ones and letting me know of any other bits that weren't quite right. All three are amazingly talented authors and bloggers in their own right and you can find them at:

Instagram.com/k.m.allan_writer
Instagram.com/oz.amelia
amazon.com/author/ruthmiranda

A huge thank you to Jessica Tahbonemah of The Magic Quill Graphics for taking my vague ideas and producing the simply stunning cover and interior illustrations. They exceeded even my wildest expectations, and if you'd like to contact her, then her email address is jesstahoz@gmail.com

Kieran Elson kindly took the author photo and if you wish to check out his amazing portfolio, go to his website www.kieranelson.com

Thank you to my wonderful street team – Michelle, Nikki and Sharman, who kindly gave up their time to go through the manuscript and give me their valuable insights and feedback.

And last, but by no means least, thank you to the author James Fahy, who so graciously agreed to "take a look" at my manuscript, and liked it so much he gave me a wonderful endorsement for the cover.

~ A Note for the Reader ~

The Forest is a very strange and in my opinion anyway, wonderful book. Based on my love of old folklore, legends and myths, especially those of Britain and Europe, elements of this fascination thread all the way through this tale of old magic. And I have drawn heavily on the legend of The Green Man, an enigmatic and iconic image that has intrigued me since childhood.

In this book I ask you to suspend belief and follow me into The Forest. Within its shady glades and shadowy heart, watch as fantastical events unfold and you are shown a tale of old magic, rich in folklore and legend.

I really hope you enjoy this book, and if you wish to contact me then please find me on Facebook - Julia Blake Author. Where I would be happy to hear from you.

You can also follow me on Instagram @juliablakeauthor and read my blogs and various book reviews on Goodreads.

Check out trailers for my books on my YouTube Channel - Julia Blake Author.

Finally, there's my website for information about me, as well as background on all my books and free tasters.

www.juliablakeauthor.co.uk

All the best ~ Julia Blake

~ *Other Books by the Same Author* ~

The Book of Eve
a tale of secrets, betrayal and love

Lifesong
our world seen through the eyes of an alien

Becoming Lili
an ugly duckling, coming of age story,
set in 90's Britain

Eclairs for Tea and other stories
a collection of short stories and quirky poems,
including the critically acclaimed, Lifesong

Lost & Found
book one in the Blackwood family saga, a punchy,
fast paced, romantic suspense

Fixtures & Fittings
book two in the Blackwood family saga

Erinsmore
a wonderful fantasy of magic, myth,
swords and dragons

~ *Table of Contents* ~

Copyright
Dedication
Acknowledgements
A Note for the Reader
Other Books by the Same Author
The Legend of the Green Man
The Tale of Mad Meg
The Wyckenwode Chant

Part One
Chapter 1 ~ The People of the Village   1
Chapter 2 ~ The Forester's Son   17
Chapter 3 ~ The Farmer's Daughter   43
Chapter 4 ~ The Blacksmith's Boy   59

Part Two
Chapter 5 ~ The Tale of Two Sisters   76
Chapter 6 ~ The Tale of Black Bridget   97
Chapter 7 ~ The Tale of the Faithless Wife   112
Chapter 8 ~ The Tale of the Changeling Child   133

Part Three
Chapter 9 ~ Sunrise   150
Chapter 10 ~ Midday   161
Chapter 11 ~ Sunset   173
Chapter 12 ~ Evening   190
Chapter 13 ~ Midnight   208
Chapter 14 ~ In the Dead of the Night   220

Part Four
Chapter 15 ~ Family   240
Chapter 16 ~ Pages of the Past   255
Chapter 17 ~ Innocent Blood   274
Chapter 18 ~ Curses and Consequences   293

Part Five
Chapter 19 ~ Sally's Tale   312
Chapter 20 ~ Completions and Connections   329

About the Author   343
A Note from Julia Blake   344

~ The Legend of the Green Man ~

The myth of the Green Man is believed to have its origins thousands of years ago, with earliest images predating Christianity quite considerably. Supposedly a pagan symbol of growth and rebirth, the seasonal cycle of nature and the life of man, this last stemming from ancient belief man is born from nature and is at one with its pace and rhythms. Primarily a British and French myth and closely linked to Celtic society, with the coming of the Roman Empire it spread as far as India and possibly beyond.

Usually depicted as an older man's face emerging from a background of forest trappings, entwined with leaves, vines and roots, he appears to be literally born from nature. However, slight variations do occur depending on where in the ancient world these symbols appear, and the nature of the belief system in place at the time of its creation. Whatever his origins and the intent behind the myth, The Green Man is widely regarded as being symbolic of man's oneness with the natural world, and, as such, makes a fitting guardian for The Forest of my imagination.

Julia Blake

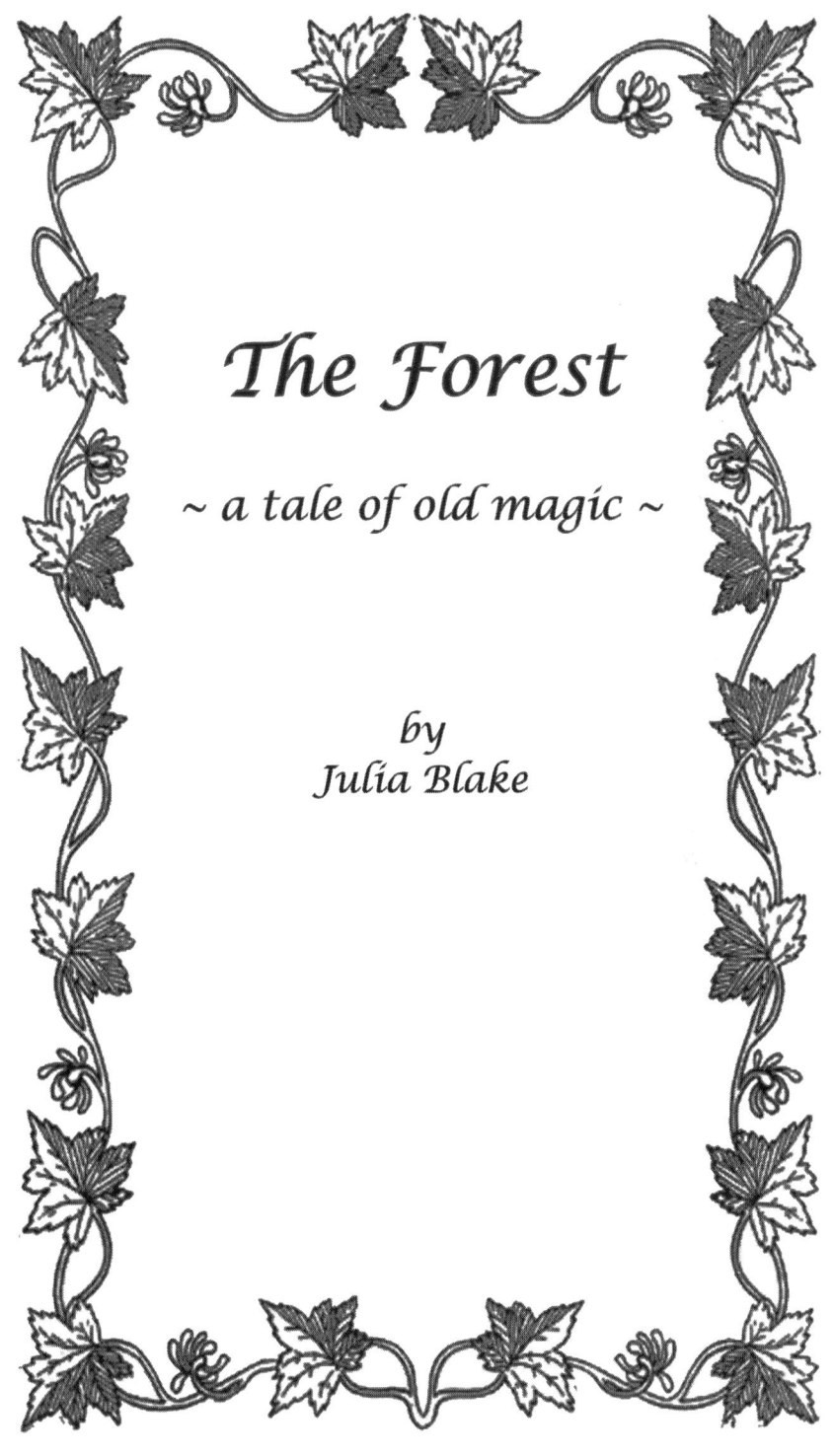

The Forest

~ a tale of old magic ~

by
Julia Blake

~ The Tale of Mad Meg ~

Everyone knew young Margaret Forrester wasn't right in the head. Pixie-mazed, they'd mutter, casting thinly suspicious glances whenever she passed by, although she mostly avoided the village, her days spent roaming the Forest, aye, and nights too. Drove her poor mother to distraction it did.

In vain, she'd take young Margaret with her to the village well where the other women congregated to do their weekly wash, her smile fixed as she chatted, putting on a brave front of respectability, of normality, when all the time...

When all the time the lass would sit there, corn silk hair escaping from whatever arrangement her mother had forced it into, skirts riding up slim, bare legs tanned from the sun, bearing the scars of many an excursion into some briar patch or other, dreamy grey eyes unfocused, fixed on some point in the distance. She sees right through a body; the women would complain, once Dora Forrester had gathered up her recalcitrant daughter and made her disappointed way home. It's as if she's seeing something, they told their husbands, shivering at the memory, something unearthly, unnatural.

She saw people in the Forest, she said, would come home with such tales of encounters and adventures her older, more practical and unimaginative brother, Tom, would snort with derision, raising brows to the ceiling. But her father would narrow his steady, grey eyes in silent speculation, before telling his son to lay off teasing the poor lass.

One day, Margaret Forrester did not come home. At first unconcerned, merely annoyed, as day turned to evening and still no Margaret, Dora Forrester felt the first small frisson of fear. Her menfolk returned from their daily work in the Forest to be greeted with tightly controlled panic, immediately took lanterns and returned to the dusky glades and shadowy life of the twilight Forest, searching until darkness fell and they were forced to retreat to the safety of the outside world.

For the next three days, they searched. Word spread, anxious villagers trooped to the small cottage by the Forest, bearing gifts of food and drink, and words of comfort for poor Dora Forrester, fair near off her head with worry.

The young Lord also joined the search; being the only other apart from the forester and his family with the ability to enter the Forest. It was he who found her wandering a sun dappled glade, eyes blank and unseeing, humming a sweet ditty of lost love that made his skin creep with unfathomable unease.

Carefully, she was carried to the Hall. A healer was sent for, but for seven days and seven nights she lay as if in a trance and spoke not a single word, her eyes wide and frightening, and apart from a little warm milk, not one morsel of food did she eat.

The Lord, having persuaded her exhausted parents to rest for a few moments in an adjoining room, sat by her bedside, wondering what fate could have befallen the lass as to leave her witless. Suddenly, her expression cleared, and she looked at him. He saw the sanity resting in those gentle grey eyes and his heart rejoiced.

"I must tell you," she whispered.

He leant closer, listening in puzzled disbelief as she murmured a rhyme, the like of which he'd never heard before.

"It must be remembered!" She clutched his arm in sudden passion, face twisted with anguish.

Moved by her urgency, the Lord sent for her parents and a scribe, and over and again Margaret spoke the words and they were copied down, exactly as she commanded. Only when she was satisfied they were correct did she fall back upon her pillow, spent and exhausted.

"But Meg," begged her mother, taking her daughter's cold, white hands in her own. "Where have you been? Who told you these words?"

"A man," she whispered. "I met a man made of leaves, with roots for hair, who looked at me with eyes that burnt like fire. He put the words into my head, told me they must never be forgotten."

Then her pretty eyes went still, and that young fey soul slipped away.

Years turned into centuries.

The tale of Margaret became a fairy tale none believed, a story to scare children at bedtime, "stay away from the Forest or Mad Meg will get you." But her words, the words she'd caused to be written down, they were not forgotten, but passed into tradition and every year, at the most important village events, are faithfully recited by the villagers. Ignorant of their true meaning or intent, they are merely ancient ritual, comforting in their familiarity.

None ever stopped to wonder at their true purpose...

The Wykenwode Chant

The Forest Queen is chosen, all hail and praise the Queen.
May her power be unchallenged, the Forest ever green.
We join together gladly, our hearts and minds as one,
We stand beneath the moonlight, and warm, life-giving sun.
Wykenwode, Wykenwode.
Defender of the innocent: Protector of the good.
Wykenwode, Wykenwode.
Defender of the innocent: Protector of the good.

In the face of mortal danger, of evilness and sin,
We stand against the darkness and know that we will win.
Against the crimes of passion, of jealously and greed,
United we must face them, for our inner strength be freed.
Wykenwode, Wykenwode.
Defender of the innocent: Protector of the good.
Wykenwode, Wykenwode.
Defender of the innocent: Protector of the good.

Link hands with your neighbour, join forces with your friend,
Face the foe united, the oldest crimes to mend.
Let the circle come together, the light of faith shine out,
Our voices sound as one, oh hear our battle shout.
Wykenwode! Wykenwode!
Defender of the innocent! Protector of the good!
Wykenwode! Wykenwode!
Defender of the innocent! Protector of the good!
Wykenwode! Wykenwode!
Defender of the innocent! Protector of the good!

(origin unknown, although traditionally
ascribed to the Mad Meg of folklore)

The Forest

~ a tale of old magic ~

~PART ONE~

*If you go down to the woods today
You'd better not go alone.
It's lovely down in the woods today,
But safer to stay at home.*

~ Jimmy Kennedy ~

*Up the airy mountain,
Down the rushy glen.
We daren't go a-hunting
For fear of little men.*

~ William Allingham ~

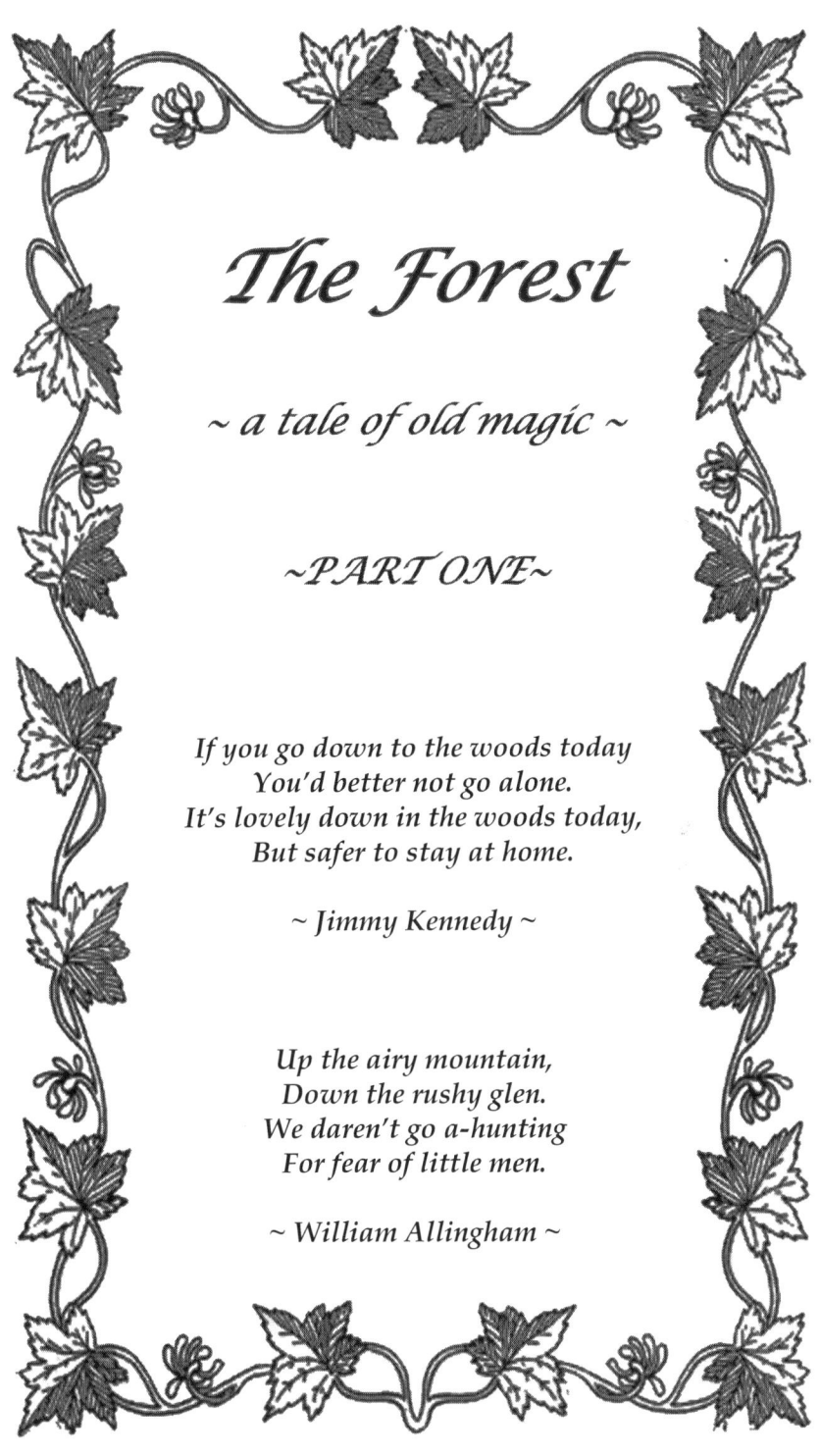

Chapter One
~ The People of the Village ~

This is a story of a curse, well, quite a few curses really, and the dreadful consequences which came about because of these curses. But to tell the tale of these curses, tell it properly that is, it's necessary to tell the story of the Forest, the two being so inextricably linked it would be impossible to understand one, without understanding the other.

Before everything else there had been the Forest. Somewhere in England, keeper of secrets, taker of souls, defender of innocence, right at the very edge of knowing or believing, there is the Forest, and this is its story.

Upon first consideration, the Forest seemed normal enough. It sprawled lazily over a roughly circular shaped portion of land, rather like an elderly lady settling herself ungainly onto the grass at a picnic, skirts spilling untidily in all directions, so did the Forest heave and flow outward, with odd stands of trees and shrubs escaping from its confines.

No one knew for sure how many square miles the Forest consumed, it defied all attempts at measuring and many had been made over the centuries. The Norman Conqueror, intrigued by the impossibility of the wild tales told of it, paid a visit to the Forest himself, it being in his mind to hunt within its leafy domain, for it was rumoured the white hind stepped through its glades and he hungered for such a prize.

Like all invasions before and all those to come, the Forest did not permit them entry. Instead it teased and tantalised, allowing entry enough to marvel at its abundance, its bushes of the plumpest hazelnuts ever seen, the tiny, succulent, wild strawberries, strangely ripe and fulsome alongside the nuts at completely the wrong time of year.

So far they ventured, until a great reluctance came upon them to go any further, the ways through the Forest seeming hazy and unclear, and his well-trained, battle-seasoned men began spooking at shadows, mumbling uneasily amongst themselves.

William, being made of sterner stuff, pushed away the sensation of nausea and ordered them on, his own entrails turning to ice as they thrust forward through an unseen wall of reluctance to emerge, blinking and confused, on the very edge of the Forest, at the exact place they'd first entered its perplexing realm.

Thrice more they tried. Each time the same thing happened. At last, William gave up, muttering obscenities about the accursed nature of this land he'd claimed as his own, half fearfully dismissed the Forest as unworthy of attention.

In records of the time it is referred to merely as The Forest and has remained so down the centuries. Many more tried to log, gauge and calculate its dimensions, all were doomed to fail, and if you do manage to find it mentioned on any map, it covers a vague portion of land, its size roughly guessed at from the dimensions of the tame, measurable, acres surrounding it.

Since written records began, and, one suspects, long before, the Forest, the village which nudges bravely at its side, the three farms encircling its girth and all the land in a vast outward explosion have belonged to one family and one family alone. The Marchmants. Although, that was not their real name, merely a name chosen centuries ago to hide their true nature.

A strange family. A family so steeped in mystery, little was known of them. No members of parliament had ever come forth from amongst their ranks, yet somehow, they'd held influence over the most powerful people in history. During the dissolution, when Henry rampaged through the country greedily acquiring land and buildings, the rich pickings of the village church were left un-plundered, the family remaining securely on its ancestral seat.

During the civil war, the village neither fought nor declared for either side, yet no retribution was ever visited upon them. They remained inviolate and unaffected, the petty goings on in the rest of the country, the downfall of kings and placing up of commoners of supreme indifference, compared to the laying down of spring barley and the choosing of the May Queen.

Through various wars no conscription notices were ever delivered to the village men. They were all needed to work the land, declared the Marchmant's, and the men were left alone, the status quo untouched.

The village was known as Wyckenwode.

A remarkably self-contained village, most of its occupants traditionally worked the land, the nearby three farms offering ready employment to all locals who desired it.

There was a school for the small number of village children, the schoolmistress seeming to be always provided from a local family, someone who'd themselves attended that very same school. Of course, the teacher must be qualified, and the school had to conform to all Board of Education standards. Whenever the position of teacher arose, the vacancy had to be advertised nationally, and it was. All the applicants being duly vetted and interviewed, but, somehow, inexplicably, once all the furore was over, it was always a local who once again shaped and moulded the young minds of Wykenwode.

There was a forge in the village, which dealt with all its needs and repaired the farms' machinery and tools. It was owned by John Blacksmith, a dark, taciturn giant of a man, his face etched deeply with the bitterness and disillusionment of life.

It was told how he'd never got over the loss of his young wife, Rosie Cairn that was. Her family had long been of West Farm and had a reputation for open, sunny natures, and many a male heart had been broken when Rosie eschewed all their advances and instead set her sights on John Blacksmith. She could do better, they'd complained. Oh, maybe not materially, after all, the Blacksmiths were comfortably off, like most of the villagers could trace their ancestry back to the forgotten times.

No, Rosie's disappointed swains grumbled, he was too old for her, too serious, too dull to satisfy laughing Rosie, sweet Rosie, happy-go-lucky Rosie. Even her parents had long and serious discussions with their beloved daughter, fearful for her future happiness.

But Rosie laughed off their concerns, adamant in her choice, she would have John Blacksmith and no other, seeing beneath his saturnine exterior something no one else could. When John tentatively, nervously, took her hand in the early days of clumsy courtship on the walk home from church, she'd sensed a great passion within John Blacksmith, a passion which scared and fascinated her.

Rosie, for all her good nature, was at heart a simple soul, her being formless and unshaped. She craved direction in her life, a sense of purpose and in the depths of John Blacksmith's eyes fancied she saw herself reflected, not as she knew herself to be, but as someone else, someone of unending beauty and unassailable dignity.

Rosie liked the woman she saw John perceived she could be, allowed herself to be loved by him, binding him to her in the most extravagant ceremony her parents could afford. She relished the admiration she saw in her former playmates faces, realising what a striking couple they made, him older and darker; her young, supple and golden.

The wedding night had come as something of a shock to naïve, clueless Rosie. Such desire, such ecstasy, such wild mutterings and dark passions. Never, in her wildest dreams, had she imagined people could do such things to each other, that she could be reduced to a sobbing, pleading, clawing creature of sensation and need in her swarthy, demanding husband's arms, his deep-set eyes glittering with the triumph of her total capitulation to him.

The village noticed the change in the young Blacksmith couple immediately. John was seen to smile, an un-heard of event, more strangely, was even known to whistle as he went about his work, a gleam of satisfaction in his eye. As for Rosie, they saw the dazed, blind look on her face, the way she constantly sought the company of her husband, could barely stand to be separated from him.

The little lad who worked for John told tales, wide eyed with incomprehension, of being sent on pointless, long-winded missions, returning to find the garage deserted, the cottage door locked. Once, he declared innocently, he was sure they'd got wild animals in there, the grunts and howls which echoed from the open bedroom window.

His elders exchanged glances, nodding sagely, eyes twinkling, none surprised, mere months after their wedding day, when young Rosie went to her mother, all a blush with shy expectancy. Soon, it was common knowledge the Blacksmith's were hopeful of a young visitor in the spring.

But even in Wyckenwode, life can be inexplicably cruel, and when Rosie died struggling to bring his son into the world, something broke deep inside John Blacksmith.

He was never seen to smile again.

He worked all hours, employing a local woman to raise his young son, Jack. Would never allow mention of his wife's name in his presence. It was to be as if she'd never existed.

His feet no more trod the path to the farm where his in-laws, Jack's grandparents lived. It was left to Mrs Dodd, his nanny, to arrange visits, when the baffled and grieving Cairns would cling to the small, living memory of their beloved daughter, and wonder at a world that could allow such things to happen.

The villagers understood, and complied with John's denial of his past. With time, it became another of the many eccentricities the village not only tolerated but seemed to positively encourage.

There was a shop within the village owned and run by the Miss Peabodys', housed in an ancient crooked building. From outside it looked too small to contain much, but, pass through its door, hear the faint tinkling of the bell in its cavernous depths, and almost immediately would be lost amongst its many aisles, its hidden nooks and crannies.

It was a shop where if you couldn't get whatever you wanted, you could always get whatever you needed, and maybe that was as it should be.

The Miss Peabodys' were sisters. They'd inherited the shop from their mother, who'd inherited it from hers, and so on back through time, an unbroken chain of female command stretching unchanged and unchallenged. By necessity of the Miss Peabodys' both being unmarried, they'd taken under their wing their niece, Nancy, daughter of their feckless brother, Joseph. Like John Blacksmith, he too lost his wife early in his child's life, and had been only too happy to hand the care and well-being of his baby daughter over to his older sisters.

Nancy Peabody commenced life much like any other little girl, but years of exposure to spinsterish dictates and morals had shaped her young mind and soul until she appeared a carbon copy of her aunt Iris, the eldest Miss Peabody. Turning her nose up at the youngsters who piled into the shop to purchase sweets and ginger beer, joining Miss Iris in condemnation of the perceived lack of morals of the young nowadays.

Miss Iris worried a great deal about the morals of others. It was both her passion in life and almost her sole occupation. She, together with her little circle of cronies, would gather weekly in an orgy of cake and gossip which satisfied immensely, yet left each feeling vaguely unwashed, as if trawling the morals of the entire village had somehow left its stain. But by the following week, any such scruples had been well and truly quashed, each member avidly bringing to the meeting the scandalous titbits, half murmured innuendoes and hints, which were the very meat and bread of their existence.

And through it all moved Nancy Peabody, handing round tea and cakes, her beetle black eyes listening and absorbing. For the most part ignored, even forgotten, she'd sit quietly in a corner, soul shrivelling into a petty, spiteful smallness from the daily doses of poison she consumed through osmosis of exposure to her Aunt Iris.

Despised by the village youngsters, Nancy had vengeance on them with small malicious acts of blackmail and exposure, her ammunition the gossip unwittingly supplied by her aunt and her cronies. To be fair to Miss Iris, such gossip was never intended to leave the sacred space of her front parlour, and she would have been mortified, even horrified, had she known of the use her obedient and demure young niece put it to.

But Nancy was sly. Long years' apprenticeship at her parsimonious aunt's knee, had taught her to be crafty about acquiring what she wanted, so Miss Iris had no idea of the depths to which Nancy's soul had sunk.

The younger Miss Peabody, Violet, was as alike her sister as cheese was to chalk, in that fundamental differences had occurred within the formation of their being to render Miss Violet a kindlier, gentler soul than her vinegar sour older sister.

Uncomfortable with speaking, even thinking ill of others, Miss Violet never joined her sister's circle for their weekly ritual of ripping the good names of the villagers asunder, her sole experience of it reducing her to quivering tears of dismay that such things could be true of her fellow villagers and friends. No, she'd exclaimed, she refused to believe such awful things, her normally timid voice for once rising in shocked objection, much to her sister's annoyance and the discomfort of the others.

In fact, so impassioned had been her defence of their neighbours, it'd quite spoilt the ladies' appetite for the delicious sponge cake Mrs Dodd had baked, and Miss Iris henceforth banned Miss Violet from ever attending another meeting. Meaning it as a punishment for her outspoken, misguided sister, she misread her down turned eyes and clasped, shaking hands for remorse, not realising the relief flooding her gentle sister's kindly heart.

Miss Violet liked things that made her laugh and books that made her cry, and her soul burned for romance. Neighbours, certainly her sister, would have been taken aback at the rich, vibrant, internal life that played out behind her sedate, pale blue eyes, anxiously blinking at the world as if constantly afraid of causing offence.

Still physically young, she'd just celebrated her fortieth birthday; Miss Violet seemed doomed for eternal spinsterhood and late at night mourned her single status, longing for something. Unwilling to admit, even to herself, what she most desired and ached for was sex.

Oh, not the brutish, physical act itself, but the love, the romance, the passion, Miss Violet perceived accompanied it. In secret, she sent away for books of a certain nature, books which would have shocked her sister to her core. These she stored under a loose floorboard in her room, consuming them late at night, her rose tinted lamp burning deep into the small hours, heart sighing over the impossible situations and seemingly untameable alpha males the heroines had to deal with.

Miss Violet's passionate nature was particularly moved by the story of John Blacksmith. The death of his young, clearly ardently loved, wife, John's removal of himself from society, seemed to her the very stuff of which classic love stories were made. On the few occasions he frequented the shop, Miss Violet fluttered and twittered in her haste to serve and make a good impression on him, pale eyes desperate to transmit her silent desire.

He remained oblivious to her. His only thought, if indeed any thought for the existence of Miss Violet ever crossed his mind, being the village was too full of annoying, interfering, old biddies.

So, sadly, Miss Violet's love remained an unspoken secret, and she contented herself with watching him from afar, pressing sweets onto poor, motherless Jack, whenever he came into the shop.

In time, her consideration of him as a surrogate for his father was replaced by a deep, maternal, concern for the lad himself. This lasted all through his youth until he emerged the other side of puberty, a brooding young man, silent and lonely, deeply mistrustful of the world and all its inhabitants. There being only three exceptions to this rule.

The brightness that was his cousin, Sally Cairn. The steadfastness that was his best friend, Reuben Forrester. The kindness that was Miss Violet Peabody.

Such were the emotions which brewed and bubbled beneath the seemingly calm, even somewhat dull, surface of life in Wyckenwode, and within its twin hearts, the pub and the church, great tragedies and romances, comedies and horrors worthy of any stage were played out on a daily basis.

The church was very old, its squat, round, Saxon tower, being only the latest structure of worship to be built upon the site; its sacredness having long been recognised by whatever religion held sway over the land, its power being shaped and reformed into whatever deities its congregation wished it to assume, blithely oblivious to such inconsequential things as race or creed.

The reverend was the latest in a long line of soul-caretakers to come from outside the village. His gentle, unassuming nature made him malleable to the demands and needs of his parishioners and they, particularly the ladies, controlled him with a subtle, almost undetectable rod of iron. In return, they let him consider his flock to be god-fearing, honest but simple farming folk, which on the whole they were, and his heart beat fiercely with the fervent love he held for them, but he did not know them.

As Reverend Arnold gaily cycled about the village, beaming with benevolent good will upon his flock, attending at the beginning and ending of their lives, officiating at their weddings, he did not see or chose not to understand, the significance of some of their quirky country ways.

The nailing of fresh, green branches from the Forest over the cot of the new born, the wild flowers from the Forest every bride wore on her brow, the pocketful of nuts and pine cones gathered from the Forest every deceased villager took with them to the grave, were merely quaint and colourful old customs, were a celebration of the abundance of life all around, a glorification of the beauty of God's world. They meant nothing, were harmless... weren't they?

Sometimes though, when Reverend Thomas Arnold walked alone from the church, skirting the edge of the Forest on his way to the village, he sensed something... something existing beyond the boundaries of his understanding. On a subconscious level, it alarmed and concerned him, but as he refused to acknowledge this fear to anyone, especially himself, he remained perpetually unable to confront it.

Instead, his pace would quicken, his breathing would catch painfully in his chest and he would find himself murmuring the Lord's Prayer over and over, as if to hold at bay... what? At this point, the good Reverend's mind would scurry back to the safety and security of abject denial.

It was just the Forest. Admittedly, it was a strange place, but then, forests very often were.

Determinedly, the Reverend would thrust away the memory of his one and only excursion into its enticingly leafy depths. Remembering, with a burst of sweat inducing adrenalin, he'd been allowed access only so far, a few hundred yards, certainly no more, before being forced back by a feeling of...

Even now, this man of God couldn't think of the experience without his bowels turning to water and his legs trembling beneath him. The feeling hadn't been malevolent, but an inexplicable urge to turn and flee had gripped him, and before he'd realised it, the Reverend had found himself careering through the trees as if his very life depended on it, heedless of direction, to erupt, breathless and panting, at the exact spot at which he'd entered.

The pub, The White Hind, arguably the true spiritual heart of the village, had been owned and run by the Blunt family for generations.

Amos Blunt, a thin, dried up, stick of a man, was fond of reminiscing to any who'd listen how, as a young lad, he'd helped his father wield the massive oak kegs down to the cellars, always claiming it'd been such exertions which had taken his father prematurely at the relatively young age of 62, leaving Amos in sole charge of the pub.

Here he'd pause, a gnarled and grimy finger scratching thoughtfully at ginger whiskers, declaring solemnly it'd be the death of him too. At this point his wife Dorcas would snort rudely, pushing past him to serve. "You're a creaking gate," she'd state. "You'll outlive the lot of us."

Dorcas Blunt was as large as her husband was slight, turning her not inconsiderable bulk sideways to manoeuvre the narrow bar, ponderous rear end in permanent danger of causing damage. Where her husband was fair and gingery, pale eyelashes and brows almost disappearing into a face splotched with freckles, Dorcas was as dark as a moonless night.

As a young girl, she'd been considered quite a looker, and Amos had puffed up with pride when her dark eyes flashed at him and she'd agreed to be his girl. Belonging to the Hunter family of East Farm, Dorcas Hunter was the best dancer within the village, and it'd been at the Autumn Festival that young Amos, face flushed with arrogant bluster, had swaggered to where she'd sat with her circle of friends and asked her to dance.

To his amazement, she'd said yes, something sparking deep within her eyes, and with a toss of her long, black hair and a swish of her womanly hips, allowed him to escort her onto the floor to the envy of all his friends.

Now, some fifty years later, there was little sign of those slim hips which had so enticed him. Somehow, with the arrival of each anniversary and the birth of each of their five children, the ravishing young girl had been swallowed up by a mountain of flesh, until now he no longer recognised her as the bride he'd so ardently desired.

As her attractiveness diminished, so had his love, Amos finally realising too late the folly of a marriage based on physical attraction alone. Poking amongst the embers of a relationship turned to cold clinker, he would ruefully wonder if this was to be the extent of his life, then would reflect Dorcas was nearly always respectful to him, kept the house as neat as a new pin, had raised their children satisfactorily, was a good help-meet in the pub, and really, what more could a man ask for or expect?

Amos felt for his wife familiarity created through long years of exposure, in that whilst he would miss her if she was suddenly not there, and undoubtedly his life was much easier with her around, it was the same casual regard he had for his dog. In fact, if brutally honest, whilst he'd shed a tear when old Prince shuffled off this mortal coil, it was highly unlikely he'd do so should Dorcas predecease him.

The pub itself was a long, low, thatched building, its origins lost in the amnesia of time. Its uneven flagstone floor and great, open fireplaces in its two commodious bars and cosy snug, spoke of a building dating back to medieval times at least. The small, leaded panes of glass at the windows let in barely enough light to see by, so, apart from days of the most brilliant sunshine, the pub was lit artificially, creating an inviting, womb-like interior to enfold and cushion its patrons within maternal protective arms.

The villagers regarded the pub as an extension of their homes, a place to meet and exchange gossip, a safe environment in which to discuss topics of interest, although rarely did these topics encompass anything occurring beyond a ten-mile radius around the forest.

And so, the seasons turned, years rolled by in this overlooked corner of England, never changing, always constant, the villager's lives measured and ordained by the planting and gathering of their crops, the birthing of their stock.

One chill autumn evening, Wally Twitchett was cycling cautiously down the lane running alongside the Forest to the village. Absently licking his lips in anticipation of his nightly pint of ale, Wally's seventy-year old heart clutched with fear as the front wheel of his bicycle slipped on the lane's surface, glittering sharply in the gleam of a shimmering wedge of moon.

Temperatures had dropped dramatically during the day until now every surface bore the hoary white mantle of frost, and as Wally wheezed, it stabbed, cold and alien, deep into his lungs. Tentatively, he put a foot to the ground.

Torn between thoughts of his lonely, but nearby cottage, and the beckoning allure of the blazing fires Amos would have lit in the pub, and almost tasting the rich, malty flavour of the locally brewed beer,

Wally hesitated, greying head bobbing in one direction, then the other, but the siren call of the pub triumphed and he continued towards the village, wobbling and cursing as the bicycle's wheels skidded and slipped beneath him.

Once again, he stopped, calling himself an old fool for even thinking of going to the pub on such a night. But Wally knew something else pulled him ever onwards, something possessing an allure more powerful than the promise of warmth and company, something even more powerful than ale.

At the thought of her, Wally briefly closed his eyes, a wistful sigh whistling through ill-fitting false teeth to hang, like an exclamation mark, before his face, clearly visible in the moonlight.

Dorcas Blunt. How long ago had Wally yearned and ached for her, captivated and tantalised by her dark eyes and flashing hips. She'd known how much he wanted her, of course she had, promised if he asked her to dance at the Autumn Festival, she'd say yes and be his girl. But, his nerve failed. As the evening wore on and he'd dithered in agonised, crushing despair, Dorcas had sat at the table with her friends, eyes growing fierce, chin lifting proudly as the evening waxed and waned and still he did not ask.

Finally, as Wally was steeling himself to take the eternal walk to her table and acquire his heart's desire, Amos Blunt had beaten him to it. With a contemptuous toss of her head in his direction, the burn of rejection in her eyes, she'd accepted Amos's offer and flounced onto the dance floor with him.

Silently Wally had left, unable to bear the pain of watching the girl he loved in the arms of another man. His dumb misery increased over the following weeks as it became clear Dorcas was being fiercely and determinedly courted by Amos. Flashy, mouthy, abrasively confident Amos Blunt, he possessed a way with words poor Wally sadly lacked.

Watching the courtship from the side-lines, Wally became convinced Amos did not truly love Dorcas, not in the way he did. That he could see no further than the exotic, dark eyed exterior, did not know the proud, romantic heart which beat wildly within.

Concerned, alarmed Dorcas was about to make a dreadful mistake, Wally confronted her, his shyness rendering him tongue tied and awkward, the speech he'd practised for days deserting him.

Instead of convincing her of his undying love and admiration, Wally only succeeded in angering and antagonising Dorcas.

Burning with the sting of perceived rejection by the only man she'd ever cared two hoots about, in a flurry of hurt pride, she went to Amos. Bitterly regretting her action when the anger of the moment cooled, and she found herself pregnant and then wed, rushed into a whirlwind marriage by indulgent parents, who blindly accepted her desperate lie of a love that couldn't wait for matrimony.

And so, Wally lost his Dorcas and with her any hope of love and a normal life, instead became shepherd at Home Farm. Throwing his broken heart into a career which ensured a persistently lonely existence, watching, heart aching, as Dorcas bore Amos sturdy ginger sons and dark-eyed daughters, seeing, in the blind misery in her eyes and rapidly increasing circumference of her waist, realisation of the dreadful mistake she'd made.

Knowing it was unfair to his heart, unable to remain away, Wally fell into the habit of calling at the pub almost every night. Busily serving, private thoughts banished to the furthest corner of a mind so used to being unloved, unconsidered, any traces of the proud wild girl she'd been were invisible, Dorcas would feel his eyes upon her from his habitual corner by the fire and, for a moment, would remember.

Occasionally, her head would lift, and their eyes would meet in a silent instant of unspoken regret. Fleeting and fragmentary, it impinged not upon their conscious minds, but Wally would make the mile bike ride home in a blaze of happiness, and Dorcas would lie in bed, listening to the night-time noises of her carelessly cruel and disregarding husband, remembering far-off, promise filled days of her youth, a beautiful smile transforming her face into what it had been.

Wally pushed on, ignoring the cold which crept insidiously through his old and patched greatcoat and nipped at his ribs, breath bruising him from the inside with each gasp for air he took.

A screech owl called, and once again Wally paused, heart giving a thud of fear, his eyes drawn instinctively to the dark mass of the Forest, even though knew he'd nothing to fear from it or its inhabitants.

Once upon a time, maybe, when he'd been young and burned with a love so intense it equalled the glare of the sun, but not now.

No, now he was too old to be of any interest. A sudden movement on the path ahead. Wally stared. Unable to believe. Unwilling to accept what his frantically widening eyes were telling his frozen brain he was seeing.

She stepped lightly onto the path from the trees, coat milky white and delicate in the fierce moonlight. Raising her beautiful head on its slender column of a neck, large dark eyes turned in Wally's direction and studied him, dispassionately and calmly, ears pricked as if she could hear the wildly pounding tattoo of his terrified heart.

For a long, eternal moment, they surveyed each other. Elegant beast and petrified man. He saw the flash of red inside her flared nostrils as she sampled the air, the thought crossing his numb mind she could smell his fear. Then she turned and walked back into the Forest, her trim, neat hooves picking their way carefully through a shaft of moonlight, and Wally watched her go, her shimmering hide a patch of brightness deep within the trees.

Suddenly galvanised into action, Wally remounted his bicycle with trembling, fear filled legs, pedalled frantically towards the lights of the nearby village, resisting the urge to look behind him. Convinced if he did, he'd see her again, standing in the moonlight, her gaze direct and all knowing, staring into his very soul.

The pub was half empty that night, folk choosing to stay home by their own fires, unwilling to venture out on such a cold and forbidding night; peering from windows at the shrouded world, shuddering as something else, something unknown and unbidden had crept into their hearts, and they'd drawn the curtains and locked their doors early as if to shut that something out.

Only a few hardy souls had ventured out, and these huddled around the fire, morose and unusually silent. The call of a screech owl in the night broke into their collective thoughts and they looked up as one entity, exchanged glances and shivered, a few muttered about graves being danced upon, before subsiding once more into brooding, sullen silence, furrowed gazes following the flames as they flickered and danced.

Long minutes passed. Suddenly, the door banged violently, Wally Twitchett staggered in, face ashen, eyes wild and staring, mouth desperately working as if he wished to speak but couldn't.

Hands clutching at his throat, he panted and rasped, legs collapsing as those nearest instinctively rushed to catch and support him.

"Lord alive, Wally? What's the matter, man, what is it?"

Amid the concerned chorus, Wally's eyes rolled back in his head. Quickly, they thrust him into a chair, hands pulling at his greatcoat, patting him frantically on the back, voices twittering with alarm as they gathered around.

"Wally?"

"He's having a heart attack!"

"Merciful heavens, someone send for the doctor!"

"Out of the way," demanded a voice, firm and commanding, and as one the group moved to allow Dorcas Blunt to pass through, a brandy glass clutched in her hand. Lightly, despite her bulk, she knelt beside Wally and pressed the glass into his hand, patting at his crinkled, trembling flesh with her own firmly rounded fingers.

"You get that down you," she ordered, her tone sounding maternal to those around, Wally heard the loving concern buried beneath, and it gave him the strength to draw himself upright, take a deep shaky breath, drain the glass in one burning gulp, passing it back with a hand that quivered a little less violently.

"I've seen it," he declared, eyes darting from one to another. "Out there, by the Forest. I saw it standing there, large as life in the moonlight."

One or two of the older villagers drew sharply back as if he were contagious, eyes fearful, expressions grim, exchanged looks of horror.

"It?" asked another, younger, villager, puzzlement obvious in his voice. "What do you mean, you've seen it? What it?"

"It!" demanded Wally passionately, clasped Dorcas' hand, trembling gaze fixed upon her worried face. "The White Hind," he finished in a hoarse whisper.

An unearthly hush fell upon the room. Even those too young to remember the last time had heard the stories and so trembled, drew nearer to one another, seeking safety in numbers.

"Oh Wally," murmured Dorcas. "Are you sure? Could it have been a stray sheep maybe; or a red deer…" her voice trailed away as Wally decisively shook his head.

"It stood no more than six feet away from me," he stated, quaked at the memory. "I saw it in the moonlight, as clearly as I see you all now."

"It's been over sixty years since the last time," someone murmured.

Mabel Dodd, the oldest villager there, shook her head. "That makes no odds," she stated firmly. "My grandmother told me it's skipped three generations before, but it always comes back. Sooner or later, it comes back. When the White Hind is seen, that's a sure sign it's going to happen again."

The villagers stared at each other in dismay.

"All we can do now is wait," declared Mabel Dodd grimly. "Wait and see."

"But it's only a legend, a story…" insisted someone weakly.

"A story?" Mabel Dodge demanded scornfully, outrage making her nostrils flare and her chest heave. "A legend? Let me tell you, Jacob Cairn, I remember the last time as if it was yesterday. If she's here again, then it's simply a matter of which ones it'll be. Which ones of our youngsters will die."

Chapter Two
~ The Forester's Son ~

Reuben Forrester had always known he was different from the other village children, but it'd never been more than a vague wisp of knowledge brushing at the edge of his thoughts, until that day at school, he couldn't have been any older than nine, when he'd heard older children bragging about how far into the Forest they'd gone.

With fearful pride they described the dell full of bluebells, the massive, fallen oak tree, with its impressive crop of spotted toadstools, the bramble bushes which yielded succulent berries in mid-April. The other children listened with wide eyed awe as their peers told of the feeling which denied them any further access, the force which had gently, but firmly, deposited them back at the outermost perimeter of the Forest.

"But I've been much further in than that!" Reuben impulsively blurted out, immediately wished he hadn't as Winston Blunt, the most bullish of Amos and Dorcas' grandsons, muscled accusingly up to him.

"Have not," he insisted. Reuben wished he'd kept his mouth shut, but something inside refused to back down, and desperately he drew up his slight form, stared into Winston's piggy eyes framed by sandy lashes and brows.

"Have to," he retorted.

"You're a liar, Forrester," Winston's face darkened with scorn. "Or perhaps I should call you Mad Meg," he taunted. "Go on admit it, you're a liar, liar, liar, look his pants are on fire!"

The other children laughed.

"I'm not a liar," Reuben blushed angrily.

Winston's smile turned into a snarl and he raised a beefy fist. "You'd better admit it," he threatened. "Or else I'll make you!"

Miserably aware he was about to get a pounding, Winston was renowned for being a bully, Reuben shrank away from the bigger boy, saw mingled looks of pity, concern and fear on the faces of the other children, knew none of them were big enough to stand up to Winston and his cronies, none of them could help him.

Suddenly, the crowd which had gathered tightly around in anticipation of a fight, parted, and the slight, dark form of Jack Blacksmith stepped from it, followed by his cousin, Sally Cairn. Exchanging quick glances, with one accord they moved to place themselves in front of Reuben, staring impassively at Winston as he blinked and frowned, confused by this latest turn of events.

"Jack, Sally," he began importantly. "Get out of the way, I've got to teach this pipsqueak an important lesson about not telling lies to his elders and betters."

"Really?" enquired Sally calmly, glancing around the hushed and expectant crowd of children. "Well, that's odd," she continued. "Because although I see a few elders I don't see any betters here, do you Jack?"

Jack looked up from examining dirt under his fingernails, scowled at Winston. A brooding, darkly violent glare, that had the older boy taking an involuntary step backwards.

"No," he agreed softly. "I don't."

"What?" Winston's mouth gaped as a red flush infused his neck and face. Aware he'd somehow been insulted, too unintelligent to understand quite how, he bunched his fists, loomed menacingly over the wiry form of Jack, who slumped, casually uncaring, still frowning at the state of his nails.

"Now see here, Blacksmith," Winston began, then broke off, large hands clutching his quivering gut which Jack had punched with such speed and agility, half the children were left unsure what exactly had happened.

"No, you see here, Blunt," retorted Jack, all casualness gone from his stance as he looked down on the groaning, gasping, bent double form of Winston. "You want to pick on someone, then you pick on me, because I ain't afraid of you and anytime you want some more, you let me know."

Winston squinted at Jack. For a split-second, Reuben thought he was going to do precisely that, but something in the younger boy's face stopped him. Instead, he glared with naked hostility at the three of them standing together in solidarity, then stumbled away, the crowd parting to let him through, his cronies, Thomas Dodd and Frank Twitchett, exchanging glances, reluctantly following.

The others slowly dispersed as it became clear nothing more exciting was going to happen, and Reuben was left, staring in silent, grateful wonder at his two rescuers.

He knew them, of course he did. You couldn't spend the first nine years of your life in such a small village as Wyckenwode and not know everyone, but he'd never been able to penetrate the charmed circle of the Cairns and the Blacksmiths, inextricably linked by ties of marriage and blood.

"Thanks," he finally mumbled. Sally Cairn flashed him a wide, sunny smile, which left Reuben warmed by its radiance, completely understanding why Sally was the most popular girl in school.

"That's all right, Reuben," she reassured. "Winston's a bully, he needed taking down a peg or two," her smile became quizzical. "But what on earth had you done to upset him?"

"He was boasting he'd got to the fallen oak tree in the Forest," Reuben mumbled. "So, I told him I'd gone further, and he called me a liar."

"Well, why did you say such a thing?" asked Sally, smile slipping. "It was a bit of a silly lie to tell, Reuben."

"It wasn't a lie," insisted Reuben hotly, cheeks flushing at the thought they too believed him a liar. "I really have gone further than that into the Forest."

"Come on, Sally," Jack spoke for the first time, shooting Reuben a vaguely contemptuous look and placing a hand territorially onto his cousin's arm.

"I can prove it!" Reuben cried desperately as they turned to go. "I can! I can!" he insisted, voice shrill with the desire to convince them of the veracity of his words.

Jack paused, glanced at Sally, looked back at Reuben, studying the younger lad intently. Reuben quailed at the darkness in the other boy's eyes, the stillness that settled onto his face, realising even though Jack was only a year older, the suffering of generations passed seemed etched into his sharply handsome young face.

"Go on then," Jack said simply. Without another word, he and Sally turned on their heels and walked away, leaving Reuben to follow or not as he pleased.

He followed them, trailing anxiously in their wake as their supple, slender forms easily climbed the incline which led up and out of the village, until finally, they stood, breathless and hot from the afternoon sun beating unremittingly on the backs of their necks, staring in silent expectation at the massed green ranks of the outermost trees of the Forest.

Wordlessly, Jack and Sally turned and studied him. Once again, Reuben swallowed down his unease, before stepping past them and leading the way into the Forest, flickering patches of green tinted light and shade dappling their faces as he led them deeper in.

They reached the bluebell dell, paused for a moment, looking around in wonder at the nodding blue heads of the wildflowers, knowing anywhere else but the Forest, bluebells should have been over long before, that it was impossible for them to still be blooming in late September.

"This is as far as I've ever been," confessed Jack, and Sally slowly nodded.

"I managed a few steps further once," she admitted, pointed towards where an old track meandered its way into the still, secret depths of the Forest. "Over there."

Both children followed as Reuben slowly crossed the dell, flowers bending and whipping back against his bare legs. Looking over his shoulder, he saw their faces widen with nervous anticipation, Sally's eyes flicking up at the cry of a cuckoo, followed almost immediately by the drumming of a woodpecker.

"This is the furthest anyone's ever been," stated Jack flatly, as they once again paused at the edge of the dell by the massive fallen trunk of an oak tree.

"Can you feel it?" whispered Sally, palms flat against the lichen smeared trunk, bending over in pain, beads of sweat springing out upon her forehead, her breathing laboured and heavy.

Jack nodded, Reuben saw with alarm the matching pain on his face. "We have to go back," he moaned. "We're not wanted."

Silently, Reuben took their hands, led them forward a slow, shuffling step and then another, feeling the clamminess of their skin as they clutched at him.

"Reuben, we can't..." whispered Sally, her skin going a pale, sickly green colour. Reuben wondered if she was going to vomit but tightened his grip on their hands, pulled them forward another step. Jack moaned softly in his throat, his eyes glazing over, the colour draining from his face, leaving lines of stress etched deeply around his mouth and eyes.

"Have to go back," he muttered thickly. "Not wanted ..."

Closing his eyes, Reuben formed a single desperate plea in his mind – *Please* - then pulled them that final step and they were through. Exhausted and panting, pulses beating visibly at their temples, they collapsed onto the loamy Forest floor, sides heaving from the exertion of those four, terrible, eternal steps.

He let them lie, watching in concern as they struggled to recover, triumphant he'd managed to bring them through, with a nagging sense of unease perhaps he shouldn't have done.

Finally, Jack rolled over and staggered to his feet, helping up Sally who brushed twigs and other debris from her dress. Together they gazed in wonder, before clustering around Reuben, eyes bright with shocked awe.

"Reuben," sighed Sally. "What did you... how did you...?"

"Told you I'd been further," boasted Reuben, savouring the supreme triumph of having Jack Blacksmith and Sally Cairn gazing at him in admiration.

"But how did you do it?" insisted Sally.

"It's meant to be a secret," Reuben shrugged guiltily. "All offspring of the forester can pass through."

"Like Mad Meg?" grinned Jack, and Reuben flushed.

"Yes," he mumbled, scowled furiously as Jack hooted with amusement.

"So," breathed Sally, looking around her with avid curiosity. "Where do we go now?"

They both looked to Reuben to guide them, and he threw his young chest out with pride.

"Come on," he said, grabbing Sally's hand and leading her down the overgrown track, so puffed up with his own importance, he failed to see the furiously angry scowl Jack sent in his direction, completely unaware of the primeval emotions he'd unwittingly unleashed within Jack's breast...

...and somewhere, deep within the Forest, further in than even Reuben had ever been able to penetrate, something stirred and awoke, its generations long slumber disturbed by the sharp, welcome tang of resentment and jealousy.

Patiently, it settled down to wait, knowing the time was not yet, but it would be soon, so very soon. And as decades could creep past and barely register upon its consciousness, waiting was something it did very well...

Being an only child, Reuben Forrester often wondered what it would be like to have siblings, brothers and sisters to share and disagree with. As he grew older, further thought maybe if he hadn't been the only one, his parents wouldn't worry so much about him.

Because they did worry. Although Reuben knew their motives were love, still their concern was claustrophobic, and at times he longed to escape, feeling the pull of the Forest lying at the bottom of the garden, its deep rustling glades and pathways offering solitude and respite from his mother's often cloying attentions.

His father too worried, although in a subtle, less demanding way, than his mother, and Reuben soon learnt not to do or say anything that would trigger his father's thoughtful, considering stare. Also knew there was much they kept hidden from his mother, much that was to be spoken about only between father and son, Reuben realising this caused worry to occasionally creep into his father's calm, grey eyes.

It began, this keeping of secrets, early in Reuben's life on the day of his seventh birthday. His mother had made a delicious birthday tea, complete with the crowning glory of a large chocolate cake, which she informed him must not be touched until his father returned from his day's work in the Forest.

In an agony of anticipation, Reuben returned again and again to the small, wooden fence which formed the perimeter of his little world. Leaning against it, straining his eyes to see into the dark between the trees, trying to urge his father home through sheer will power alone.

Each time, his mother would take his hand and lead him away, back into the small cottage which had traditionally been the forester's home since long before anyone could remember, laughing at his impatience, telling him to sit quietly with his toys whilst she finished sorting laundry upstairs.

"Your father will be home soon," she'd informed him. "You have to wait."

But Reuben couldn't wait. As soon as the creaking floorboards above his head informed him his mother was once again safely ensconced in the bedroom sorting and folding freshly dried linen, he'd slipped from the house, let himself quietly through the gate and ran headlong into the Forest, intent on finding his father and bringing him home to tea.

Further and further into the trees he'd run, seeing, not understanding, the contradictory nature of the wildlife around him. His seven-year-old eyes failing to recognise the impossibility of sloes in April, growing next to wild strawberries and alongside hazel trees already heavy with nuts.

Deeper and deeper he penetrated, until finally he stopped, feeling resistance in the air before him. Concerned but unafraid, he pushed on through. It moved around him. And Reuben was reminded of the time he'd plunged his hand into a cluster of frogspawn in the village pond, remembering how his hand had sluggishly passed through its cloying, sticky mass, resisting his advance. Still, he'd been able to move his hand through the clump to emerge onto the other side.

Shivering, he crept forward, and the feeling eased. Looking back, Reuben was surprised to see no visible barrier on the track behind him; nothing to indicate the boundary he'd penetrated, but a definite physical line had been crossed. Reuben could feel it with every fibre of his being as he curiously gazed around him, sensing the differences in the Forest on this side of the perimeter.

The air was thicker, richer; and the young boy fancied the world outside the Forest no longer existed... that time and life and progress were concepts with little meaning in this strange place. Cautiously, he walked on, sticking determinedly to the track, aware should he wander from it he'd never be able to get back. The thought of roving the Forest, lost forever in its seductively enticing depths, was enough to make him shiver, and he glanced nervously over his shoulder, almost tempted to go back. Almost, but not quite.

The air was alive with the throb and rush of birds and insects, Reuben staring in delight as a large, iridescent green dragonfly perched on a tree trunk beside him, sheer wings twitching in a patch of brilliant sunshine.

Further and further he penetrated, shoulders bowing under the timeless, ageless atmosphere of the place. Suddenly, he saw a flash of light through the trees, heard voices and emerged, blinking, into a small clearing, saw his father crouched by a fire over which hung some sort of cooking pot.

But he wasn't alone.

As Reuben approached, scared and apprehensive, the two men his father had been speaking to arose, surveyed him with a coldly dispassionate interest, which sent shivers of fear whispering down the young boy's spine.

His father stood and turned, face registering concern at his son's appearance, shot a worried glance towards the other two.

"Reuben?" he exclaimed. "What are you doing here?"

"I came to find you, father, to bring you home," stuttered Reuben. "Mother said we couldn't have my birthday tea until you got back, so I came to find you…"

His voice trailed away under the steely, level stare of the two men, noticing how strange their clothes were. Their tunics and leggings looked cut from rough, woollen blankets rather than proper cloth, the clasps at the throats of their cloaks glittered in the sunlight like gold. As they moved, Reuben saw the glint of steel at their hips and gazed, round eyed with wonder. He'd never seen anyone wearing a sword before but felt no fear, almost as if he instinctively knew, strange as their appearance was, these men meant him no harm.

He looked up into their faces, meeting the piercing blue of their eyes, noticing with surprise their long hair tied back from the angled planes of their cheeks.

"Your son, forester?" enquired one, his voice rich and low. Reuben could understand the words, but the accent was strange, as if its speaker was unaccustomed to modern English.

"Yes," agreed Daniel Forrester curtly, pulling Reuben close, enfolding an arm around him. Reuben leant thankfully back into his father's comforting solidity.

"A fine boy," the other one commented, bending, placed a strong finger beneath Reuben's chin, tilting his face to look into his eyes. "He has the look of you," he remarked, flashed a tight smile at Daniel. "He will make a fine forester when the time comes."

"Reuben will be whatever he chooses to be," Daniel retorted, his words clipped and precise.

The strangers exchanged amused glances. "His very presence so deep within the Forest, means the choice has already been made," replied the first reprovingly.

Reuben felt his father's arm tighten almost imperceptibly around him, as if seeking to protect his son from something. "Forgive me, my lords," Daniel mumbled, and Reuben squirmed with excitement. They were lords, lords of what? "He's merely a boy," he continued, an almost pleading note in his voice.

"Of course," replied the man, brow creasing in amusement. "Yet do not mighty oaks from such small acorns often grow?"

"Yes, my lord," murmured Daniel.

"Go, forester," commanded the second. "Take your son home. He is right, celebrating the day of his birth is of far more import than conversing with us."

"Thank you, my lord," said Daniel.

He gave a jerky bow from the hip, turned Reuben, and hurried him to the edge of the clearing, away from the two men with their all-knowing, ancient eyes and their strange clothing.

At the beginning of the track, Daniel stopped, swung his son easily into his arms, and Reuben peered anxiously over his father's shoulder, gaping at the empty clearing. Of the two men there was now no sign, and every trace of their fire had also vanished.

"You shouldn't have come here, Reuben," his father began. Reuben nodded sleepily, rested his head against his father's shoulder, a strange, heavy weariness wrapped itself around his body like a blanket, his eyelids fluttered shut...

"Wake up, sleepyhead, look, your father's nearly home, it's time to have tea."

Reuben blinked open his eyes, stared blearily up at his mother, struggling into an upright position from the grass where he lay. Confused, he looked around, rubbing at the damp imprint of grass on his cheek from where he'd obviously fallen asleep.

"Father?" he murmured, followed his mother's pointing finger to where his father had emerged from the Forest and was now walking down the track towards the cottage, shotgun broken and nestling in the crook of his arm, his tread even and measured.

Reuben frowned with astonishment at the familiar bulk of his father, convinced only moments earlier he'd been in his arms, sleep tugging at him, and now he lay here... on the grass in their small garden, his mother smiling indulgently at his sleepy stupidity.

"You must have fallen asleep," she remarked, lovingly helped him to his feet, hugging him tightly as Reuben stumbled, confused and befuddled thoughts struggling to make sense of it all.

"But... but..." he began, then his father was with them, letting himself into the garden through the small wooden gate, his smile warming and genuine.

"Where's the birthday boy?" he demanded, and held out his hand to reveal a small basket of tiny, wild strawberries, expectant smile slipping as Reuben continued to stare at him in stunned silence.

"Reuben?" he began in concern. "Is anything wrong?"

"He fell asleep waiting for you," his mother explained. "Truth be, I think he's still half asleep."

"Is that so?" remarked his father, handing the strawberries to his mother and sweeping Reuben up easily into his strong and warmly familiar arms. "Come on, birthday boy," he said. "I've been looking forward to a slice of that birthday cake all day," and carried Reuben un-protesting into the house.

Later that night, after every crumb of the birthday tea had been consumed, Reuben was lying in bed. Hearing his father pass by his door, he called out to him, his voice low and urgent. His father hesitated, slipped silently into the room, pushed it shut behind him and perched on the side of Reuben's bed.

"It wasn't a dream, was it," Reuben demanded.

For a long moment his father looked at him, the strong lines of his face highlighted in the moonlight peering through the window.

"Father?" insisted Reuben.

"No," he finally admitted, weariness in his voice. "It wasn't a dream, but you must tell no one, especially not other children," he paused, seeking the right words.

"You know only the Marchmant family and the forester may enter the Forest? It is not so widely known the forester's offspring may also pass through the barrier. Oh, the adults of the village know, understand and accept it is the way it is, but, tis felt the young would not understand. So, you must tell no one, do I have your promise, Reuben?"

"Of course," murmured Reuben, mind bursting with questions. His father turned sharply at the sound of his mother's footsteps on the wooden staircase, placed his finger firmly to Reuben's lips, eyes intent with obvious meaning. Reuben nodded, understanding completely what had happened was never to be mentioned again and certainly his mother was never to know.

After that, Reuben ventured many times into the Forest, sometimes with his father, but more often by himself. Growing in confidence, he wandered its overgrown trails, learning it was impossible for him to become lost within its depths, that as soon as he grew weary his feet would unerringly lead him home.

Never again did he see the two strange men, or indeed anyone else, but always felt others dwelt within the shady sanctuary of the Forest, would smell smoke and the aroma of roasting meat, but never find its source. Occasionally, he would hear laughter, the baying of hounds, would know a hunt was taking place tantalisingly close, yet was never allowed to encounter the hunters.

And often would feel eyes watching, tracking his every move as he progressed slowly through the trees, head jerking up at the sound of a twig snapping, sensing the presence of another, calling out for them to show themselves, waiting in heart pounding silence for a reply, hearing and seeing nothing.

Once, he thought he saw something from the corner of his eye, a quick flash of silvery white, but when he looked properly, whatever it was had gone.

Until his inclusion into the tight knit circle of Jack Blacksmith and Sally Cairn, Reuben Forrester had not realised how lonely he was, how desperate for the companionship of others, how isolated his mother had kept him in that little house on the edge of the Forest.

He attended the local school, as did every other child born within the village, but even that did not ease his solitude, and Reuben felt at odds with his peers. Realising they found him strange and difficult to understand, he was at a loss how to address the situation, unsure if he even wanted to, feeling a sense of apartness from the other families that made up Wyckenwode, this unconscious air of superiority further alienating him from the other children.

By the time he met Jack and Sally, Reuben had become a silent, still figure, moving unnoticed and unremarked upon through the terms, the teachers allowing him to blend into the background, never attempting to force him into pre-eminence, recognising and respecting his desire to be left alone.

Then, he met Jack and Sally. With their respect and admiration won by their adventure in the Forest, Reuben finally discovered his true soul mates and they quickly became inseparable, sharing their innermost thoughts and feelings.

Reuben discovered Jack and Sally had been close since babyhood, Jack sharing Sally's playpen and toys after the death of his mother left him in the care of a bitterly grieving father and an ageing, inept Mabel Dodd, who, although kindly, had been unable to replace Jack's mother except on a very basic, practical level.

Instead, it'd been left up to Jack's grandparents and Sally's parents to fill the gap. At this point, Reuben found although Sally referred to Jack as her cousin, Jack was strangely quick to point out Sally was in fact his second cousin. Her father being Michael, son of David Cairn, the much older brother of Rosie, Jack's mother. Quite why this was important to Jack, Reuben was at a loss to understand, but accepted it as another of Jack's eccentricities.

For Jack had many eccentricities, and sometimes Reuben despaired of ever fully understanding his new friend, whose mercurial moods were as changeable as the weather. One day, Reuben would feel Jack was the only soul, apart from Sally of course, upon whom he could always rely. The next, some seemingly innocent remark or action would set Jack's black eyes flashing with displeasure, face darkening into its habitual scowl, he would simply walk away, leaving Reuben and Sally staring at each other in exasperation.

If Jack was shadows and complication, Sally was the absolute antithesis of light and simplicity, the Cairn predilection for a sunny nature reaching a natural climax in Sally's placid temperament, unfailing generosity and sweetness of spirit, possessing the ability to coax even the surly Jack into smiles when the black dog perched on his shoulder, causing him to snap and snarl at all.

Practical and reliable Sally, Reuben loved every golden freckle on her up tilted nose, her thick, flaxen plaits reaching to waist level and her slight, sturdy body. United in mutual adoration of Sally, Reuben and Jack would cheerfully have died to protect her, although neither would admit it. Instead they teased and taunted, treating her with the friendly contempt reserved for a much beloved sister. She in turn loved them both, nagging and scolding, wrapping them up securely in her tender concern.

Together they were invincible.

The village watched indulgently, knowing where one was sighted, the others were inevitably not far away. The years prior to puberty were simple, uncomplicated ones of innocence and shared joy in each other's company, marred only by Jack's inexplicable dark moods, when Reuben and Sally learnt it was best to leave him alone, to fight his ongoing battle with whatever demon it was that rent his young soul.

With his friendship with Jack and Sally, came a slight but telling relaxation of his mother's too firm grip over Reuben. As if finally accepting her son's need for separation from her, she slowly, reluctantly, un-loosened the loving ties which had bound him so closely to her, allowing him previously unthinkable freedoms.

Relishing this liberty, Reuben discovered true independence from his parents, spending long days in the company of his friends, returning home, exhausted and happy, as the moon was rising above the Forest. Hurrying into the warm, bright kitchen, sniffing the good, solid smells of his mother's cooking, face ablaze with the triumph of his day.

Quietly, his mother would serve dinner, and listen as her son spoke of his life without her. Watching with the still, aching heart of a mother, as her only child gradually undid the ties linking her soul to his. Realising, with a pang of loneliness, that she was no longer the centre of his universe, that his feet were now firmly set on the path to manhood, and her role in the formation of his being was at an end. She was no longer needed, would never be needed in quite that way again.

Perhaps, if there'd been other children, this wrenching away of her son wouldn't be so painful, so agonising in its completeness. But, after Reuben, the cradle had remained empty of another babe to fill the aching hollow in her arms and in her heart.

Reuben's father observed the friendship of his son with the Cairn girl, and the son of the broodingly silent John Blacksmith, with mixed emotions. Reuben's happiness with his friends would have touched the heart of even the most indifferent parent, and Daniel Forrester felt the reflected glow of the intensity of his son's relationship with his friends, his slow, patient smile spreading across his face at dinner, when his son would regale them with tales of the day's small glories and setbacks.

Still, something nagged and tormented Daniel's soul. A worry. An unease this triumvirate of young people were destined for disaster. As time passed, so too did this tiny worm of discontent, this premonition of evil, grow and twist in his gut, until a frown line of inexplicable worry gouged a permanent groove between his eyes, an air of expectancy hovering within a heart beating anxiously with fear for his son.

The years passed. Reuben grew, his frame broadening until it became clear physically at least, it would be his father he'd favour, with his long limbed, muscular body, and his dark blond hair framing a strong, sensitive face. His grey eyes were the image of his fathers, as was his height. At over six foot he towered over Sally, and even the slighter Jack was forced to look up to his friend.

As they emerged from puberty and their adult physiques were revealed, Sally once commented that their ancestry couldn't have been more apparent. She, with her Saxon stockiness and flaxen blondness. Jack with his wiry frame, black hair and eyes, was the living embodiment of how she imagined the Gaelic people who'd once inhabited this land would have looked. What about me? Reuben cried. Sally had laughed, called him a Viking, exclaiming with his broad frame and shaggy blond hair, she could imagine him climbing from a long boat clutching his war axe, setting out for a spot of pillaging.

At this point, Reuben had tumbled Sally into a pile of straw, and tickled her until she'd begged for mercy, called for Jack to rescue her, but Jack had gone, storming off in one of his unpredictable and inexplicable moods, leaving the others to shrug shoulders, so used to Jack now the incident passed without comment.

As Reuben grew and matured, he realised his family, although an integral part of village life, were, nonetheless, considered apart and special from other families. He'd long known that he and his father alone possessed the ability to penetrate the Forest's defences, and that even though he'd taken Jack and Sally through, he'd felt the warring conflict within his breast at his actions and never offered to do so again. Relieved, as years passed, they did not press him to repeat the experience, instead regarded him with awe, and listened with quiet envy to his tales of the Forest and the things to be seen within its fiercely guarded boundary.

Reuben knew his father, as the latest in the long line of foresters, was regarded with an almost superstitious trepidation. The latest in a long, unbroken chain of foresters who worked deep within the bounds of the Forest, their duties were manifold: from the coppicing and maintaining of its trees, to the care of the creatures who lived within it, and to the raising of pheasant and deer for the sport of the Lords, the foresters had always been an integral part of woodland life.

This regard was further boosted by the fact Daniel Forrester regularly visited the hall to report to the Lady Marchmant, and often took her sons, the Lords Gilliard and Jolyon, hunting. Then the village would hear dogs barking deep within the Forest, for no obstacle was ever placed in the way of a member of the Marchmant family from entering its realm.

When they walked through the village, Reuben would note the respectful nods and greetings offered to his father, a warm glow suffusing him as he realised this was his own future. That he would follow in his father's footsteps and become forester, Reuben had no doubt. It was in his blood, his bones. He could no more conceive of going against his destiny, than he could of leaving the village.

Although his father's job gained him the admiration of the village, Reuben knew it brought no comfort to his mother. For as he loved the Forest with a passionate intensity, so did his mother hate and resent that which daily took her husband away from her.

Reuben would observe his mother as she worked in the garden or stood at the washing line pegging out a basketful of freshly washed linen, her eyes constantly sliding sideways to the Forest, mere feet away from where she stood. He would watch as they narrowed into serpentine slits of disapproval, her mouth thinning into a tight line of displeasure, would see the stiffening of her spine, sensing waves of antipathy arising every time she looked at its deceptively calm exterior.

From four every afternoon, the earliest Daniel would return home, she would begin to watch. Eyes constantly moving to the window, starting at the slightest sound outside, palm flying to the suddenly increased pulse in her throat as if to calm and steady it. The love of his mother for his father was akin to the cloying, neediness of her relationship with her son, but where Reuben would gently chafe against his restraints, devising small stratagems to escape, his father seemed not to notice his wife's dependence on him, or, if aware of it, seemed not to mind.

Once, believing them unobserved, Daniel paused behind his wife's chair and rested a hand gently on her shoulder, thumb stroking slowly down her neck. Reuben, watching through the partially open kitchen door, was humbled by the quick, hot, ardent look his mother gave her husband, her own hand clutching his in an agony of passion. Reuben lay thinking of it, long after he'd gone to bed, suddenly aware for the first time his father and mother did not exist purely as his parents, that they were separate entities, with thoughts and private desires about which he knew nothing. It was an awkward, startling realisation, one many never achieve, this seeing of parents as individuals.

His mother had been a Hunter, used to living high on the downs in the large farmhouse her family had inhabited for generations, and Reuben came to understand how hard it'd been for her to move from the sunlight and wind-kissed heights, where views stretched untrammelled and unhindered for miles in all directions, the Forest a mere dark smudge in the depths of the valley floor, down to a cottage at the edge of the trees. In time, he appreciated how strong her love for his father had been, that she'd packed her few belongings without a murmur, made the move from sunshine to shade, to live out the rest of her life at arms-length from that which she so feared and resented.

And so, time rolled continuously on, much as it'd done for centuries past, much as it was supposed it would for centuries to come. Life within the village was both open and closed, in that all knew your business, were intimate with every tiny detail of your family and life, still, there were secrets, bubbling away beneath the apparently calm exterior of bucolic country life.

One such secret, was one Reuben had been keeping from his family and his friends.

The secret that was Sylvie.

During his thirteenth year, when his body struggled with that difficult stage between boy and man, Reuben spent most of his time with Jack and Sally. Still the Forest called to him. Often, he'd rise from his bed at dawn, take bread and cheese from the kitchen, leave a note for his mother and slip away into its welcoming, cool greenness with a profound sense of grateful release.

Freed from all constraints, Reuben would pass through its boundaries and know himself to be truly free, apart from the unseen, ever present, inhabitants whom he'd long since grown to accept as an inevitable facet of the Forest.

Within the Forest, Reuben found all he needed, sipping icy crystal water from the streams which gurgled through its depths, gorging on the many fruits and nuts always available in plentiful abundance. Sometimes he hunted for rabbits, setting snares across their runs, checking next day to occasionally find a small, brown body caught in soundless terror, although usually, if his snare had been successful, some other predator had helped himself to his prize long before Reuben claimed it.

His time spent within the Forest honed and sharpened his natural instincts until he could identify any animal merely from the tracks it left, recognise any bird from its song, look around the seemingly empty Forest and spot instantly where a dog fox had passed the previous night, smell its rank, territorial scent and note the small but tell-tale signs of bent and disturbed undergrowth.

Sometimes, his father let him accompany him when he took the Lords Gilliard and Jolyon hunting. The first time this occurred he'd been curious about these hitherto unseen members of the Marchmant family, wondering if they were the men he'd met with his father that long-ago day in the Forest.

They had an air of familiarity, as if belonging to a distant branch of the family but were not the same men. Even though he'd only been seven, Reuben knew he'd carry the memory of their lean, hard physiques with him to his grave. Mostly, Reuben was left to his own devices within the Forest, other than the usual, vague sensation of being watched, believed he was alone.

One clear day in late spring, Reuben awoke early, the sun streaming through his curtains, beckoning as he blinked at his clock and perceived it to be a little past six. Noiselessly, he let himself from the cottage and ran down the garden, looking over his shoulder with a stab of pleasure at the dark footprints his feet had left in the dew drenched grass. Vaulting the fence easily, within moments he was deep within the Forest, shivering slightly within the shadow of trees, planning his day and deciding where to go first.

Remembering a snare set the previous day, Reuben decided to pay it a visit, to see if any rabbit had been foolish enough to blunder into its path, his mouth watering at the thought of his mother's rabbit pie.

Swiftly, he set off down the path, eyes flickering left as a rustle in the bushes alerted him to some small animal quickly scurrying for cover, then right to a flash of vivid blue in the direction of the stream, a kingfisher searching for breakfast. He paused in delight as a red squirrel dashed up a nearby tree and jumped easily to the branches of another, its lithe and graceful body almost stinging his eyes to tears as the small creature darted and leapt, full of the joy of simply being alive.

He snatched a handful of blackberries from a nearby bush, cramming them haphazardly into his mouth, grinning as dark purple juice splattered onto his shirt, anticipating his mother's groan of despair when she saw the state of it that evening. He determined to stay out all day, craving some hours of solitude, aware Sally and Jack would probably call for him, knowing they would understand when his mother explained where he'd gone. They recognised his occasional need for the Forest, accepting it as an integral part of his being.

Coming to the stream, Reuben paused for a handful of the sparkling liquid, a handy hazelnut tree satisfying the last of his hunger. Replete, he moved on to where he'd set his snare, only to stop dead in sudden bewilderment at the small mound of newly dug earth which lay where his snare had been.

Cautiously, silently, Reuben approached and dropped to his knees before the tiny grave, stretching out a puzzled hand to the posy of woodland flowers which lay atop its heaped dirt. The flowers were fresh, so Reuben knew they'd not lain there long. Perplexed, he gazed around, a sudden conviction dawning on him that he was not alone, that somewhere in the dense undergrowth, someone or something, was watching him.

Slowly, Reuben stood, eyes flicking right towards a dense cluster of shrubs, straining senses convinced that the watcher was concealed behind their leafy barricade. Casually, he wandered down the track and around the bend, silently moved into the undergrowth, noiselessly working his way back. Arriving at his destination as the bushes were rustling closed, knew his prey had stepped out onto the track. Gently parting the leaves and peering through, his eyes widened as he saw her.

He must have breathed, made some sound, or perhaps she sensed his presence. Her back stiffened, as she slowly turned from contemplation of the grave to fix her eyes upon his startled face, her expression inscrutable. For a long moment, they stood, him and her, the richly moving light of the Forest dappling their young faces, as they stared and stared.

Reuben saw a girl, no more than eleven or twelve, who for all her tender years wore an air of maturity, as if an older, much wiser soul peered through her large dark eyes, which, he noticed were fringed with silvery lashes. Her hair was long and smooth. Completely straight, it rippled over her shoulders in a curtain of silver blonde, much fairer than Sally's flaxen plaits, indeed much paler than any hair Reuben had ever seen before.

She was slight and slender, and he dimly registered her clothes were odd and old fashioned looking, her dress was made of some dark green, fine, woollen material, its hem swept the Forest floor, small leaves and small twigs caught up in its folds. Her cloak was pushed away from her shoulders, a large ornate clasp securing it firmly at her throat, and Reuben was reminded of the men he'd seen in the Forest with his father, all those years ago.

"Who are you?" she finally spoke, her voice young and breathless. It broke the spell, releasing Reuben from the trance-like state he'd been caught in.

"Reuben," he stuttered.

Her delicate, pale brows knitted together in a frown. "Who are you?" she repeated urgently. "The Forest is private, you should not be here."

"My father's the forester," Reuben replied, saw her relief and understanding.

"The forester, of course," she said. There was a lilt in her voice, and it reminded him of the French they were learning at school, the way she pronounced her words, stumbling slightly over her rs.

"Who are you?" he asked. She hesitated, smiled, a sweetly shy smile that had Reuben automatically returning it.

"Sylvie," she said, as if that was enough, as if it explained everything. Somehow, strangely, it did.

"Sylvie," Reuben repeated, and gestured at the small, flower strewn mound at her feet. "Did you do that?"

"Yes," she turned saddened eyes to him. "There was a rabbit, it was dead, so I buried it. Someone had set a snare."

"That was me," Reuben said, flinching away from her horrified expression. "I'm sorry," he added hastily, not sure quite what he was apologising for. "I was going to take it home to eat," he added.

The horror in Sylvie's expression was replaced by dawning realisation, a pitying look. "Of course," she breathed, gestured helplessly towards the grave. "I'm sorry… I did not realise… are you so very hungry?"

"What?" Reuben exclaimed, confused, realised her meaning and flushed angrily. "No, no, of course not," he snapped, wincing away from the assumption he saw in her eyes.

There was silence, as the two, young people studied each other curiously. Reuben thought how beautiful she was, her delicate fragility a contrast to the sturdy, sunny prettiness of Sally. It was like comparing night to day, he thought, moonlight to sunshine.

"I'm going to the river," he said. "Would you like to come?"

"The river?" Sylvie gazed at him curiously. "I have been trying to find it, I have been unsuccessful."

"Well, come on then," Reuben replied, instinctively holding out a hand, feeling her shy hesitation as she slowly placed her small hand in his, the milky whiteness of her skin against his own tanned and roughened palms.

That was the beginning of Reuben's friendship with Sylvie. A bizarre and secretive relationship which, for some reason, he kept hidden from all, not even telling Jack and Sally of the strange young woman he regularly met in the Forest.

It was surprisingly easy to keep the two components of his life separate. Jack and Sally accepted and understood his need for solitude within the Forest, never questioning his activities within its boundaries. And Sylvie never expressed even the slightest curiosity about his life away from their sporadic meetings.

When he was in the Forest with Sylvie, Reuben almost imagined he'd no other life beyond the solemn amusement in her dark eyes, the calming peace which wrapped itself around him in her presence.

Away from the hypnotic charm of her, it was as if she was some dim and distantly remembered dream.

Often, many weeks would pass, and he would wander the Forest without seeing her. Once, almost three months crept past, the memory of her had all but faded from his mind until he walked into the small clearing which was their favourite meeting place, and she was there. Then the fact of her filled his mind and essence until no room was left for his other life, his family and his friends.

When thoughts of her did brush across his mind, Reuben determined next time, he would question her closely about where she lived, where she came from. Somehow, when he saw her, all such strategies vanished to be replaced with the pure joy of being with her, of spending time within the Forest in her undemanding, soothing presence.

Years passed. Sylvie grew from a painfully shy, hesitant young girl to a poised and striking woman. Her rare smile a thing of such heart aching beauty, Reuben constantly sought ways to make her happy for the delight of seeing her finely drawn lips lift at the corners to form her own unique, sweet smile.

Reuben too had grown, his body broadening and thickening into his father's strong, muscular frame, his active outdoor life bronzing his skin until his grey eyes surveyed the world from a permanently tanned face. At twenty, he was a tall and handsome young man, a far cry from the undersized youngster who'd been the target of bullies like Winston Blunt. Now when Reuben walked by, many a girl's eye would follow his progress and sigh a little.

One chill, autumn day Reuben was in the Forest, for once on a specific quest to gather blackberries for his mother. The apple tree in their garden was shedding its fruit and his mother wished to bake a batch of her famous pies, and gladly Reuben had offered to fetch a basket of berries, pleased of an opportunity to escape to the Forest. As he wandered through its ripening embrace, trees and bushes heavy with the richness of an English autumn, thoughts of Sylvie flitted through his mind.

Reuben had not seen her since Spring. He remembered how preoccupied she'd seemed the last few times they'd met, as if other, more pressing matters, were weighing her down. He wondered if the burdens he'd sensed she carried, had somehow prevented her escaping to the Forest as often as she'd used to.

Reaching the place where grew the most succulent and plumpest berries, Reuben pushed thoughts of Sylvie from his mind, and set about filling the basket, fingers and lips quickly staining purple with juice from the berries he picked and those he could not resist eating.

"Reuben?"

He turned, the berry sweet on his tongue. It was her; a grown and palely silent Sylvie. As he blinked with surprise at her sudden appearance, she shuddered, tears slipping from eyes bright with unmasked fear, her slight form trembling under her warm cloak.

"Sylvie? What is it? What's the matter?"

He started towards her, purple stained fingers reaching to comfort and console. She shrank back, her expression haunted, and he was reminded of a doe he'd once seen cornered by dogs, the same quivering resignation to her fate in her fathomless dark eyes.

"I hoped to see you, to say goodbye," she murmured.

"What do you mean, goodbye?" Reuben frowned. "Are you going away?"

"I do not know," she replied. "I only know he has returned, and that which I feared can no longer be postponed."

"I don't understand," cried Reuben. "Who's returned?"

"My betrothed, my husband," she replied. It was as if the world shifted from its habitual alignment, leaving Reuben gasping in shocked horror, moved by the desolation he saw in Sylvie's eyes, the pain which lanced his heart.

"You're married?" he cried, and she flinched from the harsh accusation in his tone. "But, you never said, how… I mean, when?"

"I was brought from my home many years ago," she explained, eyes pleading with him to understand. "I was so alone, so afraid of what my future would hold. I have never met my betrothed; he was too busy in the company of the King to bother with a child too young to be his bride, so I was left alone. Gradually, as months turned into years, I pushed all thoughts of the marriage from my mind. But, news came this morning, he is returning, the wedding is to take place immediately upon his arrival."

"I see," said Reuben slowly, unsure of what to say or feel, her words so strange and alarming he could make no sense of them.

"Oh, Reuben," she whispered miserably. "I am so afraid. I am to be given to a man I do not know, a man who is over twenty years older than me. My heart cries out in horror at the thought. My mind knows I have no choice. It must be as he wishes it to be."

"Can't you tell him you've changed your mind?" Reuben asked. Sylvie stared as if he'd gone suddenly mad and deranged nonsense was spouting from his mouth.

"That is not possible, Reuben. The agreement was made between our parents and my dowry has been paid. We are married in all but the final ceremony and…" she paused, shuddering again. "The consummation," she finished in a whisper.

Heat slashed his face at her words, as images flashed through his mind, images of him and Sylvie locked together in a lovers' embrace, safe in a secret bower hidden deep within the Forest.

"Don't go back," he ordered, sudden despair making his voice harsh and strained. "Come home with me. You'll be safe there. They'll never find you, I'll keep you safe, I promise."

"Oh, Reuben," she murmured, a pretty blush highlighting her cheeks. "I wish it could be so, but they would find us. It would go badly for you and your family, you would be turned out of your home. I could never be the cause of such a thing. No," she paused, drew herself up bravely. "I must return and face my future."

"You can't go back there, I won't let you!" shouted Reuben, springing forward, clasping her hand and drawing her to him. For a heartbeat, she did not resist, instead lay her beautiful head upon his chest, her small hands resting on his arm as a deeply tortured sigh was wrung from her body.

"I must go," she finally whispered, stepping from his arms, eyes luminous with barely restrained emotion. "Farewell," she said, hand briefly touching his cheek before she turned and slipped away through the trees.

"No, Sylvie…" cried Reuben, quickly hastening after her through the trees she'd passed by mere moments before. But, she'd gone.

"Sylvie!" he shouted, head thrown back, lungs aching from the force of his cry. "Sylvie!"

His desperate shout echoed through the Forest, sending animals fleeing for cover and birds soaring upwards from the branches. Reuben stumbled, eyes wild and staring, wondering why he'd never realised how important she was to him until it was too late. She was to be given into the hands of another.

Falling to his knees, Reuben held his head in his hands and howled in despair, but his distress was cut short by another sound; a snuffling, grunting noise. It was a sound he'd never heard before, but on some primitive, survival level was terrifyingly familiar. Slowly, blood freezing in his veins with fear, Reuben raised his head.

The wild boar was squat and powerful, its small eyes fixed upon him with a malevolence that left Reuben in no doubt as to its intentions. Slowly, carefully, he began to creep backwards, hoping against hope the creature would decide him unworthy of any further action. But the boar lowered his head, and with a sudden wrenching movement, charged him.

Desperately, Reuben scrambled to his feet and began to run, stumbling and tripping over exposed tree roots and tangled brambles which thrust themselves into his path, as if some malevolent intelligence was at work. Behind him could hear the creature gaining, and frantically glanced around for a likely tree to climb, knowing should the boar catch him, its strong tusks and teeth were more than capable of inflicting serious harm.

A wall of impenetrable brambles was suddenly in his way. Unable to stop, Reuben fell headlong into their mass, crying out with pain as thorns ripped and scratched at his clothing and skin. The boar seemed to recognise its prey was caught and picked up its pace. Again, Reuben cried out, this time in fear, desperately struggling to free himself from the brambles' firm grasp, Reuben yanked backwards, yelping from the pain of a dozen lacerations as the bush refused to let him go.

The boar was closer now. Reuben ceased his fruitless struggles, stared in fascinated horror as the creature came closer, small eyes blazing with anticipation of the kill, head lowered, powerful chest muscles bunching as it rushed towards him.

Suddenly, a twang split the air, and the beast howled and keeled over, a feathered arrow sticking from its side. Reuben gazed in stunned disbelief as a man strode from the trees. Tall and rangy, his clothes were like those he'd worn so many years before, his eyes the same piercing blue Reuben remembered. Kneeling by the boar, he swiftly plucked the arrow from its side, kicking over the body to ensure it was dead before turning to Reuben, face still and impassive. He held out a hand and with an iron like grip hauled him from the bramble patch, ignoring Reuben's shout of pain as thorns were brutally ripped from his flesh.

"You are the forester's boy." It was a statement, not a question. Without waiting for a response, he continued. "You must tell your father to beware. She walks the Forest and it is time once again."

"I don't understand," Reuben stuttered. "What time? Who walks the Forest?"

"Tell your father," ordered the man. "He will understand."

He strode away amongst the trees, leaving Reuben staring in mute incomprehension.

Later, after his mother had exclaimed in horror over the ripped and lacerated state of his body, and ordered him into a hot bath laced with witch hazel, Reuben sat in the garden holding a bottle of Amos Blunt's finest brew in bloated and sore fingers. His father sat on the bench beside him, grey eyes thoughtful and concerned.

"Now," he began. "Your mother's gone to the shop, tell me."

So, Reuben told him everything that'd happened, everything except his meeting with Sylvie. For some reason, Reuben still could not bring himself to speak of her, so his tale began with the sudden and shocking attack by the wild boar, a creature supposedly long absent from this land.

His father nodded, brow creasing with concern. At the words spoken by the stranger, his head jerked up and Reuben felt a sudden stillness emanate from his father.

"They were his exact words?" he demanded.

"Yes," Reuben nodded," I was to tell you she walked the Forest; that the time had come again."

"It's as I feared," his father murmured. "Although, it's missed two generations, I'd begun to hope…"

"What?" demanded Reuben in an agony of ignorance, "What does it mean?"

"Betrayal," replied his father, cryptically. "Betrayal and jealousy. Love turned to hatred, despair and longing and death…"

"Death?" cried Reuben, sore fingers clutching at the cold bottle in his hand with such intensity, several deep scratches on his palms re-opened and began to bleed.

"Yes," confirmed his father, "Death of innocence and youth."

"But, whose death?" his son demanded.

"I don't know," his father sadly shook his head, turning to face Reuben, and clamping a hand urgently to his shoulder. "Promise me you'll be careful," he begged.

"I don't understand," Reuben began in confused bewilderment.

"Promise me!" his father insisted. "If anything troubles you, if anything unusual happens, no matter how small or inconsequential it may seem, promise you'll come to me?"

Reuben hesitated, thinking about Sylvie, wondering if he should tell his father of her, remembering the anguish which had raked at his heart. Within the Forest it'd seemed a pain too great to live with. Now, Reuben wondered curiously at his extreme reaction to her news, thoughts of her milk white beauty fading from his mind.

"I promise," he finally said. "If anything unusual happens or I'm worried about anything, I'll come straight to you." Daniel gazed for a moment into his son's eyes, then released his arm with a sigh and turned to stare intently into the Forest.

"But who is it who walks the Forest?" Reuben asked.

Long moments ticked by before his father dragged his gaze reluctantly back to his son's concerned face, and once again sighed, a heavy breath which spoke of weighty fears pulling at his soul.

"The White Hind," he finally replied, and would be drawn no more on the subject, leaving Reuben to puzzle and worry at the matter, turning it over in his mind, not speaking of it to anyone, not even Jack and Sally.

Then, a few days later, the old shepherd Wally Twitchett began to spread his tale of seeing the White Hind in the Forest and he exchanged a considering look with his father, sharing the fear he now saw behind his eyes.

Chapter Three
~ The Farmer's Daughter ~

Of the three farms around the Forest, two were high on the downs. On a clear day, it was possible to see East Farm from the highest point on West Farm, and as a child, Sally Cairn had believed these two farms represented the topmost reaches of the world.

The third farm, Home Farm, was more an extension of the estate of Marchmant Hall as it dealt with the husbandry of the Forest, selling timber and game to the local builders and the butcher, although they did raise flocks of traditional rare breeds of sheep, the wool of which was exported around the world.

West and East Farm were similar in size and layout, though the two families which for generations had farmed the land were as different as chalk and cheese. The Hunters of East Farm were an exotically dark and fiery breed. It was always said a man who took a Hunter for his bride would know unending pleasures in the night but would never know a moment's peace during the day, the Hunters being renowned for possessing both passionate natures and quick, hot tempers.

The Cairns were blessed with even, sunny temperaments, and even though Sally's mother had been a Dodd, physically, none of her had been passed onto Sally or her three younger brothers. They were Cairns through and through, from the tops of their flaxen heads to the ends of their freckled, turned up noses.

Sally Cairn loved her family and home, love forming a fundamental and integral part of Sally's life. Sometimes, she felt her very bones had been saturated in love; that it oozed from every pore, lighting her up from within, attracting others to her brightness like moths to a flame.

Her parents often fondly remarked how Sally's first word had been love, and it was a word that still trembled readily on her lips, mouth quivering with happiness and sheer delight at a world that seemed created merely to bring her pleasure.

Once, her father had taken his small daughter up to the very highest point of the farm. Clambering with her onto the strangely shaped, grassy, hummock which crowned their land, he'd held out her chubby, toddler arms to the golden, sunlit world spread below them.

"One day, all of this will be yours," he'd proudly told her. Sally had laughed aloud with joy, clapping her small hands, completely without fear as her father hoisted her aloft in his arms, accepting entirely her position as princess royal, heir apparent for several years until first one, then a further two male heirs arrived to disinherit her.

Sally hadn't cared in the slightest, knowing her true inheritance spoke to her in the rushing of the wind across the downs, the warmth of the sun on her body, the thrilling, intoxicating pulse of life which burst from the earth every Spring, awakening an answering echo in her own wildly beating heart. Understanding it was something that could never be taken away from her.

Sally's favourite place on the whole farm remained the odd, grass covered mound on the highest reaches of the down. She would often go there, scrambling up its uneven banks to lie upon its curiously flattened top, her young body as sturdy as one of the ponies which galloped freely across the nearby moor, melding into the rough grasses. She would lie, eyes closed against the sun's rays, feeling the rawness of the breeze as it swept up the down and gently seduced her willing body.

Twisting her fingers into the coarsely stubby stalks, Sally would lift herself from the earth, her weight supported by heels, hands and head alone, as if offering herself in ritual sacrifice to the sun and the elements, feeling the pull of her cotton frock as it anchored her firmly to the ground, preventing her soul from soaring free.

A true child of the light, Sally hated the dark, her fear a thing of twisted, black reality. As a baby her parents had despaired, finally relenting and installing a night light in her room; a brave little lamp which from that moment on had burned with a comforting glow.

Sometimes, waking briefly from a deep sleep, Sally would blink in the gloom, looking around her room so beloved and familiar during the day, somehow changed in the obscurity of night. Her heart would quicken, her small hand would reach out and turn up the light, a smile of relief on her lips as she fell instantly back into her dreams, thankful once again the dark had been held at bay.

Although she never spoke of this engrained fear of the dark to anyone, somehow Jack and Reuben knew, accepted, and protected her against it. Never did they expect her to join them on their midnight jaunts, when Reuben would slip soundlessly from his window, out on the branches of the ancient apple tree which tapped on the panes and provided a secure route down to ground.

Jack didn't have to rely on such subterfuge, his father never seeming to care where his son was, it certainly never occurring to John Blacksmith to check his son did indeed sleep fast in his room at night.

Occasionally, especially when adolescence loomed, and Sally began to naturally chafe against parental restraints, however loving, she envied Jack this freedom. But then she would see the wild desolation in his eyes, and feel his black jealousy when her parents exhibited by a thousand small and loving gestures, how much her well-being meant to them. At such times, Sally did not envy Jack at all, rather she railed inwardly at the careless callousness of John Blacksmith so lost in his own selfish bereavement he could not, would not, see how much his son needed him.

Sally loved Jack from the depths of her heart. More like a brother to her than her own, much younger siblings, she couldn't remember a time when Jack had not been a fundamental part of her life. He was her other half, her confidante, and her rock. For ten years they were everything to each other, finishing the other's sentences, knowing, without it needing to be spoken, the thoughts which formed in the other's mind.

And then they'd met Reuben.

Of course, they'd known of him before. The village of Wyckenwode being such a small enclosed community, it was impossible not to know intimately every resident. Still, Reuben had been something of a mystery to the other children. The very fact of him being the forester's son, apart and different from the other villagers, afforded him an instant notoriety. And then there was Reuben himself.

Silent, taciturn, with a world of secrets hiding behind those thoughtful grey eyes, Sally often sneaked peeks at him sitting so quietly on the back row at school. Never speaking unless spoken to, never venturing an opinion during lesson, even though Sally felt sure he knew all the answers.

A year younger, and of a slighter, paler build than them, Jack had always dismissed Reuben as being unworthy of their notice, silently seething with jealousy over anyone who took Sally's attention away from him. But, Sally did not dismiss Reuben so quickly, aware beneath the still, placid surface, complexities and unfathomable depths lay concealed.

Then came the encounter with Winston Blunt and everything changed.

"Look at Reuben," Sally murmured to Jack. "He's taking on Winston Blunt."

"Bloody fool." Jack shrugged his indifference to her words, eyes wandering involuntarily to the gathered flanks of fascinated children, and Sally fancied a flash of admiration sparked in his black eyes.

"We have to help him," Sally demanded. "Winston will beat him to a pulp."

"But Sally…" began Jack, then stopped, silenced by her blue eyed, coolly level look.

Sighing, he reluctantly heaved himself to his feet, following to where the children were gathering even tighter into an almost impenetrable mass, eager anticipation of a fight emanating from them in the sweet, sickly smell of pack lust.

Pushing through, Sally and Jack emerged into its epicentre in time to see Reuben throw his head up, defiance blazing from his grey eyes as Winston muscled up to him, fists clenched threateningly, his henchmen, Thomas Dodd and Frank Twitchett, looming menacingly at Winston's shoulders.

Seeing from Reuben's expression he knew he was about to get a pounding, and watching the way his slight, young body tensed and braced itself, his own hands tightening into weak parodies of Winston's, Sally felt her heart go out to him, every protective urge within her rushing to the surface.

Glancing at Jack, Sally knew even though his stance was casually indifferent, he was ready for confrontation. Not only ready, but willing, Winston being one of Jack's least favourite people. Jack hated bullies, despising those who used their strengths to prey on the weak and fragile.

As one, Jack and Sally stepped into Winston's path, their determined bodies shielding Reuben, admitting him into their charmed circle, claiming him as their own. Winston had been easily dealt with, a cleverly cutting remark from Sally to make him lower his defences, then the short, sharp blow from Jack.

As always, when confronted with the violent side of Jack's nature, Sally felt a judder of fear which forced the breath to catch in her throat, heart clenching in fierce denial that someone she loved so completely, could be the very antithesis of all she believed in, capable of such acute aggression.

Sally might very well love Jack, but was all too aware she did not understand him.

At first contemptuous of Reuben's claim to have penetrated further into the Forest than any other child, as they walked in silence towards its shady forbidden depths, Sally had suddenly known beyond any doubt that Reuben could do it. That the Forest which remained closed and secret to all, would welcome and accept this son of the forester, but never imagining the Forest would allow them access too.

It'd been a magical experience, although alarming. The stomach-churning nausea and panic as Reuben dragged them through the barricade, were feelings Sally wouldn't forget in a hurry. The Forest beyond the barrier had proved to be a special, private place, and Sally had looked in awe at its wonders, including Reuben in her silent worship.

But, when Reuben finally led them back hours later, Sally had known they'd never return, that the Forest had tolerated their encroachment this once on sufferance to please Reuben's passionate desire. Never again would they be allowed access.

Relieved once they passed back across the barricade, Sally could remember the acute sensation of unease which'd accompanied her the whole duration of the visit. The feeling of not being wanted; of hostility. How sure, how very sure she'd been, that someone or something, hidden in the impenetrable undergrowth, had watched their every move.

In unspoken agreement, none of the children ever told another soul of that day in the Forest and Reuben never again boasted of his excursions into its depths. It was their secret, and it bonded them even closer together.

After that, Reuben had naturally become one of them. Their twosome expanding easily into a threesome, although sometimes Sally knew Jack might possibly have preferred the old ways, when it'd been only the two of them. This was another reason, beside her fear of the dark, why Sally declined to accompany the boys on their midnight expeditions, believing a chance to spend time in Reuben's company was good for Jack, helped lessen to some degree his complete dependency on her.

Sally was relieved that occasionally the boys were happy to spend time together during the day without her, for Sally had a secret, one unknown to any. Not even Jack, guardian of her innermost thoughts knew of it. And if he was a little puzzled, maybe even a little hurt, that Sally sometimes declined invitations to go fishing, or out with Daniel Forrester brushing on the gorse bound moors for the Marchmant family, he attributed it to some vague girlish issue and didn't pursue the matter.

On the dark side of the Forest, beyond Home Farm, there lived an elderly spinster woman. Her name was Molly Mole, but so ancient and decrepit was her appearance, she was known to one and all as Granny Mole. It was thought at some time in her long-ago youth that she'd worked at the Hall. Her cottage being a tied cottage owned by the Marchmant estate, perhaps there was some truth in the rumour.

Although well cared for by the Marchmant estate, her log pile always full of well-seasoned wood from the Forest and her larder always well stocked with Marchmant family largesse, she didn't have many visitors. It'd been firmly believed by generations of village children that she was a witch, so they avoided her cottage with a tradition which'd become so engrained, even as adults the villagers would go the long way around to Home Farm, instead of the shorter route past Granny Mole's front door.

But Sally Cairn knew Granny Mole was no witch, at least was certain she was benign and would never knowingly do evil. The reason Sally knew this, was that for many years she'd been visiting the elderly woman whenever she could slip away unnoticed.

Sally's acquaintance with Granny Mole had come about literally by accident on her ninth birthday, when, following many broad hints and outright pleas on Sally's part, her parents had bought her a beautiful silver bicycle.

Thrilled with its reassuring sturdiness and added delights, such as a wicker basket and gloriously loud bell, Sally had decided to go for a ride there and then, unable to wait for Jack to arrive for her birthday tea and had jumped on her gift and raced away.

Zooming through the village in an intoxication of speed, skirting the Forest on the broad bridle path, she'd coasted down the steep hill on the far side, feet held high off the pedals, head thrown back in open mouthed, soundless joy at the freedom such speed afforded.

Disaster struck at the bottom. Seeing the fallen branch too late to avoid it, the brave little cyclist had hit the obstacle with a force violent enough to catapult her over the handlebars to land with a sickening thud on the path, to lie, shocked and winded, her precious bicycle twisted and bent beside her, heart pounding from the unexpected awfulness of it, knees and elbows grazed and bleeding, small particles of grit and dirt ground painfully into her soft skin.

Dazed and shaken, Sally had never experienced real physical pain, she'd opened her mouth to howl.

"Hush be, young 'un. Lie still a minute and let old Molly take a look at ya."

Shocked into silence, Sally twisted her head to see who'd spoken. Upon seeing it was an old woman who could only be Granny Mole, the woman everyone avowed to be a witch, Sally's blue eyes had opened very wide, her little heart pounding even faster, convinced the witch intended to cast a spell on her, or worse.

But Granny Mole had merely knelt beside her, muttering sourly about being too old for such things, doubting her ability to be able to get back up again. As Sally heard the rusty creaking of little used kneecaps, a wild urge to giggle bubbled up inside and she no longer felt afraid, feeling, probably quite rightly, any witch who was so inept at magic they couldn't cure their own rheumatism, was almost certainly not much of a threat to anyone else.

Curiously she looked down, and saw Granny Mole had produced a small, green, glass bottle of milky liquid from her brown sack like bag. Using a nearby handy dock leaf, she soothed it onto Sally's poor grazed knees. It'd stung terribly, and Sally had again opened her mouth to howl, only to close it in surprise as she'd realised once the initial ouch wore off, her knees felt much, much better.

Tentatively, Sally struggled into a sitting position, silently offering up her elbows to receive the same treatment. Gazing trustingly into the ancient woman's face, she noticed the milky white film clouding one eye, although the other blazed greenly, alive with cunning intelligence, set into a face so wrinkled and lined, it was hard to make out any expression, other than thin-lipped mouth currently pursed in concentration of the task at hand.

Scrambling to her feet, bracing herself to take the old woman's not inconsiderable weight, Sally helped haul her, muttering and groaning, to her feet. They stood, looked curiously at each other. Two women at opposite ends of the path of life. A spark of recognition passed between them, and Sally offered up a shy smile.

"Thank you," she stuttered.

Pleased, the old woman ducked her head, gesturing with her hand as if to wave away Sally's gratitude. "You be more careful in future, young 'un," she'd cautioned.

They'd both looked up at the sound of Sally's name being called far back along the path, and heard the approaching thud of feet. Jack rounded the bend, face anxious, an anxiety which deepened upon seeing Sally standing there, new bicycle a disregarded heap at her feet.

"Sally!" he cried, as he ran towards her.

Raising her hand in salutation, Sally turned to Granny Mole, only to find she was alone. With a speed and agility belied by her apparent age and infirmity, the old woman had slipped silently and nimbly away. Confused, Sally looked wildly around, and when Jack reached her, turned dazed and bewildered eyes to him.

"Are you alright?" he demanded, concern sharpening his voice.

"Yes," she replied. "I fell off," she added unnecessarily. She opened her mouth to tell of her encounter with Granny Mole, the village witch, but something stopped her. Some inexplicable need to keep it secret, even from Jack, gripped her, and Sally knew she'd never tell anyone of what had happened.

Gratefully, she let Jack take over. He fussed and exclaimed over her damaged bicycle, worried how her parents would take the news their precious gift was already broken.

Slowly, Jack half carrying, half wheeling, the twisted machine, Sally had limped to the village beside him. He'd taken her to his father's garage, explaining to a tight lipped and silent John Blacksmith what had happened. Anxiously, the children watched as he'd run his large, capable hands over the poor little bicycle, mouth tightening as he examined its bent front wheel, the punctured tyre and scratched handlebars.

"Leave it with me," he'd finally said. "Come back in a bit, and I'll see what can be done."

Then, Jack had taken her to the shop, relieved beyond words to find Miss Iris had gone to take tea with Mrs Dodd at the far end of the village, leaving the shop in the care of Miss Violet.

Twittering and concerned, Miss Violet sat Sally on a stool in the corner of the empty shop, and plied her with cold, home-made lemonade. Perched on the low, wooden stool, gripping the thick glass tumbler in both hands, Sally had sipped gratefully at the tart, thirst quenching, contents.

Miss Violet had examined her knees and elbows, expressing surprise she hadn't inflicted more damage on herself. Sally too looked at her wounds, strangely unsurprised the skin, previously so broken and sore, had already begun to heal, a livid pinkness showing where the damage had been done.

Silently, Sally watched as Jack performed small, kindly tasks for Miss Violet, fetching up a heavy box of stock from the cellar, sweeping the dusty wooden floor, chopping a handful of kindling, in case it turned chilly that evening and they decided to light the fire.

She saw the odd, awkward affection that existed between them, and realised from the way Miss Violet's eyes softened whenever she looked at Jack, from the rough concern in his voice, that a genuine and deep attachment existed between them. And liked Miss Violet even more for being so kind to Jack.

Sally knew, apart from herself and her family, Jack was effectively alone in the world, starved for love and affection, and was glad he could also count on Miss Violet. Then, Miss Iris had returned, and quickly, with a pocketful of sweets hastily and guiltily pushed onto them by Miss Violet, they'd returned to the garage to see if John Blacksmith had been able to salvage the bicycle.

To the children's surprise and relief, it'd been returned to almost pristine new condition. At Sally's stuttering, effusive thanks, she fancied she'd almost seen a ghost of a smile on his shuttered face. If she had, it vanished before it could form, and he'd merely grunted away her gratitude.

The children hurried back to the farm, Sally's parents none the wiser as to their adventures, where they enjoyed a marvellous birthday tea, complete with uproarious party games, in which even Jack had been forced to participate. When he'd left, Sally insisted on carefully wrapping a slice of her delicious birthday cake in brown paper, and had made Jack take it for his father. Not caring if he ate it or not, merely wishing to express by some small gesture, her appreciation of his help.

A few weeks after that, Sally found herself alone, Jack being kept back after school to complete an unfinished essay. Bored with loitering around the playground waiting for his incarceration to be over, Sally found her feet making their way through the village, along the track, over the hill and down the narrow, overgrown trail which led to Granny Mole's cottage.

The elderly woman, visibly surprised but, Sally felt, secretly pleased to see the young girl, had insisted on making her tea. A dark green, oddly smelling brew, Sally had the awful feeling it was nettle tea, but, being a nicely brought up and polite little girl, she'd drunk it, and found it strangely satisfying and thirst quenching.

How interesting that first visit had been. Sally tried hard to control her gaze, but oh, how her eyes had wandered all around the cottage's cluttered though clean interior, taking in the bundles of herbs and flowers drying in the rafters, the rows of bottles and containers on the old shelved dresser, their contents unlabelled and mysterious.

A fat tabby cat, almost as ancient as its mistress, had purred in geriatric slumber on a rocking chair. From a vast cooking pot bubbling and rattling its lid on top of the old range, Sally smelt the appetising aroma of stewing meat and vegetables.

Hearing her stomach rumble, the old woman had chuckled, ladled some broth into a carved wooden bowl, and watched with satisfaction as Sally eagerly wolfed it down with the sharp appetite of youth, her one good eye beaming her delight at Sally's praises of its flavour and the succulence of the meat.

That visit was only the first of many. As Sally grew from child to youth to woman, she would go to Granny Mole's as often as possible. Still she kept it a secret. Unsure why, Sally knew her parents would praise the kindness of their daughter, that Jack and Reuben, beyond initial surprise she'd felt the need to keep it hidden, wouldn't have cared, preferring to disappear off on their male orientated excursions in which she had little interest.

Often, Sally opened her mouth to tell, confess her secret, but something would always still her tongue, freezing the words in her throat before they could be uttered, And so the village remained unaware Sally Cairn went to visit the witch, Granny Mole.

Another interest which Sally was unable to share with Jack, was her passion for books. Attentive and intelligent, Sally was the star pupil of the tiny school, and as Jack was renowned for his total disregard for authority and anything vaguely smacking of education, so Sally was lauded for her quick wits and thirst for knowledge.

When Sally became lost in a book it was the one place Jack couldn't follow. Once, his jealousy flamed into such a passion he'd snatched the offending novel from her and thrown it into the duck pond. Stunned, hurt beyond belief, Sally had refused to speak to Jack for days. Crippled by the agonising thought he may have lost her forever, Jack had worked all weekend for Miss Violet, chopping and carting logs in exchange for a brand-new copy of the book, which he'd presented to Sally, so contrite and palely scared of her silence, Sally's tender heart had been touched and she'd instantly forgiven him.

After that, Sally had been careful not to flaunt her love of books in front of Jack, although once, when reading Wuthering Heights, she'd been unable to resist taunting him with how much he resembled Heathcliff, refusing to be drawn any further, no matter how much he'd pleaded with her to enlighten him. Finally, Jack braved the unfamiliar territory of the school library, borrowed the book, and painstakingly read it from cover to cover over the course of many weeks.

Sally, who'd long finished the book and forgotten her teasing comment, was surprised when Jack confronted her with it one evening as they were walking back to the farm. The air had been thick, full of the summer sunset, swifts darting and swooping above their heads catching unwary moths emerging from daytime slumber, the field through which they walked thigh high with burgeoning wheat.

They'd reached the brow of the hill where they always lingered to say goodbye, the lights of the farmhouse comfortingly close, when Jack turned and snatched up her hand, face fierce in the twilight, Sally shocked from her pleasant reverie by the passion on his eleven-year-old face.

"You're right," he'd declared violently. "I am like Heathcliff in lots of ways, but I would never have let Cathy go. I'd have killed that other man rather than see her married to him. In fact, I'd have killed her rather than ever lose her!"

With that he abruptly strode away, leaving Sally confused, concerned, and aware for the first time that the sisterly affection she felt for Jack was returned by him in an altogether more adult, more serious, manner.

The next time they met, Jack acted as he always did, and gradually, with time, memory of the incident slipped to the back of Sally's mind, rarely remembered, except on odd occasions when Jack's jealousy would flare, and she'd be uncomfortably reminded of it. Then she would worry. Wish life could remain as simple and innocent as it'd been when they were children.

Sally knew Jack liked and trusted Reuben. As close as brothers, they needed one another to supply constant male companionship. Sally was also aware Jack was deeply, bitterly jealous of Reuben, and that Reuben himself remained blithely oblivious to this fact.

Desperately, Sally tried to reassure Jack without ever actually expressing it, that he had nothing to fear from Reuben, that his suspicions were unfounded and his paranoia unreasonable. Mostly, she was successful. Only occasionally, upon some harmless comment or action made by either herself or Reuben, would she look into eyes glittering black with passion, heart sinking as Jack closed in on himself, turning away from them, leaving Reuben in a state of confusion and Sally wanting to shake such unworthy, nasty, thoughts from Jack's mind.

One such occasion was when they'd been laughing about their different appearances, and thoughtlessly Sally had commented how like a Viking Reuben looked. Reuben had laughed an outraged denial, pushing her over into the straw and tickling her, and as Sally had rolled and shrieked for mercy, she'd caught sight of Jack, silently watching Reuben lay hands on her, and with a sinking heart had seen the bleakness seep into his eyes.

Once, she'd tried to express her turmoil concerning Jack and Reuben to Granny Mole, stuttering out an explanation of their long friendship, which seemed to be changing the older they grew. Granny Mole had fixed her one good eye on her, and regarded her with a sadness which sent a chill down Sally's spine. For a long time, the old woman did not speak, then sighed and shook her head.

"It's always the same," she murmured. "It were passion that killed her before. It's passion that kills her every time."

"Who?" cried Sally in alarm, "Who was killed?"

"Her," repeated the old woman. "Her that walks the Forest," and refused to be drawn any further, repelling all Sally's questions until finally, exasperated, Sally had gone home. Turning Granny Mole's words over and over in her mind, she felt an echo of recognition deep in her soul, as though the old woman had been referring to something Sally should know, should remember, but couldn't, Something that lurked on the tip of her memory. But the more she tried to claw it into the light, the further it retreated into the darkness of the past.

Sally was aware Reuben went often into the Forest, and even though he spoke little of his experiences, she could always tell when he'd spent time within its boundaries. As the children matured towards adulthood, Sally found herself increasingly confused in her responses towards Reuben and the other life he led.

On the one hand, she, of all people, respected and understood his desire for privacy and some sense of an independence apart from his family, the village and even his friends. But, as Sally blossomed into a pretty and confident young woman, she grew ever more resentful of the time Reuben spent apart from them, from her, and finally began to understand and sympathise with the obvious, passionate dislike his mother had for the Forest.

That Mrs Forrester hated the Forest, Sally had always known. Not until she too began to see it as a rival for Reuben's time and attention, did she finally comprehend why.

It was a taker of men, this Forest. If the old legends were true, it did not always return those it had taken.

Again and again, during that long, hot summer of her twenty-first year, Sally would return to her secret place on top of the down. Hidden, she would lie amongst the tall poppies, ox-eye daisies and wild grasses, turning eyes intense with bewildered pain up to the rain starved sky, torn asunder by conflicting emotions, and by the battle being waged for possession of their young hearts.

Jack's black moods were growing in intensity and regularity, and it seemed each time they were together a bitter fight would ensue, triggered by nothing and leading nowhere, his accusations of neglect and preference for Reuben's company so precisely aimed to maim and hurt, that finally, in pained confusion, Sally would snap at him.

Was it any wonder she preferred being with Reuben? He didn't worry at her so, didn't deliberately fabricate small wounds and slights to justify his loss of temper. With Reuben, she could simply be herself, and not have to watch every word that issued from her mouth. She could relax, secure in the knowledge her every action and thought were not being minutely scrutinised and examined, her every sentence being picked apart for any sign of… what?

Here, Sally would stop, and Jack's eyes would spark a challenge she finish what she'd started, that what was or was not between them be finally brought out into the light and exposed for all to see. But Sally was afraid. Afraid of her feelings. Afraid she was unprepared to make such a choice. Afraid whatever she decided, one of her friends would be irrevocably hurt, their friendship damaged beyond repair.

So, her mouth would clamp firmly shut, her eyes mutely pleading with Jack not to push so hard. Jack would subside, afraid to take that final step, sharp cheekbones stained with the flush of frustrated passion, and their friendship would limp on for a few more days or weeks until the next time.

As for Reuben, Sally was unsure what his feelings about the matter were. His even, placid temperament, so alike her own, was steady and unchanging and eventually, desperate for peace and respite from the constant war now being waged with Jack, Sally sought out the company of Reuben more and more, finding solace in his undemanding, comforting presence. With Reuben she felt calm, content, not harried on the riptide of emotions Jack released within her young heart.

Yet, when she was with him, Sally would worry about Jack, her lifelong love and regard for her cousin binding her fast with unbreakable chains. Made miserable for the first time in her short life, Sally would flee to the sanctuary of Granny Mole's cottage.

Autumn came, and still nothing was resolved. The threesome continued to spend much time together, but the easy trust and companionship that'd so delighted them was gone. Instead, they surveyed each other through eyes grown mistrustful and cautious; Jack's bleak and hostile, Reuben's wary and concerned. Sally watched them both, heart slowly being torn apart with the knowledge that everything had changed.

Adulthood, with all its attendant emotional trauma, had been thrust upon them. If it was not to destroy them somehow a solution had to be found, and Sally felt the burden of responsibility weigh her down, sensing ultimately the outcome lay solely with her.

Then, everything changed.

Reuben came back from a visit to the Forest pale and shaking, skin ripped and cruelly lacerated by thorns. He refused to say what'd happened, although Sally noticed his father's eyes resting anxiously on his son. She sensed the fear emanating from Daniel Forrester, from the tense set of his shoulders knew he was afraid.

Looking at Reuben, seeing the answering alarm in his eyes, Sally became scared, not understanding why, but knowing anything which could cast shadows in the normally unruffled gaze of Daniel and Reuben Forrester, could only be bad.

Reuben too had changed. Frequently, his attention would wander, his body quivering as if waiting and listening for some signal, or some voice Sally could not hear. She realised she was losing him. He was slipping away from her, and as his eyes returned again and again to the Forest, she silently despaired.

For two days, he and his father vanished for hours on end into the Forest's suddenly sinister depths, eyes grim, mouths set into steely tight lines, shotguns tucked firmly under their arms. Sally would wait with Reuben's mother, endless cups of tea and slices of home-made cake disguising the growing terror each woman kept tightly locked away.

Only the slightest shaking of a hand when pouring out tea, the over-brightness to their smiles, revealing the depths of their fears.

Then, Wally Twitchett saw the White Hind.

Suddenly, the creeping anticipation of unease exploded into a firm conviction in Sally's mind this was what it'd been building towards. That something had been unleashed onto the village. Something ancient and implacable.

With panic gripping her heart, she ran to Granny Mole's cottage, seeking answers, unsure what questions to ask.

She found the old lady huddled by the fire, clutching her shawl to her face, muttering and rocking, backwards and forwards, her face shiny with tears. Alarmed, Sally knelt by her side, calling her name and patting her arm.

Finally, the old lady looked at her, although Sally knew only her good eye was recognising her, the other eye, its milky film impenetrable and opaque, twisted and looked away.

A wild thought clutched Sally that it was seeing ghosts and shadows from the past; things which she herself was only dimly aware of, vague echoes and murmurs which caused her to shiver with foreboding.

"She's come back," croaked the old lady, gripping tightly onto Sally's wrist. "She walks the Forest once more, and it will happen all over again. Like the time before and the time before that, all the way back to the first time."

"Who?" cried Sally, voice shrill with fear, "Who's come back?"

"My lady, my little lambkin," crooned Granny Mole, ancient and wrinkled face falling into a grotesque parody of loving concern, making the hairs on Sally's neck rise in icy terror.

"My poor lady," the old woman sighed. "Not her fault, it wasn't her fault." Her face changed, cold hard hatred settled into the lines. "It was their fault," she spat. "All their fault, but I fixed them. Oh yes, Molly Mole fixed them good and proper."

"What did you do?" Sally demanded. But the old woman was gone, lost in a twisted world of shadowed memories.

Sally sat back on her heels, confused and scared, for the first time in her life feeling completely and utterly alone.

Chapter Four
~ The Blacksmith's Boy ~

Why was it, thought Jack Blacksmith despairingly, the more you loved something, the harder you tried to hold and keep it safe, the more it slipped away through your fingers?

Once, when very young, he'd caught a butterfly in his trembling hands. Fragile and beautiful, his heart had ached with the desire to keep and protect it and he'd tightened his grip, terrified of losing it, had run to show his father his treasure, but when he'd opened his palms, the tiny creature had fallen to the floor, its delicate body broken. Jack had cried out in guilty horror that through his love, the very thing he'd been trying to prevent had happened.

The memory of that had stayed with Jack ever since, and he couldn't help thinking of it as he realised the more tightly he tried to hold onto Sally's love, the quicker it seemed to slip away from him.

How old had Jack been when he'd first understood the love he felt for her far exceeded the natural affection between family members? It seemed there'd never been a moment in his life when Sally wasn't the most important thing in it.

Effectively parent-less, Jack looked to Sally for guidance on almost every matter. Her cheerful sunny nature soothed the darkness within, calming his internal tempests, bringing joy to an otherwise bleak and colourless life.

Jack learnt at a very early age not to rely on his father for anything, his young heart hardening towards his father's indifference. Still he couldn't help waiting, hoping for a sign his father cared. As a result of perpetual disappointment, Jack erected barriers of his own, hiding his vulnerability and desperate need for love behind a façade of rebellious apathy. No one cared about him, least of all his father, so he cared about no one in return.

The obvious exception to this was Sally, later Reuben and Miss Violet Peabody. Somehow, Sally possessed the ability to see right through his disguise, to know and understand the real Jack, the lonely boy hiding behind the casually indifferent sneer he'd adopted towards the rest of the world.

Jack knew what the village thought of him, knew and secretly relished the bad boy label he'd acquired. So long as he had Sally, he didn't care if teachers found him unruly and unteachable, if the residents of Wyckenwode sighed and shook their heads whenever he walked by.

What did they know? They'd never tried to see beyond that rebellious facade to the person he was inside.

The only person who'd ever touched the real Jack was Sally, and Jack's heart beat with a fierce loyalty for his cousin.

Second cousin, he would determinedly correct himself, Sally was his second cousin, and that made all the difference. It was alright for second cousins to be in love, it was alright for second cousins to marry.

Even though Sally had always been a constant in his life, Jack still remembered the exact day, the exact moment, when everything had changed. When he realised what he felt for Sally went beyond mere cousinly affection.

It'd been the height of summer, and Jack had made his way up to West Farm looking for Sally, hoping she'd agree to go fishing with him. The sun was standing directly above him, and Jack wiped a sweaty hand over his brow, thinking longingly of the cool, green shade of the pond.

That year, a heat wave had gripped the country. All around was parched evidence of months without rain, and the habitual smile had even begun to slip from the face of Sally's father, as weeks slipped into months and still the drought continued.

Skirting the cornfield, crackly brown stalks of grass scratching and whipping at legs bare under old threadbare shorts, Jack could almost feel the countryside groaning with thirst and his dark eyes squinted against the scorching glare of the sun, concern registering on his face, wondering if this year, for the first time in living memory, the farms around Wyckenwode would have a bad harvest.

Reaching the farmhouse, Jack carefully leant his rod and tackle bag against the sun baked, clay brick walls of the old farmhouse. He walked through the open back door to be rendered almost instantly blind, as he plunged from the brilliance of the day into the comparative darkness of the kitchen.

Pausing for a moment, waiting for his eyes to adjust, Jack heard the amused chuckle of Sally's mother. Blinking, he saw her turn from sliding a tray of loaves into the bread oven to the right of the vast, old fashioned range, permanently alight whatever the weather.

"Hot enough for you, Jack?" Eliza Cairn laughed. Jack grinned in reply, wiping a hand across his brow again and blowing out his cheeks.

"It sure is scorching out there," he agreed, and she moved efficiently across the uneven flagstone floor, to pour him a glass of homemade elderflower cordial from the earthenware jug standing on the enormous kitchen table.

"There you go," she said, watching with satisfaction as Jack drained the glass in four thirsty swigs.

"Where's Sally?" he gulped around the last mouthful.

"She went to hang the washing out for me," Eliza Cairn nodded towards the open door. "One good thing about this weather, washing's drying practically as you're hanging it on the line."

Jack nodded absently, not really interested in such household details, knowing Sally's mother believed in all her children taking on certain responsibilities both around the home and on the farm, feeling it helped prepare them for lives and homes of their own.

Mostly, Jack was relieved his father hired Belinda Twitchett to do the small amount of cleaning they required, and that other than basic tidying up after himself, neither expected nor cared that his son had not the first clue how to look after himself.

Sometimes, Jack would feel a pang for the lack of parental concern this indicated, and envied Sally her loving parents, with their rules, discipline and guidance.

"Has she finished her chores for the day?" he asked anxiously.

Eliza smiled at the barely concealed impatience in his tone. "What you two got planned then?"

"Fishing, down at the pond," Jack's eyes shone. "Winston Blunt caught a huge trout there last week. I wanna see if I can beat him."

"It'll be nice and cool down there," agreed Eliza. "Tell you what," her eyes twinkled at him, "you go and help Sally finish up with the washing, and when you come back I reckon there might be a picnic for you to take."

"Thank you," said Jack, and dashed from the kitchen, leaving Eliza shaking her head, a kindly smile on her honest face as she began slicing doorsteps from one of the loaves cooling on the window sill.

Racing up the garden towards the ranks of washing lines, Jack saw white sheets billowing in the ever-present breeze that rippled over the crest of the down, like sails on a fleet of old-fashioned ships.

Squinting in the strong sunlight, trying to see Sally, his heart thudded oddly as he reached the lines and ducked between the sheets, finally spying her, kneeling on the parched, scrubby grass, intently watching something on the ground before her.

Hearing him, she looked over her shoulder, placing a finger to her lips, and Jack instinctively stilled his approach, creeping up and peering to see what was absorbing her attention so completely.

It was an ant's nest. As the children watched, a neat row of ants, military in the precision of their ranks, were busy ferrying particles of leaf into an earthy tunnel leading into the depths of the baked hard soil.

As fascinated as Sally had been, Jack leant closer, marvelling at the small creatures' strength and tenacity, before his attention was caught by something else. Sally's flaxen hair was in long, thick plaits as normal, and for the first time Jack noticed at the base of her skull where it joined the neat column of her neck, a small golden mole.

Surely he must have seen it before? As Jack stared, mesmerised, felt he was aware of it for the first time, and was suddenly, agonisingly, aware of Sally for the first time.

He gazed at the small, perfect, imperfection, partially obscured by wisps of corn coloured hair gently curling over her tanned skin.

The most overwhelming urge to touch it dawned on him, and Jack reached out a trembling finger, gently laid it directly on the mole. He felt for a second the warmth of her body, fancying he could feel the thud of a pulse through her skin.

She turned startled eyes up to him, and Jack's face flamed as he realised what he was doing, snatching his finger hurriedly away.

"It was an ant," he'd lied hastily. "You had an ant on your neck."

Sally grinned and stood up, brushing at her neck and shoulders. Taking Jack by the hand, she led him back to the farmhouse, blithely unaware in the course of one heartbeat to the next, everything had changed.

For the rest of that day as they lazed under the trees by the pond, greedily consuming the lavish picnic provided by Sally's mother, idly trying to catch a fish, Jack's eyes returned again and again to Sally's sun kissed, happy face.

Knew he was looking at her as a man would look at the woman he loved… knew there could be no other for him.

He marvelled that she seemed completely unaware of his feelings. He ached to confess his longing to her but resisted, knowing with wisdom far beyond his ten years it was too soon, they were too young, and it would only confuse and scare her. But he knew for him the die had been cast, heart soaring at the glorious inevitability of it. Sally was his, the future was settled, he would never again be alone.

The arrival of Reuben into Jack and Sally's lives caused such a dichotomy within Jack's heart, at times the overwhelming confusion would cause him to snap and snarl in frustrated, bewildered resentment.

He hated them both, hated himself for the worry and pain he saw on Sally's face, knowing he'd hurt her, yet unable to stop himself from turning on them, on her, before slinking away like a wolf upon whom the rest of the pack has turned, licking his invisible wounds in private, thinking dark thoughts to himself until the mood had passed.

But Jack liked Reuben and trusted him. After Sally he was his best friend. Sometimes, Jack would imagine life without Reuben and a wild desolation would arise within his throat, choking and strangling. Then he would seek out Reuben, foregoing Sally's company to go fishing with Reuben, sneaking out of the house with him on moonlit adventures through the fields and hedgerows around the village.

Sometimes, Jack even accompanied Reuben and his father on brushing and beating duties for the Lords Gilliard and Jolyon, and would throw out his chest, eyes gleaming with pride at the honour afforded him.

Watching the easy camaraderie between father and son, the obvious, steady love Daniel Forrester bore for Reuben, Jack would swallow down his resentment and envy, returning home to a dusty, cold house, empty of love, to a father who looked at him with eyes barely concealing their bitterness that he was alive, whilst his mother, that beautiful, two-dimensional stranger in the photographs on display in his grandparents' house, was dead.

His mother. Whenever Jack thought of her it was always as Rosie Cairn, never as his mother. In his mind, he considered her to be Sally's great-aunt, it made the loss easier to bear and he was able to study her picture, dispassionately and objectively, seeing her likeness to Sally, the Cairn eyes, the long flaxen hair, marvelling that not one trace of her was apparent in his face.

Intently, Jack would study his own reflection, unable to see Rosie in the shape of his eyes, the sensitive curl of his full mouth, the way his dark hair flopped across his brow, the wistful expression that sometimes passed across his face when he thought himself unobserved.

But his father saw. Every time he looked at his young son, a thousand fresh daggers sliced through his heart, his wounds bled anew, and John Blacksmith would turn away from Jack in silent, unspoken agony.

On those days, Jack would angrily tell himself he needed no one, neither father nor mother. The only person he needed was Sally, and would cling furiously to her, trying to keep her close, desperately seeking reassurance, not understanding like his butterfly so very long ago, that it was possible to suffocate that which you treasured most with too much love.

The day Reuben took them into the Forest, Jack had felt something enter him. Vague and ethereal, its touch was slight, and if Jack's senses hadn't been straining to feel, his emotions on a knife edge of anticipation at being within the impenetrable, forbidden Forest, he might have missed it. When Reuben took Sally's hand and led her away, Jack suffered a tiny stab of insecurity at the unfamiliarity of another boy touching her. In that small instant of raw jealousy, he had let it in it.

A miniscule, almost insignificant seed of darkness, it settled itself in the furthermost corner of his heart, and Jack felt an answering echo of suspicious envy resonate from it, then it faded, and he'd found himself caught up in the wonder and excitement of his surroundings.

But, when Jack re-crossed the boundary with the others, he'd carried this uninvited stowaway with him, unaware something had been planted, something that soon discovered its roots had found fertile soil in which to grow. Little by little, day by day, year by year, this tiny seedling matured, twisting itself deep within Jack's psyche.

Feeding avidly off the half-formed, barely noticed emotions of jealousy and resentment, it grew, spreading its spores throughout his body, until he was unknowingly riddled with cancerous growths of bitterness and anger.

The darkness spread, unchecked, feeding off its own negative energy, and Jack's grip on rationality began to slip. It became harder to fight against the insidious voice which whispered suspicions and poisoned his mind.

Battling the invader alone, Jack was unaware this foreign, invidious parasite had an ally within the village. An ally that had been patiently waiting, unknowingly biding its time, until the small seed of malcontent and resentment was finally ripe.

Jack was fourteen. An awkward age. A time between boy and man. A time during which hormones raged, savage and unchecked, and emotions seemed too much to bear. He grew almost overnight, his father constantly grumbling at the necessity of replacing clothes grown out of within weeks of purchase. Although not as tall as Reuben, still Jack gratifyingly towered over Sally, the very fact of her having to look up at him causing a dull ache to bloom in his chest.

Unaware, uncaring of his appearance, Jack was blind to the glances of the village girls, who suddenly began noticing the darkly scowling good looks and bad boy charisma of a lad previously too slight and troublesome to look twice at.

Now, as his frame developed into whipcord leanness and his face matured into a sardonically handsome expression, the village girls and young women would sigh, exclaim quietly to each other on the unfairness of the situation. That Sally Cairn, although arguably the prettiest girl in the village, had the two best looking boys permanently welded to her side and seemed to express no romantic interest in either of them.

As Jack stalked through the village early on the morning of his fourteenth birthday, his heart was singing from a combination of events which had fortuitously come together, to ensure this was going to be a very special day.

For a start, it was a Saturday, the fact of no school on his birthday being, to Jack anyway, the best present he could have. Coming down to breakfast, Jack had found his father absent. This was no surprise. Since he'd been old enough to understand such things, Jack knew the day of his birth was not an event his father wished to celebrate or even remember, knew today the garage would not open, knew his father would already be sitting by his wife's grave, face even more closed and unreadable than ever.

All day John Blacksmith would walk the fields until it grew too dark to see, before returning home to shut himself in his room, the room where he'd known such joy in the short span of his life with Rosie, heart beating painfully, slowly, as he tortured himself with memories and should have beens.

Jack knew and accepted this, in a way almost understood. The startling realisation came to him one day that should he ever lose Sally, his grief would be as intense and all-consuming as his father's. Indeed, Jack almost admired his father for the constancy and intensity of his love for his wife. Almost, but not quite.

For Jack was certain that when he and Sally had children, as Jack knew with a certainty set in stone they would, if Sally died bringing one of them into the world, that child, rather than being blamed, would be cherished and loved. Living, tangible proof of Sally's life and the great love they'd borne for each other.

Beyond this Jack's thoughts could go no further, emotions racing at the idea of being married to Sally, being with her every day, loving her, doing the things with her that led to the creation of children.

Here, Jack's face would flame with agonising confusion and he'd be stiff and offhand with Sally. His thoughts threatened to burst free every time he looked at her natural, uncomplicated face, knowing her to be innocent of his plans concerning them, and confident they would come true.

They had to, because he could not conceive of a future in which Sally was not his, a world in which he was truly alone. Events would unfold as he wished because the alternatives were too unthinkable.

On the kitchen table, rather than the cake, presents and cards which any other fourteen-year-old might have reasonably expected, Jack found instead an old envelope containing money.

His eyes gleamed as he thumbed through the grubby notes, knowing them to be for him, acknowledging they were a guilt offering from his father. Not caring, or rather, fooling himself that he didn't care.

Reaching the shop, Jack was gratified when Miss Violet fussed and twittered over him, exclaiming she couldn't believe another year had gone, pressing a large envelope and gaily wrapped present onto him, her eyes bright with joyful anticipation.

In that instant, the thought flashed across Jack's mind how pretty she was, how young, then forgot such things as he eagerly opened his card and read the message inside, feeling a warm glow at the effusive best wishes in Miss Violet's flowing script.

Next, he turned to his present, unwrapping it with a nonchalance which didn't fool Miss Violet for a moment. As the last folds of paper fell away to reveal the brand-new fishing reel Jack had been sighing over for months, startled and pleased beyond belief, he turned stunned eyes up to her gently beaming ones.

"How did you know?"

"Let's say a little bird told me." Her smile broadened, and Jack knew that could only mean she'd pressed either Reuben or Sally for ideas, touched she'd cared enough to do so.

Both a little awkward at the sentimentality of the moment, with relief they turned to the important issue of what Jack should buy for his birthday picnic, and a very pleasant quarter of an hour was spent as they considered, choosing a variety of treats. Miss Violet then offered to make up sandwiches for him, and called to her niece to keep an eye on things whilst she popped next door to make dear Jack's picnic.

Slowly, Nancy Peabody sauntered into the confined space of the shop. Instantly, the brightness left the day.

Flushing under her knowing, dark eyed, gaze, Jack nodded politely as Nancy positioned herself behind the counter and leant over it, surveying him with interest.

"Your birthday is it?" she asked.

Jack swallowed, nodded again, wondering if Nancy was aware that when she pressed her arms together and bent forward in that manner, her breasts pushed up to form a darkly enticing canyon, the scooped neck of her cotton dress gaping open to reveal their mysterious curves.

Jack's flush deepened. He yanked his eyes away and looked up into Nancy's amused expression.

"How old are you, then?" she asked languidly.

Desperately Jack wondered how much longer Miss Violet would be. Nancy Peabody had never been one of his favourite people, her sly manipulations and obvious delight in the misfortunes of others did nothing to endear her to Jack or his friends and they tended to avoid her.

"Fourteen," he stammered.

"That all?" Nancy's brows rose in apparent surprise. "Thought you were older. You look it."

Not fully understanding the implication behind her words, not sure he really wanted to, Jack ignored the comment, examining his new reel, once again touched at Miss Violet's thoughtfulness.

"So, what're you doing today then?" Nancy continued.

"Picnic with Sally and Reuben," Jack mumbled.

Nancy slowly nodded. "Always with them, aren't you?" she commented archly. "Wonder you don't get sick of each other."

"I could never get sick of Sally," protested Jack hotly. "And Reuben's my friend. They're both my best friends. You don't get sick of your friends."

His tone was fierce, and it was Nancy Peabody's turn to flush. Angry at the inference she had no friends to grow tired of, her brows drew together threateningly.

Scowling at one another, Nancy suddenly decided to take this arrogant little boy down a peg or two. Deliberately smoothing the angry lines from her face, she shrugged, apparently uncaring.

"If you say so," she drawled. "I only ask because I saw them together last night, and thought it was odd seeing as how you three are always together, it struck me as strange, that's all."

"You saw Sally and Reuben?" demanded Jack.

Nancy nodded slowly, eyes avidly watching his expression, waiting for the flash of jealousy.

A smile briefly touched her lips when she saw it, the uncertainty on his face, and the flicker behind his eyes. Slyly, her hand edged forward to gently touch his where it lay clenched on the glass countertop.

"Expect it was nothing," she murmured innocently, twisting the knife a little further. "Probably something that didn't concern you."

Jack didn't answer, lost in the hot bewilderment of emotions which shrieked in outrage, the piercing thrust of jealousy stabbing deep into his gut.

Entrenched in suspicious envy, he didn't hear the low gasp Nancy gave. Didn't see her head rear up or the taut whiteness of her skin as her mouth tensed. Didn't see the darkness flash in her eyes as she looked at him with new interest…

… and deep within the Forest, a breeze suddenly ripped through the trees, bending them before an unseen force, their leaves dancing in agitation…

Miss Violet returned with his picnic. Somehow Jack was able to fool her all was well, thanking her for the present, unable to meet her fond gaze, before falling out of shop, over bright smile dropping the moment his back had turned.

He paced the road, thoughts in a turmoil, a great reluctance growing within him to see his friends. At the same time an urge burned to grab and shake them, to demand to know why they'd been together, wanting to know why he'd been excluded.

Nancy Peabody watched him go.

Placing a palm flat against the warm glass of the window, her other hand resting against her heart as it raced within her chest in excitement, she tried to analyse exactly what had happened, aware in that instant of blinding jealously she'd triggered within Jack, that something had called to her, had crawled into her already blackened soul and made her its own.

And Nancy had welcomed it, feeling its already familiar warmth as it took up residence. Thin lips curving into a cruelly mocking smile, she watched the troubled Jack walk slowly to meet his friends, all earlier pleasure at the thought tainted with a few, well chosen, words.

Meeting Reuben and Sally at the appointed place, it was hard for Jack to maintain his resentment in the face of Sally's evident excitement, and Reuben's quiet satisfaction. They swooped onto Jack, exclaiming at his lateness, peering with pleasure into the bags of provisions he carried.

Taking him by the hand, Sally led him down the track towards the outskirts of the Forest, her palm warm and soft against his. Jack clutched with sudden despair, frantic to keep her close, to bind her to him, only releasing his grip when Sally squeaked and turned laughing eyes onto him.

Reuben fished a blindfold from his pocket which they insisted he put on, ignoring his half-hearted protests, they turned him around three times until his head pounded dizzily and he'd no idea where they were taking him, guessing it was towards the pond as the air thickened and cooled, and he heard the soft plop plop of fish catching unwary insects from the water's surface.

Hands stopped him, fumbled at the blindfold, and Jack blinked in the sudden sunlight, eyes widening at what he saw: a tent, its camouflaged sides blending neatly into the undergrowth, canvas walls rolled up to allow a cooling breeze to roll through, a groundsheet spread within, perfect for three children to use as an excellent campsite.

Beside him, Sally was almost leaping with anticipation.

"Do you like it?" she begged. "It's our present to you. It was my idea, Reuben talked to his father about it and he helped us get it. Last night, we carried it down here and set it up for you."

"Last night?" Jack asked, relief welling, the tension coiled around his gut releasing. "You both set it up last night?"

"Yes," smiled Reuben. "Never ask a girl to help you set up a tent," he advised. Jack grinned at Sally's huff of mock offence, and the entity within him subsided disappointed, but knowing there'd be other times, other opportunities to gorge on the bitter jealousy it craved and needed to exist.

His weakness discovered, Nancy Peabody never missed an opportunity after that to subtly and cunningly drop poison into Jack's mind about the relationship between Sally and Reuben. Yet it was carried out with such delicacy and precision, Jack remained oblivious it was Nancy Peabody's hand which planted and nurtured the growing paranoia he felt. That it was her satisfied gaze noting the small, but significant, ripples occasionally appearing in the placid surface of the trio's friendship.

Years passed. They all emerged, shaken and breathless, on the other side of puberty.

Nancy Peabody would lie in her narrow bed at night, pulse thumping, breath catching at the waves of satisfied delight being generated from the entity within. aware it was somehow linked to Jack, realising at a very early stage the more jealous and bitter he became, the more her own symbiotic intruder rewarded her with the most exquisite pleasure.

Occasionally, Nancy would use the innocent Miss Violet to do her dirty work, subtly planting suggestions that all was not right with Jack and his friends.

Anxiously, Miss Violet would question him, becoming flustered and tongue tied when Jack almost angrily demanded to know what she'd heard, what she'd seen, her embarrassed blushes lending credence to Jack's ever-growing conviction that Sally was pulling away from him, preferring the company of Reuben to his.

Sometimes, Jack would see himself as the others did, would see the incredulous look on Sally's face, and realise he was behaving unfairly and irrationally.

Then he'd try to contain his feelings, laughing them off as a joke, knowing from her concerned eyes he might be able to fool Reuben, but Sally knew him too well.

Other times, the black cloud would descend upon him without warning, as it did the day harmless teasing about their appearances, led to Reuben innocently pushing Sally over into the straw and tickling her. Jack watched them, his rational side knowing it was merely friendly play, but his blood boiling at the sight of Reuben touching her, of Sally's bright eyes as she'd giggled helplessly.

Jack had left, having to get away, as far away as he could, stunned by the realisation in that precise moment he'd wanted to take his father's shotgun and kill his best friend.

Scared he could be capable of such an urge, Jack savagely fought down the demon within, and for a while was successful. But the strain of constantly being on his guard proved too much, and within a few months the old feelings of inadequacy and helplessness came creeping back.

So it continued, a constant merry-go-round of jealousy and inexplicable rage, until poor Jack's head throbbed from the effort of attempting to control the ever-growing bleakness in his soul, his heart aching with conviction he was going to lose Sally to Reuben.

Time slowed, and seemed to move with a reluctance noticeable only to Jack. He couldn't shake the feeling the world was waiting for something to happen, was holding its breath in anticipation of an event of cataclysmic proportions, still in the future but drawing closer with each passing second.

Jack's memories of this period were vague and hazy, pinpoints of clarity in a mist of confused emotions and thoughts.

Like the day they were wandering past the eastern rim of the Forest when they heard a strange cry above them, accompanied by a rustling of wings and a light jingling of bells. Looking up, they saw a flash of soft brown as a bird landed on the fence skirting the edge of the trees.

They froze, each recognising this was no ordinary bird. Glancing at Reuben, Jack saw his eyes widen with incredulous recognition.

"It's a gyrfalcon," he exclaimed quietly in excitement.

"A what?" whispered Sally, cautiously peering at it more closely, sunlight glinting off her hair as she slowly bent her head to look at its feet bound in soft leather jesses. The bird shifted position, and they heard the soft ringing of its bells again.

"A gyrfalcon," repeated Reuben. "They used to be used as hunting birds centuries ago, but they're endangered now. I wonder where it came from."

"Well, someone's obviously using it for hunting," Sally took another silent step forward, and the bird surveyed her with still, cold eyes, turning its head to watch as Reuben stepped closer, seeming not to mind their proximity. Visibly holding his breath, Reuben pulled his jumper down over his hand and held it out to the bird.

Almost regally the bird inclined its head, stepped gracefully from the fence onto his arm, and settled with a grace so fluidic, Jack caught his breath at the sheer magnificence and beauty of the bird

"She's so beautiful," whispered Sally, echoing his thoughts. "Do you think she'd let me touch her, Reuben?"

"I think so," replied Reuben, frowning slightly as the bird gazed into the wind, a slight breeze ruffling its soft brown feathers.

Slowly, carefully, Sally extended a hand, and the bird turned its head to gaze impassively at her then back at Reuben, as if permission had been granted.

Gently, Sally stroked the bird's soft back, beaming a smile of pure delight at the others.

"Jack," she murmured. "Why don't you come and try, she seems really friendly."

As cautiously as the others had done, Jack made the slightest of movements towards the bird. Its head reared up in sudden panic, eyes locking onto Jack's.

With a jingle and flurry it was gone, soaring up into the sky to hang for a moment, suspended like a lark high above them, before it dove into the canopy of trees and was lost from view.

"Oh, what a shame," cried Sally, and she and Reuben chattered in a rush of excitement about the bird, speculating where it could've come from, wondering where it'd gone.

Jack remained silent, lost in realisation it'd been no coincidence the bird had flown the moment he'd stepped towards it.

For in the instant the bird raised its head and looked deep into Jack's soul, Jack had felt a great terror grip the bird, knew it to be mortally afraid of him, or rather of what it sensed within him.

Not for the first time, the shadow of fear brushed across his heart.

The year began to die, and the nights closed in.

As the long, lazy days of summer ended and his time with Sally was of a necessity curtailed, a rising tide of panic clawed at Jack's throat, choking him with a noose of despair.

Gradually, imperceptibly, Jack sensed her slipping away from him, and knew it to be entirely his own fault. Angrily, he'd rail at her for preferring the company of placid, good-natured Reuben, hearing in his own bitter, accusing words the wedge he was driving between them, unable to stop himself from demanding her constant reassurance.

Patiently, Sally would attempt to placate him. Still Jack could not let it be, pushed to the limits. In utter exasperation, Sally would finally snap and plead with him to stop, please stop. Jack would understand the pain on her face, see tears glinting in her eyes and turn away angrily.

Mostly angry with himself for upsetting the one person who meant more to him than the rest of the world put together, but also angry with Sally, for not being able to give him the absolute commitment he craved.

Worrying at it late into the long autumn nights, Jack could see no solution except one, and his heart lightened at the obvious rightness of his plan. He would finally ask Sally to be his wife.

They were young, that was true, but had been destined for one another since babyhood. Jack knew once Sally was his, the awful, gnawing bleakness within would finally be vanquished.

At last he would be happy.

Before Jack could act on his plan Wally Twitchett saw the White Hind, and suddenly everything changed.

The Forest

~ a tale of old magic ~

~PART TWO~

*"Every ancient tale has truth at its heart," I said.
"That's what I've always believed, anyway.
But after years and years of retelling, the
shape of those old stories changes. What may
once have been simple and easily recognized
becomes strange, wondrous and magical.
Those are only the trappings of the story.
The truth lies beneath those fantastic garments."*

~ Juliet Marillier, Tower of Thorns ~

*Pay heed to the tales of old wives. It may well
be that they alone keep in memory what it
was once needful for the wise to know."*

~ J.R.R. Tolkien, The Lord of the Rings ~

Chapter Five
~ The Tale of Two Sisters ~

It'd been five days since the sighting of the White Hind. Once again, Miss Iris's select circle of ladies gathered in her front parlour, and Nancy Peabody moved silently amongst them, handing out napkins and best bone china cups which Miss Iris saved for company, her eyes kept demurely on the ground.

Adept from long years of practice, Nancy blended seamlessly into the background, unnoticed and forgotten, sinking quietly into a corner, mouth firmly compressed into a tight line of anticipation, ready for the intriguing, possibly useful, information she felt confident would soon be shared, along with feather light sponge and delicate scones.

She didn't have long to wait.

"Well," Winifred Blunt exclaimed, teacup rattling dangerously in its saucer as she leant forward in slack-mouthed eagerness, matronly bosom heaving with barely suppressed excitement. "What do we all think of the news?"

The low hum of polite small talk ceased. Sliding her eyes upwards, Nancy thought how like a ferret the elderly woman looked, sharp nose twitching as if to scent the air, small inquisitive eyes with their hint of pinkness, her tight helmet of rigidly controlled curls practically bristling with self-importance.

Ninety-three, only ever admitting to eighty-nine, Winifred Blunt was the oldest women in the village, and even though had stepped down from running the pub some forty years hence when her husband had died, she was still considered a veritable matriarch. Instilling the fear of god into the village children, they'd scatter at her approach, hiding behind walls to peer out as she passed, her once legendary flaming hair faded to the dull rust of extreme old age, belying the sharply knowing gleam in her eye.

"Surely it can't be true," murmured Maisie Dodd nervously. The youngest of the group, only allowed to attend because she was Mabel Dodd's much put-upon daughter-in-law, poor Maisie was looked down on by the other ladies. Her flippant, airheaded comments usually caused many an arched brow and knowing look between the other ladies, but now Nancy noticed several looked hopeful at her words, as if they too were finding it hard to believe the veracity of events.

"It's true alright," snapped Mabel Dodd, casting her daughter-in-law a sharp look which had her subsiding, blushing furiously, into her tea. "I've known Wally Twitchett all his life," she continued. "He's not one to have flighty imaginings. He's steady, he is. No, if Wally Twitchett says he saw the White Hind, then that's what he saw."

Her mouth closed firmly over the last words, declaring an end to the matter, her chin bobbing decisively, and a sigh rippled through the room. For a moment there was silence as the ladies sipped thoughtfully at their tea, nibbled listlessly at cake, all appetite dispelled by her words.

"Yes," murmured Miss Iris. "But what will happen? Now she's returned, what does it mean?"

"Mean?" snapped Winifred Blunt. She exchanged a protracted, solemn stare with Mabel Dodd, the only other lady present old enough to know, to remember the last time the White Hind had been sighted, and the tragedy which followed in her wake. "It means death," she finished.

"Yes, but whose death?" insisted Miss Iris.

Winifred Blunt slowly shook her head, taking a long sip of tea, feeling the eyes of all fixed upon her in an agony of anticipation, enjoying her moment in the spotlight.

"Nobody knows, until it's too late," she stated. "That's the thing. Everything seems normal, life in the village going on much as it's always done. But underneath, it's brewing and bubbling, waiting, just waiting to strike. Deep within the souls of the young, it sharpens its weapon …

"What weapon?" asked Maisie Dodd, eyes wide with the delicious thrill of fear.

The ladies leaned expectantly towards Winifred Blunt, tea cups being carefully set to one side, cake crumbled into dust by nervous hands.

"Jealousy," declared Winifred Blunt decisively.

The ladies exchanged twitchy, apprehensive, glances.

"Jealousy?" queried Miss Iris, thin lips pursing into a moue of disapproval. Jealousy, in Miss Iris's view, denoted an excess of passion, and everyone knew no good ever came of that.

"That's right," Winifred Blunt nodded, scraggly chin bobbing enthusiastically, the loose skin on her face settling into even more rigidly defined lines than normal. "Jealousy," she stated again. "At least that's how it looked to me, and it's certainly what the old legends claim it is."

"So, what exactly happened?" enquired Norah Twitchett timidly. Only her third invitation to join Miss Iris and the ladies, she was keenly aware this inclusion into the inner circle had come about because of her husband's ascent into the position of head of the village council.

"It was seventy years ago," mused Winifred Blunt. "I was only a young lass myself, not even twenty." Several of the ladies exchanged mouth pursed glances, but wisely refrained from comment.

"I remember it too," interrupted Mabel Dodd. "Even though I was only ten or eleven, I can still remember it as if it were yesterday." For a moment the two old women were silent, caught in memories of long ago. Then Winifred Blunt sighed and shook her head.

"It was so terrible," she murmured. "Such a waste of young lives…"

"Whose lives?" demanded Miss Iris in exasperation.

"Why, their lives of course," replied Winifred Blunt, looking around in startled bewilderment. "Do you mean to tell me none of you know the tale?"

At the sea of shaking heads and denials, she looked at Mabel Dodd in surprise. "How can they not know?" she demanded.

"It was so long ago," Mabel Dodd chided softly. "The Family hushed it up, forbade anyone to talk about it, didn't want lots of nosy parkers asking questions, and telling lies about what had happened."

"That's true enough," agreed Winifred Blunt. "But all the same, you'd think they'd know something, would remember enough to be on their guard for the next time."

"People wanted to forget," replied Mabel Dodd. "And really my dear, can you blame them?"

"I suppose so," Winifred Blunt reluctantly conceded.

"Could you tell us the story, Mrs Blunt?" Once again, Maisie Dodd put into words what everyone was thinking.

"Well, like I said, it happened seventy years ago," began Winifred Blunt, eyes misting as her thoughts travelled backwards to the days of her youth so far away, but clearer and more vivid than events of yesterday.

"There were three youngsters," she continued, her words weaving a magic of their own as the ladies settled into their chairs to listen. "They were George Dodd and the Hunter sisters, Louisa and Jemima…"

It was commonly acknowledged in Wyckenwode, if a man's preference ran to dark eyed, dark haired and passionate beauties, then Louisa Hunter had no one to equal her loveliness, unless of course it was her younger sister Jemima.

Inseparable since birth, the Hunter girls seemed to think with one mind and speak with one voice, and as they grew into womanhood, it was said Farmer Hunter had no need to mow the path leading to the farm, because it was kept short by the feet of all the suitors who regularly climbed the hill to pay court to either Louisa or Jemima.

For all their similarity in looks, the sisters were as different as day is to night. The eldest sister, the fiery and proud Louisa, scorned any man who could not match her in wits and on horseback. Her younger sister, Jemima, was gentler and steadier, a quiet and practical girl who preferred more ladylike pursuits, she was able to see past a man's exterior to the loyalty of his heart.

It was believed Jemima Hunter would marry first, for it seemed no man would ever be able to meet all of Louisa's demanding standards. When one young man was singled out by Jemima from all the other village lads to be paid special consideration, gossip all agreed the shy, quietly good-looking George Dodd would finally win one of the sisters.

Head stableman on her father's farm, George had been in front of Jemima all her life, but she'd never noticed him until the day she'd taken her mare, Polly, out for a ride. Not a natural rider like her sister, Jemima needed a trustworthy, quiet mount, and when her father bought riding horses for his daughters, he'd chosen carefully, selecting animals which matched the different temperaments of their new owners.

Louisa's horse, Satan, was a shining chestnut brute of an animal. All heart and pounding muscles Louisa adored him, and in turn Satan worshipped his mistress, allowing no other but her to ride him, taking bad tempered nips out of the stable lad whose misfortune it was to groom him.

This was in direct contrast to the sweet tempered, dependable mare Farmer Hunter chose for his youngest daughter. On Polly's back Jemima always felt safe, until the day they rode over the moor and Polly stepped on a viper. In cold and instinctive vengeance, the reptile plunged its fangs into the horse's leg and Polly reared in mindless terror, startling Jemima who lost her seat and fell to the ground, knocking the breath from her body and severely twisting her ankle.

Shocked and bruised, Jemima huddled over the fallen body of her mare, facing the very real possibility of being stranded on the moor all night, knowing without medication her beloved mare would certainly die. Then Jemima heard a familiar voice whistling a jaunty tune and over the crest of the hill came George Dodd, her father's stableman, heading back to the farm from his day off.

Never had Jemima been so pleased to see anyone and she clutched at George's hand in desperate gratitude. As her sorry tale of woe tumbled from her lips, George's face grew serious. He knelt beside Polly, seeing from the foam flecked lips and heaving sides the mare was in a bad way.

Inwardly feeling the kindest thing would be to put her out of her misery, when he looked into the pleading dark eyes of Jemima Hunter, felt the pressure of her small, pretty hand on his arm, George swallowed his thoughts, and vowed to do everything within his power to help his master's daughter.

Leaving Jemima with the mare, he raced back to the farm as fast as he could and alerted Farmer Hunter, who dispatched four men and a low cart to collect the animal and his daughter. Louisa, upon hearing the dreadful news, immediately leapt onto Satan's back and set off to fetch Adam Forrester, for as everyone said, what Adam Forrester didn't know about animals was not worth knowing.

Polly was examined and treated by Adam Forrester. His face grim, he gave Jemima a milk white concoction which had to be forced down the mare's throat every hour. Before he left, he warned that the situation did not look hopeful, and again Jemima's eyes swam with tears. Seeing this, George's heart constricted within his chest, and when Jemima decided to sit up all night with Polly, he volunteered to assist with medicating the sick mare.

It was a long night. In between caring for Polly, Jemima found herself having long conversations with George, during which she discovered there was a lot more to the shy and modest young man. By the time Adam Forrester returned at first light to proclaim Polly out of danger, Jemima was halfway to being in love with George Dodd, and he had realised no other woman in the village would do for him.

Theirs was a conventional and steady courtship. George would walk Jemima home from church, shyly shortening his stride so she could walk demurely by his side, glancing sideways at him through her lashes, their hearts beating and cheeks flushing with the simple pleasure of being in the other's company.

Finally, George plucked up the courage to ask Farmer Hunter for his formal permission to become engaged to Jemima. After long conversations with his daughter to determine that was her wish, Jemima's father gave his permission and the pair announced their engagement at Whitsun.

At first, Louisa dismissed George as being unworthy for her sister, refusing to believe Jemima could possibly be interested in someone who, as far as Louisa was concerned, ranked far below her both socially and intellectually. Then, when their engagement was announced, Louisa railed angrily at her sister, deriding her for making such a bad choice, expecting Jemima to heed her words and follow her sister's advice, as she'd done all her life.

For once, the mild and gentle Jemima surprised her dominant older sister. Facing her down, chin held high, Jemima firmly declared her love for George, requesting her sister hold her tongue if she could find nothing civil to say about her future husband.

Rendered speechless by the battle light shining in her sister's eyes, Louisa subsided, realising her sister was in love, completely and utterly, that it would be very unwise of Louisa to force her to make a choice.

After that, Louisa was the very model of politeness to George. In time, seeing how much he worshipped her sister, and the steadfast, loyal heart which beat within his unprepossessing exterior, Louisa came to appreciate George's worth, and no more did she tease her sister at his supposed inadequacy. Maybe, there was even a little envy at Jemima's good fortune to be so wholly and assuredly happy and settled, her future fixed and unwavering, for often Louisa would take Satan and ride for miles across the wild, windswept moors, her young heart yearning for something, not knowing what.

One day, the sisters were walking along the bridle path that skirted the edge of the Forest on their way to visit old Clara Twitchett who was not long for this world, with a basket of provisions the sister's mother had packed with which to tempt her failing appetite. As the girls paced they discussed many things, wondering if Clara Twitchett's granddaughter, Winifred, would be there.

A distant cousin, as most were in the village if you followed family trees back far enough, Winifred was an especially close friend of the girls, although her forthright manner and blunt way of talking sometimes worried Jemima. They giggled about Winifred's forthcoming marriage to William Blunt, the owner of the village public house, speculating how such a mild-mannered and weak man would possibly cope being married to a girl whose tongue was only rivalled by Louisa's for its sharpness.

Suddenly, the pounding echo of hoofbeats intruded into the girls' musings, hastily they turned as two horses, racing neck and neck along the path, galloped around the corner. Jemima screamed. Louisa dropped the basket and grabbed her sister's hand, pulling her sharply towards the verge as the riders saw them, attempting to slow their wild-eyed mounts.

The horse in the lead, a glorious rich bay, swerved, pounding past them in a blur of tossed mane and wide eyes, but the other was headed straight for them. Louisa saw the rider pull desperately on the reins, his cap flying off as the horse plunged and reared upright, unseating its rider who crashed heavily to the ground.

Quickly, Louisa pushed Jemima behind her. Stepping forward, spreading her arms wide, she spoke softly and reassuringly to the animal, maintaining eye contact, watching the madness drain from its large dark eyes as it listened and responded to the calm in her voice, dropping its head to the ground, sides heaving, nostrils blowing out clouds of hot steam.

Gently, easily, Louisa moved forward, placed her hands on its face, whispering, always whispering until finally the horse stepped forward and nudged her gently in the shoulder. Lifting its dangling reins from the ground, Louisa marvelled that it'd avoided breaking one of its delicate legs.

Looking over her shoulder, she indicated with a nod that Jemima could now move to assist the downed rider. Quietly, Jemima knelt, helping him to sit, ascertaining there were no broken bones or serious injuries to contend with. Glancing towards them, Louisa recognised him as the head groom from Marchmant Hall, and her heart began to pound as she heard hoofbeats returning along the track.

They were well matched, she thought desperately. The tall, muscled animal, his glossy bay coat shining with health, and the arrogantly handsome rider. His piercing blue eyes examined her with an interest so frank, the usually unshakeable Louisa was horrified to feel her cheeks burn with the kind of blush she'd always scorned to see on other girls.

"Well," drawled Lord Marchmant, taking in the situation with a glance. "And who might you be?"

"Louisa Hunter, sir," she replied, and grudgingly dropped a half curtsey which had his strong white teeth flashing in a mocking grin.

"How's Benson?" he demanded, and Jemima looked up.

"I fear he has a lump the size of an egg on his head, sir. Is badly bruised and shaken."

"It's a damn nuisance," declared Lord Marchmant, annoyance flickering across his chiselled face. "I wanted a good hard ride across the moors. Now, thanks to you two, I suppose I'll have to turn back."

"You were riding too fast along the track," Louisa snapped, forgetting her place in her anger at his apportionment of blame.

"Indeed?" Louisa saw his brows lift at her presumption, instinctively raising her own chin to meet him, and fire blazed in her dark eyes.

"Yes, indeed, sir," she retorted. "You could have trampled us."

"And as that would have been a tragedy of the greatest magnitude, Miss Louisa Hunter," he retorted. "You have my most sincere and humble apologies." Again, he grinned, and Louisa desperately wondered if there could ever be anything humble about this man.

"This does not solve the problem of my ruined race. I take it Benson's in no fit state to continue?" This last was to Jemima, who shook her head resolutely.

"I fear not, sir," she replied, Louisa's lips twitched at the ring of steel in her sister's voice. "He is mightily confused and really needs to be escorted home."

"Damn and blast it," swore Lord Marchmant. "He's the only one who stands even a chance of giving me a run for my money. Still, nothing for it I suppose." He wheeled the bay's head around, as Louisa stepped forward and impulsively cried out.

"I will race you, sir!"

Lord Marchmant stopped and stared, Louisa fancied she saw a flash of admiration pass over his face before he shook his head. "Do not be so foolish girl, Prince would never allow you onto his back. Even if he did, you'd not have the strength to control him, not a slip of a girl like you."

"You let me worry about that, sir," Louisa snapped. Gathering up the reins, she threw her leg across the willing horse's back, mounted in a flash of white petticoat and long legs and was off, calling back over her shoulder. "Catch me if you can, sir!"

Jemima watched with apprehension as her headstrong, volatile sister galloped away from them, afraid she might be thrown, and saw the spark of lustful interest flare in the young Lord's eyes as he wheeled about his horse and set off after her in hot pursuit. Helping the hapless Benson to his feet, Jemima's heart clutched with a new and even more alarming fear.

Two months later, the village was rocked to the core at the news the eldest Hunter sister, Louisa, was engaged to be married to the dashingly handsome son and heir of the Marchmant family...

Winifred Blunt paused, cleared her throat, sipping at the dregs of her tea and pulling a face at its tepid, stewed taste. "I think we need a fresh pot, Miss Iris," she ordered. Impatiently, the other women waited whilst Miss Iris hustled into the kitchen to obey.

"I'd forgotten," mused Mabel Dodd into the expectant hush. "I'd forgotten how wild and magnificent Louisa was."

"She sounds little better than a hussy," snapped Miss Iris, hurrying back into the room, rotund blue china pot clutched in her permanently chilled grasp.

"Oh no," retorted Winifred Blunt, a wistful look settling onto her lined and mournful face. "Louisa Hunter was no hussy. She was strong-willed and fiercely independent, a woman ahead of her time. One who chafed at the restraints of the age she'd been born into. A free spirit in every sense of the word. It was no wonder young Lord Marchmant was obsessed with her. Louisa never saw herself as anything other than his equal, you see. For a Marchmant, well, that must have been a startling change."

"Did she marry him?" Maisie Dodd enquired timidly. Once again, Winifred Blunt and Mabel Dodd exchanged glances, eyes twinkling with the memory.

"Oh yes, she married him. What a wedding it was! Why, I can still remember it as clearly as if it was yesterday, such feasting, such celebrating. Louisa made a beautiful bride. Her dress was made of the finest silk and satin, her shoes came all the way from Paris. When she married into the Marchmant family, it set her high above the rest of the village. She was gentry now. Even her own family had to pay her respect." Winifred Blunt paused, considering.

"I often wonder if that's when it all began to go wrong, if that's when the seeds of discontent and jealousy were sown. Of course, Jemima wished her sister well, and of course was very happy with George. But, their own simple little wedding couldn't begin to compare with Louisa's, and the tiny cottage George took his bride home to looked like a ramshackle hovel when seen next to the magnificence of Marchmant Hall. It would've been only natural for Jemima to envy her sister, maybe a little," she broke off and frowned at Mabel Dodd.

"I can't quite remember when it was the White Hind was seen, but I do know it was your brother who saw it…"

"That's right," confirmed Mabel Dodd eagerly. "Stanley my older brother. He was working as cowman on West Farm and used to come home every Sunday, taking the shortest path which led right past the Forest. It must have been some five years after the weddings, I remember, because I'd have been sixteen and mother was making enquiries about me going into service at the Hall. That Sunday, Stanley had gone to church with us as normal, then he'd helped mother out around the house, Father's back by then being so bad, heavier chores such as digging the garden and chopping wood were beyond him. Stanley always made sure we'd enough logs chopped to last us the week," she paused, and took a sip of tea.

"I remember that particular Sunday, Stanley had left and I was helping mother clear away the tea things, when suddenly we heard pounding feet and Stanley burst through the kitchen door, white as a sheet, looking as though he'd seen a ghost, which I suppose, in a way, he had. I've seen it, he yelled as soon as he could get a breath, the White Hind. Well, mother threw up her hands and gave a shriek, father rushed into the room and there was a right to do. Father took Stanley off to the pub, and messages were sent to all the men to gather to talk about what to do for the best."

"I remember," agreed Winifred Blunt, nodding her rust coloured head vigorously. "My father and both my brothers went to that meeting. Mother and I sat by the fire and she told me the tale of the White Hind. How every generation or so it's seen, and that death always follows in its wake."

"But what about Louisa and Jemima?" insisted Maisie Dodd. "What happened to them, after they were married and after the White Hind had been seen?"

"Well, listen and I'll tell you," began Winifred Blunt importantly, and the ladies leant forward expectantly...

Another miscarriage. Jemima lay back on blood-stained sheets and turned her face to the wall, unable to bear the sight of the village midwife, silent and grim-faced, bundling up the pathetic fragment of life to dispose of.

Hot accusing tears slid slowly down her cheeks, and she stuffed a fist into her mouth to muffle her sobs, knowing George was waiting downstairs, and would be distressed to hear her suffering. Inwardly, she railed against a world which had turned its back on her, punishing her for some misdeed, although what, Jemima could not imagine.

How many hopes had there been now? How many desperately longed for dreams had been swept away in a scarlet tide? Five? Six? Jemima was unsure. The fact she couldn't remember how many scraps of life she'd lost made her bite her knuckles even harder.

Always before she'd been able to recover quickly. Her body was young and strong, her love for George, her faith one day her dearest wish would be granted, had always given Jemima the strength to carry on. But this time was different. This time Jemima had carried the child well into her seventh month, and had felt it move and stir deep within her womb.

Had allowed herself to hope.

When she'd awoken in the night, the familiar throbbing, dragging pain ripping at her innards, she'd prayed frantically that somehow it would be alright. Maybe she'd got her dates muddled and the baby was arriving when it should.

Her plea was ignored. When finally the child had passed into the light, Jemima lifted her head and looked down, seeing it was a boy child, knowing from the blue pinch to his small mouth and the firmly closed eyes, that his softly rounded body, blurred and indistinct, was merely an empty husk. The little soul who'd inhabited it for seven months was gone.

During the weeks and months that followed, Jemima knew her family were concerned for her, understood the pain George was suffering. It seemed insignificant, inconsequential, compared to her own. Each time, he awkwardly tried to reassure her he didn't care if they never had children. He loved her, said she was enough for him, and Jemima would feel the black tide of resentment well inside.

Because he was not enough for her, and by claiming it didn't matter he undermined her suffering and pain.

She both longed for, and despised her sister, needing Louisa's familiar strength, yet bitterly resentful of the fact her sister had borne two beautiful and healthy babies, sailing through pregnancy as if it were nothing, practically giving birth in the saddle. Every time she looked at the sturdy beauty of her sister's children, Jemima's blood would seethe with sticky envy.

She began disappearing for long walks, wandering through the outskirts of the Forest, her heart a painful mix of jealousy and frustrated dreams. A small, dark voice deep inside urged her on to more and more bitter and violent thoughts against her sister.

Jemima would return from the Forest, wild eyed and restless. Once back within the neat and tidy world she inhabited with George, she would vow to herself not to return to the shadowy glades with its strange rustling, those silent voices which whispered such twisted and tortured things into her heart, feeding the ever-growing seedling of bitter resentment she carried under her breast against her sister.

It was unfair. Her sister had everything. The handsome husband, the magnificent home, the wealth and power which came with being a member of the Marchmant family.

Most of all, Louisa had her children.

Jemima grew pale and slight, eyes sunk deep into shadows of long, sleepless nights and even longer days spent in anguished contemplation. Again, and again, her feet would follow the now familiar path into the Forest, feeling the wraiths it contained calling to her from the other side of the barricade.

Then, Louisa's husband went away on business. Lonely without him, Louisa began to spend more time with her family, taking her children by the hand and walking them up the hillside to visit with their grandparents, kind Uncle George, and Aunt Jemima who scared them with her silently hungry gaze, her thin angular fingers which would grip their shoulders, pinching their young skin.

With the vision accorded to the very young and the very old, the children would observe the way Aunt Jemima watched their mother. They saw the ever-growing hatred and madness in her eyes, grew afraid yet remained silent, trapped in the knowledge that even if they spoke they'd not be believed.

Jemima watched her sister. Saw the way she laughed and joked with George, and an even darker notion arose inside her. At first she dismissed it as pure nonsense, but as weeks passed and George began to spend more time at Marchmant Hall, the conviction took firm hold within her breast that her husband and sister were lovers.

Louisa had recently bought a new mare, and George had been giving her advice as to which of the magnificent stallions residing in the Hall's stables it would be best to breed her to. She'd also presented each child with a pony at Christmas, and George had taken upon himself the pleasing task of teaching his young nephew and niece to ride.

~88~

Enjoying the company of the children, secretly relieved to escape the bleakness of his own home, George was too loyal to admit aloud his concerns about his pretty young wife's disintegration into the skeletal, silent form that moved carefully around the cottage, going through the motions of being a good housewife, her fathomless, empty eyes frightening him with their desolation. Instead, he sought sanctuary in the bright cheerfulness of his sister-in-law's home, where Louisa's uncomplicated and forthright manner came as a welcome relief, the children a bittersweet reminder of what might have been.

Eaten alive with suspicious convictions, Jemima held her tongue and bided her time, both craving and dreading absolute proof her husband had been untrue and her sister had betrayed her. Then, some five months after her husband had left home, Louisa came to take tea with her sister, desperate to somehow reach through the shuttered layers, to the sweet and loving girl she felt was still buried deep within.

Jemima played her sister at her own game, exchanging polite small talk over the best china, her mouth erecting a smokescreen through which her blackened heart peered suspiciously, the creature behind her eyes watching, watching, for a sign, the slightest hint. When Louisa rose to take her leave, Jemima fancied she saw it.

Silhouetted against the bright spring sunshine pouring through the open cottage door, Louisa turned to bid her sister a fond farewell. Jemima narrowed her eyes, staring at her sister's thickened abdomen, realising with a wild, hot rush of exhilaration that her sister was once again with child. Judging by the slightness of the bulge was not far along, certainly less than the five months her husband had been away, so that could only mean one thing...

Every vestige of Jemima perished in the howl of satisfaction the creature within uttered. Black, loathsome hatred filled her veins and pounded in her temples.

Watching her sister make her way down the hill, skirts brushing through poppies and ox-eye daisies, heartsease and buttercups, wild grasses and speedwells; Jemima silently made her plans.

It was late next evening when the children's nursemaid went in search of Lady Marchmant, concern etching her brow, mouth plucked into a moue of alarm. The young Lady Marchmant had not come to the nursery to spend her usual hour with the children before they went to bed. The children looked forward immensely to this special time they spent with their mother, and had been most disappointed at her non-appearance. When the nursemaid made enquiries, no one in the Hall could recollect seeing Lady Louisa since afternoon tea, although a parlour maid did remember a note being delivered by one of Farmer Hunter's lads.

Concerned, a strange disquiet creeping along her spine, Lady Marchmant hastily sent a groom to East Farm to enquire about her daughter-in-law's whereabouts, reassuring herself that maybe Louisa had stayed to have dinner with her family, knowing if this had been the case, Louisa would have sent word.

The groom returned with news that the whole farm was in an uproar, for young Mr and Mrs George Dodds were also missing. Farmer Hunter was arranging a search party, fearing his daughter's fragile health may have led her to perhaps wander onto the moor, and that maybe George was out looking for her.

Nagging disquiet now growing into full blown alarm, Lady Marchmant ordered men from the Hall to aid and assist with the search. She, together with the maids and cooks, began an intricate investigation of the many stables and outbuildings clustered around the Hall, fighting down ever mounting fear, desperately reassuring herself all would be well. Louisa was perhaps also looking for Jemima, although a tiny insistent voice within kept demanding something was dreadfully, terribly, wrong.

Lady Marchmant would've been even more alarmed if she'd seen the events which occurred some two hours previously, when Louisa, somewhat annoyed by the presumptive tone of her sister's note, walked into the Forest to rendezvous with Jemima.

Shivering at the change from brilliant sunshine to shady cool, Louisa picked her way delicately over exposed tree roots. Feeling the child within kick, she placed a hand on her stomach, stunned as always at the rush of maternal protectiveness which swept over her. She wished she'd been able to share her glad news with her dear sister, but knew Jemima to be in no fit state to hear her sister had been blessed again, whilst she…

Louisa sadly wondered at the unfairness of life. That it denied her sister the one thing she needed to make her complete, her heart aching at the way both Jemima and poor George had suffered because of it.

Dear George. How very wrong she'd been about him, believing him unworthy of her sister, when nothing could be further from the truth. Over six long and painful years, Louisa had come to appreciate the quiet strength and inherent goodness of her brother-in-law. Was it any wonder she'd grown to regard him so highly?

Carefully, Louisa moved deeper into the Forest, heart thumping at the sudden swoop of birds in the treetops, apprehension making her palms clammy as the undergrowth rustled and whispered. A sudden foreboding made her stop in her tracks and glance longingly over her shoulder to where the light of the outside could be seen brightly shining.

Her sister's note had sounded desperate…

Calling herself a coward, Louisa squared her shoulders and continued onwards, at last stepping into the small glade where her sister had requested they meet. Jemima sat demurely on a fallen tree trunk on the far side of the glade, hands folded neatly in her lap, long dark hair unbound and spread over her shoulders.

"Jemima?" It was gloomy so deep within the Forest, and Louisa could barely make out her sister's features as she raised her head and looked at her, face glowing palely in the dim twilight. "Are you alright? Why did you wish us to meet here?"

"I wanted us to talk," Jemima finally said, and a shiver whispered down Louisa's spine at the precise, measured tone of her sister's words.

"But why here?" demanded Louisa. "I can't stay long, Jemima, it will be the children's bedtime soon and I need to get back."

"This won't take long," assured Jemima. "Indeed, I was surprised how quickly I dealt with George."

"George?" stuttered Louisa, confused and alarmed by Jemima's words. "What do you mean? What about George? Where is he?"

"George is no longer your concern, dear sister," Jemima smiled. She rose to her feet, took a step forward.

An instinctive sensation of terror screamed a warning within Louisa's body. A primitive urge to flee drenched her in adrenalin and she turned and ran, picking up her skirts and racing across the glade, hearing the rustle of her sister's skirts as she followed.

Outraged denial and panic pounded a drumbeat of terror within Louisa's heart as she plunged back down the track. Losing her footing on the slippery undergrowth, she crashed heavily to the ground, her flailing hand encountering something soft and warm.

Revulsion crawled up her throat as she saw George lying beneath a bush, his eyes open and filled with frozen pleading. The blood from *the savage gash which had practically severed his head from his body, drenched his clothes and the ground on which he lay in a thick, sticky, crimson puddle.*

Crying out in horror, Louisa scrambled to her feet, desperately wiping her hand, warm with George's blood, on her skirts, as the baby leapt with adrenalin fuelled panic within her womb. A great determination gripped her. Nothing would harm this child.

She risked a quick glance over her shoulder, to see Jemima slowly pursuing, her pace not rising above an unhurried, floating walk, a smile dragging her mouth into a macabre grimace, eyes wide and endlessly dark, as if seeing things Louisa could not. She stopped and showed Louisa the wickedly long carving knife hidden within her apron folds.

"It will do you no good to run, Louisa," she said. Louisa fancied it was not her sister's voice that cautioned her but was the tone of another. That something else inhabited her sister's body, something that would not hesitate to take her life and that of the babe within. At the thought, Louisa jumped like a cornered doe, fear lending her legs a speed she'd normally never have possessed.

On and on through the dim Forest she sped, her mind playing tricks with her tiring body. Surely she had not walked so far? Had she somehow taken a wrong turn? Was she even now running in circles, back towards her sister and the darkness within?

Finally, Louisa saw the flash of late afternoon sunlight ahead, and relief swept through her. She looked to see if Jemima followed. There was no sign of her. Thankfully, Louisa turned to make her escape and something dark and vast and ancient and immeasurably evil was there.

It seized her, forcing her to the ground. She fought against it, feeling waves of jealousy and spiteful resentment pour from it in a foul, stinking miasma which choked and twisted in her throat. Louisa screamed in dreadful agony. When she looked up, Jemima was there, arms reaching to enfold her sister in a loving embrace ...

Arriving home unexpectedly, young Lord Marchmant was alarmed to discover the Hall ablaze with light. As he and his entourage rode through the wide-open gates, maids, stable lads and cooks alike scurried away at his approach, faces taut and grey in the gloom. Reaching the steps, he leapt from his horse and went in search of his wife, looking for an explanation. Instead he found his mother, and at the sight of him, Lady Marchmant reached for him in anguish and in a few terse words told of the mysterious disappearance not only of Louisa, but her sister and brother-in-law too.

Heart clenching with fear for his wife, Lord Marchmant swung back into the saddle, earlier fatigue forgotten, and barked out orders to his retinue to join the search parties, to look everywhere, to not stop until Lady Louisa was safely home again. His mother stood on the steps and watched them go. A terrible dread descended upon her that they were too late, and she railed against the White Hind, the outrageous curse she'd levelled upon the village and the Marchmant family.

The sun was rising over the downs when Lord Marchmant wearily turned his horse's head home, the taste of failure bitter in his mouth. Of Louisa and the others there'd been no sign. Like his mother, he remembered the sighting of the White Hind and cold dread gripped him.

Alone, he'd become separated from the rest of his party sometime during the long dark night, Lord Marchmant crested the hill and began down the slope towards the Hall, passing the small cottage where Jemima and George lived. He decided to stop and see if they at least had returned home.

The cottage door was ajar. He entered, eyes blinking in the gloomy interior, dimly made out a slight figure sitting at the table, and a wild hope soared in his heart.

"Louisa?"

"No, sir," came the soft reply. "It's Jemima."

"Jemima?" With two strides he was upon her, resisting the urge to shake her by the shoulders. "Where the devil have you been, Jemima? Half the village is out looking for you!"

"The devil?" Jemima raised her head at last. In the thickening light of dawn, he saw a strange deadness behind her eyes. "Not the devil, sir, although perhaps very like."

"What?" he demanded, then rushed on impatiently. "Where is she? Where's Louisa?"

"You should thank me, sir," she murmured. "She wasn't far enough along, so it couldn't possibly be yours."

"Do you know where she is?" he demanded, worry spiking his words with roughness. "I'm extremely concerned about her. If she's been out all night, in her condition..."

"Condition?" he saw her shock. "You knew of her condition?"

"Well, of course I knew," he snapped. "I am her husband, she told me she suspected we may have been blessed again the night before I left."

"But, but, she did not look that far along..." stammered Jemima.

"Louisa never does," he retorted impatiently. "Now, I'm begging you Jemima, if you know where she is, you must tell me!"

"The Forest," Jemima murmured.

He turned and left the cottage, not seeing the look on Jemima's face as the madness drained from it and horrified realisation dawned. Clutching her hands to her throat, she fell to the floor, howling like a wounded animal, listening to the fading hoofbeats and knowing he was too late.

Reaching the edges of the Forest, he slowed his horse to a walk and paced its outskirts, unsure where to commence looking, all the while hearing a voice urging him to hurry, hurry!

Finally, he came across a bloodied trail emerging from its depths, followed as it led across a meadow heading towards the Hall. And there, practically in the centre, curled up in a bed of poppies and ox-eye daisies, heartsease and buttercups, wild grasses and speedwells, he found her.

Stumbling from his horse, unable to believe this pale, blood-drenched stranger was his beautiful and vivacious wife, he gathered her to his chest. Seeing the gaping wound in her stomach through which her lifeblood had slowly leaked away during her long, agonising crawl, he realised she'd been trying to get home to their children, to him. Bitterly, he cursed himself for having gone away, for not being here to protect her.

Her eyes fluttered, there was a flash of recognition, and her hand grasped at his jacket, pulling him down, her last breath whispering into his ear. Her words were faint and wavering, but he heard, jaw hardening as the only woman he'd ever loved told him the name of her murderer with the last dregs of her strength. Then her dark eyes grew still and he knew she was gone. A great sob rent his soul as he clutched her fiercely to him, before he staggered to his feet, placed her gently on his horse's back and took her home.

When they finally came for her, Jemima was ready.

Lord Marchmant, followed by a group of his loyal men, faces shattered by the loss of their much-admired lady, forced open the locked door of the cottage. They found her twisting slowly in the *breeze, the rafter to which she'd fastened the rope creaking under the weight, her face discoloured, eyes bulging.*

Furious she'd so neatly escaped the brutal retribution he'd consoled himself with planning on his way back to the Hall, his wife's slight form clasped tightly before him, deaf to the shocked murmurs of his men behind him, Lord Marchmant harshly barked out an order to cut her down.

His eyes fell upon a scrap of paper placed neatly in the centre of the table. Snatching it up, he read the final confession of Jemima Hunter Dodd, face creasing into lines of understanding as he read her words; of her growing despair at the countless miscarriages, the jealousy against her own sister, the hatred that grew from this jealousy, her terrible suspicions that an intimacy existed between her husband and Louisa and the proof she perceived to have discovered of such an intimacy.

Finally, she spoke of the dark malevolence that dwelt within the Forest. Of how it'd goaded and manipulated her into committing such a terrible deed. Of how she'd lured first her husband and then her sister into the Forest, and how she'd murdered them both.

Lord Marchmant railed against the terrible curse that'd blighted his family and the village for so many generations. A curse which had caused the violent deaths of three more of its innocent young, including his own beloved wife.

Winifred Blunt ceased talking. A hush fell upon the assembled ladies, and Nancy Peabody saw tears openly rolling down the cheeks of Maisie Dodd. Many of the ladies looked decidedly ashen-faced at the bloodthirsty conclusion to the tale so expertly told in Winifred Blunt's creaking voice, even Miss Iris, her normally disapproving expression for once softened, seemed affected by the tragic story.

"Is that how it always happens?" Maisie Dodd whispered.

"Not always exactly like that," Mabel Dodd explained. "My mother told me time before it was two Blacksmith brothers, both in love with the same girl. When she married one of them, no one realised how affected his brother was, then the White Hind was seen. Next thing, the eldest Blacksmith boy and his wife are dead at the hand of the youngest Blacksmith boy, and he's killed himself."

"And my grandmother told me time before that it was two village lasses," added Winifred Blunt. "Both firm friends since birth, when one married and the other didn't they began to drift apart. Then the White Hind was seen, and a few days later they were all dead,"

"So, what can we do?" breathed Maisie Dodd in awe.

"Do?" barked Winifred Blunt. "Do about what?"

"Well, do to stop it, of course," cried Maisie Dodd, clasping hands to her rapidly heaving breast.

"There's nothing that can be done," declared Mabel Dodd bluntly. "The White Hind's been seen, and there's an end to it."

"But… but, there must be something we can do." Maisie Dodd insisted forcefully, for once ignoring the withering glance her mother-in-law sent her. "We can't sit here and do nothing, simply wait for more of our young people to be killed! There must be some way of breaking this terrible curse."

"But what is there to do?" Winifred Blunt demanded. "It's the way things are, and we must simply accept it." Her mouth snapped closed into a firm line, and not one lady dared to comment any further. Even Maisie Dodd, her burst of rebellion seemingly at an end, subsided into a resentful silence.

After the ladies had gone and Nancy Peabody had helped Miss Iris to silently clear away the tea things, she went to her room to reflect on all she'd heard. Sitting at her small dressing table, Nancy gazed unseeingly at her dark reflection, aware of the thumping of her heart, and the singing of the blood in her veins.

Somewhere, buried inside her, lay the blackness. She now knew and recognised that what lived in her had also once resided in Jemima Hunter, driving her to madness and murder. Fear arose in her gullet, but she swallowed it down. Knowing herself to be stronger than poor Jemima, Nancy Peabody was confident of her ability to control it, whatever it was. A glow arose in her eyes and she met her own gaze proudly in the mirror.

And deep within the Forest, something stirred and moved sluggishly in on itself, knowing all the pieces were in place and it was time for the game to commence once more.

Chapter Six
~ The Tale of Black Bridget ~

Six days since the sighting of the White Hind. The village buzzed with wild speculation and fears, whispered in corners and spoken of more openly in the private sanctity of the pub, where the men huddled, grim faced and brooding, over tankards foaming with the pub's own ale. Rather bizarrely named the Witch's Brew, it'd been traditionally brewed on the premises for centuries, using a well-guarded secret recipe passed down through generations of Blunts.

Back and forth the debate would rage, always returning to the burning issue, who would it be this time? With growing concern, parents warned children, fear causing voices to sharpen in dire cautions and promises extracted to be careful, take care, watch out. Anxious mothers advised daughters to think twice about that nice young village lad they'd been stepping out with. Fathers lectured lusty young sons on the dangers of too much passion.

All the time, the village waited and watched and wondered and worried.

The tale of the Hunter sisters and the dreadful fate which had befallen them, spread like wildfire through the village. The ladies who'd been present at its telling, re-told the tale with many embellishments to husbands and older children, pressing home its appalling warning to sulky daughters and resentful sons, chafing at the restrictions placed upon them.

Miss Iris, in turn, repeated the tale word for word to her sister, and even though she'd no children to be fearful for, Miss Violet had taken Jack to one side and told it to him, pleading with him to take care and to please be cautious.

Touched by her concern, feeling a frisson of recognition at the black voice Jemima Hunter had claimed coerced her to such appalling deeds, Jack promised Miss Violet to be wary and ever vigilant, always on the look-out for… what? At this point mothers would sigh and fathers would bluster, unsure of how to answer such a reasonable question, the truth being that none knew what form the next incident would take, or how to recognise the signs. Or indeed if the signs were acknowledged, whether any actions could be taken to prevent the cycle repeating itself.

Less alarmed than most, knowing his son intimately and recognising for the darkness to take hold there must be some kinship within its victim, some seed of negativity present for it to latch onto, Daniel Forrester, nonetheless, exchanged long and serious words with his son. He was reassured by his son's answers, but was mindful as Reuben was able to enter the Forest, he was more likely to be exposed to the sickness that lay at its heart.

Had Reuben been honest with his father, confided in him about Sylvie and that he'd taken Jack and Sally into the Forest, his father would've been more adamant in his warnings, and mayhap events would've played out differently. He did not know. So, fate twisted along its narrow track, with no hindrances being placed in its way, no circumstances occurring to force it down a different path.

Tired of the frightened, speculative looks his mother continually bent his way, sick of the brooding, heavy atmosphere within the little house by the Forest, Reuben took his shotgun and decided to go and check the current batch of pheasant chicks.

Already having taken over many of his father's responsibilities, the previous summer Reuben had been officially recognised by the Marchmant family as apprentice forester, it being understood that one day he would assume his father's mantle as caretaker of the Forest. As such, Reuben was paid accordingly, enjoying the sensation of receiving an adult wage in return for adult duties.

Wandering through the Forest, Reuben was aware of a difference since the sighting of the White Hind six days previously. Every time he entered the Forest it seemed to hold its breath, and Reuben could almost hear the trees whispering a litany of woe.

The air was thick, pregnant with expectation, so charged and emotional that Reuben could sense the gathering storm and his hand would tighten on his gun, eyes flicking from cover to cover as leaves rustled in the still, hushed day. The creatures of the Forest ceased their usual incessant chatter, as if they'd gone into hiding, remaining quiet and motionless in their burrows, dens, and nests, battening down the hatches and preparing for it.

Whatever it may be.

He paced silently down familiar tracks, recognising how everything was the same, all was different. Reaching the clearing where the pheasant chicks were housed, they were being hand reared to ensure maximum survival ready for the Lords' to hunt, Reuben stopped short in horrified dismay.

Of the hundreds of small, peeping chicks he'd been charged with caring for, not one was left alive. At the sight of their tiny ravaged bodies, hearts and heads ripped and mangled, carcasses tossed hither and thither, Reuben felt a wild rage sweep through him. Leaning his shotgun carefully against a tree, he crouched by the pens, assessing the damage, and trying to see where the predator had gained entry. Grey eyes creasing in incredulous surprise, he realised every pen was still securely locked and fastened, no holes visible in the wire to explain the carnage meted out to the defenceless chicks.

"A pitiful sight," said a rich, loamy voice behind him. Reuben jumped to his feet, desperately reaching for his gun, as the tall, rangy figure of the man whose timely intervention had saved him a savaging by the boar, stepped into the clearing. His casual pace and easy manner belied the wariness behind his eyes, the tautness of muscles, as though expectant of danger.

"Did you do this?" demanded Reuben in outraged sorrow, gesturing at the killing pens.

"Nay, lad." The man's eyes flattened, insulted by Reuben's wild accusation, his expression softening as he took in the young man's shocked, defensive attitude, the gun clutched in shaking hands and the bright sheen of denied tears in his eyes. "This is not the work of a man," he continued.

"Then what creature could possibly do such a thing?" interrupted Reuben. "There's no sign of anything but the chicks being in the pens, so how did it get in and out again?"

"It was no creature either," stated the man. "When I said it was no man, I meant it truly. She has a black, wicked temper, and when roused none is safe before her fury. Neither man, woman or creature, could stand before her or defy her foul intent."

"I don't understand," began Reuben, "Who? What she? Are you saying a woman did this? But none save the Marchmant family and the forester can enter the Forest, so where did she come from?"

"There is much you have to learn, young forester," replied the man. "I have been watching you since birth, and know your heart to be pure, your spirit to be strong. Still, it is ever the innocent who suffer. Time and again, the strength of evil has proven too much for even the shining light of goodness to overcome."

"What do you mean?"

"Come," ordered the man. "Let us leave this place of death and I will tell you what I can. I fear tis not much nor may it aid you, for it was ordained long ago that none of the folk trapped within the Forest may ever attempt to pervert the course of destiny."

"Trapped?" enquired Reuben, following the man gladly from the clearing, wondering what his father would say at the news of the loss of the whole brood of pheasant chicks, "What do you mean, trapped?"

"Lad," replied the man affably, "As you know, this Forest is a strange, uniquely charmed place, and has always been a sacred and most holy site. It was that strength of natural forces which granted the curses life. Still, the Forest did what it could to protect innocence. Within its boundaries, those of the Family whose lives she tried to take eke out an existence of sorts."

"Wait a minute," demanded Reuben, mind bulging at the man's astonishing, unbelievable, but strangely credible words. "Are you saying what I think you're saying?"

"Do not question me any further, lad," ordered the man as they entered another dell, and Reuben was greeted by the odour of wood smoke, saw a ring of stones containing a crackling, smouldering fire, and smelt the delicious aroma of roasting rabbit suspended over the heat on a spit. Hurriedly, the man turned the rabbit and examined it, pulling at some of the flesh with a broad hunting knife taken from his belt.

"Sit," he ordered. In a daze Reuben obeyed, sinking onto a fallen log dragged close to the fire to provide a handy seat. He watched as the man pulled the rabbit off the spit and divided the meat onto two pewter plates, and handed one to Reuben with a hunk of rough, seeded bread and a flagon of ale, which was rich and sour on his tongue.

Hungrily, Reuben accepted his simple meal and feasted gladly, realising his appetite, jaded by the stresses and worries of the past few days, was back with a vengeance. For a time there were no sounds in the clearing other than the crackle of the fire and the noises of men eating with gusto.

The man placed aside his plate, empty but for bones, and gestured to Reuben to do the same. "Now then, lad," he began. "I have a tale to tell you, and you must listen closely, for it is important. How much is true and how much of it is false, I cannot say. I only know 'tis ancient, and my surmise is it alludes to how this all began."

"What tale?" asked Reuben in confusion. The man gestured impatiently for him to be quiet and into the stillness of the dell, began to speak.

Once, long ago, according to the customs of the land, a young noble Lady was sent away from her home across the sea to be the bride of the great Lord of the Forest. She was still very young, a mere child, so her concerned family sent to accompany her a wise and learned widow woman. She had been the Lady's nurse and companion since her birth and loved her as her own. Also escorting the Lady was the wise woman's only daughter, and a young foundling girl. The wise woman had taken over the raising of this child when her parents had perished of sickness many years earlier.

Thus, it was, the wise woman treated all three young girls as her daughters, her own child and the foundling girl acting as personal maids to the young noble Lady, familiarity effectively lowering all barriers between them, until the three young women felt more like sisters, than mistress and servants. Especially had a loving regard arisen between the Lady and the young foundling girl, and the Lady bestowed on her many small gifts of regard.

The name of the wise woman's child was Bridget. By a strange twist of fate, this was also the name of the foundling and the girls became known as Black Bridget and Fair Bridget, because as the wise woman's daughter was dark of brow and hair, her eyes black as pitch, so the foundling girl was bright and golden, with eyes the colour of a summer's sky, and a merry smile of delight always quivering on her soft lips.

Black Bridget was considered by many a beauty, but her permanently displeased countenance and sulky scowl which marred her flawless skin caused many to turn from her, naturally repulsed by the slick lies and small deceptions which she delighted in practicing on her fellow servants. In particular did she despise Fair Bridget, believing unjustly that the hapless girl had stolen the mother love Black Bridget felt by rights belonged to her. She also believed their mistress looked more favourably upon the girl.

In this last, she was correct. Alone and friendless in a strange and unfamiliar land, a country whose customs and language seemed brutish and unrefined, compared to the sweeping grace and culture of her childhood home, it was only natural the poor Lady preferred the lively, uncomplicated and friendly company of Fair Bridget, to the darkly brooding and spiteful ways of Black Bridget.

Unaware of the growing resentment within Black Bridget's heart, the Lady only knew Fair Bridget's companionship eased a lonely and frightened heart. When the Lady had a secret, it was to be expected that it was into the sympathetic ear of Fair Bridget she whispered, instinctively knowing should Black Bridget have knowledge of it, the secret would be used as a weapon of spiteful manipulation against her.

The Lady's secret was harmless enough, but given her status of birth, the fact she was the Lord's future bride was one she and Fair Bridget knew must be kept close to their hearts. The secret was this: since her arrival, the Lady had been privately meeting with the forester's son deep within the Forest.

A comely and honest lad, he'd never treated the lady as anything other than an honoured friend, and the Lady, in turn, never gave any indication she felt otherwise for him. But deep in her heart burnt a true and abiding affection for the boy.

As they grew into adulthood, the lad became a tall and handsome man, taking over as forester when his father became infirm, and the lady would feel her heart beat with a woman's love every occasion she saw his face. She would tell herself it must be the last time they met, yet when they parted, her heart yearned to be in his company again.

After several years, during which the Lord was absent with the King and did not return home, a messenger arrived, saddle sore and weary, the news he carried truly terrifying the Lady. The Lord was on his way home, and had sent ahead to warn that immediately upon his arrival they were to be wed.

Scared and confused, the Lady fled into the Forest to seek solace with the forester, and he in turn offered her sanctuary. Although it was what the Lady desired more than anything, she knew it could not be. Her betrothed was a powerful man from a mighty family, and she feared the consequences for her handsome love should she flee to him. Also, the weight of duty and family honour burnt hotly within her womanly breast, and as she thought of the shame such an action would bring her family, reluctantly the young Lady did refuse his offer and sadly left him alone in the Forest.

Her wedding night arrived, the Lady needing all the comfort and solace the wise woman and Fair Bridget could give her. With a quaking heart and troubled soul, she let them place her within the bridal bed and leave her to her fate.

The gods were kind to her. Her husband, although considerably older than her and a soldier much roughened by many years of warfare, was a kind and decent man. He recognised his new bride's fear and was touched by her vulnerability, his mighty warrior heart falling instantly in love with her youth and fresh beauty.

Gently, he took her hand and sat with her, talking softly so as not to alarm her. When eventually he made her his own, the Lady was surprised to find her terrors had been groundless, and a great regard and liking for her husband was born that night.

Many months passed, Fair Bridget would wander the Forest picking the wild flowers her Lady so loved to adorn her chambers with, and often would be joined by a young, handsome forester, eager for news of his former friend. His mind being much reassured by reports Fair Bridget willingly supplied of her mistress's happiness with her husband, and how her innocence and sweet nature had tamed the wildness of the Lord. Gradually, the young man came to look upon Fair Bridget with more than friendship, and she would return to her Lady, cheeks flushing prettily from the memory of softly whispered compliments.

Thus it was inevitable that the day came when Fair Bridget approached her mistress and asked permission to marry, not realising the jolt of dismay which pierced the Lady's heart. Then, she remembered her position, her own satisfactory marriage and wished Fair Bridget every joy and happiness, insisting upon arranging the *wedding ceremony and breakfast for her favourite maid. Amused and indulgent, her husband ordered a suckling pig and a cask of finest ale to be present at the celebrations ensuring a gay and happy time was had by all the guests.*

Now, you may be wondering what had happened to Black Bridget. The maid had not been idle, and some months hence had also married, her choice being a handsome, but weak, manservant of the Lord. Easily managed by his sharp-tongued and cunning wife, this hapless man had good cause to regret succumbing to the lust aroused by Black Bridget's flashing dark eyes and lush, firm body.

Happy with the new status afforded her by marrying higher up the serving echelon, Black Bridget had felt herself well pleased until Fair Bridget married the forester and she attended their wedding. The fine ale sour on her lips, she reflected bitterly on the miserly gift her mistress had bestowed upon her, and a renewed tide of black, jealous bile arose within her against her mistress and Fair Bridget both.

This situation was not improved when her mistress pleaded with her Lord for permission to renew and renovate the sweet little cottage traditionally the abode of the forester and his family. Unable to refuse his wife anything, he'd laughingly agreed.

Visiting Fair Bridget in her cheery abode, seeing her revel as mistress of her own home, the envy bit keenly. Black Bridget's resentment against her mistress grew into a deep-seated loathing, and she longed for revenge to recompense her imagined wrongs.

Then, Black Bridget realised she was to be a mother, and for a few weeks was appeased by the fuss and attention accorded to her. All too soon, Fair Bridget also discovered she was with child. Once more, Black Bridget felt a quiet rage consume her that a foundling girl, a nobody, should again steal the affection and attention of her Lady and her mother.

Shortly after, the Lady announced she was with child and the whole castle rejoiced. Seeing the besotted awe in the Lord's eyes, Black Bridget knew she must discover a mightily powerful weapon if she wished to blacken his wife's character and good name enough to make him turn her away.

Then, one day, quite unexpectedly, she found it.

Black Bridget's babies had been born four weeks previously. Twins, a boy and a girl, identical in dark, good looks, their young bodies ruddy with health and vigour. Although Black Bridget enjoyed the admiration delivering such a lusty pair of babes had brought, the children bored her. Being a mother, with all its attendant chores, was not a role she relished, and she was forever foisting the children onto her mother and slipping away, seeking the rough lovemaking of the Lord's men-at-arms.

One bright, chill day in October, Black Bridget was adjusting herself back into her dress, when she looked through the open stable door and spied her mistress heavy with child, slipping quietly into the Forest. Stepping over the heavily snoring body of the man she'd used this time, Black Bridget followed her curiously, instinctively making her tread light and staying hidden from view.

Deeper and deeper into the Forest the Lady went, finally reaching a pretty clearing where she sat upon a fallen log, as though waiting for someone. Concealed behind a bush, Black Bridget also waited.

She did not wait very long. Stepping from the trees came the forester, Fair Bridget's husband. The Lady gave a glad cry and ran to him, clutching his arm and urging him to sit beside her on the log. Straining her ears, Black Bridget could not hear their words beyond a murmur but her dank and twisted soul gladly supplied them, placing the language of love and longing on their lips. When they finally arose, and parted to go their separate ways, Black Bridget chose to ignore the chaste handshake of goodbye, the entreaty to pass her regards to his dearly beloved wife and the happy innocence of the whole encounter.

Late that evening, the Lord angrily stormed into his wife's chamber, and before the horrified gaze of Black Bridget's mother, raged and demanded to know if his wife had made a fool of him with the forester, threatening to have the young man disembowelled before her if it be the truth.

Terrified for herself and for her friend, his wife bravely stood her ground, vowing and declaring, the light of truth shining in her eyes, that nothing beyond honourable friendship had ever existed between them. Did her Lord not remember their wedding? Was he questioning her virginity that night? His accusations not only insulted the love and honour she bore for him as her beloved husband, but also slandered the deep and abiding sisterly regard she felt for Fair Bridget.

Confused, and deeply moved by her words, her husband left the room. Anxiously, the Lady sent her nurse after him to further plead her case and make such reassurances as should be necessary.

A short time later, Black Bridget hurried into the room, sent by her mother she claimed, to warn my Lady that her husband's rage had grown apace. Even now he was rousing his men to go with him to the forester's cottage, where they intended to drag the hapless young man into the Forest to execute him, after first removing the offending portion of his anatomy.

Appalled and horrified, the Lady wasted no time in throwing a cloak about herself and hurrying out into the stormy night, reassured by Black Bridget that if she took the path straight through the Forest, she would reach the forester's cottage before her husband and thus could warn her friend to flee.

Seating herself before the warming fire, Black Bridget held her hands to the blaze, her blood throbbing with exhilaration. After waiting in comfort for a few moments, she went to find the Lord, informing him with downcast eyes and trembling lips that her mistress had fled into the night, fleeing to her lover, before she left confessing the child she carried was not her lord's, and that she was fearful he would dash the child's brains out as soon as it was born.

Incredulous at her report, the Lord called back the wise woman, repeating what Black Bridget had claimed. Her mother's eyes grew hard as iron as she gazed into her daughter's soul and saw the foulness within. For it was a little-known fact the elderly woman, who'd loved and raised the Lady from birth, was truly a white witch, and as such, had the power to determine truth from lies.

In a passionate fury, she raged and struck at the evilness and depravity of her own child, assuring the Lord with words of absolute truth of his wife's innocence. Horrified, he realised his dearly beloved had been driven out into the cold night, into a deep and inhospitable Forest, where even now the trees were bending under the gathering winds of a mighty storm.

Quickly, he ordered every able-bodied man to horse; telling them their mistress was ill and had wandered away into the Forest. With rising panic, he commanded his best hunters to take their dogs and search for her. Holding a tiny pair of his wife's slippers in his large hands, he clutched them briefly in self-accusing agony, before handing them to the chief huntsman for the dogs to sniff.

Assuming, his wife would be heading to the forester's cottage to warn them, the Lord mounted his fastest horse, risking life and limb thundering along the track skirting the edge of the Forest, arriving at the home of the forester and Fair Bridget as a full moon arose in the dark, storm tossed night, its silver countenance savagely lashed by scurrying clouds.

Dismounting, he pounded on the door, hoping against hope his Lady would be so easily found, his heart aching with the need to urge his apologies upon her, and to carry her back to the home they'd begun to make together.

Gaining no answer, the Lord thrust the door open and strode into the snug kitchen, his ear instantly caught by animal like screams coming from upstairs. Fear gripped his innards as he fled up the narrow staircase to discover a scene of natural mystery and powerful forces.

The forester knelt between his wife's straining, blood stained thighs, leather sleeves rolled firmly to his elbows, as Fair Bridget screamed once more and twisted in mortal agony. The Lord stared in wonderment as the forester gently turned the tiny head of the child and eased it from its mother, expertly tying and cutting the cord, massaging his wife's belly until the afterbirth, dark with the blood of creation, passed from her.

He washed both mother and child tenderly from a bowl of warm water, stuffing clean padding between Fair Bridget's thighs to absorb the blood, and handed her the child, which squirmed and nuzzled at its mother's breast. Then, and only then, did the forester look up and see the Lord concealed in the shadows of the doorway.

Any last vestige of doubt the Lord had fled when faced with the quiet, steady love in the man's eyes for his wife and child. No man, he reasoned, upon being confronted by his lover's powerful husband, would be able to resist the smallest flicker of fear showing in his eyes. The forester's gaze was level and calm, not the slightest alarm showing within those grey depths.

The Lord was momentarily humbled, until the ever-present fear for his wife arose. He quickly explained his Lady was lost in the Forest, alone and scared, heavily burdened with child. He feared the worst, and begged the forester to help, as with his superior knowledge of the ways and meanings of the Forest, the Lord felt his wife's chances of discovery would be greatly improved.

The forester looked concerned. His eyes went to his newly created family lying in maternal bliss upon the bed, and the Lord understood he was torn, wishing to help, but reluctant to leave. The two men stared silently at one another, the Lord aware he could simply order the forester to obey, yet was unwilling to do so, respecting the other man's right to choose.

Suddenly, there was noise and movement in the kitchen, and the next moment the wise woman was in the room. Crossing swiftly to the bed, she ensured Fair Bridget and the child were well, before turning to the forester. Go, she ordered him, find my lambkin and bring her home. 'Tis no night for any to be so abandoned within the Forest, yet alone one as tender and vulnerable as my lady.

Urged also by Fair Bridget, who caught his arm and entreated him with tears in her eyes to find her poor Lady, the forester nodded to the Lord, and the two men left the room.

All night they searched. Through the blackness, the sheets of rain, the brilliance of the lightning which rent the sky time upon time, thunder rumbling as if the gods of the skies were displeased.

Dawn came and the storm eased. After returning to the castle to break their fast and pack more supplies, the men once more plunged into the Forest, finding the trail easier to follow by light. Gradually, they wound their way deeper and deeper into the Forest, knowing by the tortuous twists and turns of the trail, that once the Lady realised she'd strayed from the track, her wanderings had become frantic and fearful.

Then, finally, as the sun broke through the dense canopy overhead, they found her.

Curled in a sweet bower of hazelnut branches and wild strawberries, she lay as if asleep. Her beautiful gown was begrimed and splattered with mud, stiffly drenched with the blood of the child she'd delivered alone during the long, dark night. Still and cold, it lay beside her, its small, untested soul now residing in the same place as its poor, destroyed mother.

Giving a great cry of grief, the Lord fell to his knees and gathered the cold bodies of his wife and daughter into his arms, his noble heart breaking, guilt he could ever have doubted her forcing bitter tears of contrition to flow unchecked down his cheeks.

Sorrowfully, the forester stood respectively to one side, tears at the lonely death of his little friend also wetting his face. United in mourning, the two men wept for the senseless demise of youth and innocence, until finally, a great anger arose within the Lord. Lifting the empty bodies of his family, he gently gave them to the forester, ordering him to carry them carefully back to the castle.

Confused, the forester enquired as to the Lord's intent, understanding gripping his heart at the mighty Lord's ground out answer. Revenge! Silently he watched, clutching tightly his precious burden, as his Lord swung easily onto his horse and set out for the castle as fast as he could safely go.

As his horse's hooves echoed on the track, so did the Lord's mind and heart pound with the need for vengeance, and the darkest hatred for Black Bridget arose within him. Many and awful were the torments he planned for her, and around him the Forest stirred and trembled, reflecting his tortured mind.

Finally reaching the castle, the Lord strode in search of her, shouting orders to all he saw that she was to be found and brought to him immediately, dragged in chains should she resist. So awful was the look on his face, so terrible the light in his eyes, all who saw him trembled and ran to do his bidding.

But, for all their searching, no sign of Black Bridget was ever found, and the Lord's thirst for revenge was left unquenched. Long did he question her mother, the wise woman, satisfied by the answering spark of hatred within her eyes, should Black Bridget ever approach her mother for aid, she would be sorely disappointed by her reception.

The Lord never remarried. Towards the end of his days he became apt to wandering the Forest, until at last, one evening in October, he did not return. Searchers, led by the forester, found him curled in endless sleep in the same bower where his Lady had met her end, a peaceful smile of bliss on his face. Gently, they bore him back to the castle, where the new Lord, his younger brother, was informed of the sad tidings. And so life continued.

As to Black Bridget's children, the Lord could not bear sight of them. They were fostered to families in the village, and the wise woman, their grandmother, watched over them from afar, anxious to see if any of their mother's depravity had been passed down to them.

Black Bridget herself was never seen again. Superstitious villagers would mutter about the evilness that stalked the Forest, and it became a place to be avoided, mothers warning their children to be good or else Black Bridget would come and take them away. Thus, her name and deeds passed down into folklore, until eventually none remembered they'd ever been real.

The man stopped talking. Silence fell upon the clearing. Reuben blinked and looked away from the man's steady blue gaze, confused by what he was feeling, his mind crying out in fear for Sylvie. As he'd listened, a dreadful conviction had arisen that the Lady in the tale could surely be no other than her. When the man told of the Lady's secret meetings with the forester's son, Reuben's suspicions were confirmed, and he shuddered to learn of her fate.

"Is it true?" he asked desperately.

"I do not know." The man shrugged, his eyes compassionate. "I believe much of it has been embroidered and added to over the years, but believe the heart of the tale to be true. I believe in the existence of Black Bridget, have felt her malevolence within the heart of the Forest, lurking like a spider in its web, waiting to trap the unwary in silken skeins of jealousy and suspicion."

"But how can she possibly still be alive?" cried Reuben. "This tale happened centuries ago. How can they, I mean she, still be living in the Forest?"

"Human emotion is one of the most powerful forces on earth," replied the man calmly. If he'd noticed Reuben's slip, he did not mention it. "Feelings can remain long after the physical entity has dissolved. Even normal folk in the real world can sometimes feel the residues of intense emotion, so imagine how it must be in such a place as the Forest."

"But what can I do?" demanded Reuben almost angrily. "It's all very well telling me long, elaborate stories, but what can I actually do to stop it happening?"

"I do not know, lad," replied the man and sighed, weather-beaten forehead creasing in a frown of concern. "I do know something feels different this time. There is an intensity to the Forest, as if forces are aligning themselves for a confrontation. When the time comes, I and the others, if we are able, will do all we can to help."

"Thank you," mumbled Reuben, unsure what else he could say.

"I must go," stated the man, rising to his feet. Reuben stumbled to his, gazing miserably at the tall stranger as he placed a comradely hand on Reuben's shoulder.

"I can tell you this, lad," he began seriously. "Very soon you will have to make a choice. Once made, you must be true and faithful to it. Never falter in your decision and do not allow others to doubt the fidelity of your soul. Never forget, this creature feeds off the jealousy and uncertainties buried deep within every one of us. Do not supply it with further ammunition."

"I... I won't..." stammered Reuben, as the man kicked dirt onto the small fire and tapped the rabbit bones onto the ground. He wiped his plates with grass and stuffed them into a small leather bag, which he swung easily onto his back.

"Farewell lad," said the man. "I trust if we meet again it will be under happier circumstances."

"Goodbye," mumbled Reuben. "Wait," he cried, "I don't even know your name?"

The man paused at the edge of the clearing, turned to face him, blue eyes contemplative as if debating the wisdom of imparting such knowledge, then nodded once and smiled.

"Lucian," he finally replied. "It is Lucian. Fare thee well, Reuben," and he was gone, vanishing completely and utterly into the Forest as if he'd never been. When Reuben looked down, it was to find the fire also had disappeared, with only the lingering scent of wood smoke on his clothes and his own full belly as proof the meeting had ever taken place at all.

He returned home, head full of the encounter. Later, after a tense and silence laden meal with his parents, he slipped out of the house and met with Sally and Jack, telling them the tale as best he could remember it, watching their faces as they listened, shock and pity in their eyes.

As they spoke together, for a few short moments their petty jealousies and bitter misunderstandings were placed to one side, and Reuben rejoiced that it was like old times, when three had thought and acted as one. But, when they finally parted to go to their separate homes and he walked home alone in the growing dusk, it occurred to him for all their renewed closeness, he still hadn't confided in them about Sylvie.

Chapter Seven
~ The Tale of the Faithless Wife ~

Seven days since the sighting of the White Hind. Sally Cairn's head ached with the burden of anxiety and worry her well-meaning parents loaded onto her, as lovingly, tenderly, they nagged and fretted, until it was a relief to mount her bicycle and go to work.

The acknowledged brightest child in the village, precisely what was to happen to Sally when she left school had been a source of many heated, private discussions between her parents. Her mother was determined her daughter should marry and soon, fully expecting either Jack or the forester's son to ask for her, superficially happy with either, her private preference for Reuben.

Dearly though she loved Jack, Eliza Cairn knew there was much that was disturbed about the boy, and instinctively felt that any wife of Jack Blacksmith's would have a troubled and fretful time of it. No, better her happy little Sally married the nicely normal Reuben, to lead a quiet, uneventful and contented life.

Sally's father felt differently. Fiercely proud of his clever child, was determined she wouldn't go to work on the land or bury herself in wedded life too quickly, tentatively even suggesting that maybe she should look for work outside the village, only to have his wife round on him in horror. Leave the village? Their Sally! The very idea of it reduced his normally implacable and staid wife to tears of dismay, and Farmer Cairn stood down in resigned sadness, leaving the decision up to Sally.

Then, fate intervened. Lady Marchmant paid one of her sporadic, spontaneous visits to the school. Quietly sitting in on some of the lessons, she observed and listened in silence, her once piercing blue eyes now faded to softer hues, sharpening as Sally answered question after question, her intelligence clearly obvious.

A few days later Lady Marchmant paid a visit to Sally's parents.

She needed a new secretary, she explained, her clear cut, refined tone standing out against their rounded, country burr. Someone young and smart. Someone willing to learn and able to use her initiative. Someone like Sally, perhaps.

Leaving Sally's parents speechless, Lady Marchmant urged them to consider the idea, discuss it with Sally and let her know shortly. Sensible of the honour being accorded their family, Sally's parents fell upon her the instant she returned from school, bombarding a stunned Sally with the news.

It really needed very little discussion, because what else was Sally to do? What other occupation in the village would be worthy of a girl who consistently scored top marks in class? A girl whose clear, analytical mind had already considered her future options, considered and rejected them as being too mundane and boring. No, at the thought of working at Marchmant Hall every day, Sally's eyes began to gleam, and it was a well satisfied Cairn family who retired to bed that night.

Eliza Cairn had hugged herself with joy at the status working for the Family would accord her only daughter. Farmer Cairn had been quietly pleased his Sally's talents had been recognised and rewarded. As for Sally, she'd viewed her potential career with a mixture of trepidation and anticipation, longing for daybreak to come so she could share her exciting news with Reuben and Jack.

Predictably, Reuben had been delighted for her, his open, honest face beaming with shared joy and pride at her achievement. Jack had been defensive, sulky at the thought of sharing her attentions with one more thing, and it'd nearly led to a row, with Sally cross at having the shine of her news tarnished in such a way.

Finally, Jack was forced to admit how limited her options were, facing the choices Sally starkly pointed out to him. Either she worked locally for the Marchmants, or sought employment in a far off town, he swallowed his objections and wished her luck.

Sally had been working for the Marchmants for nearly two years now, and every day she grew to love her job more. At first she'd been nervous, apprehensive of making a mistake, but as her confidence grew, so did Lady Marchmant trust her more with the intricate workings of the Marchmant Estate, Sally realising just how influential and global the Family and its connections were.

Although the main family had always dwelt at Marchmant Hall, side shoots of the family tree and distant members had migrated around the world. Now, the spider web of influence stretched into every country of any worth, it not being uncommon for Sally to correspond with a second cousin twice removed who, although a member of the US Senate, owed a greater allegiance to the Family.

Like the ever-spreading roots of some invasive, tenacious weed, tendrils of control and authority twisted and entwined themselves into every organisation of power Sally had ever heard of, and quite a few she hadn't. It startled, maybe even on some level alarmed her, how powerful the manipulative strength of the Family was.

As she cycled to work that morning, the wheels of her bicycle turning steadily on the track running alongside the Forest's perimeter, Sally was intensely aware of its dark, looming mass, and unconsciously, her eyes would continually flick to its shady depths. Before, the Forest had been merely a feature of her every day, familiar journey to work. Now, it seemed unwelcoming, alien, a dark and mysterious place appearing suddenly sinister.

With the Forest so prominent, her thoughts automatically turned to the strange, sad tale told them the previous evening by Reuben. She wondered about it, about the even stranger storyteller, Lucian. Who was he? Where did he come from? Rather, she thought, when did he come from? From Reuben's description, he sounded like a member of the Marchmant Family, although Sally had never heard tell of anyone called Lucian in any of its branches, and determined as soon as she reached the Hall, to pay a visit to the Family Tree.

The Family Tree was an amazing piece of genealogical artwork. A vast and ever growing mural, it spanned an entire wall of the central banqueting hall, showing the history of the Marchmants spreading back over centuries, listing every Marchmant who'd ever lived. Sally knew if this mysterious Forest dweller was indeed Family, he'd be shown on the tree.

Propping her bicycle against the wall, Sally let herself in the kitchen door to be greeted by the cook, Brenda Dodd, with a cheery good morning, a cup of tea, and the news that Lady Marchmant had left a list of arrangements for the festival on her desk to be dealt with.

Every year on the twenty-second day of October, Marchmant Hall threw open its doors and a great festival was held in the banqueting hall. Thinly disguised as a Christian harvest home, the Festival had long been a part of Wyckenwode's life. Its origins shrouded in the obscurity of time, none knew if there was any significance to the date, and most villagers regarded the Festival as an opportunity to throw off the burden of work and responsibility for one night. Traditionally, the Festival was an occasion of feasting and drinking, with the pub supplying the ale and spiced punch, the village ladies providing the food.

Tending to see the festival as an unofficial competition, many a lady had her pride bruised or inflated by the reception her beautifully prepared cakes, pies and pastries received, and Sally knew even her own mother was not immune. For the past week, the farmhouse kitchen had been aglow with the comforting aroma of good, honest home-cooking.

As at the May festival, a Queen was chosen. But instead of a crown of white blossom, the Autumn Queen would be honoured with a wreath of dried corn, flowers and fruits, representing the villagers' gratitude for the bounty of the Forest and surrounding fertile lands.

Last May, the Spring Queen had been Peggy Hunter, and it'd been with a thrill of excitement that Sally had accepted the honour when offered to her by the Village Council. Alfred Twitchett's red shiny face beamed with benevolence as he'd taken her hand, and in a stiff, formal voice requested she be Queen of the village for the next six months, until the May Queen took over. Stammering with gratitude, Sally had accepted. Since then, her mother had been all-of-a twitter, busily making Sally's gown, mouth full of pins, eyes shining at the honour shown her daughter.

Thanking Brenda Dodd, Sally gratefully took the earthenware mug of tea and wandered into the banqueting hall. Struck anew by the beauty and complexity of the Family Tree, she wondered who made the additions. Although she'd never seen anyone working on it, whenever news was received of a birth, marriage or death within the Family, no matter how far flung or tenuous the blood connection, by the next day the information had been incorporated into the Tree, the paint of the latest addition looking as ancient as the very first.

Blinking in the sunlight pouring through the windows, Sally stood before the Tree and ran her eyes over its myriad of branches, searching for the name Lucian. Eyes narrowing with the intensity of her task, she followed each branch to its natural conclusion, going back, generation into generation, until finally she found him.

In the mid twelfth century, heir to the Marchmant Estate, Lucian. There he was. He was real. He'd existed. Sally frowned. Although Lucian's date of birth was plainly listed, beside what she assumed to be his date of death was written the single word *taken.*

No other explanation was offered, merely that simple, ambiguous statement. Running her eye over the main trunk of the tree, Sally saw, with a thrill of icy realisation, the same word appearing again and again. Always next to the heir. Always when he was in the prime of his life.

Counting backwards, she realised no less than twenty-three heirs had, over the course of the centuries, been apparently taken, although taken by whom or for what purpose, it did not say.

"Where were they taken?" Sally muttered. "Who took them?"

"Talking to yourself, Sally?" enquired a dryly amused voice from the door. Sally, abruptly jolted from her musings, turned sharply to see Lord Jolyon leaning against its frame, his smiling blue eyes studying her with interest.

"My Lord," stuttered Sally, flushing under his mocking gaze.

Of the two Lord Marchmants, Sally found the sombre manner of the older son, Lord Gilliard, easier to be around. As heir to the whole Marchmant Estate, Lord Gilliard took his duties seriously, and Sally's dealings with him were always of a practical, dryly matter-of-fact fashion. But, his younger brother, Lord Jolyon, was a different matter altogether.

Taller, handsomer than his stern and foreboding older brother, Lord Jolyon treated life as one great adventure to be enjoyed. His prowess at riding, hunting and shooting were legendary, as was his reputation for enjoying the company of ladies, and the Hall often rang with laughter of the crowds of young people he'd invite to stay.

Once, taking a message to the stables, Sally was mortified to come across Lord Jolyon and a married lady guest, emerging, giggling and rumpled, down the hayloft ladder. Sally had felt her cheeks flame as Lord Jolyon met her gaze with a coolly sardonic one of his own, daring her to comment, to judge. But Sally fled back to the house, original mission forgotten in a rush of humiliation.

Now, embarrassed and wrong footed, Sally's quick brain for once left her floundering and she gaped at him, cheeks firing under his knowing, mocking gaze, those piercing blue eyes for which the Marchmant's were famous, laughing at her obvious discomfort.

"I'm sorry, Sir," she finally gulped. "I was looking up someone on the Family Tree."

"Really?" his eyes expressed casual interest. "And who might that be? Some far flung, third cousin, twenty times removed, whom I've never heard of and have absolutely no interest in meeting?"

"No, Lucian," Sally blurted out, instantly wishing she'd had the sense to remain silent.

Lord Jolyon's nonchalant manner vanished abruptly, eyes now sharp and interrogating, they pinned her where she stood.

"Lucian?" he snapped. "And how do you know about Lucian?"

"Reuben Forrester told me about him," she replied, flinching away from his stare.

"And how does he know about him?" he demanded.

"He met him in the Forest and he told him a tale." Sally's garbled explanation sounded nonsensical, even to her own ears.

Lord Jolyon enquired no further. Instead he nodded thoughtfully, beckoning abruptly to her.

"Come," he ordered. "You need to speak to my Mother."

Following his tall, imposing back, almost running to keep pace with his long-legged stride, Sally's heart knocked against her ribs with trepidation, and she wanted to cry out to him to slow down, to wait while she caught her breath. After rushing up broad flights of stairs and hurrying along dark, twisting corridors, they arrived at the door to Lady Marchmant's chambers, Sally panting and breathless, Lord Jolyon annoyingly cool, calm and collected.

He rapped presumptuously on its thick panelling, barely waiting for the muffled invitation to enter, before pushing open the door and striding into the large room, dragging the reluctant Sally behind him.

"Jolyon?" Lady Marchmant's bewilderment was obvious as she looked up from her place on the sofa before the fire, Sally barely having time to register the empty breakfast tray on the small table beside her, before Lord Jolyon thrust her forward, kicking shut the door behind him so hard it rattled in its sturdy frame.

"Whatever is the matter?" Lady Marchmant cried, a spark of fear leaping into her eyes. "Gilliard?" she cried. "Where is he? He hasn't…?"

"No, Mother, it's alright," snapped Jolyon, impatiently. "He's fine. Or at least he was the last time I saw him, five minutes ago at breakfast. No, it's her," he jerked his head towards Sally. "I think she has something to tell us."

"Sally?" Lady Marchmant turned her attention towards Sally, who clutched her hands nervously to her chest, unsure what to say. At her obvious distress, Lady Marchmant's expression softened, and she patted the sofa beside her. "Please Sally, sit, then maybe you could explain what all this is about?"

Nervously, Sally obeyed, shifting uncomfortably on the brocade surface, squirming under the intensity of two sets of blue eyes.

"Tell us, Sally," Lord Jolyon commanded. "Tell us this tale the forester's lad told you. A tale told him in the Forest by Lucian."

"Lucian?" Sally saw the shocked light which leapt in Lady Marchmant's eyes, the swift, knowing look which passed between mother and son.

"Tell us," Lady Marchmant briefly touched her arm. Hesitantly, with many false starts, Sally did.

As Sally stumbled to the end of the tale, finishing with the fostering of Black Bridget's children, and the superstitious belief she still somehow walked the Forest, Lady Marchmant nodded in understanding, eyes clouded and unreadable.

"I see," she finally murmured, smiling at Sally. "As you have shared your tale with us, perhaps it is only fair I give you one in return, Sally."

"My Lady?" enquired Sally, bemused.

"Do you think that's wise, Mother?" asked Lord Jolyon. His tone was casual, but Sally heard the underlying note of alarm.

"Oh, I think so," replied Lady Marchmant slowly. "I think Sally may need all the help she can get, and maybe this old story will be of some use. Although, I must warn you, I do not know how much, if indeed any of it, is true. That is for you to decide."

"Please, my Lady," began Sally, hesitantly. "What is this tale?"

"It is called the Tale of the Faithless Wife," replied Lady Marchmant. "And it begins …"

Once, long ago, there lived a mighty and noble Lord, who although had gained much honour and recognition in the service of the King, found his thoughts turning to a new task. That of taking a bride and continuing his illustrious family.

To this end, the Lord looked far and wide for a lady of impeccable name and ancestry, eventually deciding on the daughter of a rich nobleman over the sea and made advances to her family to see if they were agreeable to such a match. After much negotiating and correspondence between the two families, a dowry was agreed upon, and the Lady Blanche, for that was her name, set out on the long journey to her new Lord's castle.

Accompanying the Lady was her waiting woman, an elderly and wrinkled crone who'd been the Lady's nurse since birth, and a young man-at-arms, sent to serve as her bodyguard. Now, there were two things that needed to be known about this entourage, two things which, had the Lord but known, he'd have sent them all straight back to her father's house, the Lady included.

The elderly waiting lady was not the harmless old nurse she appeared to be, but was in fact a powerful and cunning witch. And the young bodyguard was the lover of the Lady Blanche, for the Lady Blanche, despite her spotless reputation, was a wicked and wanton woman. One whose voracious appetite for the hot passionate lust of young men, had led to the loss of her virginity to her father's groom at the tender age of thirteen.

Working her way through almost the whole retinue of her father's estate, the offer from the great Lord had appeared as a gift from the gods, and her father lost no time in agreeing to the Lord's terms, offering a handsome dowry to be rid of such a troublesome daughter, before news of her activities rendered her completely unmarriageable.

Faced with a choice of disinheritance and being cast out, or marrying the foreign Lord, Lady Blanche had sulked and protested, but realising her father was in earnest, chose the lesser of two evils. Her only concern, voiced privately to her nurse, being how to fool her new husband she was still a virgin, and as they approached the Lord's castle this was a problem the nurse had still to solve.

On reaching the castle, Lady Blanche was appeased by its size and grandeur, realising with a stab of pleasure that her new position, should she overcome the small problem of the wedding night, would be very satisfactory indeed.

As the bridal party rode tiredly into the large courtyard, the Lord's servants rushed to greet them, taking the exhausted and travel stained Lady Blanche to her chambers. They apologised for their Lord's absence, explaining that he'd been called to the King's side on urgent business but would endeavour to return presently, his desire being the wedding take place immediately upon his homecoming.

Relieved for a few days in which to conceive of a plan, the Lady Blanche and her nurse sat before the fire, anxiously thinking of ways in which to fool her husband. For though the nurse was a witch of no small power, once innocence has been lost it is impossible to regain. Now that Blanche had seen the status and wealth being offered her, she was determined that nothing would keep her from attaining it.

They were interrupted in their foul plotting by the arrival of the young maid who'd been assigned to care for the Lady Blanche. Young, fresh and innocent, the maid was a local lass from a nearby farming family, going by the name of Sarah. As soon as the nurse laid eyes on her slight, womanly figure, so alike that of her mistress, her eyes gleamed with the germ of an evil plan.

When the Lord returned, he was delighted to discover his future bride to be a ravishing beauty, her modestly downturned eyes and maidenly blushes awakening yearnings of protective love deep within his breast. All through the wedding feast he hungrily watched her, eager to dispense with the ceremonies and take his intensely desirable wife to bed.

Later, the bride was taken away by the nurse and young Sarah to prepare her for the bedchamber, the Lord following a respectful time later, a contingent of his own men-at-arms, the young, foreign bodyguard amongst them, accompanying him.

Gladly accepting a cup of wedding mead from the bodyguard, the Lord downed it in one swallow, causing much good-natured joshing and laughter amongst his men. Feeling strangely disorientated, the Lord entered the dimly lit bedchamber alone to find his bride lying in bed, awaiting him.

The wedding night was everything the Lord had desired it to be and more. How tenderly his new bride had lain in his arms, her maidenly blushes stirring his blood to new heights of passion, and when he finally breached her maidenhood, her cries of pain were heard and cheered by the waiting men outside.

When the Lord awoke in the morning with a strangely sour taste in his mouth and a thick, throbbing skull, the Lady Blanche was innocently asleep beside him. The bloodstained sheets on which they lay were duly displayed in the banqueting hall as a testament to his new bride's virtue.

Of course, no one cared that the little maid, Sarah, had quite a different awakening that morning. Dumped on the rude pallet in the tiny room she shared with four other maids, she also had a sore, pounding head, and a foul, lingering taste in her mouth. Even more worryingly, she had no memory after putting Lady Blanche into her bridal bed and taking a sip of wine to celebrate the nuptials.

As poor Sarah struggled to make sense of the fragments of passionate memory which floated on the surface of her mind, she wondered at the tender, newly sensitised state of her maidenly parts, little guessing her most precious possession had been cruelly stolen from her.

Weeks passed, and Lady Blanche soon began to fret at the restrained, unimaginative lovemaking of her elderly husband. Even though she knew herself to be playing with fire, could not resist seeking out the young bodyguard, contriving ways in which to secretly meet with him.

Her blood throbbing with the desire to feel his taut, young flesh against hers, his firm, passionate lovemaking aroused such desire within her, that Lady Blanche was deaf to her nurse's entreaties to cease such a dangerous activity. Craving him, she took greater and greater risks merely to satisfy her appetite.

Meanwhile, the nurse realised another problem had arisen. Discovering Sarah crouched in vile misery over the night pail retching until her insides were dry, she instantly understood her night of unremembered passion had left the hapless maid with child.

Speaking in hushed whispers to her mistress, even the hardened old woman was shocked when Blanche casually ordered her to murder the girl in the Forest and leave her body for wild animals to devour. Although feeling a pang of sympathy for their innocent victim, the nurse realised they may not have any other option and began to contrive ways in which to carry out the foul deed.

Luckily for Sarah, Lady Blanche discovered she was also with child, it being either that of the Lord or the bodyguard. As the bodyguard was a lusty, dark-haired lad with grey eyes, and the Lord's family were all possessing of piercing blue eyes, the ancestry of the child would be all too apparent, and the nurse convinced Lady Blanche that having access to a true child of the Lord would be too valuable a commodity to waste. Thus, Sarah's life and that of the child within her, were spared.

Lady Blanche called her bodyguard to her, and ordered him to make much of the maid Sarah; to woo her so she would quickly agree to marry him, for she realised time was of the essence. Even though the maid, in her ignorant innocence did not suspect she was with child, it would not be long before others recognised her symptoms, and she was sent back to her family in bewildered disgrace.

Petulant and reluctant, the bodyguard at first refused, but Lady Blanche and the old wise woman so threatened and terrified him, he eventually agreed. That evening, he sought out the company of the young maid, gave her so many compliments and attentions, her head was quite turned, and in her naivete, she believed herself favoured by him.

The young man in turn began to enjoy the simple honesty of the maid, comparing her to the jaded wantonness of his mistress. His task at first abhorrent, quickly took on a more pleasing aspect, although he wisely hid this fact from his mistress, understanding she would be mightily displeased if he allowed her knowledge of the love he now bore for his sweet Sarah.

And so, the bodyguard and the farmer's daughter were married. A few weeks later, when the young bride blushingly sought out her mother, and with downcast eyes and a sweetly hesitant voice described her symptoms, it was assumed their union had been instantly blessed and all rejoiced.

All except the Lady Blanche.

Cumbersome with her own advancing pregnancy, sick to her stomach, Lady Blanche quickly wearied of her maternal state and the cloying attentions of her delighted husband. She also missed the excitement of her young lover's arms, for although she frequently tried to arrange a rendezvous with him, he showed a curious reluctance, explaining his new wife was of a suspicious nature, and he could not risk exposing his Lady should Sarah ever suspect her husband to be her lover.

Frustrated with the situation, but unable to fault his logic, Lady Blanche could do little but fume and fret, her bad temper snapping over at her Lord, who withdrew himself from her company, *indulgently explaining to himself and others it was a common fact that women in such a delicate condition often behaved thusly.*

And so the months dragged by and news came that young Sarah had gone into labour.

Dispatching her own woman to aid at the birth, along with Sarah's mother and the local midwife, the wise woman returned many hours later, to inform Lady Blanche that Sarah had been delivered of a baby boy, who although small, appeared healthy.

A few days later, Lady Blanche's own pains began. Telling no one, she sent for her wise woman, and the two secretly made their way to a place deep within the Forest which the wise woman had already prepared. There, Lady Blanche gave birth easily, her child also being a boy, although a good deal larger than Sarah's had been, already, even newly born, appearing much older. From the tuft of dark hair and shape of his face, the Lady and her nurse knew him to be the son of the bodyguard.

Quickly, the wise woman took the infant and set out to implement her evil plan. Watching from the Forest's edge, she observed Sarah happily going about her housewifely tasks in the cottage she lived in with her husband, who'd already gained much favour in the Lord's eyes, and thus been rewarded with a home in which to live with his family.

Waiting until the girl was occupied hanging out linen, the wise woman slipped silently into the cottage where in a moment she switched the two children, before hastening back to the castle and her Lady's chamber unobserved, where Lady Blanche was waiting.

Sending word to the Lord that the Lady Blanche was in labour, the wise woman hurriedly ordered boiling water, fresh linens and towels to be delivered to the Lady's chamber, before locking the door. There, the two foul conspirators remained, Lady Blanche amusing herself mightily by emitting such gruesome screams and moans, that the servants listening outside trembled, and ran to report to the anxiously awaiting Lord how badly it went for her Ladyship.

Finally, many long hours later, the wise woman ceased dropping sleeping potion into the child's eyes. He awoke, screamed long and lustily for his mother, Sarah's, breast, and the whole castle breathed a sigh of relief the Lady had been safely delivered.

The Lord hurried to his wife's bedside, eyes widening with appreciation at the sight of the strong, healthy lad, whose countenance bore plainly the marks of his ancestry, and his love and desire for his beautiful wife was strengthened anew.

Meanwhile, the bodyguard had returned home to the little cottage, where he'd known such contentment and happiness with his wife and new baby son, to find Sarah sobbing fit to be tied, crouched over a cradle in which lay a strange child.

Seeing his own likeness in the face of the unknown babe, the bodyguard knew it to be his son. In an instant he saw the whole evil scheme laid out before him, and was sickened to the core at the part he'd played. Humbly, he placed himself at his wife's feet, confessed all to her, feeling the knife wrench in his heart as her eyes widened with incredulous horror and she turned away from him.

As he knelt, listening to his wife's frantic sobs and the ever-increasing screams of the hungry newborn, the bodyguard felt the enchantment the Lady Blanche held over him dissipate like morning mist. He determined to take the only honourable course of action left to him, and in a low voice spoke softly and tenderly to his wife, explaining his plan. As his dearly beloved voice penetrated the depths of her heart, her tears ceased, and where a great loathing for him had sprung, now an intense fear grew and in dismay she clutched her hands together.

She rose to her feet, took up the child from the cradle, and placed it to her full and aching breast. Satisfied, the child's screams stopped. She looked at her husband across the new babe's suckling, announcing her intent to accompany him, so adamant in her resolve nothing he could say would dissuade her. Thus, when the child had fallen into a contented sleep, they carefully wrapped it against the chill of the October evening and set out on the short walk to the castle.

When they arrived, it was to find the whole castle in an uproar of celebration at the safe delivery of the son and heir. Poor Sarah's soul quaked at the thought of her darling babe being passed off as Lady Blanche's. but she spoke not, settling the child of her husband securely against her breast, her generous mother's heart holding no blame or rancour against the innocent creature.

The bodyguard sent a message that he wished to converse with the Lord privately on a matter of extreme importance. Still, it was a full, long hour before the Lord came to the small anteroom where they waited, and in all that time not one word did Sarah speak to her husband. Quietly, he mourned the loss of her love.

Jovial, full of good humour, at first the Lord could scarce believe the words the young bodyguard spoke to him. When at last he comprehended the full horror of the tale, he cried out in appalled amazement, demanding to know if the bodyguard was mad. Looking into those steady, grey eyes, saddened with his betrayal of a Lord who'd never been aught but fair to him, a great rage overcame the Lord. Pulling free his sword, he rushed at the young man determined to strike his head from his body.

Making no attempt to save himself, the young bodyguard did not flinch, and the Lord may have been successful in his intent, had not Sarah, giving a cry of denial, interposed herself and the wailing infant between her husband and her Lord.

Hastily, he stayed his sword, it not being in his nature to harm an innocent woman and child. Angrily, he cried to Sarah to remove herself, asking how she could possibly wish the life of one so treacherous to be saved.

Falling to her knees at his feet, Sarah gazed up in the Lord's eyes, and, in a voice which never wavered, answered him thus.

"Because I love him, my Lord, and true love is something which cannot easily be forgot or brushed aside, even if the one you love has treated you with such shabby contempt, as to be lower than the humblest thief. My husband has assured me since making vows of fidelity to me, he has been ever constant and faithful to that vow. In that I must believe. I also truly believe him innocent of this latest evil ploy of the Lady Blanche and her wicked serving woman. I know him to be guilty of much whilst under the influence of that most wicked of women, still do I love him and will continue to do so until the last beat of my poor, much maligned heart. And I do beg you for his life, my Lord."

At her words, the Lord turned away in anguish. For in that instant he'd looked into her eyes, seen the depth of her passion, and had understood what it was to truly love another more than oneself. Throwing down his sword, he clamped a hand to the bodyguard's shoulder, feeling the young man's body shudder with emotion at his wife's impassioned plea. Earnestly, he bade him take his wife home, ordering him to love and protect her for the rest of his days. The young man assured him he would.

Then the Lord went in search of his wife.

Entering her chamber, he found Lady Blanche seated in a chair by the fire, her serving woman combing her long shining hair, the child asleep in a cradle at her feet. Seeing his wife in all her ravishing beauty, for once the Lord did not hunger for her, instead he thought of the simple, unwavering faith and love of the young maid Sarah for her husband, and almost did he envy the bodyguard.

Lady Blanche greeted her husband. Alarmed by the coolness of his reply, her eyes met those of the wise woman, knowledge of their exposure passing in an instant between them. Casually, the woman did step away from her mistress, hand fumbling under her apron to pull out a small leather pouch, and in one quick movement opened the bag and flung its contents onto the fire.

In an instant, the room was filled with thick, pungent smoke, so dense and heavy it was impossible for the Lord to breathe easily or see any further than the end of his nose. Choking and gasping, he fell to his knees, hearing the pitiful mewling noises of the nearby child. Desperately, he grasped the cradle and pulled it towards him, snatching up the distressed child, groping his way to the door, to emerge, retching and straining, into the hallway.

Thrusting the screaming child at a passing maid, he called to the guard in the hallway, asking if he'd seen the Lady Blanche and her serving woman. Alarmed by his Lord's red streaming eyes and wild expression, the guard stammered out an affirmative, explaining the two women had hurried down the stairs towards the great hall mere moments before.

His rage mounting, the Lord hurried after, gathering his men around him as he went, wall sconces dancing desperately in the rising gusts of wind which whispered through the ancient castle, speaking of a storm brewing outside. In the great hall, the Lord informed all that Lady Blanche had been discovered to be a witch, along with her wise woman, and that the pair must be caught and burnt, or else none in the castle would be safe.

Alarmed mutterings spread. Nervous men-at-arms fingered their sword hilts, privately wondering how much use they would prove against witchcraft, but obediently followed their Lord out into the courtyard, where storm-ripped clouds scurried overhead, alternately hiding then revealing the full, yellow moon.

Calling to his huntsmen, the Lord bade them fetch their dogs to track down this most treacherous wife and her evil accomplice, knowing if any could find the pair in the wild rides of the Forest, it was this family, who were much skilled in the arts of the hunt. Dark of brow and eye, the Lord's huntsmen could track the swiftest falcon on the wing, follow the scantest of trails, had never been known to lose their prey, and the Lord was confident they would catch the pair before morning.

All night the search continued. Teams of hunters led the men-at-arms deeper and deeper into the inhospitable Forest, the dogs straining this way and that to pick up the scent, the mutterings of the superstitious and fearful men growing.

They'd turned into a pair of owls, the whispers grew, even now perched high in safety, round eyes watching the efforts of the men below. They'd turned into wolves and raced away onto the wildness of the moors. They'd turned themselves into trees, waiting to snatch up any who fell behind. At this last thought, the men grouped closer together, anxiously eyeing the storm-tossed, mighty trees.

The Lord and the young bodyguard were in the same party. Back and forth within the Forest they roamed, following first one trail then another as the dogs ranged all over, baying their confusion to the moon, noses down and tails up in an attempt to find the scent.

Finally, one sharp nosed hound sent up the call and darted away, closely followed by the Lord and the young bodyguard. For long moments they followed the hound's cries, straining to see in the fickle moonlight, trying to hasten, and at the same time watching their footing, roots and scrubby undergrowth rising beneath their feet, as if the trees themselves were attempting to trip the unwary.

Crashing into a small clearing in the heart of the Forest, the two men paused to catch their breath, as the moon sailed from behind a bank of black clouds. And there, silhouetted perfectly in a shaft of silvery light, stood a white hind.

Poised, one foreleg raised, it looked at the men, and in an instant the young bodyguard knew it to be the Lady Blanche. Thinking only of the pain caused to his Lord and wife by this woman, he snatched up his bow, and shot an arrow which pierced the animal's breast.

It screamed, high and anguished, a woman's cry, and the bodyguard knew he'd been right. Then it bolted from the clearing and the moon once again vanished, plunging them into darkness.

The two men rushed to where the hind had stood, as the storm cloud broke and torrential rain crashed onto the Forest, drenching all in an instant, and The Lord knew to pursue the creature any further would be futile.

Over the next few days, the hunters would again and again venture into the Forest, in a vain attempt to discover either a body or a fresh trail, but no sign of either Lady Blanche or her wise woman was ever discovered.

It passed into legend that they still walked the Forest and it became a place to be avoided. Mothers would caution their children, to not venture too far into its temptingly shady depths, or else the evil Lady Blanche and her witch will take you.

The Lord married again, a comely, merry daughter of a nearby nobleman, and found uncomplicated happiness in her arms, all rejoicing as several sturdy sons and pretty daughters arrived, and the castle was a happy place again.

As for the young bodyguard and his faithful wife Sarah, they continued to dwell in the little cottage by the Forest, the Lord appointing him chief forester, assigning this role to him and his family for all eternity, as well as ownership of the cottage.

The two babes, both innocent victims of Lady Blanche and her evil serving woman, were raised by the bodyguard and his wife. Not by a single word or look did they ever learn from their parents the truth, believing themselves true brothers both in blood and spirit, and never had two children been as close. By the Lord's orders, no mention was ever made of the parentage of the children, and over time people forgot.

Generations turned. Life went on as it had before the arrival of Lady Blanche, but each October when wild Autumn winds begin to bite and frost dusts the ground, it is said the White Hind walks. In her wake trails jealousy and mistrust, and folk's thoughts must be guarded, for then does she seek out the petty meanness of the soul, it is meat and drink to her, and thus does she feast.

Lady Marchmant stopped talking. Sally was intensely aware of the aching silence in the room, broken only by the soft pop and hiss of logs moving in the grate, and the creak of the chair as Lord Jolyon leant forward, his blue eyes intently watching her.

"Is it true?" Sally finally murmured, needing to break the quiet, but unsure what to say.

"No one knows," replied Lady Marchmant, smiling into Sally's confused face. "Perhaps there's a germ of truth at its heart, for I believe most folklore to have some lingering memory of fact."

"The White Hind," said Sally. "What does it mean? Can it be stopped?"

"I do not know," Lady Marchmant's brow plucked into a frown of concern. "I do not know if there is anything to be done."

"When Lucian spoke to Reuben, he told him something was different this time, that there's an intensity in the Forest that's never been present before. He promised Reuben when the time came, if they were able to, he and the other Forest folk would try to help."

"Others?" Lord Jolyon interrupted eagerly. "He claimed there were others?"

"Yes," replied Sally confused. "Although who and where they came from, I don't know. If this Lucian and the one who vanished in the twelfth century are the same man, how is that possible?"

"All things are possible within the Forest," claimed Lord Jolyon.

Lady Marchmant placed a comforting hand over Sally's cold, trembling one. "Every now and then, a Marchmant heir is taken from us. They disappear into the Forest and are never seen again. Rumours abound that they still walk its depths, and foresters claim there are men, strange men, living within its vastness."

"But what takes them?" demanded Sally.

"There is a sickness which lives at the heart of the Forest, Sally," Lady Marchmant bit her lip, glanced at her son. "A darkness so consumed by spite and envy an innocent soul such as yours could not possibly hope to fathom its motives. It preys on vulnerability, that much we know. Where it came from, and what it truly is, no one can tell." Lady Marchmant paused, gazing into Sally's open, trusting face.

"You must have great courage, Sally, and complete faith in what you believe in. I wonder, could you have been like Sarah in the tale? So certain of her husband's love she believed his word, even in the face of such overwhelming betrayal?"

"I... I don't know," murmured Sally uncertainly.

Lady Marchmant leant against the richly brocaded fabric of the sofa, her face lined and ancient, Sally glanced at Lord Jolyon in concern as he rose, bending to press a loving kiss on his mother's forehead.

"Try to rest now, Mother," he ordered. "We still have the ordeal of the Autumn Festival to endure, although I feel perhaps you should cancel it. I am sure, given the uncertainty of the time, all would understand your motives in doing so."

His mother's eyes gleamed with a flash of her usual spirit and she pulled herself upright, clutching wrinkled hands to her chest.

"Cancel the Autumn Festival?" she cried indignantly. "Why the very idea! No indeed not, we shall not even consider such a thing. Now, Sally," she turned her attention once more upon her secretary. "Go and attend to the matters I left on your desk, and I shall speak with you about them before you leave."

"Yes, Lady Marchmant," replied Sally.

Outside in the corridor, Lord Jolyon firmly but gently closed the door, and laid a restraining hand upon her arm.

"My Lord?" Sally enquired, startled.

"Take care, Sally," his normally mocking tone for once as solemn as his brother's. "Something is coming," he continued, "and I fear it will concern you. I worry for your safety."

"My Lord," Sally murmured again, eyes wide with anxiety.

Lord Jolyon's expression softened. Suddenly, his face loomed large, and his mouth, hot and demanding, pressed a swiftly branding kiss onto her own lips, softly pliant with shock. Before she could think or speak, he'd gone, moving swiftly away down the corridor, leaving her stunned and immobile, her mind twisting over all she'd heard and learnt, hand creeping with wonderment to where she could still feel his touch, scalding and disturbing.

She stood, for many long minutes, until Brenda Dodd, coming upstairs to retrieve Lady Marchmant's breakfast tray, disturbed her, and Sally fled to busy herself about her tasks.

That evening, she met with Reuben and Jack and told them the tale, imparting the news to a shocked but unsurprised Reuben, of the origins of the one called Lucian.

"I did wonder," he murmured, grey eyes thoughtful. "His clothes, the way he spoke. But, if he was a ghost, he was the most real one I ever thought to meet."

"Maybe he's not a ghost," commented Jack, who'd remained silent throughout the whole tale. The others looked at him in quiet enquiry, and Jack struggled to put his thoughts into words.

"What I mean is if this darkness, this thing, whatever it is, takes the heirs, maybe it doesn't kill them, but keeps them suspended somehow, alive only not ageing. So long as they remain within the

Forest they have a life, of sorts. But I'm willing to bet, as nobody else can ever enter, so they can't ever leave."

"If that's true," Sally murmured, looking at Reuben and shivering. "Then those poor people. Imagine it, trapped forever in the Forest with that monster. Perhaps there's something we can do to help them."

"At the moment," interrupted Jack dryly. "I'm more concerned with how we can help ourselves. These stories are all very interesting, but do they actually tell us anything?"

"I'm not sure," replied Sally slowly. "I think, apart from the report about what happened to the Hunter sisters, which I believe to be mostly accurate, the tales about Black Bridget and the Lady Blanche can't possibly both be true."

"I should think not," agreed Jack hotly. "They're completely different."

"No," disagreed Sally, "they're not. If you look at them carefully, both have points of common interest. I mean, both agree the Lady who married the Lord came from over the sea, I think, given the period of history in which the events happened, she was French. Both tales agree that the Lady had at least two servants; one a wise old woman who was either a good or a bad witch, depending on the tale, the other an innocent, simple maid, as represented by Fair Bridget in one tale, and Sarah in the other."

"And Black Bridget?" Reuben asked.

"I'm not sure," Sally replied slowly. "I can't decide about her. Also, there's a common theme in both about childbirth and abandoned children. Black Bridget left her twins without a backwards glance, the Lady Blanche also left behind a child, so maybe that element has a germ of truth in it."

"Abandoned children?" interjected Jack sharply. "Isn't there another tale? About a child who gets swapped or something? I'm sure there is, I'm sure I remember being told the story a long time ago, when I was very young," he screwed his eyes up intensely, shook his head and sighed. "It's no good," he admitted. "I can't remember anything other than that."

"Sleep on it," suggested Sally. "Maybe it'll come back to you. Then there's the young man, the forester's son in one tale," here she glanced at Reuben, who flushed slightly and turned away, thoughts of Sylvie whispering through his mind.

"And the young bodyguard in the other tale," continued Jack, thoughtfully. "Yes, I see what you mean. But what does it mean?"

"I don't know," moaned Sally, rubbing at her temples. "I've thought about it all day until my head feels ready to explode, and still can't understand why we've been told these tales. Both Lucian and Lady Marchmant claimed they might help us, but I can't see how or why."

Much later that night, long after Sally had gone to bed and fallen into an uneasy dream in which she was being consumed by a black, oily cloud, she awoke suddenly in the chill hinterland before dawn, looking wildly around her room which seemed unfamiliar and menacing, even in the usually comforting glow of her night light.

Sitting up, her nightgown sticking to her back in a sudden rush of cold sweat, Sally wondered what her friends would have made of that fiercely possessive kiss bestowed on her by Lord Jolyon. She shuddered at the thought of Jack's reaction, a protective urge moving over her at the idea of her Jack, made vulnerable by his black moods and intense jealousy, exposed to the dark creature which dwelt within the Forest.

Snuggling back down into bed, Sally comforted herself with pleasant thoughts of the imminent Autumn Festival, picturing herself in her gown, and imagining the faces of Reuben and Jack when they saw her in her planned finery. At last, a small smile tugging at her mouth, Sally slipped once more into sleep, her dreams this time of a more comforting nature, her last conscious thought before slumber dragged her under, being that Blanche was French for whiteness and purity, and she wondered at its significance.

Chapter Eight
~ The Tale of the Changeling Child ~

Eight days. Jack Blacksmith almost wished it would hurry up and happen, whatever it was, so oppressive and suffocating was the atmosphere within the village. He felt it during the usual silent breakfast with his father, John Blacksmith's face more withdrawn and shuttered than ever, a wild urge rising within him, to grasp his father by the shoulders and shake him until he roused from his self-imposed purgatory. To make him notice, really notice, what was happening around him.

As he walked through the hushed village streets seeing the scared expectant expressions, he felt a vague contempt for people who seemed content to merely sit and await their fate. Like a lot of sheep, he thought angrily, a lot of bloody sheep baring their necks obediently to the wolf's ravenous jaws.

He stopped briefly at the shop, relieved Nancy was absent, unable to understand the dark, obscene connection existing between them, a bond which always left him feeling contaminated and stained from her knowing dark eyes and mocking smile.

Each time Jack laid eyes upon Nancy Peabody, the need to escape to the clean, wholesome presence of his Sally became overwhelming. Desperately, he'd cling to Sally's company, tightening the links of blood, familiarity and friendship, until he knew he risked choking that which he treasured most in the world.

Absently, he brushed away Miss Violet's twittering anxieties, thankful for her concern, long exposure to it rendering him almost deaf to her hesitant, breathless voice. Once again, she cautioned him to take care, and once again he chose not to hear or respond, beyond a muttered promise to be vigilant, ever on his guard.

Clutching the paper bag of the violet creams his grandmother was so partial to, Jack hesitated outside the shop, shading his eyes against the glare of the low October sun, and set out on the steep climb to West Farm. Under the guise of going to pay a visit to his grandmother, in reality Jack was hoping to snatch a few precious moments with Sally upon her return home from work.

Tomorrow was the Autumn Festival.

Although Jack's heart swelled with pride his Sally had been chosen over the other village girls to be queen, he couldn't shake the nagging thought that Sally's moment of glory would somehow be his downfall and his pulse thumped erratically in his ears, making the world tip and shudder with nausea inducing vertigo.

Reaching the farmhouse, Jack rapped on the back door and let himself in, bending his head to clear its ancient low lintel. He found Eliza Cairn, flushed and warm from the range, placing a large sponge cake upon a wire cooling rack. She looked up at his entry, and for a moment Jack imagined a flicker of something - annoyance, unease, impatience - indefinable and fleeting. It rested for a brief second behind her eyes, then was gone, and she was once again his cousin by marriage, Sally's mother.

"Jack," she exclaimed brightly, wiping a flour stained hand across her shiny brow. "What brings you here?"

"Thought I'd visit with Gran for a while," he shook the bag by way of explanation. "I bought her some violet creams."

"Dear boy," replied Eliza Cairn fondly, and nodded towards the parlour door. "She's in there, sitting by the fire... oh, and Jack..."

Jack hesitated, hand on the door knob, face and brow lifted enquiringly towards Eliza. "Today's not such a good day," she continued hesitantly, saw by his face he understood. "Don't expect too much, will you Jack?"

"I won't," he promised, and walked into the room.

Approaching eighty, Amelia Cairn had always enjoyed the rudest of health until the loss of her husband. Although appearing to outwardly cope with admirable resilience and fortitude to his death, it was not long before the family started to notice small but telling changes, the apparently inconsequential memory lapses, the forgetting of close family names.

When Sally left to go to work one morning and found her great-grandmother, nightgown clad, wandering around the hillside, the family realised Amelia Cairn's symptoms were more than a natural outpouring of grief. The village doctor paid a visit, and upon his diagnosis of Alzheimer's the family and village rallied around, arranging a rota of constant loving care so Amelia Cairn could live out the rest of her existence safely, and with as much dignity as her condition would allow.

Therefore, Jack was unsurprised to find Norah Twitchett sitting on the sofa, knitting contently, keeping a close eye on his grandmother. She'd recently developed an alarming tendency to try and stoke the fire herself, giving Eliza Cairn palpitations at the thought of the elderly, confused lady going up in flames.

"Good day, Mrs Twitchett," Jack said politely.

Norah Twitchett's eyes twinkled as she bundled up her knitting, pushing it back into the commodious bag tucked by her side.

"Jack," she murmured fondly. "Come to visit your Gran, have you? That's a good, kind boy."

"How is she?" Jack asked, eyes fixed upon the blankness of his grandmother's face, heart sinking at the complete lack of recognition.

"Not so good," Norah Twitchett confirmed Eliza Cairn's diagnosis. "But at least she's in a quiet mood, not like some days..." her voice trailed away, not needing to complete the sentence for Jack had been present and could remember the times when Amelia Cairn's normally placid soul seemed racked with unseen demons and unknown tortures. The days she screamed and sobbed for release, clutching with inhuman strength at her son and grandson, begging them to help her.

"Why don't you go and have a cup of tea," offered Jack. "I'll sit with her."

"If you're sure," Norah Twitchett needed no second bidding and hustled from the room, eager for some of Eliza Cairn's legendary cake, and perhaps a good gossip over what offerings would be forthcoming from which village lady at the Festival tomorrow.

Slowly, Jack sat on the rug before his grandmother, the fire warm on his cheek, watching the shadows the flickering light cast onto her parchment lined face. After a long moment, his grandmother's head turned. She looked into his eyes, and Jack's heart jolted at the thought his grandmother was seeing right to the very core of him.

"Gran?" he whispered. "It's me, Jack, I've come to see you."

"Jack?" she murmured, a beatific smile spread over her thin lips. "Why, little Jackie, have you come to see your old Gran, there's a good boy."

"That's right, Gran," Jack confirmed, heart sinking, realising his grandmother's mind was back in the past, seeing him not as a darkly handsome young man of twenty-one, but the little motherless boy brought to the loving sanctuary of his grandparent's farm by Mabel Dodd.

Lonely and love starved, how Jack had looked forward to those visits, his small face lighting up with pleasure at the sound of his grandmother's voice calling to her little Jackie to come and see what delights she was keeping in her apron pocket.

Swallowing down his disappointment he thrust forward the paper bag, and Amelia Cairn's eyes lit up with the innocent greed of a child being offered her favourite treat. Her crevassed hands fumbled to open the bag.

For a moment the room was silent, save for the crackling of the fire, and the soft rustling of the paper bag as she clawed at the sweets. She gave a little sigh of happiness and stuffed two into her mouth at once, gesturing to Jack to take one.

"You're a good boy," Amelia Cairn eventually murmured, patting him vaguely on the head. "A good boy to visit your old Gran and bring her such a nice treat."

"I love you, Gran." Usually uncomfortable with such terms of endearment, Jack couldn't remember the last time such a sentiment had issued from his mouth, and it would've been hard to state who was most surprised at his words. But then, Amelia Cairn smiled and pulled her grandson closer, bony arms briefly encircling his strong, wiry shoulders before she sat back, eyes twinkling with some semblance of old, long-forgotten animation.

"I know what you'd like," she declared gleefully. "I'll tell you a story, shall I? My little Jackie does love to hear stories, and I know which one you like the best."

"It's alright, Gran," began Jack glancing at the clock, seeing it needed but half an hour before Sally would arrive home. Jack wanted to talk to her privately, was afraid if his grandmother embarked on a long and winding tale, Sally would be back, and the opportunity lost.

"This is the tale of the changeling child," his grandmother announced, and Jack's eyes grew sharp at the mention of the story he'd so desperately tried to recall the previous evening.

Making no further protestations, he settled comfortably at his grandmother's feet as her eyes grew soft with loving memories, her thin fingers gently stroking his hair, Jack listened as his grandmother told him a tale he'd not heard since he was a small child.

Once upon a very long time ago, a wise and powerful fairy lived in the centre of an enchanted wood. Neither good nor bad, this fairy shunned all contact with humans, believing them too easily swayed by their emotions. Although she was certainly not evil, the fairy was not one of those that rushed around performing good deeds, and instead lived alone, quietly and contentedly, with the woodland creatures and her thoughts.

One day, the fairy grew weary of her lonely existence, disguised herself as an old beggar woman and hobbled to the edge of the wood, determined to venture into the world of humans to see if it'd improved at all in the centuries since she'd last paid a visit.

Appearing ancient and decrepit in her resemblance to a crone, the fairy lay upon the track and waited to see what would happen. Soon, a party of richly dressed noblemen rode by. They laughed cruelly to see such a pile of wretched humanity, pulling their horses aside and leaving her where she lay.

The fairy's temper boiled at the realisation humankind was still as uncaring and cruel as before, and she decided to return to her wood and not bother with the world of men. Then she heard light footsteps approaching and lay down again, appearing to all intents and purposes a poor old beggar woman in distress.

The footsteps came closer, a sweet voice enquiring if she was ill and the fairy felt someone sit beside her, small hands patting at her arm. Opening her eyes, the fairy saw a sunny smile of concern set in a merry face so adorned with golden freckles gleaming in the sunlight, it appeared the young maid was bathed in gold.

Gently and tenderly, the young woman helped the fairy into the shade of trees around a nearby spring. Fashioning a large leaf into a drinking vessel, the kindly maid assisted the fairy to drink of the cool refreshing water, begging the fairy to partake of her midday meal, which although a simple one of oatcakes and fruit, was fresh and wholesome. The fairy accepted all the maid gave her, croaking her thanks in the cracked voice of the very elderly.

As she was about to reveal herself and reward her kindly rescuer, the sound of hooves echoed on the path, and a young male voice called out to them, enquiring of the maid if all was well and if there was aught he could do to assist them.

The maid leapt to her feet and gave a low curtsey. The fairy surmised the young man to be someone of importance and looked with great curiosity into his face. In the same instant did the fairy lose her heart to this most dashing and handsome of mortals, finding his piercing blue eyes and noble countenance most pleasing.

When he swung from his horse, he offered to escort the maid and her invalid charge wherever they wished to go. The fairy determined to make this mortal her own, and to that end allowed the young man to help her onto his horse. Croaking out thanks to the young maid, she begged the lord, for that indeed was who he was, to convey her to the edge of the wood where she lived.

Once they reached the enchanted wood, the young man tenderly helped the fairy down and was vastly surprised to find her transformed into the beautiful and bewitching fairy. When she took his hand and led him deep into the wood he had no choice but to follow, so beguiled was he by her loveliness and magnificence. There, in a bower of sweetly twining wild roses, the fairy did keep the lord for three days and three nights. He was her lover, and the fairy did conceive of his child.

At the dawning of the fourth day, the fairy reluctantly guided the young lord back to the edge of the wood, for were she to keep him with her any longer he would become so dazed by her presence his mind would be forever confused. With many a lingering kiss she left him, believing her soul would crack with grief.

As she walked through the trees, the fairy heard sounds of sobbing and came upon that very same young maid who'd helped her, sitting by a small stream, weeping as if her heart was breaking.

Having a fond regard for the young woman, the fairy appeared to her. The maid was amazed and afraid, until the fairy spoke kindly to her, then the maid was comforted, and the fairy did ask what ailed her.

The maid told how she and her young husband, the woodcutter, were sorely troubled because their marriage had not been blessed with a child. The fairy's usually unmovable heart was touched, and she placed a hand upon the maid's belly, promising before the rise of the next full moon she'd be with child.

But, there would be a price to pay.

So grateful was the maid, she foolhardily promised to meet any demand the fairy should make and so the deal was struck. The maid returned home. True to the fairy's word, before the month was out she grew to suspect she was with child. She and her husband rejoiced much, and the maid did forget her promise to the fairy.

The months turned, and the maid gave birth to a fine, strong babe as fair and golden as the maid herself. A little daughter, whom they named Sunniva, which means gift of the sun.

More time passed. The young woman and her husband believed themselves most fortunate in their pretty, happy little daughter. Life was simple and good. Until one dark and dismal morning, when the maid went to lift her daughter from her wooden cradle and instead of her sturdy, golden child found lying in her place a dark and sickly looking infant with locks of midnight black and a small, scowling face, out of which stared a pair of intensely piercing blue eyes.

The maid knew by the otherworldly cast of the child's face and the colour of her eyes, this child must surely be the result of the union betwixt the fairy and the young lord. Only then did she remember her promise, and wept bitter tears of pain for the loss of her child.

Years passed. The woodcutter and his wife raised the changeling child as if she was their own, yet still the maid remembered her Sunniva, and often did wonder if she'd ever see her face again.

Meanwhile, the dark child they'd named Bridie grew into a tall and passionate beauty. Fiery of temper and generous of heart, her adopted parents could not help but love her, despite the pain over their stolen child.

Deep within the wood, the fairy had also been raising a child. Knowing a fairy child to be best served by a mortal upbringing, she'd changed the babes soon after birth, taking the maid's daughter as her own. Loving the bright, sunny child and caring for her in true fairy tradition, she taught her the ways of the wood and the habits of the creatures that dwelt within.

But Sunniva, truly a daughter of the sun, pined and fretted for the open, sky bare downs, and when the child was seven summers old, the fairy knew she could keep her no longer and bade the child put on her cloak. With a heavy heart, for she'd grown to love the girl as much as a fairy could, she took the child back to her parents.

Great was the rejoicing in the woodcutter's cottage, when the maid opened the door to a midnight knock and there stood a child, whom she knew instantly to be her own. Much did she weep and enfold her daughter in her arms. Sunniva also did know these to be her own true family. Soon her life in the wood began to seem as a dream. The woodcutter and his wife were happiness itself with their two fine daughters, each as different from the other as night to day.

The years passed, and Sunniva and Bridie grew as close as any real sisters, vowing they would never be parted.

One day, when the sisters were just come of age, they went to the wood to gather fruits. There the lord of the castle did spy them, becoming instantly enamoured with the golden loveliness of Sunniva. Even though the lord was nearly two score years older than her, still he was tall and handsome and Sunniva looked with equal love upon him.

Thus, the simple woodcutter's daughter was taken to the castle to become his lady, and at Sunniva's insistence, Bridie did accompany her.

Time passed. All was happiness for the young sisters, except for one matter. Within the castle dwelt a widowed aunt of the lord. A proud and spiteful woman, she'd long determined her own daughter should marry the lord and be lady of the castle. Upon his marriage to Sunniva, she was greatly angered that a girl of lowly birth should aspire to such heights. As her hatred for the sweet tempered Sunniva grew, she determined upon a plan to remove Sunniva and install her own vapid and plain daughter in her place.

She began to drip poison into her nephew's ear about his young and beautiful wife, murmuring lies and defamations so subtle the lord was unaware of her intent. When Sunniva discovered she was with child and the whole castle rejoiced, then did the aunt insinuate and whisper obscene allegations of faithlessness, casting doubt upon the child's parentage.

Bridie too had married, a bold and brave soldier who owed much faith to his lord. He knew of old the widowed lady's character, and often did caution Bridie to warn her sister to be on her guard, being fond of his naïve and trusting sister-in-law and not wishing to see any harm come to her.

But Bridie, much distracted by the birth of her own sickly and frail son, failed to heed his warnings. Poor Sunniva was thus completely unprepared, believing her lord to be as loving and trusting of her as she was of him.

When her time came, and she gave birth to the much longed for son and heir, her dismay and shock were great when the lord ordered her and her child be thrown into a dank cell. Facing charges of treason on the grounds of the child not being his, she was to be executed that evening.

Hastening to tell his wife the dire news, the young soldier found her mourning the death of their son. When he fell to his knees by the cradle woefully imparting his dread tidings, a great rage gripped Bridie. She took up the body of her dead son and made her way secretly to the dungeon, there did she order her sister to exchange the babes through the bars, promising to get her son away to safety, and that she would return for Sunniva.

Hurrying into the woods, Bridie sent up a desperate plea for aid. Such was the pain in her heart that the fairy heard and flew to her side, face darkening and eyes snapping flames of rage at the news her dearly beloved adopted child was to be executed. She took Sunniva's son from Bridie, and told her what she must do to prevent such a thing.

So well had the venom of his aunt worked, the lord was deaf to the pleas of his previously beloved wife, and Sunniva was dragged into the courtyard to be hung.

In vain did the young soldier, Bridie's husband, plead for her life, recounting tale after tale of examples of the widow's perfidy, until at last the lord ordered him be put to death first.

And so it came to pass that Bridie returned too late to save her brave love. Her grief knew no bounds as she rushed to his side, cutting down his body with his own sword. Sunniva wrenched free of her captors and embraced her sister, still holding Bridie's dead child, so tightly bound in swaddling clothes none could see the deception the sisters had practised.

Bitterly, their tears mingled as they wept, and almost was the lord's heart moved by their plight. But then he remembered his aunt's words and ordered Sunniva be put to death, warning Bridie should she interfere she would be next, and the guards snatched the dead child from Sunniva's arms.

Seizing Sunniva, Bridie drew from her pocket the dust her mother had given her, muttering words of power and sprinkling them both with this magical powder. In an instant, they turned into does. With one bound they leapt over the heads of the startled and terrified soldiers, and dashed away into the wood.

Angered by their escape, the lord ordered his hunters to set loose the hounds. Deeper and deeper into the wood these great, vicious beasts did track the sisters eventually cornering them by the edge of a wide, rushing stream crossable only by a fallen tree. Bridie urged her sister across, and once Sunniva was safe on the other side, did knock the tree away and turn to face the dogs alone.

Realising her sister was not following, Sunniva bounded back to the stream, and there saw a dreadful sight: her sister being ripped apart by the mighty, ravenous jaws of the hunting hounds, returning to her human shape as she died.

Sunniva, still in the guise of a doe, gave such a cry of despair, her adoptive fairy mother heard and flew instantly to her side.

When she saw her poor, mutilated child, the fairy's rage knew no end and she struck until every hound lay dead. Gently, she lifted Bridie in her arms, brought her to Sunniva's side. She lay beside her dead sister, wept bitter tears and lamented so passionately, that the ancient, timeless powers of the wood heard her plea, and offered Sunniva a bargain.

They would restore her sister to life again, yet Sunniva must forevermore stay as a doe, and neither sister would ever again be able to leave the confines of the wood. Gladly did Sunniva accept, and to her great joy, Bridie was reborn and stood smiling before her.

To protect her beloved children, the fairy caused a mighty barrier to be placed around the wood which none could cross. But Bridie passionately begged her mother to allow members of the lord's family to enter and the fairy agreed, realising Bridie wished for revenge upon the lord and his family for the murder of her husband. Every few generations, she would take a son and heir for her own and never again would he return to his family.

The fairy gave Sunniva's son to the woodcutter and his wife to raise as their own. As he grew to manhood, he often entered the wood, as was his right as the son and heir to the lord, and would spend time with his gentle mother, Sunniva, who remained in the form of a doe and grew ever kinder and sweeter in spirit and heart.

But, as centuries passed her sister Bridie grew ever more dark and twisted, her intense hatred and loathing of the lord, his family and the people of the castle who had not interceded to save her husband, growing unchecked, until it consumed and saturated every waking thought and sleeping dream.

In vain did gentle Sunniva plead with her sister to let go of such anger. Eventually, the two sisters who'd previously been so close as to be one, grew so they could not bear to be near one another. Thus, in loneliness, did they pass the rest of their eternal days.

As his grandmother's quavering voice fell silent, the spell her words had cast twisted and caressed Jack's mind until a soft sigh had him turning sharply. Sally perched on the edge of the sofa, expression thoughtful, and Jack felt a plunge of disappointment that his plan to speak with her alone had been thwarted.

"Granny Amelia," began Sally hesitantly.

Amelia Cairn looked up, eyes for once focused and knowing, as if her mind had found a tiny chink in the fog of gentle amnesia and was peering through it, desperately clinging to lucidity.

"Sally, my dear," she cooed. "I didn't see you come in."

"Where did you hear that tale Granny Amelia?" Sally pressed urgently. Jack saw his grandmother's eyes cloud with confusion and knew they were losing her. "Granny Amelia?"

At the barely suppressed strain in Sally's voice his grandmother frowned, as if struggling to remember, tugged by the ring of importance in Sally's tone.

"My great-grandmother," she finally mused. "When I was a child, she told it me. She said it'd been told her by her grandmother, and so on, back through the generations. It's a very old tale, she didn't know how old, only that her grandmother claimed it was true..." her voice trailed away, and she looked around querulously.

"Where's my tea?" she demanded fretfully, shrivelled fingers plucking anxiously at a loose thread on the arm of the chair. "It's tea time, and they know I can't bear my tea to be late. Where is it?" she raised her head, fixing Sally with a pleading stare.

Sally swung from the high arm of the sofa. "Don't worry Granny Amelia," she comforted, voice taking on the brightly reassuring tone all now adopted with Amelia Cairn when it was plain she was lost in the landscape of her affliction. "I'll go and sort out your tea now." Sally left the room.

Instantly, another change came over Amelia Cairn. Her eyes lost their childlike bewilderment, and her expression was so crafty, and so filled with naïve cunning, Jack blinked in surprise.

"Well, that got rid of her," announced his grandmother, her delight at her own scheming evident as she patted Jack's hand, eyes twinkling conspiratorially. "I've got something for you," she whispered, delving deeply into her apron pocket. "Something I know my little Jackie wants more than anything else in the world."

For a moment, so intense was the feeling of nostalgic déjà vu, Jack was convinced his grandmother would produce a gobstopper or some other treat from his youth. Instead, she pulled out a carefully folded, rose pink, linen handkerchief, which she passed to Jack with all the importance of a queen bestowing the highest honour upon her most faithful knight.

Puzzled, Jack took the small bundle, his eyes meeting his grandmother's as she chuckled softly.

"Open it," she urged. "Quickly, before they come back."

With fingers that shook, Jack unfolded the handkerchief, there, nestled safely within its lavender scented folds, rested his grandmother's engagement ring. Stunned beyond words, Jack's eyes flew to her face, then back to the ring sparkling prettily in its old-fashioned setting, back up to his grandmother's face again, words choking in his throat.

"I know what you want," whispered Amelia Cairn. "I've always known what you want. But you must act fast. You must get her promised before the Autumn Festival ends."

"But, Gran..." began Jack in amazement.

"No buts," she insisted urgently, hand closing so tightly over his, the ring bit deep into his clammy palm. "She must be promised to you by midnight tomorrow, do you understand? You must make her yours in every way. Only then will you both be safe."

There was movement and noise, the other side of the door. Quickly his grandmother pushed him lightly away, and Jack stumbled to the sofa pushing the ring deep into his pocket, his gaze locking with his grandmother's in an agony of unspoken questions and doubts. The door flew open, Sally Cairn and her mother entered bearing trays of tea things, and Jack saw his grandmother retreat behind her eyes. The moment of lucidity sliding away in the face of childish greed for her tea.

Later, after an evening spent in the uncomplicated and merry company of Sally and her family, an evening during which Jack observed all, but felt himself strangely detached, his answers brief and monosyllabic. Ardently, he gazed at Sally, feeling the ring burn through the fabric of his pocket, until he was convinced when he undressed that night he'd find an indelible brand from it on his skin.

Hungrily, he watched her. Aching to think by this time tomorrow, she'd be his. Promised to him. Wearing his ring. And maybe, somehow, Jack could contrive a way for them to become one, for he'd no doubt that'd been his grandmother's implication.

His cheeks burnt at the thought, and he shifted uneasily in his seat, thankful for the drapes of the red and white gingham tablecloth which hid his desire.

Once, he glanced up from his thankfully private thoughts to find Eliza Cairn looking sharply at him, her normally placid and straightforward expression altered to one of intense suspicion.

He gazed levelly at her, meeting the cautious accusation in her eyes with candid innocence, staring her down, until finally her gaze dropped, and she turned from him, addressing the need of another family member for more potatoes and the moment passed.

Now Jack was leaving, and Sally had offered to walk him to the gate. Although Jack knew it was merely because she wished to speak with him about the tale they'd heard that evening, still he rejoiced because it meant he'd finally be alone with her. His fist closed urgently over the ring in his pocket.

It was a still, silent evening. The two looked up as one at the almost full moon as it slipped up and over the edge of the down, looking so close, Jack fancied if he reached high enough he could grasp it, bring it down to earth to them, and make a gift of it to his Sally. Heart thumping with hot, anxious love, he listened to Sally's words, comprehending nothing.

"Another story about betrayal, jealousy and swapped children," she puzzled. "What does it mean, Jack? What can it all mean?"

"I don't know," he murmured, mind in a frenzied whirl. They were almost at the gate. Now was the moment. Now was his last chance. Desperate to stop her talking, he reached out a hand and urgently gripped her arm.

"Sally," he began desperately. She stopped, turned to face him. "Sally," he tried again.

The time upon him, his tongue was stricken with paralysis and he swallowed painfully. In the silvery glow of moonlight he saw her face, and it was the face of a stranger, wearing an expression of anxious denial. Then she smiled, and was his Sally again.

"Yes, Jack," she replied gently. "What is it?" Her tender concern gave him the nerve to continue.

He stepped closer, liking the way her head automatically tipped back to look up into his face, her smile soft and tender. When his arms went around her, she did not protest or pull away. It seemed she came gladly to him.

He bent his head. Finally, finally, his lips closed impatiently over hers and desire and love and want and need and lust and longing and fear, all combined in a heady rush of passion, and Jack groaned with the terrible beauty of the moment, the culmination of a lifetime of loving her.

For a second, all was well. His heart soared with exhilaration, and his hand moved of its own volition to cup one small, soft breast. He heard her gasp, felt her pull away, and desperately tried to drag her back, needing to keep her locked in the moment with him.

Slowly, inexorably, she disentangled herself, gently stepping back, face flushed in the moonlight. Jack saw the dazed desire in her eyes, and for an instant gloried in the realisation she wanted him as much as he wanted her. It gave him hope and courage.

Stumbling over his words, he yanked the ring from his pocket, fell to his knees in front of her, handsome face twisted in an agony of anticipation and need. He held out his hand, the ring and its glory shining brightly in the silver moonlight.

"Sally," he gasped, "please, I love you so much, marry me."

She remained silent, staring first at him and then at the ring. He wished he could see her expression, but her face was shadowed, unmoving. Urgently he continued, filling her silence with hot, ardent, needy words of his own.

"It's always been you, Sal, you know it has. I've always loved you, right from the start. I can't imagine life without you, I love you so much. Please, Sally, say you love me too. Please, say you'll marry me, and we'll always be together. Please…"

He heard the pitiful pleading in his voice, winced away from it, despising himself for his weakness, yet unable to stop, Tears splattering onto his hollow cheeks, his voice hoarse with longing.

"Sally, you have to marry me! You've got to!"

"Got to?" Finally, she spoke, her voice low and husky. "Oh, Jack," she murmured, and knelt slowly and carefully before him, taking the handkerchief clutched in his other hand, softly and kindly dabbing the tears from his face.

"Jack, my dear," she said. "I love you so very much. You've always been in my life, my dearest friend and cousin…"

"Second cousin," he automatically corrected, and saw her rueful smile in the gloom.

"You're in my heart and in my soul," she continued carefully, treading lightly through the minefield of emotion he'd spread before her. "But, I don't know if the love I feel for you is the sort a wife should feel for her husband. It's so sudden, so unexpected…"

"It's been a whole lifetime," he cried in indignant agony.

"For you, perhaps," she agreed. "For me it's been a minute. Of course, some part of me may have suspected, but I think I always denied it could be true. That you could love me that way."

"I've always loved you," he declared, the words of Wuthering Heights floating in his mind. "I am you, and you are me."

"Oh, Jack."

She sighed again, leant forward and embraced his burning, shaking body in an oddly cool and steady hug. Jack fancied he felt her detach from him, stepping back from the love and passion he offered her so completely.

"Sally," desolation closed his throat.

Gently, but firmly, she placed her fingers on his lips.

"Not now, Jack," she cautioned. "I need to think about all this. I must be certain. It's a big step. You have to give me time, Jack."

"But there is no time," he despaired. "You have to be promised to me, you have to be mine…"

"Why, Jack?" He heard the surprise in her voice, knew she couldn't understand.

"Please," he tried one last approach. "You want time, I understand that, but please, I must have your answer before midnight tomorrow. Can you do that? Can you tell me you'll be my wife at the Autumn Festival, so we can announce it to everyone? Then everyone will know you're mine. I'll be safe."

There was a long silence. Sally sighed and rose slowly to her feet, brushing leaf mould from the front of her long, warm coat, fussily picking twigs and grass from her sleeve.

Jack knew she was delaying her reply. Hastily scrambling to his own feet, he fought to still the raging need to simply take her, to make her understand, with force if necessary, the rightness of their union, the completeness that could only be achieved if she was his. Finally, utterly. In all ways possible.

"Goodnight, Jack," she murmured, turning away from him, back towards the comforting solidity of the farmhouse, crouching squat and solid up the hill, its windows blazing with the light of home.

"Sally," he begged hoarsely. She hesitated, half glanced back, her smile solemn and final.

"I'll give you my answer tomorrow, Jack," she promised. At the relieved, expectant smile which broke across his face slowly shook her head in correction. "I'll give you my answer tomorrow, Jack," she said again, "whatever it may be."

Walked away from him without a backwards glance.

Jack's heart cracked with frenzied grief, yet still a wild hope remained Sally would say yes. That in front of all the villagers who'd dismissed him as wild and rebellious, an unloving and unlovable boy, she'd prove that the man loved, and was loved in return.

But, overlaying this feverish optimism was an even greater fear that Sally would reject him, a lifetime spent in loving would come to nothing. He'd be alone, completely and utterly alone, not even deserving of the hope of Sally's love.

He watched as she entered the sanctity of her home, not glancing back, the solid, wooden door closing firmly behind her.

Jack stood desolate and empty in the moonlight, his young, passionate heart throbbing and aching. A part of him wished he could call back the words, return to a time when hope still lived. But, it was too late.

He had cast the die. Now could only wait to see how they fell.

The Forest

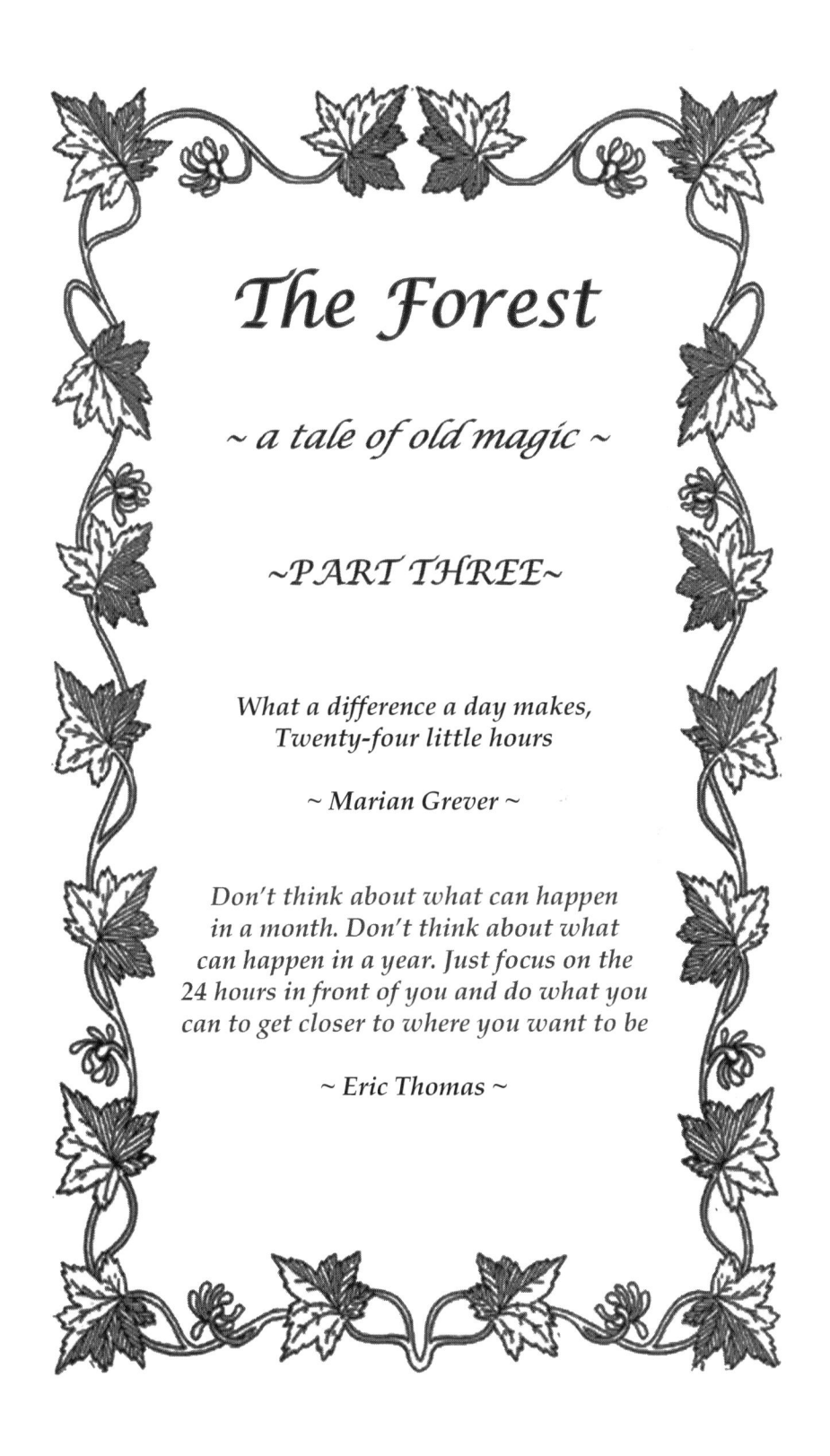

~ a tale of old magic ~

~PART THREE~

*What a difference a day makes,
Twenty-four little hours*

~ Marian Grever ~

Don't think about what can happen in a month. Don't think about what can happen in a year. Just focus on the 24 hours in front of you and do what you can to get closer to where you want to be

~ Eric Thomas ~

Chapter Nine
~ Sunrise ~

It was the morning of the Autumn Festival. Into the pre-dawn hush of the still village came the tiny sound of a door being quietly opened and closed, and Nancy Peabody emerged onto the deserted village high street. Shivering in the chill October morning, her sharp, beetle black eyes darted around, ensuring none were watching, that no hardy soul had ventured early from their bed to witness Nancy Peabody's departure from the village for the last time.

Dawn. Sally Cairn rolled over in her narrow, virginal bed, staring helplessly at the slanting ceiling mere feet above her head. Behind her lay a night of restless tossing and turning, before her a day which represented the greatest honour of her young life. Overshadowing the joy that thought should bring, was the darkly intoxicating rush of Jack's proposal.

With a suppressed groan, Sally clasped her hands to her mouth, thoughts returning to that unexpected, unsurprising encounter in the moonlight by the rickety, wooden gate. Sally's young, untried body ached at the memory of his mouth on hers, his arms holding her tightly, the shocking thrill of his palm on her breast.

With a stab of confused shame, she remembered those few, wild moments when she'd responded to his urgent need, her body straining to meet his, senses overwhelmed by the uncontrollable urge to pull him to the ground, to feel his weight move over and within her. Sally's cheeks burnt fiercely in the dim glow of her night-light at the memory.

Turning onto her side, pulling her legs fiercely up to her chest, Sally's mind returned to her dilemma. Until last night, the thought of loving Jack in any capacity other than dearly beloved friend and cousin, had never entered Sally's imaginings. Then, he'd kissed her. His firm, sensitive mouth awakening responses beyond her wildest dreams, his young, strong body calling to the sleeping passion in her own. Sally had almost succumbed, had almost surrendered her own desire to his. Almost, but not quite.

What had stopped her from lying with Jack there and then? Or at least from giving him the answer he so ardently longed for? Sally was unsure, but knew something inside had cried out in denial of Jack's love. Something had held her back, something was unsure. Maybe something was still waiting. But waiting for what?

Unbidden, the memory of Lord Jolyon arose in her mind, the look in his eyes before he'd kissed her, and the feel of his hand on her face, his mouth on hers. Sally's eyes went very wide at the thought, her breath stilled, and her soft lips parted on a sigh of unconscious pleasure. She rolled over, stretching out her limbs in supple, easy contentment, her eyes alighting on the gown hanging in readiness on her wardrobe door.

She thought of the night to come, of being arrayed in such splendour, of feeling beautiful, and of knowing herself to be the envy of the other girls, her heart skipping with a girlish thrill of excitement.

She lay quite still, eyes tracing the lines and folds of the gown, its silken perfection bearing testament to a mother's love that'd tenderly and painstakingly handsewn every stitch. The notion arose in her mind of how it would be to have Lord Jolyon look at her in that gown. Look at her, perhaps, in the same way he'd looked at her that other time.

Sally imagined Jack looking at her, the quick, hot jealousy she knew would flare should he realise she was desired by another man. A man who ranked so far above poor, lowly Jack, Sally felt mean even comparing one to the other. She knew the only way to appease Jack's fears would be to capitulate to him, to agree to be his wife and wear his ring, and announce to all her total commitment to this one man in denial of all others. Maybe, possibly, go somewhere private with Jack and finish the matter begun last night.

As her thoughts cartwheeled back to the possibility of being intimate with Jack, Sally Cairn groaned in mortal dilemma, curled herself up into a tight ball, and willed herself to sleep, sternly instructing her frenzied, racing mind to ignore the painful, insistent pounding of her newly awakened body.

Not seeing another soul, Nancy Peabody purposefully made her way to the very edge of the Forest, pausing in the grey, oddly hushed beauty of the frozen world. Hoarfrost crackled underfoot, every blade of grass and fallen twig lay shrouded in a white mantle of encroaching winter, the sky above lowered threateningly.

Nancy hesitated. Some small vestige of who she might have been pleading with her to turn back, to return to her safe bed, and accept a simple but honest life as just another village girl.

Even as the thought formed, angrily Nancy Peabody did push it away, refusing to give countenance to the idea, hungrily reaching for the darkness within, its blackness now her only source of encouragement and sustenance. The voice became loud and strident in her head, forcing her on, ordering her into the Forest.

Deeper and deeper she went, eyes curiously noticing the cold glory of the ancient Forest as the trees creaked and shivered in the approaching dawn. Nancy Peabody had never entered the Forest before, something always keeping her from its mysterious depths. Now she strode forward confidently, feet deliberate and brisk as if they automatically knew the way.

Eventually she stopped, the unseen barrier before her. Wonderingly, Nancy Peabody placed her hand flatly upon its insubstantial solidity, thoughts confused as to what to do next.

Then she looked… saw it… and finally understood.

Excitement at the coming festival awakening her early, Eliza Cairn stretched beside the comforting bulk of her husband, hearing his rumbling snores with an exasperated smile of affection. Moving closer to him, seeking his warmth, she lay with her spine pressed against his. Familiar with the feel of his wife's body beside him, Farmer Cairn mumbled in his sleep, moving to accommodate her.

Comfortably positioned, Eliza Cairn allowed her thoughts to return to the troubling scene she'd witnessed from her bedroom window last night, and a frown settled upon her homely face. Innocently, she'd gone upstairs, as was her tradition every night, to close the curtains against the penetrating chill. For some reason she had lingered at her own window, the only one in the house which afforded a clear view down the path to the gate.

She'd seen them, apparently indulging in a few moments of friendly farewell conversation, but something about the anguished set of Jack's body caught at Eliza, and she'd pressed her face to the glass, cold against her flesh, cupping a hand to the side of her eyes, and straining to see the slight figures, distinct in the blaze of silver moonlight flooding the countryside, casting long shadows over all.

Eliza Cairn inhaled in shock at Jack's fiercely possessive embrace, trembling as she'd watched her daughter return it for a brief, but telling, moment. Then Jack had fallen to his knees, offering something up to Sally. Eliza Cairn watched, heart in mouth, as her daughter knelt before him, relief swamping the mother at the resoluteness she sensed emanating from her daughter. Sally embraced Jack, an embrace which, even from a distance, Eliza Cairn could see lacked the passion of before, then she had arisen, turned away from him.

Jack had pleaded with her. Even without being able to hear his words, Eliza Cairn could feel their beseeching intensity. Sally had paused, spoken to him over her shoulder, before striding away, passing out of her mother's line of vision, and Eliza had heard the slam of the back door.

From her vantage point she'd watched, silent sympathy misting the windowpane, as Jack slumped against the gate, dejection apparent in every line of his body. Finally, he'd pulled himself upright and walked away into the night. Eliza Cairn had returned downstairs to her family, scrutinising Sally with newly opened eyes, observing with an aching heart the over-brightness in her daughter's smile, and the glimpse of confused misery behind her eyes.

When Sally excused herself to go to bed early, Eliza caught her up in a fierce hug, whispering if there was anything at all troubling her, Eliza would always be willing and ready to listen, heart cracking as Sally's gaze slid sideways from her mother's, voice brittle with denial of anything other than simple tiredness behind her decision to seek her bed at such an early hour.

Now, Eliza Cairn shifted uncomfortably in her own bed, uneasy with what she'd witnessed, its implications for her beloved Sally, and the nice, safe life she'd envisioned her leading. She remembered the passion and intensity of Jack's darkly handsome face aglow in the unearthly moonlight, and thought about the White Hind, about all the old stories and legends.

An icy fist of fear fastened itself around Eliza Cairn's heart, and her mind tumbled over itself, contriving plots and schemes to keep her daughter safe, even considering sending Sally far away until this was all over.

Somewhere, a bird sang, followed by another, and Eliza Cairn realised the long night was over, the day of the Autumn Festival was upon them. Her mind travelled across the agenda of events planned with precise, almost military, detail and a vague thought coalesced and shifted in her thoughts.

She rolled onto her back, eyes narrowing in concentration as a plan offered itself. She followed it through to completion, seeking flaws and finding none. Sliding gently out of bed, not wishing to face her husband's questioning, Eliza Cairn hurriedly pulled on her thick, woollen dressing gown, and set out to put her plan in action.

Mesmerised, Nancy Peabody stepped closer, feeling the treacly resistance of the barrier against her body. Far on the other side, the black amorphous presence swirled and moved, its form constantly in flux as it melted into smoke one moment, the next coagulating into a shape vaguely reminiscent of a human, before disintegrating once more into a heavy, tarry substance that oozed across the Forest floor.

Totally unafraid, eyes wide and unseeing, Nancy Peabody placed her palms flat onto the barrier, leaned into it as far as she could, and when the nausea of resistance rose in her throat, persisted.

Slowly, almost imperceptibly at first, the dark, shapeless thing moved to meet her. Its edges drawing in, tighter and tighter, it came closer to where the girl hung, suspended in the barrier.

Nancy felt the forces of the Forest gathering to repel her. Grimly, she clenched her teeth, digging her heels into the mud of the Forest floor, straining forward with all her might, veins at her temples throbbing in taut relief as the scream was ripped from her soul.

John Blacksmith woke abruptly from a deeply disturbing dream, his normally steady heart pounding fiercely in brutal, unfathomable fear. As usual, his night had been spent with the fanatically preserved memory of his wife, face relaxing into unfamiliar lines of joy as he'd clasped his beloved Rosie in his arms, lain with her in this bed, their kingdom for too brief a time. On this night, though, something had been amiss. For once his Rosie hadn't clung to him with passionate ardour.

Instead, she'd pulled away, beautiful, unlined and ageless face stern and unforgiving. In vain, he'd tried to pull her back to him, body straining and aching to keep her close, voice cracking with dismay as he'd called her name. Steadily, she'd moved back, shaking her head, tears of bitter sorrow streaming in rivulets down her cheeks.

In his dream, John Blacksmith begged her to tell him what ailed her, watching, unable to hear or understand, as his wife's eyes pleaded piteously, and she'd wrung her hands in agony.

Shouting her name, John Blacksmith wrenched himself upright in bed gasping with fear, the echo of his shout sounding in his ears. It seemed to him, as he'd jerked awake, he'd heard another shout close by. A despairing, pain-wracked, scream, it'd made all the hairs on the back of his neck stand up, and it took him a few, panic-stricken moments to realise that wild yell had come from his son's room.

Rising from his rumpled bed, John Blacksmith moved silently from the room, and cautiously opened the door to the small room where his son slept. A shaft of watery, early sun was oozing through the clumsily drawn curtains, and in its insipid light he could see Jack, lying on his back, apparently sleeping soundly. As John watched, Jack's face twitched, moved in extreme agitation, eyelids betraying by their never ceasing flickering, that dreams of alarming ferocity were stalking his son's slumbering mind.

Briefly, John wondered if he should wake him, his hand reaching to pull his son back into the world of the living, then it dropped back to his side. Unable to touch the boy he'd had no physical contact with in twenty years, a boy whose very features, even in sleep, were so stamped with the image of his dead wife John Blacksmith turned away in soul wrenching pain, and quietly left the room.

Closer came the darkness. It was upon the barrier, flowing easily up its dense resistance. Nancy watched in silent awe as its shape solidified. She saw its true form. Looking deep into its eyes, she felt her own grow huge as the form pressed against the perimeter.

Suddenly, gloriously, it broke through. Nancy cried out in unbearable ecstasy as she felt it penetrate her body. Finally, finally, they were one. It was all she'd ever dreamt it could be, and more.

Her eyes turned midnight black as everything that made up Nancy Peabody was consumed and amalgamated. Gladly, she felt it slip warmly into her thoughts and assume control, welcoming the strangely familiar, already beloved voice as it hissed.

"Where is the other? I need him if I am to be completely free. Where is he?"

Choking, Jack clawed his way up from sleep and away from the awful thing that had pursued him through his dreams, heart hammering against his ribs in a frenzied tattoo of terror, skin clammy with fear, eyes instantly wide and staring.

"No!" he moaned, gaze ricocheting off the walls of the familiar space which had been his room all his life, seeing everything, recognising nothing. With shaking hands he switched on the lamp, flooding the tiny, cheerless cell with its warm, comforting glow. Marginally reassured, Jack drew his knees to his chest, fingers massaging the soreness in his temples.

Cautiously, he poked at the memory of the dream. Darkness and desolation, an all-consuming, hungry rage, jealousy, hot and violent, its sticky aftertaste lingering in his mouth.

Jack moaned softly, burying his head in his hands.

Somewhere, something was waiting for him. He knew it, could feel its calling, could feel the thing inside him responding and answering. A part of him longed to give in, to simply accept and go to it. Still, Jack held it down with thoughts of Sally, of how it had been last night, holding her slight, supple body in his arms, feeling her warmth close to his chest.

Was it his imagination, or did the darkness retreat slightly from the thought? Encouraged, Jack allowed his memories free rein, lying back, and luxuriating in the glorious wonder of Sally, his Sally. Of the way she'd held and kissed him, the deep, untapped wellspring of passion he'd felt within her untouched body as she'd moved against him.

Jack allowed himself the conviction she would say yes. That tonight, at the Autumn Festival, during her shining moment of glory as crowned Queen of the village, she would accept Jack's proposal.

He would be her king, and Sally would be his love, forever and ever. But… but… what would happen should she reject him?

As the small, insidious, negative thought slithered through Jack's mind, the thing gave a great roar of triumph, and with a rush reclaimed all its old, briefly lost territory. Jack curled into a ball, sobbing in denial, as familiar insecurities welled and gushed, and he began to shake with the strain of resistance.

Gradually, sweat beading his brow from tension, Jack fought back into himself. Clinging to the hope of Sally, much as a drowning man might clutch at a fraying rope, he pinned all hopes of salvation on its rapidly perishing strands, and faced the awful realisation that should Sally say no, the darkness would win. He would truly be lost for all time.

Deep within the Forest, Lucian raised his head, feeling the atrocious outrage vibrating along every ancient line of power which crossed and connected within the Forest. Swiftly, he rose to his feet, buckling on his sword belt and slinging his quiver over his shoulder. The moment was almost once more upon them. Fervently, he prayed this time would be different, mouth thinning into a grim line of determination as he pulled his cloak around him against the chill of the early hour and set out to locate the others.

Intimately in tune with the Forest, his body connected in long tradition of blood and history, Daniel Forrester felt the disquiet emanating from the trees, and looked sharply around, sensing rather than seeing or hearing the disturbance which pulsed and throbbed from every branch, shrub and creature. Beside him, Bess stiffened, staring intently down the track ahead of them.

Watching her, Daniel knew from the hackles rising in instinctive fear on her neck, the ears cocked, nose forward stance she'd adopted, that Bess could feel it too. A powerful unease had him turning and setting off briskly the way he'd come, back to home and security.

He'd not go into the Forest today.

Hurrying along the track leading to the Forrester's cottage, Eliza Cairn found her eyes more than once sliding sideways to gaze in anxious trepidation at the Forest. Not one for fanciful imaginings, her solid, practical soul more at home in the kitchen or helping on the farm, still, Eliza felt a million eyes watching from concealment.

Unconsciously, her pace quickened. At last, with a sigh of relief, she reached the point where the track diverged, the left branch leading into the leafy domain of the Forest and its creatures, the right to the reassuring solidity of the forester's cottage. Standing at the juncture, Eliza Cairn hesitated, glanced fearfully along the left-hand track, eyes narrowed in startled surprise. Why, she thought to herself, wasn't that Nancy Peabody? Squinting to see in the low gathering October sunrise, Eliza Cairn shaded her eyes with her hand, and peered closer.

"Nancy?" she called, hesitantly. "Is that you?"

The figure between the trees stopped, and slowly turned. Conviction grew in Eliza Cairn's heart that it was Nancy Peabody, but something about the stillness of the shape, the calm, almost menacing way it was watching her, made Eliza Cairn draw back with a gasp, clutching her coat tighter to her chest.

"Nancy?" she called again, more uncertainly this time. With an acute feeling of relief, Eliza Cairn saw the shape seem to abruptly come to a decision, turn sharply on its heel, and vanish into the gloom between the trees,

Suddenly Eliza Cairn found her feet hurrying as if of their own accord along the rough track to the forester's cottage, for the first time in her placid, uneventful life, knowing what it was to be afraid.

Exiting the Forest at a point next to his home, Daniel was surprised to practically walk into Eliza Cairn rushing along the track, peering anxiously back over her shoulder as if she were being pursued. She let out a shriek of genuine fear at his sudden appearance, eyes widening with shock, hands clutching at the missed heartbeat within her chest.

It dawned on Daniel Forrester that something had scared the normally unshakeable Eliza Cairn, and he gripped her shoulders reassuringly, ordering, "Watch yourself, woman."

At his familiar, rough tone, Eliza gave a great start, palpable relief flooding her eyes. "Daniel Forrester!" she exclaimed crossly, clutching almost desperately at his arm. "What on earth do you mean by creeping up on a body like that? Why, you very nearly gave me a heart attack. What are you doing, out and about so early?"

"Never mind what I'm doing," he retorted. "What on earth brings you so far out of the village at this ungodly hour?"

"I need to talk with you," Eliza Cairn insisted urgently. Daniel's brows drew together in concern as she stepped closer, and began to speak in hurried, low tones.

Stretching lazily in bed, Reuben Forrester wondered what had awoken him so early, especially as the Autumn Festival was a day's holiday for the entire village, so there was no need to arise.

Pulling the blankets up to his nose, breath misting warm on his hand, Reuben tried to remember the dream, which had held him in such a vice like grip a part of him had feared he'd never awaken.

It'd been about Sylvie, that much he could remember. In his dream, he'd walked with her again in the leafy glades where they'd met as children. She'd seemed sad, and he remembered begging her to tell him what was wrong, but she'd merely shaken her head, long silvery hair flowing in a nimbus of pale light, her beautiful face mournful. Her hands had gently touched his face, eyes studying him intently as if committing his features to memory.

Then he'd awoken. For long moments, Reuben hovered in no man's land between sleeping and waking, annoyance at being plucked so prematurely from his dream causing his body to twitch fretfully under the covers, and the sleep yawning in his ears meant that it was a while before he realised the half-murmured voices he'd imagined had followed him from his dream, were real voices coming from outside.

Curiously, Reuben slithered out of bed, wincing as the frigid air of the bedroom struck at his sleep warmed body. Shivering, he crept to his window, pulled aside the curtain, and peered owlishly into the thin light of early morning.

To his intense surprise, it was his father and Eliza Cairn, Sally's mother, talking in low, urgent whispers. Reuben blinked in stunned shock, wondering what bizarre catastrophe could possibly have

~159~

occurred to necessitate the visitation of Eliza Cairn, at an hour more usually associated with larks, than social calls.

Flinching his bare feet away from contact with cold floorboards, Reuben strained to hear, the voices an obscure, unfathomable murmur. Frustrated, he was reduced to watching their body language, noticing that it appeared to be Eliza Cairn who was doing all the talking, her stance one of entreaty. Daniel Forrester looked steadily at her, nodding his head, apparently brushing aside her thanks as she clutched at his arm in gratitude.

Her business seemingly concluded, Eliza Cairn nodded to Daniel, and hurried off along the track, her head continually turning to look at the Forest, trepidation obvious in every line of her body.

Hugely curious, Reuben watched until she crested a small rise and could be seen no more, then glanced down to find his father standing below, gaze fixed upon his son, an oddly intense expression on his face. Reuben's eyes locked for an eternal moment with those of his father.

Daniel broke contact first, jerking his head away, snapping Bess to his side with a click of his fingers, Reuben saw him vanish from sight, heard the soft sound of the cottage door closing below.

Shaking with cold, Reuben sought the refuge of his still warm bed, logic insisting he try to return to sleep, but his mind refusing to comply, his body twisting into positions of curious contemplation as he reflected on the bizarre scene he'd witnessed. Wondering what it meant. Wondering if he dared question his father about it.

And in her small, snug cottage, Molly Mole abruptly awoke to find fresh, hot tears caressing the lines of life grooved deeply into her aged face, heart beating hot and fast with the knowledge that it was time. The players were in place. Once again events would unfold to their inevitable, tragic conclusion.

Chapter Ten
~ Midday ~

The shop bell tinkled and Miss Violet Peabody looked up, kindly face creasing into a genuine smile of welcome as Jack entered. "Jack," she exclaimed, unable to explain the relief which clutched her heart at seeing him. "What can I do for you today?"

"Bread's mouldy again," he remarked, pulling a rueful face. Miss Violet clucked her tongue in annoyance at John Blacksmith's lackadaisical housekeeping but remained silent, not wishing to provoke Jack into one of his black moods. Instead, she hurried to pull a crisp, freshly baked loaf from the basket and wrapped it almost tenderly in paper, waving away his money when he pulled a handful of change from his pocket.

"Something to go with it," she murmured fondly, cutting a slab of the mature cheddar supplied to the shop by East Farm. Jack flashed her a warming smile, gratefully taking the bag of bread and cheese, his stomach, empty since his meal with the Cairns the previous evening, lurching at the thought of the wholesome food.

"No Nancy today?" he enquired with studied casualness, glancing around as if half expecting her to appear from nowhere.

"No," Miss Violet paused, frowning, a trickle of concern whispering across her features. "I don't know where she is, she was up and gone early this morning." Her voice brisk, Jack heard deeply buried dislike for her niece beneath her words.

"I expect she'll come back when she's ready," Miss Violet reassured herself. "She knows we only keep the shop open until one on Autumn Festival days, I expect she wanted to avoid having to work, I suppose that's it. Yes… that'll be it."

Jack glanced up at the concern which had crept into her final words. "You think she's alright though, don't you?" he asked, not understanding why his heart suddenly beat faster, or why his palms clutching the bag became clammy, as if with apprehension.

"Oh yes, I'm sure she is," Miss Violet hastily chased away her fears. "It's just, with this whole White Hind business, well, I worry about you, young people. Especially you, Jack."

There, it was finally out in the open; Miss Violet's acknowledgement that something about Jack gave her cause to fear for him over any other village youngster, and that she realised the black dog of insecurity which had stalked Jack his entire young life made him an easy target.

Sally Cairn stood in the centre of the vast banqueting hall, turned slowly in a complete circle, hands on hips, head tilted back, gazing with a proprietary critical eye at the wreaths and garlands which now festooned and cheered the usually solemn and silent space.

This year, Lady Marchmant had turned over the role of decorating the great hall to Sally, and she and a team of village youngsters had worked long hours making garlands of autumn foliage studded with dried fruits, seed heads and pine cones. Each table bore a centre arrangement of corn and autumn flowers, and safely out of harm's way, strung over the rafters, Sally had arranged great swathes of brambles all groaning with plump berries.

The effect of natural fertile abundance was one Sally was pleased with, believing it to be beautiful in its simplicity, and she ached for evening for all to see and admire.

"You've outdone yourself Sally," remarked a familiar voice lazily.

Sally turned sharply to see Lord Jolyon leaning casually against the doorpost, face creased into an admiring smile. His gaze, a piercing, penetrating blue, roamed over her features in a way that had the blush springing easily to Sally's cheeks remembering the last time she'd seen him. That unexpected, incredible kiss, which'd left her young heart shaking, and her bemused mind spinning.

"It all looks amazing," he continued, eyes flicking around the hall before coming back to rest on her prettily flushed face. "Beautiful," he drawled, and Sally's blush intensified at the double meaning in his eyes.

"Th-thank you, my Lord," she stuttered, feeling provincial and stupid, gloriously desirable and hopelessly inadequate, all at the same time. "Everyone's worked so hard." Her voice trailed away as he sauntered slowly towards her, intent evident in his face.

"My Lord..." she stammered. Then he was before her, hands slipping warmly up her arms, touch burning through the cotton of her simple frock. Her head tipped back to gaze up helplessly at his superior height, throat suddenly dry as he trailed a finger down her flaming cheeks.

"The power of a maiden's blush," he murmured.

"My Lord..." she stuttered again.

He bent his head, and Sally's eyes fluttered down in total capitulation as his strong mouth closed over her softly compliant one. The kiss moved over and through her, glory exploding in her mind. Strong arms encircled and enforced. She was his captive, unable to escape even should she want to, because he was her lord, she was his subject, and still the kiss went on.

Finally, he let her breathe again, held her as she went limp and pliant in his arms, amusement etching his brow at the obvious, dazed confusion in her eyes. Tenderly, he cupped her face in his hands, his expression one of fond indulgence.

"I wonder," he murmured, "Would a man ever grow weary of counting the freckles on your face, Sally?" She stared at him, eyes wide with shock, bewildered mind trying to make sense of his words.

"Tonight, Sally," his voice was rich with promise. "Tonight, you will be crowned Queen and the first dance belongs to me. After that, well, that is to be your decision."

He released her.

Sally staggered, bereft by his absence, one hand flying to her mouth to touch the imprint he'd branded onto innocent lips, the other clutching at her chest where her heart tumbled over itself.

"Tonight, Sally," he said again.

It was both command and pledge. Numbly, Sally nodded. Satisfied, he ran a hand lightly over her shining braid of hair and left her, standing alone in the vast hall, skin throbbing from his touch, confusion warring in her mind at the thought of the decision she must make tonight. Of the two very different men unknowingly battling each other for dominion over her heart.

Banding together in unspoken agreement of safety in numbers, Lucian and the others trod softly along the Forest's tracks, seeing nothing untoward but feeling with every fibre of their being the menace dripping from each branch and shrub. Under its sticky, encompassing layer, Lucian sensed the Forest gathering its defences, knew ancient powers were stirring, attempting to repel the infestation of evil.

He prayed for once the Forest could halt events before they reached their usual, tragic conclusion, but feared deep within his heart that the Forest may only be able to restrain it as before, limiting the damage to the loss of three young souls, containing the infection within itself and maintaining the barricade, keeping the rest of the village safe.

He paused at a slight sound ahead, held up a hand to halt the others, ears straining to hear as it came again. A twig cracking in the undergrowth. His eyes narrowed as bushes parted and a young woman stepped forward, her long dark hair rippling in the breeze.

Lucian started in surprise, wondering if despite her darkness she could possibly be a Marchmant, for no other could have penetrated this far into the forest.

"Fair maid," he began. "how came you so deep within the Forest? Tis not safe here. You must return to the village and your home."

For a moment she stood, immobile and silent, eyes bent upon the Forest floor, then gave a low chuckle which stilled his heart and froze the blood in his veins.

"Oh, but I am home," she declared, and he recognised the voice. She raised her head. He saw her eyes, dark fathomless discs that showed not a glimmer of white or any other colour but the black of malevolence, his heart stopping with sad realisation that the thing had claimed its first victim.

"It's her," Lucian heard one of the others exclaim. Before he could stop him, the man raised his bow and an arrow sang through the air, burying itself into the maiden's chest with a dull thud.

She staggered back, looked with mild surprise at the feathered shaft sticking out from her breast, and smiled at the men watching in aghast silence. A terrible, awful smile. She plucked the arrow from her body, examined it, and Lucian saw she was unharmed. No blood oozed from the fatal wound.

She stepped forward, and they involuntarily fell back. The smile stretched across her still, impassive face. Wide and mirthless, it struck dread into the hearts of the men. Lucian felt their terror and realised there was no point in trying to stop the creature. It was invincible, at least within the confines of the Forest.

He motioned soundlessly to the others to pull back. A tide of relief swept over them as they crept stealthily backwards, eyes fixed upon the young woman who stood, watching them leave, head cocked to one side, smile fixed and unwavering. As they finally turned and fled from the clearing, Lucian heard her voice behind them, sweet and low, and his spine tingled with panic inducing horror.

"Bye Baby Bunting, Daddy's gone a hunting, to fetch a little rabbit skin, to wrap my Baby Bunting in."

Her mocking laughter followed them, fear for their eternal souls lending wings to their feet.

Down in the permanent chill of the cellar beneath the stone-flagged floor of the pub, Amos Blunt was stealthily loading up bottles of his latest home-brew. Rich, earthy brown in colour, it was a lethal concoction and Amos felt a stab of pride as he carefully pulled the last bottle from its hiding place, slipping it noiselessly into a stout cardboard box.

The kegs for the festival had been delivered to the Hall several days previously, it needing time for the beer to settle, and he'd paid a visit to the Hall that morning to tap them, ready for the all-night consumption the Autumn Festival inevitably turned into. But this other brew, this heady fermentation which Amos boasted could make a man drunk merely by inhaling its aroma was special, only to be offered to a select few. Amos rubbed his hands together in gleeful anticipation of the admiration it would instil, relishing the thought of superiority over his fellow villagers.

Staggering under its weight, he muscled the box close to his chest, pacing his way carefully to the steep stone steps. Even though Dorcas was over at their daughter Mathilda's house, looking after the little 'uns so Mathilda could take the cakes and scones she'd baked up to the Hall, Amos still moved warily, afraid of the trouble he'd be in should his wife return home early and discover him.

Concerned about the potency of his home-brew, Dorcas had banned him from making it several years hence, not realising in doing so she'd merely driven the practice underground, thus increasing its appeal. Amos conveyed to a chosen few by a series of well-practised nods and winks, whenever a fresh batch was ready for furtive consumption.

He slunk cautiously through the kitchen and out the door, thankfully loading the box into a waiting wooden crate mounted onto an old set of pram wheels he'd prepared for the journey. He kept the contraption hidden in an old outhouse Dorcas never entered, owing to the combined deterrents of her own bulk, and a deep-seated fear of spiders.

Chortling at his cleverness, Amos set off through the silent village, bottles dancing merrily in the box, soon reaching the edge of the Forest nearest the Hall. His delight grew as he carefully pulled the wagon into cover of a thick bush, checking no trace of it could be seen from the track.

Congratulating himself on the brilliance of the hiding place, he fussed over the positioning of the stash, completely unaware of a figure, still and menacing, hidden behind a nearby tree.

Watching. Waiting.

"Are you still here Sally?" Sally jumped from the wreath she'd been needlessly fiddling with as Lady Marchmant swept elegantly into the banqueting hall.

"My Lady?" she stammered.

Lady Marchmant's eyes moved expansively round the hall, her expression one of delighted surprise. "Why, it looks marvellous in here, Sally, simply marvellous. You've done an excellent job."

"Thank you, my Lady," replied Sally, cheeks again pinking from the compliments of a Marchmant.

"But what on earth are you still doing here, Sally? It's gone midday, you know. I'm sure you have plenty to do at home before tonight."

"Yes, my Lady. If you're sure you have nothing else that needs doing?"

"No, my dear, Mrs Dodd and a whole army of village ladies are downstairs in the kitchen busily preparing a veritable feast. I am sure they are more than capable of coping without your help," Lady Marchmant paused, smiling fondly at Sally. "Go home, Sally, my dear. Prepare yourself to accept your crown as Queen of the Autumn Festival."

"Yes, Lady Marchmant," Sally returned the smile of her employer and scurried from the hall, unwilling to admit, even to herself, that she'd been lingering, deliberately stretching out her last few duties in the hope Lord Jolyon would return.

Glancing out of his study window, Lord Gilliard smiled as Sally Cairn wheeled her trusty bicycle around the corner of the house, pausing to button up her coat against the biting chill of the raw October day. What a bright and happy child she was, he thought indulgently, always smiling, always in a good humour, really it quite lifted one's spirits merely being in her company. He watched as she glanced at the Hall's façade, biting her lip, eyes scanning its many windows as if searching for something.

Suddenly she started, a deep pink flush rising on her cheeks. Seemingly abashed, she dropped her gaze to the ground, wheeling the bicycle rapidly away from the Hall as if mistrusting her ability to ride. Curiously, he looked where she'd looked, and saw his brother leaning against the glass of the upstairs landing window, face inscrutable as he watched Sally leave.

In a flash, Lord Gilliard saw and understood. A rare spurt of temper exploded in his mind and he stormed from the study, seeking his brother, determined to discover if what he suspected and feared was true.

His brother had not moved from the position. Gilliard hesitated a moment, unsure whether to speak or leave things well alone, but an image of Sally's face, devastated by heartbreak, arose before his eyes. Newly resolved, he spoke, his words quick and fierce.

"Sally is a dear child. I would hate to see her hurt."

His brother half turned. Gilliard saw a flash of something settle in his eyes, before the old, mocking expression was back and Jolyon shrugged dismissively. "In case it's escaped your notice, she's not a child anymore."

"No, she's a naïve and vulnerable young woman," snapped Gilliard. "She wouldn't understand the way it is with you, Jolyon!"

"And how is it with me, dear brother?" drawled Jolyon casually.

"You use women for your pleasure and discard them when you grow bored of them. I would hate to see Sally treated so shabbily."

"I've never had any complaints from any of the ladies I've previously kept company with," denied Jolyon, his tone finally registering a faint note of annoyance.

"They were all sophisticated society women, most of them married," snapped Gilliard waspishly. "They knew and understood the rules of the game. Sally doesn't, she'd think you meant it. Then, when you left her high and dry, what would become of her?"

Jolyon was silent for a long time, eyes thoughtfully scanning the path down which Sally and her bicycle had disappeared. He finally turned and faced his brother, his eyes for once serious, and Gilliard stepped back from the pain and resolve he saw reflected there.

"Oh, brother," murmured Jolyon sadly. "did you never stop to think maybe, this time, I mean it?"

Perched on a conveniently fallen tree trunk, Jack hungrily ate his impromptu picnic, stomach growling its appreciation of the thickly satisfying bread and crumbly, flavoursome cheese, which he'd simply pulled apart with his fingers and consumed. He was unwilling to return home to the despairing, grieving atmosphere of the house where he lived with his father, unable to bear it a moment longer.

Brushing crumbs from his trousers, Jack looked up at the crunch of bicycle wheels on the track, heart lurching within his rib cage as Sally rounded the corner, cheeks pink with the exertion of pedalling, wisps of hair escaping her braids in the slight breeze lovingly caressing her body.

Stepping forward, Jack raised a hand. Sally put a foot down to stop her progress, and an almost guilty look scuttled across her face before her usual smile spread. She glanced at the hunk of bread and cheese he still held in his hand, eyebrows raising with amusement.

"Lunch?" she enquired.

Jack shrugged. "Breakfast," he corrected.

Sally sighed, shook her head in exasperation. "Jack," she began fondly, then gasped as Jack urgently grabbed the crossbar of her bicycle. Seeing the alarmed, fearful look flicker across her face, he cursed himself for scaring her, forced his knuckles to relax on the shiny metal, and placed a reassuring smile on his mouth.

"About last night..." he began.

"I said I'd give you my answer tonight, Jack, at the Festival," she snapped. "You have to give me more time."

"I know, I know, and I will," he hastened to placate her, fearing a Sally whose eyes flashed with annoyance, unused to seeing anything but calm friendliness in her expression towards him. "I just wanted to say... well, I know I'm not much, Sally."

At her instinctive reaction, he placed a hand over hers. "It's true," he continued bitterly. "After all, what am I? The bad boy of the village, always in trouble, disliked and distrusted by everyone except you and Reuben. Oh, and maybe Miss Violet."

"That's not true, Jack," Sally insisted hotly, springing to defend him as she always did, even against himself. "If you gave people a chance to know you, to understand the Jack I know and... love," on the last word her eyes slid away from him and the hope which had leapt, withered quietly away.

"What I wanted to say, Sal," he continued desperately, "is that I've always loved you and I always will. If we were married, I'd work as hard as I could to look after you. Give you a good life. After all, the garage will be mine one day and it makes a good living. You'd want for nothing, I'd see to that."

Sally's face softened, and for a single quiet moment there was harmony between them.

"Bless you, Jack," she murmured. "I know I'd be safe with you." She leant forward, gently her lips brushed his cheek, and as she tried to pull away, he clutched at her neck, dragging her lips to his.

Once again, Sally was consumed by the bottomless well of Jack's passion, his desperate longing rising in a great tide of lust and need which threatened to sweep her away. Sally moaned lightly against his mouth and his hands grasped hungrily at her arms, drawing her closer. Heat, intense and primal, flash fired between them, and Sally was lost.

Fingers gripping his hair. Pulling almost to the point of pain. Pulling him closer to her. Pulling him so her chest was crushed against his. Racing heartbeat to racing heartbeat. Mouths feasting.

Consuming. Hungrily gobbling each other up in an explosion of want that left her mind spinning out of all control.

How long, she had no idea. Time ceased to exist. There was only this raw, aching urge to be possessed by him. Still, an insistent voice clamoured to be heard, begging her to stop, consider, be cautious.

The handle of the bicycle, cold and real, pressed firmly into her stomach and Sally crashed back down to earth with a shocked and despairing gasp, ripping herself away from the iron circle of his arms, a tiny cry of denial forcing itself from her throat. Almost angrily she yanked her bicycle backwards, glaring at him.

"Sally," he began helplessly, tears of frustration and rage spilling from his eyes. "I'm sorry… I didn't mean… Sally!"

"I can't think, Jack!" she cried, wheeling her bicycle away and shakily trying to remount. "When you… when we… I can't breathe, Jack. You don't let me breathe."

"I'm sorry," he said again, hands falling futilely to his side.

"I'll see you tonight, Jack," Sally snapped, as she rode away from him, back ramrod straight with displeasure. Jack let her go, knowing he had no choice, fighting down dark images inside which showed him racing after her, dragging her off that infernal machine, carrying her deep into the Forest, ripping away her clothes, her protests and then… oh sweet bliss… losing himself in her again and again, until she saw and understood this was how it was meant to be. She belonged to him for all eternity.

Thrusting away the thoughts, sweat beading on his forehead, Jack gave a hoarse growl of fierce denial, hands clenched into tight fists, veins pulsing in his temples.

"No!" he cried. "I am not this! This isn't me!" He flailed at the trunk of the nearest tree, punching out his aggression, over and over until his knuckles were raw and bloody, his heart pounding in despair.

He moaned, staggering back and coming to his senses again, staring in horror at his lacerated and bleeding hands. "Someone, help me, please."

But no help came. Tearing off a length of his undershirt, Jack used it to staunch the worst of the bleeding. Still shaking, he set off for home, hoping to reach it unseen and unquestioned by those who would assume the worst.

Silence whispered through the Forest after he'd left.

The undergrowth moved, and from its depths stepped Nancy Peabody and the entity within, now so entwined through what she was and what she'd been, the point where it left off and Nancy began would've been impossible to find. A satisfied smile spread across the girl's face, a smile which erupted into an evil bubble of laughter.

"Oh, how perfect," the entity cried. It was Nancy Peabody's voice it used, the malevolence of its soul flavouring the usual youthful tones with ancient vengeful bile.

"How absolutely perfect! He's in love with the Cairn girl, and not just in love, but obsessed…"

"… fanatical," agreed Nancy. The being scanned her memories and feelings, showed her a dozen instances where the fact had been presented clearly to her, and she'd simply not seen, not realised.

"Of course," she continued. "It's so obvious now you've shown me. But, how is this…?"

"…useful to us? Think," whispered the voice. "He is the one I need to be completely free of this accursed Forest. But he is strong, oh so strong. Much stronger than you were, and he resists me. As long as he hopes for the love of this girl it empowers him, but, if he should discover she loves another…"

"… or could be made to believe she does…" finished Nancy Peabody slowly, "he would despair, and that dark and empty space inside him…"

"… would be filled by me. I would own him. He would do my bidding. For the first time my powers would be strong enough to break free, and then… oh yes, and then I will be avenged."

"And what of Jack?" enquired Nancy Peabody suddenly. She felt the surprise of the thing, its amusement tingling through her body.

"So," drawled the entity, "you have an urge to take that young man and make him your own. After all, I suppose he is very handsome…"

"… Yes," conceded Nancy Peabody unashamedly. "I want him, I desire him. Give him to me when you've finished with him."

"My child," murmured the thing almost fondly, "you can have any other man you want. For although this body we inhabit is that of an untouched maiden, still you can remember all the passions and lusts I enjoyed in my short lifetime. The wild thrill of taking an honest man away from his true love. The challenge of tempting him that has bound himself with a vow of fidelity until he forgets all pledges, all promises and can only think of you, of being your lover. Those dark, hot nights when pleasure is yours for the taking. Oh, my child, there is much to teach you. So many lustful, wild tastes and sensations."

"Yes," moaned Nancy Peabody, supple body stretching in the glow of arousal. "Yes, that's what I want," she sighed. "I want it all, and I want it with Jack. Give him to me, I will make him my lover and use him as I will."

"No, my child," murmured the voice. "You cannot have him."

"But, you said, you promised," cried Nancy angrily.

"You may have any man you desire, my child, except him. I have other plans for him. By the time I am finished with him, he will be of little use to you."

"But I want him," pouted Nancy Peabody. "There is no other man I want."

"Really?" enquired the voice mildly. "Do not lie to me my child, I know there is another, worthier by far than that pitiful, pathetic blacksmith's son."

"Do you mean, Lord Jolyon?" Nancy asked, shocked a fleeting imagining enjoyed for the merest of moments before being buried forever, was now being exhumed and held up for close inspection. "But that's… I mean, that's…"

"… Impossible?" enquired the voice in chilly amusement. "Nothing is impossible my child. Once Jack has submitted himself willingly to me and my power is no longer halved, I can annihilate the entire Marchmant clan with a thought if I so wish. But, if it pleases you, I may spare Lord Jolyon and he can be your plaything."

Nancy Peabody swallowed. Already aroused by the dark images of violation she'd witnessed the entity place into Jack's fertile imagination, by promises of sexual liberation, she felt her entire body throb and pulse in anticipation.

"Yes," she stated firmly. "You promise to give Lord Jolyon to me, and I will do anything, anything at all, to help you."

Chapter Eleven
~ Sunset ~

Reuben straightened his tie in the mirror, whistling softly to himself. He fussed with the unfamiliar knot, ran a finger inside his collar, pulling against the slight choking sensation being restricted in formal wear always gave him.

Finally giving up on the tie, deciding it was as good as it was ever going to be, he stepped back and surveyed himself critically in the mirror. The suit was new, a soft, pearly grey colour and was easily the most expensive thing he'd ever owned. Turning his back to the mirror, straining to see over his shoulder, Reuben was forced to concede his mother as usual had been right. It'd been worth every penny, and Reuben's good-natured smile broadened as he considered that tonight he looked almost handsome.

"Reuben," his mother's voice floated up the narrow staircase, "whatever are you doing up there? Come on down and let us have a look at you."

Grinning, Reuben ducked through the low bedroom door, clattering busily downstairs to find his parents waiting for him in the hall. His mother looking softly beautiful in a green velvet dress, which reflected off the creaminess of her skin, making the usually unnoticeable emerald glints in her eyes blaze in the dim lamplight.

"Mum," he exclaimed, taken aback how young and pretty his mother appeared. "You look beautiful."

"Oh," his mother gave a half laugh and clasped her hand to her chest, pleasure at his statement radiating her features. Daniel Forrester gazed proudly at his wife, a slow smile including Reuben in its caress as he tenderly helped his wife into her warm coat.

"Yes," he agreed, smoothing the garment over her shoulders. "She does."

"Get away with it, the pair of you," his mother bridled, but her eyes sparkled and her hand crept to enclose her husband's, before she frowned, and stepped forward to lovingly adjust Reuben's tie.

Patiently he indulged her, fidgeting from foot to foot until she was satisfied with it, noticing his father's fingers tugging at his collar, and recognising the gesture as a mirror image of his own.

"There," his mother stepped back surveying him, head on one side, eyes warm with maternal pride. "You'll do," she declared. Relieved, Reuben reached for his own warm coat from the rack.

With the setting of the sun, the warmth of the October day had vanished into a brittle chill, the landscape standing out stark and cold under the glare of the new moon, its penetrating light casting long, sharply etched shadows.

Reuben shivered as his father opened the front door. "It's turned really cold," he murmured. "Best you take extra blankets. We don't want the Autumn Queen to arrive with frostbite."

His parents glanced at each other.

"Yes," agreed his father, "Best you do take extra blankets."

"What?" asked Reuben, confused, "What do you mean?"

"We thought it would be nice," continued his mother. "Seeing as how you and Sally are best friends, if instead of your father, you went to collect her and take her to the Festival."

"Oh, but," began Reuben. "It's traditional for the forester to escort the Queen to the Festival. I'm not the forester, I'm just…"

"As good as," his father stated calmly, and his mother swiftly handed him a pile of blankets, warm from the airing cupboard.

"There you go," she said, matter-of-factly. "These will keep Sally nice and snug."

Reuben realised this was a decision already discussed and decided upon, the further thought dawning this may have been the purpose of Eliza Cairn's daybreak visit.

"What about the crown?" he asked.

Daniel carefully lifted a cardboard box from the hall table. "It's alright," he reassured. "It's here. We'll take it with us, so it'll be there when you both arrive."

Reuben hesitated, eyes on the box, remembering the long hours he and his father had spent carefully constructing the wreath with which the Autumn Queen was traditionally crowned, reflecting although it'd been his father's cleverly patient fingers which had shaped and fashioned the crown, it'd been Reuben's intimate knowledge of Sally that had guided them.

"Go on," urged his mother. "Go and get your Queen. We'll see you at the Hall."

"Right, I'll be off then," Reuben agreed, not understanding the reason for his hesitation. He turned from their smiles and went out into the cold Autumn air. The stillness of the night settled around him as he pulled on thick gloves, and crossed to where Farmer Cairn's placid old horse, Captain, was tethered. The farm cart he was harnessed to was a comforting bulk in the moonlight, the garlands and wreaths festooning it standing out sharply as spiky shadows.

As was custom, Reuben and his father as well as creating the crown, had also decorated the cart which was to carry the Queen to the Festival, draping and concealing its humble outline with great swathes of evergreen finery, the spokes of its wheels were adorned with seasonal flowers and fruits, the whole a reflection of the wonderful bounty of the time of year. A carriage of plenty, on top of which would sit the Autumn Queen.

Mounting the seat, Reuben folded the blankets onto his lap, attempting to keep them warm for the short trip onto the downs to West Farm. He shook the reins and clicked to Captain, whose ears flicked back before his great hooves paced patiently and the cart moved off along the track.

Glancing back, Reuben saw a brief silhouette of his parents as they stood in the doorway watching him go. Then the door closed, and they were swallowed up in the darkness of the night, as they set out in the opposite direction towards the Hall and the Festival which would already be in full swing.

Raking fingers which shook with barely suppressed nerves through his haphazardly arranged hair, Jack scowled at his reflection, fighting down the nausea which threatened to well, telling himself sternly it was going to be alright. He'd simply go to the Festival and wait for Sally to arrive, stand and watch her being crowned, his young heart nearly bursting with pride, then must watch whilst she had the first traditional dance with Lord Marchmant, and the next with the forester who'd escorted her to the Festival.

That was alright. Jack didn't know the Lord Marchmants, of course he didn't, they occupied a world so distant from his own they may as well reside on another planet but knew enough to be grateful Lord Gilliard was the eldest son and not Lord Jolyon.

Jack had heard rumours of the way Lord Jolyon was with the women he brought down from London, and was glad, very glad, that tradition stated the heir opened the Autumn Festival dancing with the Queen. Then she'd dance with Daniel Forrester. That was alright too. More than alright. Daniel Forrester, with his calm, grey eyes which crinkled at the corners with quiet humour and his possessive wife, was no threat to Jack, no threat at all.

So, she'd dance the first duty dances and then… and then, Jack would move in. He'd bow to her, real gentlemanly like, Jack instinctively knew tonight Sally would like that. He'd request the pleasure of a dance, then she'd be in his arms and they'd dance. She'd smile at him. Jack would know everything was alright, that she'd forgiven him for his clumsiness. They'd talk. He'd ask her again. This time she'd give him her answer, and it would be yes.

Jack placed both palms on the dusty wood of the chest, leant forward, scrutinising himself in the murky depths of the infrequently cleaned mirror, and smoothed out his expression, trying to see himself as Sally would. Tugging awkwardly at the lapel of the simple black jacket he'd bought specially, wondering if perhaps he should have a tie to fasten at the throat of the plain white shirt, he swallowed hard, trying to dislodge the lump wedged in his throat. No, a tie would only add to his misery.

Checking the laces on his freshly polished shoes were securely tied, Jack bounded downstairs, suddenly energised to be gone, and paused outside the door to the front parlour. Hearing no sound from within, he knew his father sat there in soul searing, lonely agony.

It'd been at an Autumn Festival that his father and mother had first been drawn to one another. Like Sally, his mother had been crowned the Queen, and John Blacksmith had taken one look at her flushed, radiantly happy face and had been a lost man.

Since her death, John Blacksmith had never attended another Festival, Jack had always gone alone. Tonight he hesitated, a sudden urge gripping him to go to his father, to beg him to come with him, to leave this silently mournful house and be with his neighbours, to have a drink with them. Maybe to not exactly forget the past, but at least come to terms with it.

Jack waited, his hand on the door handle, but the still quietness emanating from the room was too much to breach. Eventually, reluctantly, he turned away.

Cautious in unfamiliar heels, Miss Violet left the sanctuary of her bedroom and picked her way gingerly downstairs, where her sister waited in brow raised, purse lipped disapproval.

"What on earth are you wearing?"

Miss Violet had expected condemnation. Still, it stung. She blanched, twittered anxiously, her gaze moving down her frock, shiny with newness, nervously smoothing non-existent creases.

"It's new," she began apprehensively. "I thought... I mean..."

Miss Iris waited, eyes flinty, as she surveyed her sister. The frock, its colour hovering somewhere between silver and lilac, cut on the bias so it hugged her sister's slight contours, emphasised the womanliness of her figure in a scandalously obvious way. And as for the matching shoes with their spaghetti thin straps and impossible heels... it wouldn't do, it simply wouldn't do at all.

As for the rest!

"What have you done to your hair?" she snapped, peering at Miss Violet in the dimness of the hall lamp.

"Curled it... a little..." stammered Miss Violet, hands flying desperately to curls which had so lifted her heart when she'd peered anxiously at her reflection in the bedroom mirror.

"And are you wearing make up?" her sister demanded, the horror in her voice placing her sister's crime on a level with manslaughter.

"Not much," Miss Violet tried to defend herself, "Only some lipstick, a little something on the eyes."

"Mutton dressed as lamb," Miss Iris sniffed, cold judgemental gaze raking her sister from the top of her newly curled hair, to the peeping toes of her ridiculously impractical shoes. "Mutton. Dressed. As. Lamb!" she enunciated again.

Miss Violet blinked in silent misery, the tears her sister could always engender threatening to well.

"And now we're going to be late," continued her sister, "Thanks to you."

"L-late?" stuttered Miss Violet. "It's not so late, I mean, it's…"

"We're going to be late because I'll have to wait whilst you go upstairs and brush out your hair, wash your face, take off those ridiculous clothes and put on something more in keeping with your age and status."

"Take it off?" repeated Miss Violet. "But… but… I…" she visibly quailed as Miss Iris's brows rose into high archways of questioning disapproval, as if daring her sister to stand up to her, to refuse to be cowed, to rebel against her petty dictatorship.

For a moment, Miss Violet toyed with the idea, desperately wanting to keep her pretty gown, the womanly fusses which made her feel so young, so pretty. But… forty years lived under the heel were too much to cast off in a moment. Reluctantly, lip quivering, Miss Violet turned to obey her sister's command.

The loud rapping at the door made them both jump, and Miss Violet hesitated, hand clutching at the reassuring solidity of the wooden banister. Miss Iris frowned at the door, glanced accusingly at her sister.

"Who on earth could that be?" she demanded.

"I… I don't know…" Miss Violet shrugged helplessly. With an impatient tut, her sister swept regally down the hall and threw open the door to reveal Jack Blacksmith, eyes nervous at being confronted with the older of the Peabody sisters, gaze moving by her to where in the dim light he could make out the shadow of Miss Violet.

"Yes?" enquired Miss Iris, tone vinegar soused.

Jack recoiled, squared his shoulders, and met her gaze in a manner most impudent, thought Miss Iris fiercely. "Miss Violet?" he questioned.

"Yes, Jack?" the dark shape at the foot of the stairs queried softly. "What is it?"

"I've come to escort you to the Festival, Miss Violet," he stated, thrusting forward a small posy of violets, heads drooping slightly from the chill of the evening air.

For a heartbeat, the silence was complete. Then Miss Violet moved swiftly, face alight with joy, touched at this small gesture which so effectively cancelled out the rancour of her sister's comments.

As she stepped under the porch light, Jack's eyes widened when he took in her changed appearance. a low spontaneous whistle erupting from his lips. Miss Violet blushed prettily, head ducking with pleasure at the unfamiliar compliment.

"Miss Violet, you look beautiful," he cried. Her blush deepened, whilst the disapproval on her sister's face etched so deeply, it seemed certain to leave permanent grooves in her sallow skin.

"Why, thank you Jack." Miss Violet accepted his posy, burying her nose in its delicate prettiness, catching a lingering echo of scent.

"Are you ready to go?" he asked. For a second Miss Violet faltered, eyes sliding nervously to her sister, almost tasting the condemnation which rolled from her in sharp, acrid waves. Then something seemed to harden in Miss Violet's soul, her spine straightened, and her eyes twinkled.

"Yes," she stated firmly. "I am. Let me fetch my coat." Swiftly, she took a thick coat from the rack, startled when Jack easily took it from her and held it aloft so she could slip her arms into its warmth. All the time, her sister stood in dumbstruck disbelief. For once her ready tongue unable to find the words, she could only watch as her sister finished buttoning up her coat and stepped forward gladly taking the arm Jack offered, shooting Miss Iris a smugly superior look, before setting off along the village high street, wobbling slightly in her heels.

Jack's arm was firm, his pace carefully measured to match hers. Gradually, Miss Violet became used to them, automatically throwing her weight slightly back to compensate, unaware that this in turn thrust her slight hips and breasts forward and caused her spine to arch.

As they walked through the village, exchanging friendly greetings with other villagers also on their way to the Hall, Miss Violet was only aware she'd never been so happy, and had never felt so completely a woman.

In the darkness Amos Blunt tripped over some unseen obstacle, cursing freely and voraciously, swiping ineffectively at the mud clinging to the knees of his best trousers. The hiding place where he'd stashed his bottles of precious home-brew, so close to the Hall in daylight, now seeming an unbelievable distance.

Anxiously moving bushes aside, shining his torch carefully into their depths, he began to panic he might not find it, and at the thought of those waiting at the Hall, expectant expressions turning into barely concealed sneers if he went back empty handed, Amos Blunt cursed again. He checked himself with excitement as the torchlight shone on the corner of the old pram carcass, glinting off the thick, green glass of the bottles.

It was alright, he'd found it. Amos sighed with relief, bending to locate the old bit of rope, anxious to get back to the Festival and sneakily distribute his contraband, all under the ever-watchful eyes of his wife, of course.

A movement behind had him straightening, frowning in the darkness, shining his torch into the dark spaces between the trees. "Anybody there?" he enquired.

There was nothing but the rustling of the trees in the sigh of wind which whispered past him. He released the breath he'd been unconsciously holding, and turned back to the task at hand.

No, there it went again. This time when he spun round, torch held aloft, heart clenching painfully behind his ribs in sudden and acute fear, the movement continued. The bushes parted as someone stepped out from the trees.

"Who's that?" he cried in panic, shining the torch into the girl's face. He recognised her as she stood unblinking in the glare of the light. "Why, Nancy Peabody? What on earth are you doing skulking around in the trees? You nearly gave a body a heart attack."

Still she stood. Unmoving. The motionlessness of her body sending a frisson of fear skittering down his spine. Slowly, unconsciously, he took a step back, calves connecting violently with the box of home-brew, which rattled menacingly.

"What are you about, lass?" he demanded, trying to inject a note of almost uncle-like joviality into his voice. "Are you off to the Festival? Well, come on, I'll walk you there. That's where I'm going myself, I had to fetch some… some more beer, in case we run out, you know…"

He forced a laugh. It died into a thin gasp as still she did not speak, only stared impassively at him.

Then, finally, she moved. A step forward, which logic said should not terrify him so. Somehow, it did. As her hands reached for him he instinctively cowered away, a whimper wrenching itself from a suddenly numb throat.

"No…" he begged, eyes widening as pain lanced his soul. "What are you doing, no…"

He cried out as the entity reached deep within and drank of him. Feasting on his smallness, his pettiness, his arrogance and bluster, his selfishness. All the stains and blemishes which made up Amos Blunt. Sucking him dry. Taking all that was rotten. Feeling the heat as it absorbed and assimilated. Not stopping until he was completely drained. Then she dropped him and he fell to the ground, dry bones rattling inside the desiccated husk of flesh, eyes turned inward, mouth pulled back in a deathly grimace over yellow teeth.

"He's dead." Nancy Peabody stared with fascination at the thing that moments earlier had been the publican. "His soul, so rotted, corrupt, so small and mean. It felt good taking it into us, and yet…"

"… it is not enough," finished the entity silkily. "He was a mere appetiser. Something to soothe our palates whilst we wait for the main banquet."

"The main banquet?" whispered Nancy Peabody, eyes glittering darkly under the moonlight.

"That exquisite shaft of pure jealousy, the deliciousness of feasting on the fears and insecurities of an uncertain lover," the entity sighed in an ecstasy of anticipation. "Just wait, my child. Wait until you first taste the sublime essence of one who believes their lover to have been false. There is no thrill like it."

"But who…?" began Nancy Peabody.

"… I am unsure," whispered the entity. "The Blacksmith's son is a certainty. We cannot consume him though, I need him. His strength, his despair, it will be the key to my complete freedom. But there will be another… there always is…"

Reuben Forrester drew the horse to a standstill at the top of the path leading to West Farmhouse, swung himself easily down from the cart, bounded up to the low wooden door and rapped his knuckles on its broad surface.

There was a moment's stillness, a sense of movement inside, then the door was thrown open and Eliza Cairn was beaming at him, seemingly completely unsurprised it was Reuben and not his father who'd arrived to escort her daughter to the Autumn Festival. Reuben remembered again her visit to his home and wondered, but before he could comment, Eliza Cairn was ushering him into the house where he was met by Farmer Cairn, who did look somewhat perturbed to see him.

"There you are," Eliza Cairn remarked brightly, speedily pulling on her warm coat and nudging her husband to button his. "Well, she's all ready for you," she continued, gesturing towards the stairs. "You go on up, you know which room. We'll see you both soon." Before her husband or Reuben could comment or complain, she'd hustled Farmer Cairn out the door and closed it firmly behind them.

Under the bright glare of the harvest moon, Farmer Cairn surveyed his wife with the closest to annoyance he'd ever come in their twenty-five years of marriage. "Would you mind explaining to me precisely what is going on?" he ordered, and his wife flushed at the unfamiliar tone in his voice.

"I mean, you've practically thrust that young lad at our Sally. Sending him up, alone, to her room. I know it's only Reuben, and I don't know of a steadier or more dependable lad, but all the same, woman, I really think…"

"Would you rather it was Jack?" his wife demanded. He stopped mid-sentence, mouth gaping, brows knitting as he absorbed, considered, and understood the meaning behind her words.

"Well, Jack's a good lad…" he began uncertainly.

"Good enough for our Sally?" his wife pressed for an answer.

"No," slowly he shook his head in agreement. "Not for our Sally, not him. He's got… troubles, has that boy. I wouldn't want any daughter of mine to have the kind of life I think his wife will lead."

"Exactly," agreed his wife calmly, pulling on rabbit fur lined gloves, mouth a moue of satisfaction that her motherly instincts had been justified by her husband.

"I felt that way too," she continued. "So, I went to see Daniel Forrester this morning and had a little chat with him. No, as you said, Reuben's as steady and dependable a man as you could hope to find. He'll make a reliable husband and that's what Sally needs."

Farmer Cairn stared in silent admiration at the Machiavellian manipulations of his wife, musing how she never ceased to amaze him. With a silent and humble gesture he offered her his arm, which she accepted with a graceful dip of the head.

Eliza Cairn didn't know. How could she? That the other man contesting for ownership of her daughter's heart was not the even-tempered, trustworthy Reuben Forrester, but the flamboyant and wilful Lord Jolyon. That should Sally wish it, a glittering future as a member of the Marchmant family was within her grasp.

If Eliza Cairn had been privy to this knowledge, it's likely she'd have hurried her daughter to the Hall herself, ready to throw her into Lord Jolyon's arms if that's what it took to ensure her daughter's future as Lady Marchmant.

But she didn't know. Allowing herself a tiny smirk at her own cleverness, Eliza Cairn moved closer to her husband, shivered against the chill of the evening, and allowed herself to relax, looking forward with the eagerness of anticipation to witnessing the crowning of her beloved and precious daughter as Queen of the village, her mother's heart swelling with pride at the thought.

Reuben paused outside the door to Sally's room, swallowed, wondering why his mouth felt suddenly dry and his heart had taken it upon itself to unexpectedly pulse as though fearful, which was ridiculous. After all, it was only Sally.

He knocked gently, and at her invitation, opened the door and entered the room, ducking his head to avoid knocking his brow on the low lintel, an automatic gesture learnt over the years, though Reuben couldn't remember the last time he'd visited it. Eliza Cairn had not exactly forbidden it, but certainly seemed less inclined to send either himself, or Jack, up to Sally lately. Rather, she'd bidden her to come down, as if preserving the domain of a girl newly grown into womanhood.

Sally stood before the window watching the night, didn't turn at his entry, and Reuben had a moment to gaze in stunned surprise at her appearance. So like Sally. So not...

As his dazed mind took in the long sweep of silken gown the colour of a new guinea that reflected and warmed her rosy skin, its fluid lines elongating and emphasising her womanly shape, Reuben wondered how he could've been so blind. Right under his nose, Sally had grown up, had matured into this beautiful and self-possessed woman.

The biggest shock was her hair. Surely Reuben had seen it unbound before? He couldn't remember. At the sight of those long, corn coloured locks freed from their habitual plaits, rippling in satiny lengths over her shoulders to almost waist level, he swallowed again, struck dumb by her glory.

Into his stillness she spoke, voice low and thoughtful

"Has Daniel Forrester arrived, Mother?" Reuben started back into himself, his own voice rough and uncertain as he answered inelegantly.

"Yes, I mean, no, I mean, well, it's me, Sally."

She turned. He wondered desperately what she'd done to make her skin so creamy, her eyes so deep and blue. Then she smiled, her expression showing her pleasure at his presence, and held out a hand to him, warming him with her delight.

"Oh, Reuben," she exclaimed softly. "Have you come with a pumpkin carriage to take me to the ball?" She laughed. He laughed with her. The awkwardness of the moment was past. He was Reuben, and she was Sally. It was as it should be. Joyfully he took her hand, her skin soft beneath his work roughened fingers, and led her downstairs, out into the velvety black of the night.

Carefully, he settled her onto the seat of the cart, and fussed with blankets until she declared herself warm enough to survive a trip to the North Pole. He laughed again, light headed with relief, over what, he couldn't say. He swung himself onto the seat beside her and took up the reins. She smiled at him in the darkness, face calmly glowing under the sudden, fierce light of the new moon as it sailed majestically from behind a cloud. With a click to the patient Captain, he took her to be crowned Queen.

Miss Violet was having the time of her life. Entering the great banqueting hall on the arm of a young and strong man had left her fluttery with feminine delight, and she positively glowed with happiness as he settled her solicitously at a table, and went to fetch her a glass of punch.

Watching him push through the crowds to the makeshift bar, Miss Violet became aware of the watchful gaze of Dorcas Blunt, sitting alone at the other end of the table, a grandchild sleeping soundly in her arms. Miss Violet looked at the baby, wrapped safely in the repose of absolute innocence, and felt something shift in her heart. It occurred to her how much she longed for a child of her own, and her eyes sought out the tall figure of her surrogate son, smiling as she saw Jack exchange greetings and good-natured joshing with some village lads, who appeared to have taken up permanent residence at the bar.

Turning back, her gaze met that of the publican's wife. She flushed, intensely aware that her arrival with Jack could perhaps be misconstrued, and wondered whether to say something to try and clarify the situation. Whilst her mind was trying to formulate the words, Dorcas settled the baby gently into its pram, tucking a downy blue blanket around its tiny form, and shifted her not inconsiderable bulk to the empty chair next to Miss Violet's.

"You look different tonight," was her abrupt opening sentence. Miss Violet, flustered, groped for an appropriate reply, but once again Dorcas Blunt pre-empted her, nodding her head in slow appraisal, expression registering her approbation.

"It's an improvement," she commented, eyes twinkling almost mischievously. "Should set the cat amongst the pigeons."

Glancing hastily up, Miss Violet surprised upon the faces of many of the men surrounding them an expression of interest, and realised, much to her amazement, it was directed at her, She blushed to think that men who'd spent the last forty years not seeing her, should suddenly be aware of her existence.

"Where's Amos?" she asked, desperate to direct the attention away from herself.

The light left Dorcas Blunt's face, her expression became closed, unreadable, mouth pursing into lines of disapproval. "Oh, he's gone to get that disgusting home-brew of his which he thinks I know nothing about," she replied tersely. Miss Violet bit her lip, uncertain of the correct response to give, relieved when Dorcas sighed and shook her head.

"Bloody fool," she declared bluntly. "Thinks he can pull the wool over my eyes, but I know him too well, too well," she repeated bitterly. Miss Violet frowned at the underlying misery her sensitive ears detected beneath the other woman's words, but remained silent, watching as Dorcas Blunt's eyes roamed over the already crowded hall.

All around, friends and neighbours laughed and joked with each other, the imperceptible, but ever present, boundaries beginning to crumble as the drink flowed, the village band played, and the floor filled with eager youngsters and a few, more sedate, older villagers.

Suddenly, Dorcas Blunt's gaze stumbled, and Miss Violet's own eyes widened. Surely not? Looking at the publican's wife with newly sensitised vision, realising she was right, she wondered exactly how long Dorcas Blunt had been in love with Wally Twitchett. Years maybe, possibly even decades. Her romantic heart throbbed in thrilled, silent sympathy.

On an impulse, she placed a kindly hand on the other woman's arm. "Why don't you go and ask him to dance," she suggested softly.

Dorcas Blunt turned startled eyes, words of misunderstanding and denial quivering on her lips. Something in the calm steadiness of Miss Violet's regard made her pause. Her gaze flicked longingly to Wally Twitchett, sitting alone at an empty table, an untouched pint in front of him, head bent in morose misery.

"My husband..." she began.

"Is not here," interrupted Miss Violet. "Besides," she continued. "It's only a dance, where's the harm in that? Go on," she insisted as Dorcas Blunt still hesitated. "I'll watch the baby."

"Thank you," murmured the other woman simply, and with a grace which belied her size, she rose and crossed to his table. Miss Violet watched, easy tears pricking at her eyes, as Dorcas Blunt bent, murmured something into Wally's ear which had him turning and staring at her in incredulous shock, before scrambling eagerly to his feet, and offering Dorcas his arm.

It should have been ridiculous, Miss Violet mused, the scrawny old man with the protruding Adam's apple and craggy nose, stepping out lightly to the strains of an old-fashioned waltz with a woman more than three times his size. It wasn't. Instead it was dignified and beautiful, and Miss Violet silently wished them the joy of that illicit, stolen moment. A single dance to compensate for the long years of loneliness.

They travelled in silence. The newly arisen moon hanging so low overhead, Reuben felt he could reach and pluck it from the sky. He wondered what Sally was thinking, wondered if she was nervous about the evening ahead, if maybe he should say something to comfort and reassure. He cleared his throat, considered his words;

cleared his throat again. Sally's head turned to regard him, face still and impassive in the moonlight.

"Nearly there," he said, wincing at the fatuousness of the comment.

"Yes," she replied, voice low and featureless.

Curiously, Reuben glanced at her, noting the downward sweep of her lashes, her small teeth worrying at her bottom lip, her hands clenching and unclenching in her lap, with an intimacy created from years of acquaintance he realised her mind was troubled, instinctively drew the horse to a halt, and turned to face her.

"Sally?" he asked, voice calm and kindly. "What's the matter?"

She didn't speak. To his dismay her face crumpled, and she shook her head. "Oh, Reuben," she whispered sadly. "I'm in a dreadful mess, I don't know what to do. I just... don't know what to do."

Reuben dropped the reins and gently took one of her hands in his. Sally looked at him, seeing his dearly beloved, good natured face creasing with concern in the shadows, knew, even though she couldn't see them, his grey eyes would be crinkling at the corners, the way they always did when he was troubled or perplexed.

"Tell me," he said simply.

Jack finally made his way back to the table, bearing a glass of spiced punch for Miss Violet and a pint of Amos' best for himself. Forcing his way through the ever-thickening crowd and sitting beside her, he gulped gratefully at his pint as Miss Violet sipped nervously at the punch. Her sister had never allowed her anything stronger than ginger ale before, and her nose wrinkled at the strength of the potion. Resolutely, she took a second, larger sip, and decided that upon closer acquaintance it was really rather pleasant.

"Sorry I took so long," Jack apologised, "but they're short staffed behind the bar. Amos has disappeared somewhere, no one's seen him for ages, and they're struggling to keep up." Miss Violet nodded her acceptance of his explanation, eyes automatically sliding to where Dorcas Blunt and Wally Twitchett had moved easily into another dance, faces still with the cautious enjoyment of those who knew their pleasure to be unwise and ephemeral.

"Sally will be arriving soon," Jack remarked casually. With her newly discovered awareness, Miss Violet heard something behind his words, glancing at him sharply.

"Daniel Forrester went to collect her," Jack continued, his words a study in nonchalance. "So, they should be here soon."

"But I've seen Daniel Forrester," Miss Violet commented softly, eyes narrowing with concern. "Look, he and his wife are sitting at that table over there, with Alfred and Norah Twitchett."

Jack started, droplets of his ale spilling onto the wooden table as his head jerked around to follow the direction of her words. Miss Violet watched with bemused unease as his face reddened, then paled. Frantically, his head snapped to-and-fro, scanning the crowd, searching fruitlessly for someone.

"Jack," she exclaimed, laying a soothing hand upon his black clad forearm. "Whatever is the matter, my dear? What's wrong?" He stared at her as if she were a stranger, and she recoiled from the despair in his eyes.

"Where is she?" he asked helplessly.

It was as if a light exploded in Miss Violet's brain. In an instant she understood. His eyes slid by her, relief flickering briefly in their depths to be almost immediately damped down again with confused disbelief, and he reached out, clutching at the couple now passing their table.

"Aunt Eliza," he begged. Looking up, Miss Violet saw Farmer Cairn and his wife pause, turn as one entity to study Jack, saw by the way their guilty glances met, and parted, that a decision concerning Jack had been resolved between them. Her heart moved silently within her breast, as her hand unconsciously slid down his arm to lightly rest over his clenched fist.

"Jack," exclaimed Eliza Cairn over-brightly, "are you having fun?" The patronage in her tone grated on Miss Violet's ear, but Jack appeared not to notice, gaze leapfrogging over their shoulders to search the empty doorway behind them.

"Where's Sally?" he asked, making no attempt to conceal the need in his voice. The Cairns exchanged another look, moving closer to present a united front, and again, Jack appeared unaware of the solidarity of their body language.

"Don't you fuss, she'll be along any moment," Eliza Cairn reassured, turning to her husband with an artificial smile. "We really should get ourselves a seat, you know how crowded it gets."

Darting an almost sympathetic look in Jack's direction, Farmer Cairn allowed himself to be propelled across the floor to where the

Forresters' awaited them, Miss Violet observing in silent sympathy as Jack slowly sank into his chair, the hurt bewilderment on his face almost childish in its naivete.

"I don't understand," he murmured. "Where is she? If Daniel Forrester's not bringing her, who is?"

The sting of chill night air beginning to penetrate, even through the layers of blankets, Sally talked and told Reuben everything, of Jack's surprise proposal, his desperate plea she give him her answer tonight, the shock of Lord Jolyon's implied promise, her confusion over the whole situation.

Her voice raw with honesty, Sally held nothing back, except the passion she'd felt in each man's arms, this she kept to herself. A strange shyness rendered her reluctant to disclose, even to Reuben, the full extent of her body's capitulation to Jack's desire, the almost overwhelming submissiveness she'd experienced when Lord Jolyon had kissed her.

"I don't know what to do, Reuben," she cried finally, voice throbbing with despair. "Which one should I choose, Jack or Lord Jolyon? I know they'll both be there tonight. Both expecting an answer. I simply don't know what to do. Please help me, Reuben. Which one do you think I should choose?"

He sat, head bowed in thought, hand clasped warm and steady over her own, then sighed a deep and gusty exhalation, as if the answer was simplicity itself and she a fool for not realising it.

"Oh, Sally," he murmured, almost reproachfully, the strength of their friendship warming the tone. "As far as I know, there's no law stating a woman must be married before she's even twenty-two." In the glittering brilliance of the moonlight his eyes were ripe with friendly amusement.

"So," he continued prosaically, "who says you have to choose either of them?"

Chapter Twelve
~ Evening ~

A stir, a murmur of interest, a parting of the crowds nearest the door, the instruments of the village band were silenced, and all around people craned their necks, straining to catch the first glimpse of their Autumn Queen.

Beside Miss Violet, Jack tensed, trembling like a whippet sighting the hare. Through the press of eager villagers, Miss Violet caught sight of Eliza Cairn and her husband scrambling excitedly to their feet, an expression of fierce pride emblazoned all over the usually placid features of Sally's mother. Even Farmer Cairn allowed the sentiment of the moment to show in a lopsided, self-conscious grin.

The band broke into a traditional melody, composed so long ago its origins were lost in the amnesia of centuries. It was always played when the Autumn Queen first appeared before her loyal subjects.

As its gay lilting refrain tumbled amongst them, Miss Violet rose involuntarily to her feet caught up in the excitement of the moment. She knew it was only young Sally Cairn but felt a rush of nervous anticipation, as if a real monarch had descended for one evening to mix with the commoners.

There was a gasp, a sigh, and they saw her being escorted regally into the hall on the arm of a furiously blushing Reuben, good-natured face stretched so far in a delighted grin, Miss Violet smiled back, sharing in his overawed joy at the honour afforded him.

And then there was Sally.

At the sight of their young, radiantly glowing Autumn Queen, the hall fell silent, paying hushed reverence to her glorious beauty as she passed by, silken gown rustling. Its colour was reminiscent of the autumnal blaze of chrysanthemums, or the glow of crisp, crackling leaves, swirling from their parental trees to heap in flaming drifts.

She was so beautiful. As she passed by their table without so much as a sideways glance, Miss Violet looked at Jack and found him gazing after Sally with a world of expression in his dark, normally hooded eyes.

Her heart ached for his love, fervently praying Sally could return it, could love Jack with all the intensity and passion he so craved. If she couldn't...

Here, Miss Violet's thoughts broke off in a confused scatter, unwilling to pursue the awful consequences of Jack being denied Sally's heart.

Reuben led Sally carefully to the decorated platform at the far end of the hall where Lady Marchmant and both the young lords waited, together with Alfred Twitchett, puffed up with self-importance as head of the village council.

At the foot of the steps he paused, bowed solemnly to Lady Marchmant, the Lords Gilliard and Jolyon and to Alfred Twitchett, who inclined his head and stepped forward, holding out a hand to Sally. She curtsied gracefully to Reuben, thanking him for his role in acting as her escort, made her way slowly up the steps to take Alfred Twitchett's proffered hand.

He turned her slowly to face them. The band fell silent. Miss Violet held her breath, fancying all over the great hall decorated so beautifully for the occasion, that every other villager was doing the same. She was intensely aware of Jack, his stillness, eyes fixed unwaveringly on the glowing figure of Sally.

Only a few yards away in real terms, she seemed so distant as to be completely out of reach to mere mortals. Unobtainable. As untouchable as a fantasy woodland queen from myth and legend.

Daniel Forrester held out the box to Reuben, who removed the lid and reached inside for the wreath. He held it up first for the approval of the masses, before handing it to Alfred Twitchett who was puffed up even more with importance if that was possible.

Slowly and reverently, he took the intricately woven circlet, gently placing it upon Sally's gleaming head.

"My Lords, ladies and gentlemen," he began.

Out of the corner of her eye, Miss Violet saw the lips of Norah Twitchett moving silently, almost imperceptibly, as if prompting her husband. She swallowed down a sudden urge to giggle.

"My Lords, ladies and gentlemen," he said again. "My friends and neighbours, I hereby present to you our beloved Autumn Queen. A living symbol of the bounteous wonder of the land we live in which supports and nurtures, even throughout the bleakest and most unforgiving of winters. To the spirits of the Forest, and the elements of the honest, fertile farmland, we give thanks."

Across the other side of the hall, Reverend Arnold frowned at Alfred Twitchett's use of the word spirits, thus implying more than one deity, his delusion after so many years still being the Autumn Festival was one of thankfulness to his God, the crowning of the Queen a mere quaint, rustic custom.

"We give thanks for another harvest safely gathered in," Alfred Twitchett continued sincerely, if a little woodenly. "And we give thanks that we are all gathered here, safe and in good company. Secure in our fond companionship, able to face come what may in the future, knowing our friends and neighbours will always be there to guide and protect us."

Miss Violet spotted Dorcas Blunt and Wally Twitchett exchange the briefest of telling glances. It triggered the memory of the inexplicable disappearance of Amos Blunt, and a vague flicker of concern dashed across her thoughts. It was unlike him to miss such an important occasion, and she wondered if he'd been taken ill. Alfred Twitchett held up his hands to quell the tumultuous applause, and all thoughts of the absent publican fled her mind as he began the ancient Festival ritual.

Miss Violet felt her lips move automatically, voice rising in unison with the villagers as they chanted words handed down through the centuries.

Steeped in folklore, legend spoke of a forester's daughter of long ago, Mad Meg, who'd been lost within the Forest for three days. When she'd finally emerged, senses addled, not one word would she say, except that a being made of leaves had taught her the rhyme and she would sing it, over and over.

It'd been handed down through generations until now it was part of village tradition, and Miss Violet felt a jolt of connection with her neighbours as the old words bound them inexplicably together.

The Forest Queen is chosen, all hail and praise the Queen.
May her power be unchallenged, the Forest ever green.
We join together gladly, our hearts and minds as one,
We stand beneath the moonlight, and warm, life-giving sun.
Wykenwode, Wykenwode.
Defender of the innocent: Protector of the good.
Wykenwode, Wykenwode.
Defender of the innocent: Protector of the good.

In the face of mortal danger, of evilness and sin,
We stand against the darkness and know that we will win.
Against the crimes of passion, of jealously and greed,
United we must face them, for our inner strength be freed.
Wykenwode, Wykenwode.
Defender of the innocent: Protector of the good.
Wykenwode, Wykenwode.
Defender of the innocent: Protector of the good.

Link hands with your neighbour, join forces with your friend,
Face the foe united, the oldest crimes to mend.
Let the circle come together, the light of faith shine out,
Our voices sound as one, oh hear our battle shout.
Wykenwode! Wykenwode!
Defender of the innocent! Protector of the good!
Wykenwode! Wykenwode!
Defender of the innocent! Protector of the good!
Wykenwode! Wykenwode!
Defender of the innocent! Protector of the good!

Their voices rose, the last lines traditionally being delivered in an almost warrior like bellow, fit to chase away whatever demons lurked about the village. A spontaneous outburst of clapping, cheering and foot stamping greeted the end of chant. Then Sally stepped forward to make her acceptance speech.

"My dear subjects," Sally's voice was sweet and clear, no trace of the nerves she must be feeling evident on her glowing face, "I thank you for the great honour you have shown by bestowing on me the title of Autumn Queen. I promise to rule fairly and wisely, being sensible of the needs and privileges of my fellow villagers. I Promise to display all due allegiance and service to our most benevolent of hosts, the Marchmants." She inclined her head gracefully towards Lady Marchmant, who dipped her own regally in return.

"My wish is for all to show their gratitude of the marvellous bounty which has once again been accorded us by the Forest and the lands around it. A magnificent feast has been prepared for all to enjoy, and it is my command that no one retire from this glorious occasion until every morsel has been consumed, thus showing a proper appreciation and acknowledgement of our supreme good fortune."

Sally curtsied very prettily to them all, took two graceful steps back and settled herself on her flower bedecked throne. The villagers cheered themselves hoarse, the band burst forth into a joyous melody, and the press of bodies on the dance floor moved steadily and carefully back until a space roughly square had been created.

Miss Violet let out her breath in a painful gush, quite what she'd been expecting to go wrong she didn't know, but it was definite relief she felt as she turned to sit. A gasp of surprise rippled through the crowd. Quickly she looked up, not seeing what had caused such consternation, yet following Jack's wide-eyed stare of incredulous disapproval, she saw Sally being bowed to by Lord Marchmant, as customary.

But, instead of the staid and sober heir Lord Gilliard, it was his wild and feckless younger brother, Lord Jolyon who'd placed himself before Sally, bowing to her courteously, hand held out to escort her onto the dance floor.

Disapproval spread through the crowd like wildfire. Miss Violet could scarcely bring herself to look at Jack, as Lord Jolyon, face smugly triumphant, led a plainly bemused Sally onto the dance floor, glaring impatiently at the band until they re-gathered their startled wits, and began to play a piece of music traditionally played for the Autumn Queen and Lord Marchmant to formally open the Autumn Festival.

Glancing at the platform, Miss Violet saw Alfred Twitchett's head bobbing uncertainly, at a loss at what to do after such a breach of protocol and procedure. Lady Marchmant and Lord Gilliard exchanged looks of concern, Lord Gilliard's face darkly tight with suppressed fury. And as she watched, he whispered something into Lady Marchmant's ear which had her eyes widening, her look skittering towards Sally and her younger son with something approaching fear.

Curiously, Miss Violet watched as Lord Jolyon and Sally reached the floor, where he bowed courteously, and Sally responded with a decorous and measured curtsey. The music played, the couple danced, and Miss Violet suddenly became aware of what a beautiful pair they made, Sally's slight, petite figure almost trembling in the firm and masterful grip of Lord Jolyon. He bent his head towards her face, teeth flashing white and even in his square jawed, rakishly handsome face, and murmured something intended for Sally's ears only.

Miss Violet's heart wrenched at Jack's involuntary breath of horror as Sally's eyes met those of the Lord and she blushed, in the way a woman only does when she is being made love to by a man whose attentions are not entirely unwelcome.

Beside her, Jack sank into his chair, and Miss Violet silently placed a sympathetic palm on his trembling, suddenly cold hand, waiting with patient resignation as he fought to bring himself under control, glaring at the couple through anguished eyes.

"It means nothing," he muttered. "It means nothing. It's one of Lord Jolyon's whims. He means nothing to Sally. She's never spoken of him. She hardly knows him. It means nothing." His gaze once more bore into the happily dancing couple, the brooding hostility it contained enough to render Lord Jolyon dead on the spot, should such power be present in a look.

Helpless to comfort him, Miss Violet saw the expression on Eliza Cairn's face, the stunned dawning of understanding, the calculating look which slid across the homely features of Sally's mother, and her heart sank further for Jack.

Outside, in the cold darkness of the Forest's outer reaches, Nancy Peabody and the entity listened to the happy strains of music drifting to them across the starched crispness of the frosty night. Did Nancy Peabody feel a pang deep down inside for what might have been? Did some element of her not completely tainted with the stain of evilness, sigh wistfully that she should have been inside the hall with her family and neighbours, enjoying the simple and uncomplicated pleasure of a rustic gathering?

If she did, it was quickly dispelled. "Come," hissed the entity, "We must get closer, I feel it coming, it's so close now, so very close…"

Obediently, Nancy Peabody set off towards the bright lights, gay music and happy buzz of voices, which beckoned and beguiled.

Jack was in the middle of a nightmare. There could be no other explanation for the sequence of horrendously unexpected and freakishly awful events, visited almost non-stop upon his unprepared and unbelieving soul.

First had been the shock of it being Lord Jolyon who led Sally out to dance, and not the safe and sombre Lord Gilliard. Jack's cheeks burned with the memory of seeing Sally's face, flushed and excited, gazing up in dewy-eyed supplication at the young hellraiser of a Lord. And Jack didn't know what Lord Jolyon had murmured to put such stars in her eyes, but could guess, his black fury churning and broiling with impotent rage.

Then, Sally had danced with Reuben. That at least was to be predicted, he'd been the forester who'd escorted her, still, Jack's teeth ground painfully together at the merry, uncomplicated pleasure they seemed to find in that dance. Then, Sally had danced with Alfred Twitchett, as befitted a man in his position. Then Lord Gilliard had claimed her hand. Sally had then danced with her father, and had insisted on dancing with Daniel Forrester.

All the while, Jack fretted and fumed with impatient need, until finally he'd cornered her, giving her no option but to allow him to lead her onto the floor, thankfully filled with others all merrily enjoying themselves as the ale flowed and the music soared.

At first, they danced in total silence. Having longed for this moment all day, Jack found himself strangely tongue-tied. He cast his eyes around desperately, seeking inspiration from the other revellers. Briefly, his eyes lingered on the surprising sight of Dorcas Blunt dancing in the arms of the ancient shepherd Wally Twitchett, wondering if Amos Blunt had returned from his mysterious travels, then his eyes bent to Sally's cautious expression and any other thoughts flew from his mind.

"You look beautiful," he murmured, and Sally smiled gravely.

"Thank you," she replied primly. For a moment her eyes twinkled at him in the old way, and his heart stumbled in its tracks, knocking violently against his ribs.

"You look awfully handsome too," she teased. "I like your new jacket."

"Sally," he began in an agonised rush, "have you, I mean, have you thought any more about what I asked? You promised me an answer before midnight, and I wondered… well, I have to know Sally, please, it's killing me!"

Sally sighed. Gently, tenderly, her hand lifted to softly caress his hollow cheek, her eyes warm with emotion. Jack swallowed, feeling the whole of his future pivot on that moment, on the answer he could see trembling on her lips. And suddenly he was afraid …

Happily sipping her fifth glass of punch, feeling its warming, liberating effects, Miss Violet glimpsed Jack and Sally talking earnestly together on the dance floor over the shoulder of Bernard Dodd, who was trying to impress her with tales of his exploits. She saw Sally's hand creep to caress Jack's face as she murmured something to him in a voice so low he had to bend to hear.

Miss Violet strained to see his expression, hoping for a happy ending to Jack's lifelong loneliness, catching her lip between her teeth as he moved back from Sally and studied her, his look neither sad nor joyous, merely perplexed. He then reached for her hand and spoke urgently to her, almost shaking in his intensity. Miss Violet saw Sally nod reluctantly, as if agreeing to something she was unsure of, then the music ended, the couple parted, swept away into the crowd of happily inebriated villagers, and Miss Violet saw them no more.

Nancy Peabody had reached the relative security of the Hall's outbuildings, when the sound of someone approaching had her slipping silently into the deep shadow of a wall. Watching cautiously, her eyes widened as she recognised the slight figure which crept past in the moonlight, making its way carefully to the great barn.

Obeying the silent command of the entity Nancy Peabody silently followed, easing through shadows in pursuit of the figure which never wavered in its path, nor cast a single glance over its shoulder.

Reaching the barn door, the figure paused, pulled at the handle and created a gap big enough to slip through.

Nancy Peabody stopped, unsure.

"Well, well," murmured the entity within. "This is interesting."

"What do you want me to do?" asked Nancy Peabody anxiously.

The entity gave a rasping chuckle.

"Wait," it commanded. "Wait, watch and listen. I have a feeling this may turn out to be very useful, very useful indeed."

Sally pushed the heavy door of the barn closed behind her, peering into the gloom of the stable, grateful for its warmth after her brief exposure to the chill night air outside. Was he there?

He'd told her to meet him here, said he would leave first so as not to arouse suspicion. She'd watched him go, never betraying by a flicker as she'd danced with another, that her choice had been made. That here, now, tonight, Sally Cairn intended to follow her decision to its inevitable conclusion.

There was movement in the shadows, Sally's breath caught on a little gasp of fear. He stepped into the shaft of moonlight. It was alright, he was here.

"No one saw you leave?" she asked anxiously, relaxing as he shook his head, eyes never leaving hers in the silvery moonlight, the emotion written plainly across his face.

"I love you!" her cry was spontaneous, involuntarily.

"I love you," he replied, the hoarseness of his voice leaving no doubt as to the veracity of his statement. Tears slipping hotly down her cheeks, she stepped towards him as he stepped towards her, hands and mouths meeting in a glorious union of perfect harmony, and Sally felt the rightness of the connection, her soul sighing in supreme benediction.

She laid her head trembling upon his chest, fearful when she thought of how close she'd come to choosing differently, eyes brimming with the intensity of the moment.

"I love you," she murmured again. "Oh, how I love you!"

Deep within the Forest, Lucian crouched by the warming firelight holding out fingers numb with cold, his brow knit into a worried frown. All day they'd patrolled the peculiarly empty groves and glades of the Forest, the complete lack of animal or bird life worrying him immensely. He'd heard the comments of the others, knew them to be afraid.

He sighed, tried to relax. Perhaps nothing was going to happen. Perhaps this time the creature would be unable to find more victims, as had occasionally occurred over the centuries. His gut would not accept this, and unease skittered nervously along his spine.

"Look," breathed one of the others. Lucian looked up sharply, hand automatically moving to his sword hilt, to relax in an exhalation of relief which hung before him in the night sky.

"My Lady," he rose to his feet and bowed, followed by the others as they scrambled to their feet. A rough and rag-tailed army, he reflected grimly, but all that stood between the creature and her foul appetites.

The White Hind poised delicately at the edge of the clearing, her large dark eyes liquid with emotion. Lucian felt a judder pass through him at the sorrow emanating from her still serenity as she stepped lightly away, pausing to look back at them, her intent clear. Lucian gestured to the others to quickly gather their belongings. Swiftly, without comment, they followed her gleaming hide glimmering silver in the moonlight, leaving the clearing empty behind them.

Slowly, carefully, Sally climbed the hayloft ladder behind his dark shape, gratefully accepting his hand to guide her over the top. Standing amongst the piles of soft, sweet smelling hay, her heart thumped with dizzy excitement as he quietly pulled the ladder up behind them, turning to face her in the moonlight.

Reverently, gently, he lifted the wreath from her hair and placed it safely to one side, and ran his trembling fingers through her gleaming locks. Sally saw him swallow hard, emotions threatening to choke him at the thought of the love they'd been so blindly unaware of, the opportunity so nearly missed.

She shivered at the vagaries of fate and stepped closer, longing for his touch, the reassurance of his arms, thankful in that same instant he'd assured her she didn't have to marry either Jack or Lord Jolyon. The conviction had come upon both that neither could bear it if they were to marry any but each other.

Sally had become intensely aware of his hand on hers, her startled gaze had flown to his, seeing its reflection in his eyes, and they'd stared with disbelief and growing elation.

"So," Reuben had commented mildly. "That's that, then."

"Yes," she'd agreed quietly, with a wildly mounting joy. "It is."

They'd journeyed the rest of the way to the Hall in silence, and every time Sally had turned wondering eyes towards him, it was to find his also bent on her, his face quietly joyous, expression incredulous at their newly found happiness.

During their one dance, Reuben had murmured the suggestion of this rendezvous into her willing ears. In an agony of impatience, Sally had resignedly waited through all the duty dances she must first undertake to prevent her absence being remarked upon.

Trying to avoid dancing with Jack, Sally finally realised it was a trial she must face, else he'd never stop looking for her. That out of the many crowded into the banqueting hall, he was the one who'd notice the coincidental disappearance of both herself and Reuben.

So, Sally allowed him to capture her, following him unresistingly onto the massed dance floor, feeling her heart throb with her guilty secret, as she looked into his desperately hopeful eyes, realising that one sentence from her would have the power to dash his dreams forever.

She dreaded being the cause of so much pain, but knew that eventually Jack would have to be told. He would have to know whom she'd chosen, that what he'd always instinctively feared and fought against in the face of all her adamant denials, or in spite of them, had come to pass. Their triangle had resolved itself into a twosome, with Jack left stranded and cold on the outside.

But, not now. Now, Sally craved aloneness with Reuben, needing solitude and peace to work through this brilliantly complex, utterly simple truth. She loved him, he loved her. That was the all and the end of it. A fact so blindingly obvious, she wondered why they'd never realised it before. But perhaps it was all the sweeter for the sudden unexpectedness of discovery, and her young heart yearned to be close to her newly found lover.

He stood, silently watching. Sally raised her chin proudly, aware that he was letting the final decision be hers, and realising it was this which'd stopped her from committing to either Jack or Lord Jolyon. Neither had been prepared to allow Sally any degree of control over her own actions. Jack attempting to force her with his own overwhelming passion, Lord Jolyon trying to seduce her with his sophistication, dazzling her with his status and power. Now Sally finally understood what she'd craved and demanded from her lover had been equality, and autonomy.

She raised hands steady and sure to the lacings of her gown, untying them decisively, eyes never leaving his face, until at last she stood before him, naked and proud in the moonlight. A soft sigh escaped Reuben's lips upon being faced with her flaxen, neat beauty, her long soft hair rippling over her shoulders, a flush mounting her cheeks as his gaze consumed and absorbed her.

"My Lady Godiva," he murmured with loving amusement, gathering her up in his arms, feeling her mould to his body, supple and pliant. "Oh, my Sally, my love," he groaned.

Gently, she helped him to undress, and together they sank onto the scattering of warm blankets he'd collected from the cart and lain on the hay in anticipation of her arrival. Softly he pulled a cover across them to protect them from the nip of the October evening.

It was a good first loving for both, filled with aching tenderness and a love sweetened with an inexperienced awkwardness. When finally they joined, Reuben swallowed her cry of shocked pain with a kiss so gentle and passionate, Sally clung to him, her skin rasping against his, each pore absorbing and remembering every second, every touch, every sensation.

Afterwards, they lay closely clasped in each other's arms, Sally's head resting sweetly on his chest, hearing the thud of a heart that beat exclusively for her, his arms warm and strong about her, knowing nothing, not man nor beast, could ever separate them.

Dimly, they heard sounds of the Festival, knowing this paradise was temporary, that soon they must re-clothe themselves in respectability, re-join their families and friends, and face up to the scrutiny of eyes used to picking meat from the scantiest of bones.

Sally shivered at the thought of their shiny new love being held up for inspection, her eyes heavy and moist with love for him, but his gaze was serious, and a tiny flicker of fear touched her heart.

"What is it?" she murmured. "What's the matter?"

"There is… something," he confessed, for some reason remembering Lucian and his words of advice. At Sally's sudden stillness, his arms tightened instinctively around her, then he told her of Sylvie, holding nothing back, Sally at last learning of the strange fey child he'd met in the Forest, of the reserved and lovely woman she'd grown into.

A sharp wrench of jealousy, raw and unfamiliar, pierced her soul and quietly, hesitantly, she asked...

"Do you love her?"

"No, no," he hastened to reassure, voice rich with sincerity. "I love you, oh Sally, only you." She heard, believed and relaxed once more into his arms. "But I did wonder," he confessed slowly, "whether Sylvie could possibly be the lady in the tale. I must admit, it sent a shiver down my spine when Lucian told of her being heavily pregnant and lost in the Forest. I couldn't help fearing he was telling me what was going to happen to Sylvie..." he paused, then continued, voice puzzled.

"I mean, what did happen to her? Oh, it's confusing. Logically I know if the tale is about Sylvie, it happened centuries ago and she's long dead. She's some kind of, I don't know, ghost I suppose. But when I'm with her, she's seems so real. She's a friend. I care about her, would hate for anything bad to happen to her, and what happened to the lady in the tale is about as bad as it can get, isn't it?"

"Hmm," agreed Sally quietly, keen mind worrying at the problem. At the same time, Reuben's smooth skin was an enticing distraction beneath her fingertips, the novelty of lying in her lover's arms sleekly happy from the act of love making, so delightfully new and fascinating she was finding it hard to pay attention. She raised herself above him, long hair forming a silken curtain, tenderly and slowly pressing kisses, butterfly light and arousing, over every inch of him she could reach.

Reuben struggled desperately to cling to his thread of conversation. "Do you think there's anything we can do to change what happened?" he murmured, groaning as Sally's lips worried deliciously at his shoulder; small sharp teeth nipping and nibbling at a body so newly introduced to the ecstasy of physical pleasures.

"Don't know," she sighed, crying out in delighted joy as he rolled her abruptly onto her back, his weight covering her, the sharp leap of arousal as his hands explored and his mouth followed.

"Find my little lambkin," Reuben muttered, as Sally's senses were about to be completely overwhelmed in a sticky tide of sensual pleasure. He blinked with surprise when she stilled and pushed him aside, raising herself on one elbow to glare at him in sharp attention.

"What?" she snapped. "What did you say?"

"Erm, nothing," stuttered Reuben in disappointed surprise.

"Yes, you did," demanded Sally. "You said, find my little lambkin, or something like that. Where did you get that from? Who said it to you?"

"Lucian," replied Reuben, and frowned. "It was in the tale he told me, it's what the old wise woman said when she told the forester to go with the lord into the Forest and find the missing lady. Why do you ask? Is it important?"

"I don't know," mused Sally slowly. "I've heard it before…" she paused, bit her lip. "I have something to tell you too," she said, then confessed about her visits to the village witch, Molly Mole.

Reuben stared, amazed she'd kept such a secret all these years. "Lambkin is what Molly called the mysterious woman who walks the Forest," Sally concluded, and they exchanged a long look.

"It could be a coincidence," he murmured.

"It could," Sally shrugged impatiently, "But I'm betting it's not."

Reuben considered, grey eyes taking on an intensity which had her heart suddenly pounding, her limbs melting like butter on a hot June day as his hands roamed suggestively over her body. She reached for him and he was ready, once again coming together in a mindless joining of body and soul in which all consideration was lost in an endless sea of pleasure and satisfaction.

Forgetting themselves, their voices rose in gasping, wondering cries of climatic rapturous delight, unaware of a figure, dark and silent, which slipped unnoticed into the barn, and stood beneath the hayloft listening, head tipped to one side.

"This is your weapon," hissed the being insistently to Nancy Peabody. "Use it!"

Jack was in despair. It wanted but a few minutes to midnight and still Sally had not given him her answer. In ever growing panic, he searched for her through the inebriated, deafening roar of the celebrating villagers, mind returning to their dance when he'd asked her again, remembering the way she'd looked at him, cautious pity in her eyes, the promise she'd made that before midnight she would finally give him her decision.

He trusted Sally; of course he did. Why couldn't he find her? Upon reaching the bar again with still no sign of her, his heart thumped in nervous anticipation, sweat breaking out on his forehead as the room swayed sickeningly.

Agonisingly aware that unless he got out of the stifling atmosphere of the hall there was a very real possibility he was going to faint, Jack brutally shoved and pushed his way through the crowd, ignoring the shouts of annoyance he left in his wake. Staggering into the courtyard, gulping at the frigid air, feeling it clutch his lungs in its icy grip, he doubled over, clenching his eyes firmly shut, grasping his knees with clammy, shaking hands.

Footsteps sounded softly on the cobbles. Suddenly hopeful, Jack squinted into the shadows, making out the slightness of a body. Even though he knew it wasn't her, he couldn't help the despairing cry which fell from his lips.

"Sally?" The figure hesitated, stepping forward into the harsh silvery light cast by the bright, low hanging moon. "Nancy?"

"Yes, Jack," her voice was low. It sounded like Nancy, yet in some odd, indefinable way, it didn't. Jack frowned. Was there something not right about her eyes?

"Have you seen Sally anywhere?" he demanded. Nancy Peabody started. It seemed to Jack her glance flicked guiltily over her shoulder, and his suspicions, never far beneath the surface, leapt into prominence.

"Well?" He straightened, growling accusingly. "Have you seen her or not?"

"Seen her, no," murmured Nancy Peabody quietly. To Jack's sensitive ears a world of meaning lay behind her words. "But, I've heard her…"

"What? Where?" he snapped. When she seemed to hesitate again, he reached for her shoulders and shook her in his despair. "Tell me!" he ordered.

Nancy bit her lip, casting her eyes down in an apparent agony of indecision. "Trust me, Jack," she said finally. "It's best you don't know. Return to the hall, I'm sure they'll be back in soon…" she stopped on a breathy gasp, as if realising she'd said too much.

Jack pounced upon her words, heart hammering with premonition that his worse fears were about to be realised. "They? Who's she with, Nancy? You must tell me. Where is she?"

"In the stable," Nancy stuttered, falling back with a little cry as Jack released her, and strode on shaking legs towards the large barn. Behind him, Nancy Peabody smiled an awful, triumphant smile, following him gleefully as he reached the large double doors and quietly slipped inside.

Inside, all was dark and peaceful. Jack paused, blinking in the gloom, listening intently. Hearing nothing, he was about to turn on Nancy Peabody in anger at another of her schemes to torment him, when it came. A low, soft sigh, then a voice. Her voice. Jack turned to stone, hands clenched into fists by his sides, as his whole life came to an abrupt and violent end.

"I wonder what time it is," Sally mused. "I really should be getting back." There was a rustle of hay, and Jack sensed movement above him, instinctively casting his eyes upwards, he listened.

"Don't go," came the softly murmured reply, and the coldness of betrayal bit as Jack recognised the voice. Still, he listened.

"I have to," Sally's voice was heavy with regret and she sighed again. Below, Jack heard the unmistakeable sound of lovers kissing and caressing, the old wooden boards of the hayloft creaking as they moved into each other's arms.

"I love you," Reuben murmured. Jack's heart froze into a solid slab of horrified regret as he awaited her reply, knowing what it would be, unable to believe in the end she hadn't chosen him.

"I love you too."

Everything that was good and honest in Jack shattered in that instant, and a grim helplessness drenched him at the softly whispered sighs of the lovers, knowing as Sally's gasp of delight was answered by Reuben's groan of pleasure, that it was too late. Her heart and her body had been given to another, and any sweet hopes that Jack may have had were trampled into dust.

He turned and walked away, back out into the courtyard to where Nancy Peabody waited, her expression of malicious expectation replaced in an instant with one of loving concern.

"Jack?" she whispered. "Are you alright? Oh Jack, I'm so sorry… you're too good for her, much too good, she's a…"

The derogatory words were choked in her throat as Jack grabbed her and dragged her up off her feet.

~205~

"Don't you say anything about her to me!" he threatened. "You don't know her, Nancy Peabody, so don't you dare say anything against her!"

"Alright," she snapped, and fought free of his grip, casting him a look of bitter resentment as she straightened her coat. "I thought it was a bit unfair what they said about you, that's all…"

"What?" Jack stared at her, skin creeping in anticipation of further treachery. Desperately, his head begged him to walk away, and not listen, to refuse to allow himself to be manipulated by a woman long despised and mistrusted. He couldn't. He had to know. Hating himself, he heard his own voice, strangled and low.

"What… what did they say about me?"

"Reuben asked Sally what she was going to do about you. She said you'd be easy to manage, her puppy dog she called you, and then… they laughed. They laughed at you Jack, I heard them. They were still laughing about it when he… when they… Jack!" she cried in an agonised whisper, as he pushed past her and strode away into the dark.

"Jack, wait!" She caught him by the arm, hauling him around to face her. Seeing the awful, grim expression, the fathomless depths of pain in his eyes, the entity inside exalted and chortled with glee.

"Where are you going?" she begged, injecting a note of touching concern into her voice.

"Home," he snapped, pushing her roughly to one side. This time she let him go, watching with satisfaction until his shadowed form vanished into the night.

"What now?" Nancy Peabody whispered, and the entity sighed with pleasure.

"He'll be back," she vowed confidently. "It's almost midnight, he'll be back."

"What do you want me to do?"

"Wait…" hissed the entity. "Just wait…"

Halfway home, Jack came to his senses, staring in bewilderment at the alien, sinister landscape glittering sharply with silver edged frost, startled at the harsh cry of a screech owl as it flew from a nearby tree, intent on murdering some unsuspecting creature.

Sally had laughed at him. Her and Reuben together, wrapped in each other's arms, him buried deep inside her body. She'd called him her puppy dog, dismissed him from her mind, merely an annoyance to be made into a joke for her lover's amusement.

Falling to his knees in despair, Jack fumbled in his pocket, angrily yanking out his great grandmother's ring placed there so confidently in a previous life. When hope still lived and his young heart throbbed with ardent love for his Sally.

All hope was gone now. Shattered. Broken by the careless laughter of lovers and their words as reported by another. Jack's head snapped back. A howl of disbelieving agony was wrenched from his soul to rasp through the still night air.

Waiting patiently outside the hall, Nancy Peabody heard it, and smiled with ecstatic satisfaction.

Within the Forest, as close to the barrier as it dared go, the other half of the entity squirmed and writhed in an agony of anticipation. Soon, it promised itself, soon the event it'd waited and planned for over too many centuries to remember would occur.

Anger spilled into Jack's blood raging through the icy numbness of despair, a forest fire blazing out of control. His hand closed over the ring, felt it bite into his palm, drew back his fist and hurled it with all his might in the direction of the small stream which tumbled alongside the road.

At the splash he knew it to be lost forever, along with his hopes. In that instant, the ancient clock on the church tower begin to strike midnight, and fury gripped him, souring his stomach so the rich malt of Amos' beer churned in his guts. Leaning forward, Jack retched out his disappointment, his pain.

In its place surged a white-hot anger. An all-consuming, passionate thirst for vengeance.

Hatred for Reuben leapt into his soul and his brain. Deep within, he threw open the prison bars of the thing he'd fought to keep contained for so long, felt its power, its twisted thirst for revenge, and welcomed it. The bloodlust consumed and assimilated, until there was nothing left of Jack except that which the creature within allowed him to keep.

Jealousy. Pain. Anger. Hatred. Vengeance.

And the clock struck the twelfth hour.

Chapter Thirteen
~ Midnight ~

Somewhere, a door slammed. John Blacksmith jolted awake in his chair, the dream in which his wife once again pleaded with him, her face twisted into a mask of despair, scuttling away into the furthest corners of his mind.

Annoyed, he pulled himself upright, saw by the mantelpiece clock it was gone midnight, and listened, waiting to hear Jack's footsteps on the stair, wondering why he was back from the Festival so soon. Normally Jack stayed until the very end, going to either the Cairn's or the Forrester's for breakfast.

There was no sound. Curiously, he rose and crossed to the door, stepping out into the small hall, craning his neck to stare up the stairs at his son's shut fast bedroom door. For a moment, John Blacksmith toyed with the idea of going up and speaking to him, to perhaps try to break through the barrier he'd erected long ago.

At a loss to understand his dark and brooding son, seeing so much of Rosie and himself contained within the lad, John Blacksmith had not been wholly unaware of Jack's misery the last year. But, at the thought of facing those condemning eyes, seeing his dead wife peer accusingly at him from their depths, John Blacksmith faltered, and instead shut himself back in the front parlour, poking savagely at the dying embers of the fire, cursing himself for being such a coward as to be unable to comfort his son.

They had loved again. Sally rolled away from Reuben, cheeks flushed, eyes shining, hearing their ragged gasps echoing in the stillness of the stable, and wondered if she'd ever felt happier. A thought of Jack sliced through her contentment, and guilt tugged at her heart.

"I need to get back," she declared firmly this time. She sat up, brushing at hay caught in her tangled hair, looking around to locate her discarded gown.

"Must you?" murmured Reuben, stroking a finger lovingly down her spine, making her shiver. She cast a look of such intense passion at him, he sat up, and caught her mouth to his in a kiss of promise.

"I have to go," Sally whispered into the kiss. "I promised Jack I'd speak to him before midnight to give him my answer. He'll be waiting, and looking for me. I'm dreading telling him. He's going to be devastated."

"I know," Reuben pulled away, expression sobering as they surveyed each other in the moonlight. "I hate it, that he's going to be hurt. I wish there was any other way, I feel so guilty, he's my best friend, but… but… Oh Sally, if the only other way is not to have you, then it's a way I can't even consider."

Another kiss, and Sally almost succumbed. But, the thought of Jack refused to go away. Reluctantly, she stumbled to her feet, legs quaking beneath her, and a pleasant soreness bore witness to her loss of innocence.

Quickly, she pulled on her underclothes, aware from a rustling beside her that Reuben was also dressing. When she slipped her gown over her head, he helped her re-lace it, large hands clumsy at the unfamiliar task. Her skin moved at his touch, heart soaring at the thought of long years of dressing and undressing with this man, of the many joys and wonders that lay ahead for them.

Borrowing his pocket comb, Sally struggled with hair now snarled into a veritable nest of knots and tangles, breath catching in little huffs of pain and frustration at the impossibility of the task.

Solemnly, Reuben retrieved her wreath placing it reverently upon her head, and when his large hands rested briefly on her shoulders she felt his warmth and drew strength from it.

"Tomorrow," he promised her. "Tomorrow I will come and speak to your father."

She nodded, unable to speak, and in that instant heard the clock strike the half hour, wondering if it could possibly be gone midnight already.

"Yes," she agreed hastily. "Come tomorrow, early evening, give him time to sleep off tonight. But now," she continued, "we must get back. It's late."

"You go first," commanded Reuben. "I'll wait ten minutes, then I'll follow."

He replaced the ladder. They descended carefully until they stood amongst the silent horses, hearing the creatures' soft breathing as they moved towards the door. Reuben pulled it far enough open so she could slip through, neither seeing the dark silent shape outside, slipping soundlessly back into the shadows.

"I love you," he said, "Until tomorrow."

"Tomorrow," she whispered. "I love you too, I always will, I promise." One last kiss, piercingly sweet despite its brevity, then she was gone. He watched her walk away in the moonlight, turn the corner and vanish back into the hall. For a second he heard the roar of voices from inside, then all was silent, and he settled down to wait.

Miss Violet had been searching for Jack. Absently at first, idly wondering where he'd disappeared to, then with increasing concern as she'd realised not only Jack, but Reuben and Sally too were missing. All three of them, vanished without trace.

Three of them? Three of them! Miss Violet's heart stopped for an agonising eternal moment, and she wondered frantically if she should tell someone, say something. But who and what? Sighing with relief she saw Sally, flushed and slightly rumpled, slip unnoticed into the hall, catching up a discarded cup of punch from a nearby table. She mingled seamlessly with the crowd, and if Miss Violet had not seen her enter, would've believed her to have always been there.

Quietly, Miss Violet watched as Sally sat at a table, eyes constantly straying back to the door, wondering why Sally seemed so altered, so changed, her face glowing with radiant happiness, young supple body arching with limber contentment into the hard-backed chair, eyes downcast musing over private thoughts.

Waiting until an appropriate time had elapsed and he could make his way back to the ongoing festivities, Reuben occupied himself with shaking hay from the blankets and rugs, placing them back into the cart, ready for the homeward journey.

Murmuring to Captain, he fondly patted the old horse on the neck, who sleepily flicked his ears back and rumbled an acknowledgement, before returning to snatching wisps of hay from the net hanging on the wall.

Deciding enough time had passed, Reuben silently creaked the door open and slipped outside, pausing for a moment to glance at the midnight sky, grinning his happiness at the diamond scattered blackness, and breathing deeply of the frigid air, its icy tentacles slicing painfully into his lungs.

Sally was his, completely and absolutely, Reuben wanted to shout his elation at the shining face of the moon. Tonight, the knowledge was theirs and theirs alone. Tomorrow, he'd walk up the hill to West Farm, pay his respects to Farmer Cairn and officially ask for his blessing and permission to marry his daughter, as was customary. Then the whole world would know, and he and Sally could make plans to wed. At the thought, Reuben's smile broadened.

Coldness. The solid press of metal on his spine. Confused and alarmed, Reuben spun round. Dark, impenetrable eyes, Jack's eyes as Reuben had never seen them before. Black, malevolent, implacable. Reuben started back in surprise, gazing in incomprehension at the shaft of the shotgun glinting in the moonlight, levelled firmly and steadily at his heart.

"Jack…" he began.

"Be quiet," ordered Jack.

Reuben felt a grip of fear at the sound of his voice. It was Jack's voice, but it wasn't. There was something, some indefinable timbre to it, that had every hair on the back of Reuben's neck rising instantly and silently, a macabre manifestation of the warning shouted by every one of his straining senses.

"You took her," Jack said, words rendered sinister by the deadness of the tone they were delivered in. "You knew I loved her. You knew she should have been mine. It was the way it was meant to be. Yet you took her from me."

"Jack, I'm sorry," began Reuben helplessly, guilt lacing his words with a passionate intensity. "We couldn't help it. We fell in love."

"You took her from me," Jack continued, as if Reuben had not spoken. "You took her, so now you must pay." Reuben stared in horror at the gun as the full meaning of Jack's words sunk in, instinctively moving back.

"Stay where you are!" ordered Jack. Desperately, Reuben searched the face of his best friend, looking for a flicker of the old Jack, of his boyhood companion. There was none. A stranger faced him, a stranger intent on ending his life, and Reuben shuddered with fear.

"No, Jack," he said, voice firm, not betraying the terror churning beneath the surface. "No, Jack," he said again. "You don't want to do this. I understand you're upset and angry, but if you do anything... stupid... here tonight, you'll regret it for the rest of your life."

"No, I won't," retorted Jack flatly. "Because with you out of the way, Sally will turn to me for comfort. It will be as it should be. As it would have been, if you hadn't come between us."

"If you kill me," Reuben cried desperately, "do you think Sally will ever forgive you? They'll come for you Jack, they'll take you and lock you up for a very long time. When you finally get out, you'll be an old man and Sally still won't want anything to do with you."

"Ah, but that's where you're wrong," replied Jack. For the first time emotion crept into his voice, and Reuben winced away from the spiteful cunning which laced the words. "You see," continued Jack, prodding Reuben in the chest with the gun, "no one's going to know it was me. Let's go," he prodded again, this time a sharp painful thrust which had Reuben falling back, trying desperately to see if the safety was still on, realising with a sinking heart it wasn't, and that Jack's finger hovered a hairsbreadth away from the trigger.

"I'm not going anywhere with you," he declared bravely, bracing his feet into the ground, staring directly into the bottomless pits which were Jack's eyes. "If you want to shoot me, then you're going to have to do it here and now, and everyone will know. You won't get away with it."

"Move," said Jack, a vein throbbing in his temple, lines of strain around his mouth.

"No." stated Reuben determinedly. "I won't make it easy for you."

Jack paused, smiled an awful, emotionless smile which did not reach his eyes. "Have it your way," he shrugged, raising the gun.

Reuben braced himself, waiting for the impact, knowing at such close range it could not fail to kill him. An image of Sally flashed through his mind as she'd looked, flushed and rosy from their lovemaking, and regret seared his soul.

There was a sense of movement behind him, Reuben half turned to the slight figure which had arrived soundlessly at his back. Pain exploded in his head, and the world went dark as he fell to the ground and knew no more.

Nancy Peabody stared dispassionately at the prone figure at her feet, idly fingering the half brick now splattered with blood with which she'd rendered Reuben unconscious, and looked at Jack, her eyes clouding with anger.

"You fool," she commented icily. "You were ordered to bring him to the Forest, not shoot him here. We may still have need of him."

"He wouldn't come," Jack lowered the shotgun disappointedly. "What else was I supposed to do?"

"Well, he'll come now, won't he," declared Nancy Peabody flatly. "Bring him," she commanded. "And for heaven's sake, put the safety on that thing before you shoot yourself."

She tossed the brick to one side and crossed noiselessly to the door of the hall, creaking it ajar and peering in for a long moment. She turned to stare icily at Jack, who hurried to obey, leaning the gun against the wall as he hefted Reuben effortlessly over his shoulder, some part of him marvelling at the superior strength he now possessed.

"Come," stated Nancy Peabody, taking the gun herself and leading them into the darkness.

So much time had gone by, and still he didn't come. Sally throbbed with an impatience to see him, for their eyes to meet across the throng, for the intensity of their love to be transmitted in that one brief look.

She tapped her fingers anxiously on the wooden table top, sipping absently at her punch, barely registering its spicy warming taste. Still he did not come. Lost in thought, Sally didn't notice the seat next to her being pulled out, a figure easing itself into place.

"Is everything alright, Sally?"

"What?" Sally turned distracted eyes up to Miss Violet, and frowned as she noticed the erstwhile dowdy shopkeeper's altered appearance. "Yes, I'm fine… everything's fine… but, you… Miss Violet, I've never seen you look like this before. You look… beautiful."

"Thank you, Sally," Miss Violet flushed at the latest of many compliments she'd received that evening, but awareness of the concern in the younger woman's eyes nagged, and gently she repeated her question.

"Is everything alright, Sally? Only, I couldn't help noticing how distracted you seem. I've been looking for Jack, he seems to have vanished. When I realised you and Reuben were missing too, well, I couldn't help but worry…"

"Jack?" Sally turned alert eyes onto Miss Violet. "Jack's missing? How long? How long has he been gone?"

"Why I'm… I'm not sure," murmured Miss Violet, taken aback at Sally's vehemence. "It's hard to tell in this crush. I certainly haven't seen him for at least an hour."

"Oh," Sally mumbled, once more her gaze bent onto the table, a deep frown ploughed a furrow between her eyes. Miss Violet felt a frisson of fear, inexplicable and unfounded creep down her spine, and laid a hand upon Sally's arm.

"Sally…" she began, and paused, realising the girl was no longer listening, but was staring intently at the door. Following the direction of her look, Miss Violet saw the small, pinched face of her niece briefly peer in, her expression one of unconcealed contempt as her eyes swept dismissively over the rowdiness of the villagers.

Sally flinched as Nancy Peabody's glance rested on them, and Miss Violet quaked at the implacable coldness of the stare, before her niece's lips twitched briefly upwards in a superior smirk, and she was gone. Shaken, Miss Violet turned to Sally, her own confused and troubled thoughts reflected on the young woman's face.

"Miss Violet," began Sally abruptly, as if a decision had been reached. "Can you keep a secret?"

"Of course," murmured Miss Violet automatically, taken aback at the question.

"Jack asked me to marry him," Sally began.

"I guessed he intended to," Miss Violet nodded. "I know how much he loves you, Sally. May I ask… what was your reply?"

"I... I haven't given it to him," Sally said, a look of guilty anguish flickered across her features. "But... it's going to be no."

"I see," replied Miss Violet crisply. "Poor Jack. He will, of course, be devastated. But you must be true to your heart, Sally, if you don't love him..."

"There's more..." interrupted Sally desperately. "Tonight, here, well, in the stables, Reuben and I, we... we discovered how much we love each other, and we... well, we..."

Miss Violet understood Sally's frantic blushes, and her heart bruised for poor, rejected Jack.

"Oh, my dear," she murmured. "I don't know what to say."

"But don't you see?" cried Sally. "You say Jack's been missing for an hour? What about if he went to the stables? What about if he saw or heard... us? What then? There's three of us, Miss Violet. There's always three in the tales. The White Hind has been seen. It always brings death in its wake, and jealousy is always the cause. Oh Miss Violet, I'm so afraid... what if...? And just now, you saw her, you saw Nancy. Her eyes. The look she gave me, it scared me so."

She pushed her chair violently away from the table, rose to her feet, shaking with the force of her terrified convictions. "I'm going to look for them," she declared.

Concerned, Miss Violet stood, placing a comforting hand on Sally's trembling shoulder. "I'll come with you."

Sally turned grateful eyes up to her. "Thank you," she said. Quietly, without fuss, the two women slipped out of the hall and into the chill autumn night.

Outside, all was still and quiet. Miss Violet shivered at the abrupt change of temperature whilst Sally, seemingly oblivious to the cold, picked up her skirts and ran to the stable, pushing open the door and rushing inside.

"Reuben?" she called hopefully. "Reuben are you still here?"

Silence greeted her words, apart from the stamping of the horses and the earthy sounds of them breathing. Sally walked to the cart, peering at the blankets and rugs now neatly folded onto the seat.

"Where is he?" she cried, turning on Miss Violet in an agony of fear. "Oh, where is he?"

"I don't know," Miss Violet shook her head. "Maybe he went home?"

"He wouldn't," Sally insisted. "Not without telling me. He wouldn't go home and leave me alone. No, something's happened to him, something bad." Her voice broke on a sob, and she pushed frantically past Miss Violet, rushing once more into the courtyard, her foot kicking at something loose on the cobbles.

"Look!" she cried. Miss Violet hurried to her side, their eyes meeting in shared and instant concern at the half brick in Sally's hand, blood now staining her palm.

"He's been hurt." Sally's voice rang with utter conviction. Mutely, Miss Violet nodded, her face pulling into tight lines of dread. "I'm going to look for him," Sally declared.

Desperately, Miss Violet clutched at her arm. "We can't," she cried. "Not dressed like this, not unprepared. Think Sally! We need sensible shoes, warm clothing, and we need torches." She tightened her grip on Sally's arm until she saw the sense of her words penetrate, and reluctantly Sally nodded.

"But we must hurry," she demanded. "If Jack's found out about us and taken Reuben somewhere, he's already hurt him. Anything could happen. He could even…" she stopped and swallowed, eyes huge with panic. "Oh, Miss Violet, if anything should happen to him…"

"We'll find him," declared Miss Violet firmly. "We'll find them both!"

Strangely, it occurred to neither woman to seek help from those within the hall, as if instinctively knowing that whatever aid the reluctant villagers may offer, it would be ineffective against the forces they faced. Clutching Sally's hand, cold and clammy, in her own, Miss Violet led the way back to the village. The ten minutes it took to reach the shop seemed an eternity, and Sally shivered in anticipation as Miss Violet hastily unlocked the front door, and ushered her into its welcoming warmth.

"Straight up the stairs," she ordered. "I'm sure I can find some clothes to fit you. We're about the same size." At her words, Sally glanced wonderingly at the radically altered Miss Violet, marvelling she could've been so blind to the creaminess of her skin and slenderness of her form, her eyes flashing blue sparks as she pushed her long wavy hair over her shoulders. Hurriedly she pulled out thick skirts and sweaters, woollen stockings, and stout, waterproof shoes for them to change into.

Back downstairs, Miss Violet dragged thickly lined jackets from the peg, shamelessly tossing her sister's to Sally, who belted it hurriedly around her, and followed Miss Violet into the shop where she yanked two large torches from a shelf, ruthlessly ripping open packets of batteries and thrusting them into the torches. Their powerful beams lit up the interior of the cramped and overloaded shop as she switched them on. Handing one to Sally, she stuffed handfuls of fresh batteries into their jacket pockets.

"Now," cried Sally, with barely concealed impatience as Miss Violet locked the door behind them, "we've wasted so much time. We must find them!"

"No, wait," said Miss Violet, her gaze travelling the deserted, dark street where one lone light glimmered forlornly at the very end. "There's one thing we must try first. Jack may have gone home. We need to check there."

"There's no time," insisted Sally hotly. "We must go, come on."

"No Sally, wait," cried Miss Violet.

But Sally had gone, her anxiety reaching fever pitch she rushed away down the street. Miss Violet hesitated, watching the light from the torch bobbing as Sally ran, and almost followed her, but something pulled her back, back towards the light. With one last agonised glance after the fleeing girl, she turned and hurried in the opposite direction.

Although he'd attempted to force himself back into his dream, sleep eluded him, and John Blacksmith muttered curses under his breath, calling himself a fool, stomping morosely over to the sideboard, and angrily yanking a bottle of brandy from the tray, sloshing it heedlessly into a glass.

Raising it to his lips, he stopped and frowned, as a small, almost timid knock came at the front door. Straining to listen in the aching stillness of the house, half convinced he'd imagined it, but no, there it came again. Moodily, John slammed out of the room and crossed the hall with one bound, flinging open the front door so abruptly, the slight figure on the step jumped back in obvious fright.

"Oh!" she gulped. In the light spilling onto the street, John Blacksmith saw it was the interfering old biddy from the shop, Miss Violet, or whatever her name was, but tonight she did not seem so very old. For once, he found himself noticing the appearance of somebody else, briefly wondering what on earth she'd done to herself.

"Yes?" he barked, feeling satisfied when she visibly blanched. "What is it?"

"Jack's missing," she murmured. "We... that is, I wondered if he'd come home?"

"Not that it's any of your business," he snarled, "but he's home and in bed."

"Oh," she cried again. "That's a relief... you're sure he's home?"

"Well of course I'm sure," John growled, wondering if he were in the grip of a bizarre and surreal nightmare in which his neighbours were behaving as if possessed. "I heard him come in, didn't I? Well, that is, I heard the door slam."

"So, you didn't actually see him?" Violet persisted, a strange dread making her press her point home, even in the face of such downright hostility and rudeness.

"I told you, didn't I woman?" barked John, his impatience rising like a tidal wave. "Now, go about your business and leave me to attend to mine." He went to slam the door in her face, but a foot, determined despite its smallness, wedged itself firmly in the way, and a hand slapped onto the wood, shoving it violently back. John stepped away from the flaming passion in her eyes, from a voice that thundered in a previously never-before-used tone.

"JOHN BLACKSMITH! WHERE IS YOUR SON?"

John gulped and quailed, for once silenced by the force of another. As he stared at her slight form, her chest heaving with barely suppressed gasps of frustrated rage, he felt a chill creep into his soul. Her manner, the air of apprehension she wore like a mantle, impressed upon him a sense of panicked urgency.

"What's wrong?" he asked slowly, his voice for once lacking its usual curtness. "What's happened?"

"There's no time," she cried frantically, and his unease grew. "Please, please, go and see if Jack's in his room."

Thrusting his glass into her hands, John turned wordlessly on his heel and hurried upstairs, returning seconds later, face now as drawn and grim as her own.

"He's not there," he stated flatly. Violet groaned with despair, unthinkingly tossed back the contents of the glass, coughing as its rawness caught at her throat. "Now, would you mind please telling me what on earth this is about?" John demanded.

Violet ran a trembling hand over her face, unsure where to begin.

"Jack's in love with Sally Cairn and was going to propose to her tonight. Only Sally's in love with Reuben Forrester. We think Jack may have found out, because they're both missing. When we went outside to look for them, we found a brick, with blood on it, and we're afraid… I mean, what with the White Hind being seen and all, we're afraid Jack's hurt Reuben. And now Sally's gone off on her own to look for them, and that makes me even more afraid. Because, well, because you know the stories… it's always three and they always end up dead, and, oh, I'm so… so afraid, so scared for them…"

Her words disintegrated into a sob. As John stared in dismay, helpless in the face of female tears, his own concerns threatening to overwhelm him, a sudden thought struck. Quickly, he turned to the door of the cupboard under the stairs and yanked it open.

"He's taken my gun," he declared flatly. His eyes met those of Violet's, saw the dawning realisation of horror in her gaze, and grimly reached for his coat.

"Let's go," he said.

Chapter Fourteen
~ In the Dead of the Night ~

At the edge of the Forest, Sally checked her headlong flight, gasping for air, lungs aching from the cold, apprehension gripping as she realised Miss Violet was nowhere to be seen. She was completely alone. Alone in the darkness of her nightmares.

Cautiously, fearfully, she shone her torch through the trees, heart hammering as shadows leapt, innocent branches and shrubs becoming monsters and ghouls, waving their clawed arms as if to clutch her to their breast. Sally jumped, sternly reprimanding herself for being such a child, to be so scared of shadows and imagined horrors.

Silently she stood, ears straining to hear, and it came to her how hushed the Forest was. Nothing stirred, not a leaf nor a creature. No owl screamed, no fox barked, this total absence of life seeming to assume monumental importance.

Shivering with fear and cold, Sally tentatively stepped into the Forest, unsure whether to call out Reuben's name or not. Fearing that by betraying her presence, she may startle Jack into doing something rash, maybe hurting Reuben again, maybe even…

At the unwanted notion, Sally swallowed hard, thoughts in a whirlwind of despair and confusion. Two men were lost to her. Two men she loved with all her heart, albeit in very different ways. At the idea one might die at the hands of the other, all because of her, Sally fought to hold back a sob.

Resolutely, she straightened her spine, and tightened her grip on the torch. She wouldn't break down, would find them if she had to search all night, wouldn't think any more on what might happen, for that way lay madness. Sally knew she needed all her wits about her tonight. If tradition was to be broken, the creature that walked in the obscurity of the Forest defeated, she couldn't afford to despair.

Stumbling over exposed roots, her progress hampered by the darkness within the trees, Sally fumbled her way further into the Forest, the torch's powerful beam illuminating bushes and undergrowth.

Briefly, she blessed the practicality of Miss Violet, realising if she'd rushed headlong into the Forest clad only in her flimsy Autumn Queen gown, she'd have quickly been forced back through exposure and lack of light. Sally wondered where Miss Violet was, wishing she was there, longing for the older woman's calm steadiness.

On and on Sally travelled, searching the Forest as far in as the barrier before sweeping back outwards again, believing instinctively, it was to the Forest Jack would have brought Reuben, praying he hadn't forced Reuben to take him through into realms of the Forest where she could not follow.

Working steadily eastwards, Sally came to the part of the Forest closest to the Hall. She paused, gaze moving to take in Marchmant Hall ablaze with the lights of celebration, wondering whether she should return to the Festival and seek help.

Yes, perhaps many would block their ears, not wanting to hear, choosing to close their minds to what was occurring, maybe even thankful it was finally happening whilst their own children were safely in their sight.

But Sally knew Daniel Forrester would help, and realised he was the one they should've turned to first. After all, Reuben was his son, and Daniel had access to the Forest. If that was where they were, he could follow them.

Resolved, Sally turned her feet towards the Hall and started forwards, only to stumble and fall over something concealed in the shadows of a nearby shrub.

Shaken and winded, she rolled onto her side, groped frantically in the darkness for the torch which had gone out as she'd dropped it, and with shaking hands switched it on, directing its beam towards the shrub, curious to see what had sent her flying in such an abrupt manner.

Yellow, desiccated, parched flesh. A mouth that grimaced, stretched over brutally protruding teeth. Limbs twisted and cracked, still attempting to ward off the foul atrocity which had been visited upon it.

Sally cried out in horror, scrabbled frenziedly backwards, recognising it as Amos Blunt. Terror clawed at her throat, stopping her heart. She inhaled painfully, clutching a hand to her chest, struggling to breathe.

"Don't worry," said a calmly amused voice. "He can't hurt you. He's dead, quite quite dead."

Shocked beyond words, Sally shone her torch wildly upwards, its beam illuminating a familiar face. Swallowing a jolt of almost hysterical laughter at the incongruity of seeing Nancy Peabody, not a hair out of place, sitting neatly on a tree stump, legs folded demurely at the ankles, and watching Sally's consternation with obvious enjoyment.

"Nancy?" Sally cried. "Nancy Peabody? Where are they?"

"Where are who?" enquired Nancy politely.

"Reuben and Jack," Sally snapped, "Where are they?"

"Oh, back there somewhere," indicating the Forest behind her with a casual wave of her hand. "But you don't need to worry about them anymore."

"What?" Sally stammered, the surrealism of the situation rendering her capacity for logical thought practically non-existent. "What... what do you mean by that?"

"Because I'm going to kill you now," announced Nancy Peabody, as calmly as if informing Sally of a proposed walk before tea.

Sally froze, brain screaming at her body to run. Move. Do something. Anything. Her legs were incapable of obeying, and she could only watch, numb with terror, as Nancy Peabody rose gracefully to her feet and stepped towards her.

"I promise it won't hurt," she murmured, paused, and considered, her head on one side. "Well," she amended thoughtfully, "it might hurt. It depends on how much badness there is inside you. Now, Amos Blunt there, well, it hurt him dreadfully. But then, you see, he really was a nasty little man, so petty and spiteful. I truly feel I did the world a service getting rid of him.

"You... you killed him?" Sally gasped.

Nancy Peabody nodded, dark eyes glittering in the moonlight, Sally realised with a shock of horror that there was no white to be seen anywhere in the other girl's eyes. Just endless, fathomless black.

"What are you, Nancy? What have you become?" Sally cried out in deeply buried recognition.

"Vengeance!" hissed Nancy Peabody in a voice no longer hers. "For so many centuries I have waited for this moment, struggling to be free, trapped within that accursed Forest. Every generation I reached out with my mind to see if they had been returned to me, that which were taken. Always I have been disappointed, having to content myself with feeding off the jealousy and envy of the poor, stupid fools from the village. But now, finally, the bloodlines have come true and they are re-born, both of them, at the right time. I found them, they are mine."

"I don't understand!" Sally cried, as something nagged and tugged at her memory. A thought, a remembrance, elusive and fleeting, it refused to be captured.

"And you!" the thing inside Nancy Peabody snapped, turning her fury back to Sally. "You, it was always you. You were the favourite. You got everything, everything that was mine by right. Well, not this time. This time I shall kill you and destroy all that you hold dear."

Before Sally's terrified eyes she grew, her face changing. Horribly, suddenly, Sally saw the evilness uncloaked, screamed with terror, knowing her last moment on earth was now. The darkness flowed from Nancy Peabody's mouth, spewing towards her in a foul, dense miasma of malevolence and Sally fell back, choking on its stench.

A blur of silver, a flash of white, something bounded from the trees knocking Nancy Peabody to the ground. The entity reared up as a twang rang into the night, and an arrow sang through the air and buried itself in her back.

The spell broke. Sally jumped to her feet, seeing the intelligent liquid eyes of the White Hind as it turned and raced back into the sanctuary of the Forest. Saw, deep within the trees, a man with long hair flowing over the bunched muscles of his arms, as he lowered the bow which had unleashed the arrow.

"Run!" he bellowed.

Sally turned and ran, hearing the furious howls of the creature behind her, desperately heading for the lights of the Hall and help.

They'd been searching the outer perimeters of the Forest for an eternity, Miss Violet's despair rising as they penetrated deeper and deeper into its glades and clearings, always being brought up short by the barrier.

Ablaze with incandescent fury, John Blacksmith pounded his fists on its impenetrable surface, pressing his body against it until his face blanched, his eyes bulged, and Miss Violet pulled him away, fearful he might vomit or pass out.

Still they kept on. Every time Miss Violet stumbled, John Blacksmith's hand was there, steady and firm. As her feet tripped, so did her heart, old, long forgotten passions stirring and clamouring within her soul.

The scream, compelling, faint and far away, rent the stillness of the night. Shocked, they clutched at one another, faces pale and drawn in the torchlight.

"Over there," John Blacksmith gestured with the torch. Not waiting for her assent, he took her hand and pulled her through the undergrowth, new purpose lengthened his stride.

Miss Violet stumbled in his wake. Pride forbidding her to ask him to slow down, she gritted her teeth and kept up, ignoring a stitch in her side, the adrenalin pumping through her body endowing it with fresh energy.

Sally ran faster than she'd ever run in her life, and still the thing pursued her. She'd switched off the torch to make herself less of a target, knowing the entity would realise precisely where she was heading. Despair ripped Sally's soul at the triumphant cackle of laughter close, oh so close, behind, realising Nancy Peabody was almost upon her.

The moon sailed behind clouds, plunging all into darkness. Hopelessly, Sally changed direction, veering northward, racing silently down the steep incline back towards the Forest.

Praying the creature would believe her intent was still to reach the Hall, Sally flung herself into the trees and came to rest, leaning against a stout oak tree, fighting to quieten her breathing, every fibre of her body straining to hear, senses quivering in the silent-as-a-grave Forest.

The moon re-emerged from its covering. Cautiously Sally peered around the edge of the tree, eyes wide as they scanned the now floodlit open ground beyond. Seeing no sign of it, yet hardly daring to hope she'd lost it.

All was still, all was silent. Thankfully, Sally pushed herself away from the comforting roughness of the trunk, wondering what to do. Fearing the creature was now between her and the Hall, she decided to head back to the village, hopeful of finding Miss Violet, sure the entity would be unable to venture so far from the confines of the Forest.

"Boo!"

Once again Sally's scream divided the night, as Nancy Peabody was there, right there! Eyes sparkling with malicious amusement as Sally sobbed with fear, falling to the ground. Blackness swirled and oozed around the other girl, as she smiled a calm smile of cruel madness.

"Why did you run?" she asked. "It was really such a pointless thing to do. You can't escape me, no matter how hard you try, so you may as well resign yourself." She paused, head on one side, mouth pouting into a mocking facsimile of sympathy. "But don't fret so. At least you and your lover had some time together."

"Reuben?" stuttered Sally. "Where is he? What have you done to him?"

"Nothing... yet," purred Nancy Peabody. "I haven't decided if he could be useful to me or not. I think, on reflection, probably not. You certainly make a pretty pair though, just as before. Simply too good to be true, positively brimming over with the milk of human kindness," her face twisted into a sneer.

"You won't make very enjoyable eating at all, not like Jack, oh..." she sighed with pleasure. "If I were only able to consume him, how simply delicious he would be. So much pain, so much insecurity, jealousy and envy, and all caused by you. Really, my dear, you should've accepted him, then none of this would've happened."

"I love Jack very much," declared Sally stoutly. "But not in that way..."

"Oh, come now," interrupted the entity dryly. "It's just us girls, you can admit it to me. You've thought about it, you must have... after all, he's young, virile and oh so handsome," Nancy Peabody's eyes flickered briefly closed and her hands roamed over her body.

"I'm sure he'd be an outstanding lover. All that passion and brooding violence would have to go somewhere. You've imagined, don't deny it. The thought of his hands on your body, the look on his face as he possessed you, that intensity of emotions, so very nearly brutal. After all, that's what women really want, isn't it? Not namby pamby milksops like the forester's boy …"

"No," interrupted Sally sharply, feeling, with a pang of outraged betrayal, her body react to the entity's words, memories tumbling through her mind of the times Jack had kissed her. "No," she cried again. "I love Reuben, we're meant to be, we fit together…"

"You disappoint me, Sally," sighed the entity, turning its awful blank gaze onto her. "You really do. I thought maybe you, out of them all, would be the one to break the mould, dare to change history. But here you go again, loving the nice, safe, comfortable one. Oh Sally, Sally, I expected more from you."

"What do you mean?" stuttered Sally in confusion. "I don't understand."

"Of course, you don't," snapped the entity waspishly. "After all, your man has never given you any reason to doubt him, has he? I don't suppose your precious Reuben would even contemplate seeing another woman behind your back," it broke off, eyes rounding with shocked knowledge.

"So, there is someone else," it mused. Unbidden, the thought of Sylvie had tickled through Sally's mind, a flicker of uncertainty, tiny and insignificant, lifted its head. For the first time in her life, Sally had the vaguest notion of what it was to doubt another, to wonder about their actions, to feel jealousy.

"Yes…" breathed the entity. "Oh, yes, that's it. Embrace that spark of disquiet. Feed it with suspicion. Fan the flames with mistrust. Blow onto its glowing embers with the breath of jealousy. Oh, feel it! Feel it grow and burn, deep within your soul. Feel your gut churn and broil with dark imaginings of him with her… feel it, feel it!"

"No, please…" begged Sally, closing her eyes, pressing her hands to her head in agonised denial. The images refused to go. Frantic thoughts tumbled and twisted, dark and bitter. Had Reuben told her the truth? Was it merely concerned friendship he felt for Sylvie? Or was there more?

After all, he'd freely admitted they'd often met in the Forest. That she'd grown into a beautiful woman. How beautiful? Maybe so beautiful no man could resist her. Maybe she'd not been his first lover, as he'd claimed. Maybe he and Sylvie had… deep within some Forest bower… He could quite easily have… How would she know… She only had his word… no, no, no!

Sally's mind twisted away. Her eyes snapped open, seeing with distracted horror the black cloud which oozed eagerly from Nancy Peabody. Foul and oily, it surrounded her with its evil presence. There was no escape this time, no one was coming to rescue her. Soon she'd be as Amos Blunt, drained and shrivelled.

"Reuben!" she screamed despairingly.

Suddenly, it didn't matter whether she'd been his first love or not, he loved her now, forever, of that Sally was absolutely convinced.

With conviction came calm acceptance, total faith in the man she'd given her heart and soul to. Softly she closed her eyes, awaiting her end, wishing she'd been able to save Reuben, wondering where he was, and if he was alright.

"Oh, Reuben, my love. I'm so sorry I couldn't save you. I believe in you. I love you…"

The entity hissed violently. Opening her eyes, Sally saw it fold over onto itself, its surface sizzling as if burnt.

Disbelievingly, she scrambled to her feet, cautiously, carefully, stepping towards the clear pathway through its foulness, so unexpectedly opened before her.

Tentatively, slowly, she moved until she was free, her love and faith in Reuben still blazing within her soul like a brilliant beacon.

Again, the creature writhed and hissed, and Sally stared in confusion, unable to accept its attack had been halted, wondering what'd occurred to divert its attention.

Stumbling, Sally came to her senses, turned and fled, in her panic not knowing where she ran, only knowing by some miracle she'd once again been spared. Fearing the entity's incapacity would be only temporary, soon, all too soon, it would be recovered and intent on the hunt, with Sally its terrified prey.

Pain. A world of pain in his skull. And fear… although fear over what, Reuben couldn't remember. He groaned and tried to move his head, wincing from the resulting explosion of agony. Painfully he opened his eyes, vision blurred and indistinct, darkness and images juddering sickeningly. He blinked rapidly, eyes welling with hot tears of distress.

Slowly the world righted itself into an image of Jack sitting on a fallen tree opposite, a shotgun lying across his knees, face impassive and unreadable. He simply sat and watched Reuben in silence.

"Jack," murmured Reuben groggily. "Help me, please."

Click. Slowly, his eyes never leaving Reuben's face, Jack eased the safety off the shotgun.

With that small metallic sound, memory came roaring back. Reuben winced away from his former friend, his fingers delicately exploring the raw wound on the back of his head, remembering before she'd struck him, the triumphantly malicious smile of Nancy Peabody.

"Where is she?" he asked, struggling to sit, clutching at a nearby tree for support, the world swaying giddily. "Where's Nancy?"

"Gone to find Sally," replied Jack dispassionately. A new fear, primal and raw, gripped Reuben's heart and he stared at Jack in horror.

"Why?" he demanded in anguish. "If she hurts her..."

"She won't," assured Jack, then stopped, a flicker of doubt in his eyes. "She wouldn't..." he said again slowly, more as if to reassure himself than Reuben.

At Reuben's sudden movement he swung the gun onto him. "Don't," was all he said.

At the utter conviction in his voice, Reuben eased back, gaze never leaving the smooth shine of the shotgun.

"So, what's Nancy's role in all this?" he asked in as reasonable a tone as he could muster. "I mean, I can understand why you're upset, Jack. I can, I really can," he added hastily at Jack's impatient gesture. "But Nancy, what's any of this got to do with her?"

"Everything," replied Jack and grinned, a mirthless, bleak smile which didn't reach his eyes. "She has everything to do with it, she always has."

Running, gasping, panting, clutching her side which throbbed with a stitch of exertion, Sally was almost beyond her limits of endurance. Suddenly, in the darkness before her, she saw a light; a coloured, beckoning, calming light, and realised she'd reached the church.

Sobbing with hope, Sally staggered through the ancient gravestones and pushed on the great wooden door, feeling a shot of relief as it swung creakily open. She fell inside, closing and locking it behind her with the huge, black key.

Breath loud in the awed silence of the ancient place of worship, Sally leant back against the door, praying its foot of solid oak and thick stone walls would be enough to keep the creature out.

Jumping in horror as an icy cold tendril touched her heel, she backed away, eyes wide with terror at the sight of the thick blackness which crept and slithered under the door, slowly but steadily threading its way through.

"Sally my dear, is everything alright?"

At the gently concerned voice, Sally started in fright again, spinning round as Reverend Arnold made his way down the aisle, kindly face creased with anxiety, his hands reaching to her in comfort. Giving a wild sob, Sally threw herself at him.

"It's coming for me," she cried. "It's going to kill me."

"What is?" he exclaimed, alarm sending his bushy eyebrows so far up they almost met his untidy, snowy white thatch of hair. "Whatever are you talking about, Sally?"

"Evil," she choked. At his instinctive gesture of denial, she pulled at his arm, dragged him back to the door, and showed him the foul, black cloud which slimed through the scant, inch wide crack between stout English oak and the stone lintel, worn smooth from generations of parishioners' feet.

"May all the Saints preserve us," he cried in horror. "What is it?"

"The creature from the Forest," she explained. "It's broken free. Somehow, it's gained control of Nancy Peabody and it means to kill me. Jack's under its spell. He's taken Reuben somewhere, I couldn't find them."

"Nancy Peabody? Miss Violet's niece?" demanded the good Reverend in alarmed incomprehension. "No, no, Sally; that I cannot believe. Have you perhaps had a little too much of that excellent, though I must say, rather strong punch Amos had made for the Festival?"

"No," denied Sally. At his mention of the former publican, she shook with remembered horror and gripped at his sleeve. "Amos Blunt," she cried. "He's dead. I found him in the Forest. That thing had sucked all the life out of him."

"Dear Lord," the Reverend exclaimed, casting another worried glance at the cloud which had now doubled in size. He ushered Sally back along the aisle. "Now sit, my dear," he ordered. "Take a deep breath and tell me everything."

"There's no time," Sally cried impatiently, aware it wouldn't be long before the entity gained admittance. "Please, you must believe me. That thing is evil. It'll kill us if it can. Just like it did Amos!"

The good reverend's eyebrows wandered across his face in consternation at her words, and Sally shook his arm in pleading despair.

"It attacked me in the Forest. It almost killed me, but I got away…"

"How? How did you escape?"

"I don't know…" began Sally, then cried out in horror. "Look, Reverend, look!"

The creature in its entirety was now within the church. They backed away until their spines touched the coldness of the stone altar, and Sally grasped for the comfort of the Reverend's hand, eyes flicking desperately around the small stone church for another way out but there was none. The entity was between them and the only door. They were trapped.

"Courage, my child," cried the Reverend. "Have faith in the Lord, he shall deliver us from evil."

"Faith," murmured Sally, understanding exploding in her mind. "Reverend Arnold," she exclaimed, turning to him in excitement. "How did you come to the Lord? I mean, how did you find your faith?"

"My faith?" he queried, plainly puzzled.

"Please," she insisted, one eye on the agonisingly slow, but relentless, progress of the creature up the aisle towards them. "It's important."

"Well," began the Reverend uncertainly. "I was a young man, much like any other I suppose, selfish in my desire for advancement, my ambition blinding me to the needs of others. Until one night the Lord spoke to me. He showed me the smallness of my heart. Let me taste of his greatness. In that instant, I knew I must dedicate my life to him, that my faith in him must be complete and absolute. And, in nearly forty years, I have never had cause to regret that decision."

"Good," exclaimed Sally, clutching his hand, dragging them a step nearer to the entity. "Remember that faith, Reverend. Hold onto it. Let it fill your soul and your mind until nothing else matters…"

"But my dear…"

"Just do it," cried Sally.

The good Reverend asked no more questions, closed his eyes and began to pray, the words of the Lord's Prayer at first wavering and unsteady, but he did not falter. As his tone grew in strength, so did the conviction and passion behind the words and Sally knew he was speaking with the pure, true voice of his faith.

She faced the creature and allowed thoughts of Reuben to flood her body, the memory of his face, soft with the tenderness of the love he bore for her, his eyes looking deep into her soul when they'd first joined, the sacred wonder she'd seen reflected in his gaze.

Her love for him, her absolute trust in his fidelity and honesty with her heart, took away her fear. Bravely, chin held high, the good Reverend's hand clasped firmly in hers, Sally walked straight into the heart of the creature.

As before, it hissed like water on a hotplate. With a jolt of life renewing hope, Sally saw it fold up over onto itself creating a safe passageway right through the centre of its amorphous fluidic mass. It fretted and bulged at the edges, plainly incensed it couldn't reach them, emitting sibilant hisses, it hung, suspended, mere inches away.

"Yea though I walk through the valley of the shadow of death," intoned the Reverend. Sally felt a flicker of irony as they crept through the centre of the creature, the good Reverend's eyes still firmly closed, his hand clutching trustingly at Sally's.

They emerged on the other side of the creature, Sally still clinging desperately to her belief in Reuben, allowing positive thoughts of his love, and the life they would have together, flood her body with hope.

She led the Reverend to the door and fumbled with the oversized key, and on hearing the sound his eyes flew open. He glanced over his shoulder at the quivering mass, apparently frozen in place.

"Thank the Lord," he murmured in relief. "Did I not tell you faith in him would save us, Sally?"

"You did, Reverend," she agreed. "But it's not only faith in God, it seems to be a true belief in anything or anyone. It doesn't matter what it is, so long as you truly believe with all your heart. It doesn't understand such emotions. All it knows is envy, hatred and jealousy, all negative emotions. That's what it wants. That's what it feeds on."

She pulled the door open, jumping back as Nancy Peabody erupted into the church, nails hooked into claws, face distorted with fury, mouth stretched in a grimace of evil rage.

Crying out with shock, Sally fell back under the attack and Nancy was upon her, hands fastening around Sally's throat, tightening painfully with unnatural strength.

Choking and thrashing, Sally fought frantically to free herself, bringing her knees up and kicking at Nancy's body, clawing her face in an attempt to loosen her grip. But it was no use. The hands closed even more firmly, Sally's vision blurring as she gulped for precious air.

Suddenly, Nancy cried out in shock and keeled over sideways clutching at her head, releasing Sally, who rolled over, panting hoarsely, as Reverend Arnold dropped the large, heavy candlestick with which he'd struck Nancy Peabody and dragged her to her feet.

"Quickly," he cried in horror. "Already she recovers."

Sally let him pull her from the church, barely registering his cool actions in taking the key from the door, slamming and locking it from the outside, moments before a heavy body hurled itself at the other side. There was a howl of furious disbelief as Nancy Peabody once again found herself on the other side of a locked door.

Staggering, throat raw and head pounding, Sally was half carried, half led through ancient gravestones until the coldness of the night air shocked her into some semblance of alertness, and she drew him to a halt.

"I have to find Reuben and Jack," she insisted.

The Reverend shook his head in fear, glancing back at the church, the increased violence of Nancy Peabody's attack on the door bearing witness that once again she and the entity were joined.

"That door won't hold for long," he cried. "We must get to the Hall. It's not safe out here alone."

"There's no time," Sally replied desperately. "It may already be too late, Jack may have already... I have to find them, I have to try. You go to the Hall, Reverend, speak to Daniel Forrester and tell him what's happened. He may know what to do."

"Truly," agreed the Reverend. "If anyone knows of the Forest and its inhabitants it'll be him. But come with me, Sally..."

"I can't, I have to find Reuben," she insisted again. The Reverend saw from her face that no amount of persuasion would change her mind, so he nodded and patted her hand reassuringly.

"Take care, Sally," he ordered. "I'll fetch help, but just take care."

"I will," she promised, and hurried away from him into the darkness, towards the menacing gloom of the nearby Forest.

Reverend Arnold watched her go until he could see her no more, then a shriek of demonic rage and a renewed battering upon the door set his heart thudding with fear, his feet quickly moving in the direction of the Hall; to the sanctuary and the help he hoped to find there.

Pulling the torch from her pocket, Sally was relieved to find it still worked, its steady beam saving her from many a stumble as she worked her way back through the Forest. Beyond its warm, yellow glow, the dark lurked uneasily, and Sally's eyes ached from constantly flicking to the imagined movements and half-seen images which tortured her from the shadows.

Something moved in the gloom between the trees.

Sally stopped, heart hammering against her ribs, eyes throbbing as she strained to see, fearing Nancy Peabody had escaped the church and was even now waiting to pounce, lurking soundlessly in the dimness, the foul creature which owned her soul whispering commands of vilest intent into her willing heart.

The patch of lightness moved towards her, and Sally froze with terror as it came closer. Ripples of silver and cream shifting in a shaft of moonlight angled through a gap in the canopy, casting welcome illumination onto the ethereally beautiful shape of the White Hind.

Sally stared, mouth falling open in silent homage to the glory of the animal. Hide milk white and perfect, neat hooves stepping precisely onto the leaf strewn Forest floor, it stopped, one leg lifted in a pose of enquiry, its eyes dark with intelligence.

Sally gazed into those eyes. Any thought of fear left her mind, and when it stepped away, glancing back over its shoulder, Sally understood, and followed without thought or caution.

Deep into the Forest it led her, almost to the barrier itself. Still Sally followed, trusting implicitly and instinctively it meant her no harm, that such a gorgeous creature could only be a force for good, the very antithesis of the black malevolence left behind at the church.

Finally, the White Hind halted, turned, looking at her with an expression of such sorrow, Sally felt tears start to her eyes and held out a hand, wanting to comfort and reassure.

Then, a voice low and steady, but so achingly familiar and dear, spoke from beyond the trees, Sally's head turned hopefully in that direction and when she looked back, the White Hind had gone, melted away into the shadows as quietly as it had come.

Treading softly, Sally moved in the shadow of the trees, peering cautiously into the small clearing beyond, a shaft of relieved joy piercing her heart when she saw Reuben, sitting with his back to her.

In the brilliant moonlight which flooded the clearing, making it almost as bright as day, she saw the ugly gash on the back of his head, and the blood which matted his hair and stained his jacket.

Opposite him, perched in casual comfort upon a fallen tree, sat Jack. Sally stifled a gasp at the sight of the shotgun lying across his lap, the way his finger idly caressed the trigger, his dark eyes fixed unerringly upon Reuben's face, expression immobile and impenetrable.

Reuben spoke again, his voice low and urgent, and Sally strained to hear. "What do you intend to do, Jack? We can't sit here all night."

"We will if necessary," Jack's voice sounded odd, Sally thought, remembering how Nancy Peabody's had been. It was Jack's voice, but in some strange, indefinable way, it wasn't.

"Why are you obeying her orders, Jack?" Reuben's voice was calm, but Sally heard the strain behind the words and wondered what to do, eyeing the shotgun fearfully, afraid if she revealed her presence, it could provoke Jack into using it.

"After all," Reuben continued reasonably. "You've never liked her, have you, Jack. In fact, I'd go as far as saying you've always hated her. So why listen to her now? Why let her order you around like some kind of lackey?"

"Shut up," demanded Jack, gesturing with the shotgun towards him. "You know nothing about her, Reuben, nothing, so shut up."

"I know she's out there now, hunting Sally. What happens if she catches her, Jack? What then? Do you seriously trust her not to hurt Sally? Because I certainly don't."

"She wouldn't," insisted Jack. "She promised..."

"And you believed her?" scoffed Reuben. "Then you're a fool, Jack, that's all I can say. A fool. Are you really happy to trust Sally's life on her word?"

Jack said nothing, merely glancing at Reuben, then looked away as if supremely unmoved by his words. From her vantage point though, Sally saw the uncertainty on his face, and realised that Reuben was reaching him, slowly picking a way through the creature which had swathed Jack in layers of malignant hatred to touch the real Jack inside.

Sally realised this was Reuben's intent: to somehow tap into the Jack who passionately loved her, the Jack who could never bear to see her injured in any way. Sally bit her lip, watching in silence, praying Reuben would be successful.

"What will you do, Jack?" Reuben continued relentlessly. "How will you live with yourself if she hurts Sally? What about if she kills her? What then, Jack? How can you live in a world with no Sally? Knowing she's dead because of you? She suffered because of you. That she..."

"Enough," snapped Jack, flashing the gun in Reuben's direction. "She won't hurt her," he insisted again, lowering the gun and staring at his friend in obvious anguish. "Will she?"

"Of course not, Jack," purred a dreadfully familiar voice behind Sally. She yelped as Nancy Peabody seized her by the arm and pushed her into the clearing, where the two shocked men scrambled hastily to their feet.

"Here she is," sang Nancy. "Safe and sound as promised. Although I really don't know why you're making such a fuss about her."

"Sally," cried Reuben. Next moment Sally was in his arms, her bones melting with relief at his touch before she was dragged away by the steely grip of Nancy Peabody, who thrust her towards Jack so violently Sally stumbled and fell against him, the coldness of the gun against her arm.

"Jack," she sobbed, noting with dismay the newly set rigidity of his jaw, and realised that seeing her in Reuben's embrace had only served to strengthen the entity's hold over him. "Please don't do this," she continued hopelessly. "Jack, think about what you're doing. We're your friends... please, Jack..."

He moved away from her, face set as stone. Behind her, Nancy Peabody laughed, a chillingly evil laugh which spoke of triumphant pleasure.

"It's no good," she crowed. "He can't hear you, Sally Cairn. You had the opportunity to stop all of this, but you chose the wrong man. So, the circle spins and the same old story is told. But this time, there is a difference. That which was lost has been found. That which was ripped away, has been restored. Now, I will be free of this accursed Forest. Come!" she shrieked, whipping round and staring to where the barrier, invisible and impenetrable, hung in the air.

"Come!" she cried again. "It is time!"

Something moved thickly, deep within the Forest. On the other side of the barrier, it oozed and slithered through the undergrowth, Sally's heart stopping in terror as it paused, its blackness swallowing the moonlight wherever it fell upon its shifting, smoke like, surface. She recognised it as being the same as the entity which was inside Nancy Peabody, but this was bigger. Much bigger. Three, four, five times the size of the creature which had cornered them in the church.

Taking the shotgun from Jack, Nancy Peabody propelled him towards the creature. Like one in a dream, he complied, moving until he collided with the barrier and hung in its embrace, body writhing with pain as the creature on the other side flowed upwards, probing and pushing, trying to find a way through.

Then, to Sally's fearful disbelief, it found a pinprick of entry.

Slowly at first, then gaining in speed, it tore and ripped at the barrier, pouring through the hole it'd created. And Jack was waiting for it with head thrown back, eyes and mouth open wide, palms placed flat on the barrier as if in supplication.

"No, Jack!" screamed Sally, realising too late what was happening.

"Get back!" yelled Reuben and made to dash forward. Nancy Peabody raised the shotgun, and at the look in her eyes, Reuben subsided, watching with Sally in helpless horror as the darkness crept into Jack and he took it all, eyes bulging as the entity engulfed and swallowed him from the inside out, Sally sobbed at the sight of Jack being taken so far away, she knew he'd never find his way back.

Finally, the last whiplash of creature was through and into Jack. He staggered, bloated with the enormity of the burden he now carried, slowly straightened, the movement that of one worn out from long years of toil.

He turned and faced them. Sally sobbed anew at the total blackness of his eyes, the blankness of his expression, and heard Reuben gasp with horror. Desperately, her hand groped for his, holding it tightly, knowing the end was near for them, not seeing how anything could save them from the awfulness of the creature's intentions.

"At last!" roared the creature in Jack's voice. "At last all of me is free of that accursed Forest. For so long, I have been trapped within its boundaries. Unable to escape. Unable to take my revenge on those who ended my life and condemned me to eternal damnation!"

It paused, holding out a hand to Nancy Peabody, who picked her way daintily, almost primly, across the uneven Forest floor to stand beside it.

"See," commanded the creature. "Both my children are restored to me. I have waited centuries for the bloodlines to run true, finally they have. The two halves I placed fragments of my essence into, even as my enemy devoured me, are once again united. I am free!"

The last words were bellowed in exact synchronicity by Jack and Nancy Peabody. Reuben and Sally stared, frenzied minds trying to make logic of all they had heard and seen, and it struck Sally how alike Jack and Nancy Peabody were. Both so dark, so slight of build, their Gaelic blood bore witness to in their facial features, so alike they could be...

"Twins!" she exclaimed.

"What?" Reuben looked at her in confusion.

"Twins," she cried again. "They're twins. Look at them, look how alike they are. Why did we never notice it before?"

Reuben looked and saw, yet could not understand. "But they're not," he insisted. "We know they're not. We know their families, Sal, it's not possible."

"I know," agreed Sally. "But somehow, they are..."

Jack laughed a low, terrible laugh which bore no trace of him at all. "Pitiful little fools," it mocked. "How your tiny brains struggle to understand. I wish I had time to explain but have waited so long for vengeance that none shall delay me."

"What of them?" asked Nancy Peabody, turning her malicious gaze upon Sally and Reuben.

"I am free now," declared Jack, levelling a thin, mirthless smile upon them. "I have no more need of them. Soon, I will have a whole village full of petty and corrupt souls to gorge upon. What need have I of them? Kill them," he ordered. Obediently, Nancy Peabody raised the shotgun.

"Run!" yelled Reuben. Sally found herself pushed before him into the trees, barely managing a step before the gun exploded, its blast reverberating shockingly through the silent Forest.

Together they collapsed onto the cold dampness of its hard, unforgiving floor.

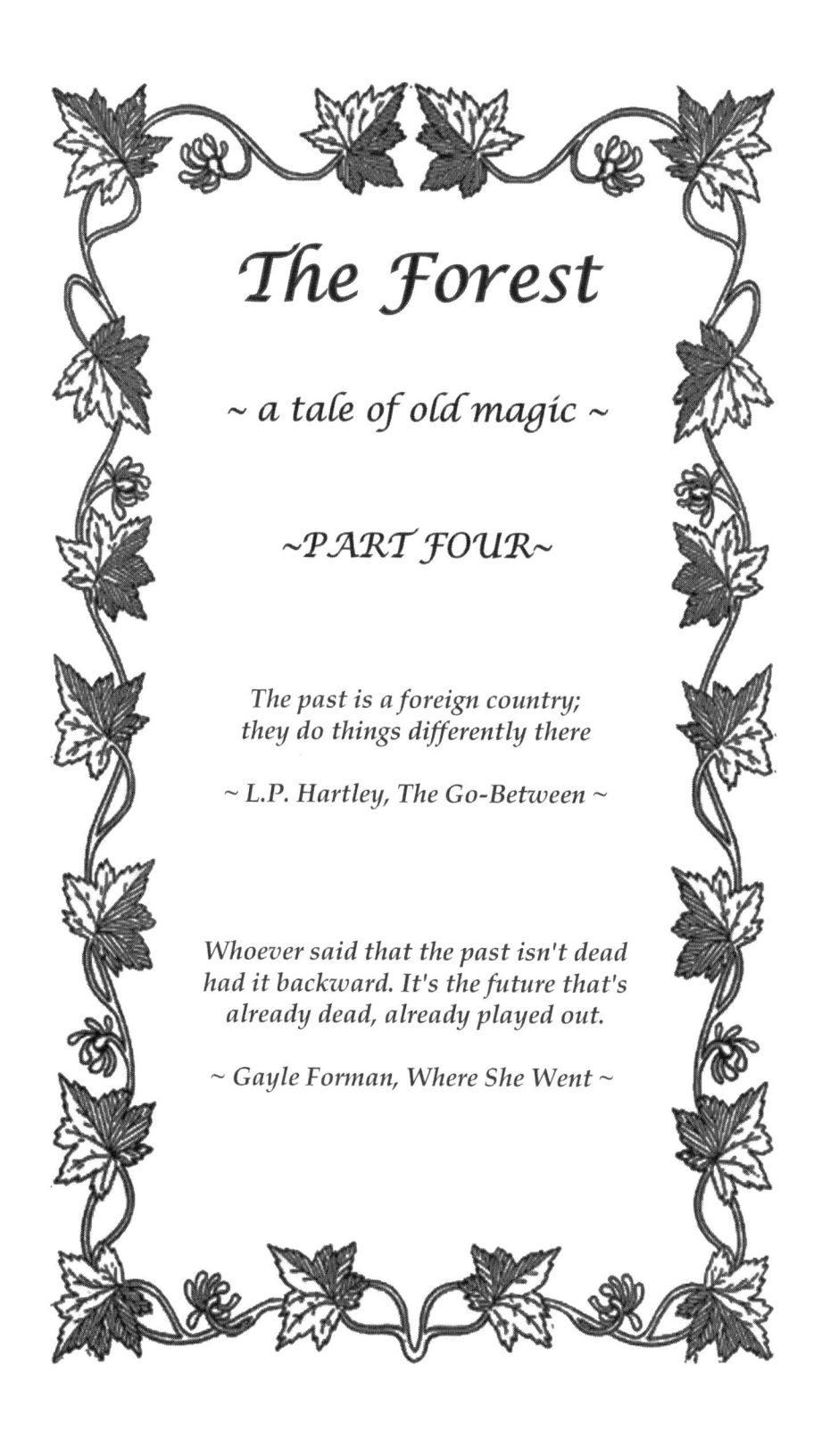

The Forest

~ a tale of old magic ~

~PART FOUR~

*The past is a foreign country;
they do things differently there*

~ L.P. Hartley, The Go-Between ~

*Whoever said that the past isn't dead
had it backward. It's the future that's
already dead, already played out.*

~ Gayle Forman, Where She Went ~

Chapter Fifteen
~ Family ~

Miss Violet cried out in shocked alarm as the roar of a shotgun echoed through the Forest. John Blacksmith paled, his strong face tautening into lines of grim horror, instinctively clutching her hand as they stared at each other, ashen with fear, the after echo of the retort hanging in the still, frigid, night air.

"Oh no," he murmured. "Not that, not that…"

Deep within the Forest, Lucian and his men froze, eyes wide with the knowledge they were too late. Galvanised into action, the White Hind leapt past them and set off towards the barrier.

Shaking himself back into his scattered wits, Lucian gestured impatiently to his men, who swallowed and muttered amongst themselves, gripping their weapons with renewed vigour, seeming to feel, as he did, that this time was different. This time there was hope. Or rather, had been hope corrected Lucian silently to himself, wondering if the blast of the shotgun signalled an abrupt halt to their fervent desire to end this nightmare.

"Come," he said simply. To a man, they followed, hurrying after the White Hind, Lucian wondering what she intended to do, always supposing if they were not already too late.

Shock. Panic. Confusion. Reuben's weight prone and heavy, crushing her into the dirt. Desperately, Sally slid from under his motionless body, sobbing in horror as she rolled him over, trying to see if he was hurt, stunned she herself seemed uninjured.

Blood, so much blood, it flowed in a steady, sticky stream from a gaping wound in his side. In the moonlight, Sally could see his face, pale and still, and she clasped him to her, ripping material from her skirts lining, adrenalin lending her hands the strength to tear through the cloth. Urgently, she attempted to staunch the flood, realising when Reuben pushed her in front of him, that he'd deliberately placed himself between her and the bullet.

Anger, white and hot, flared in her breast, and she glared at the impassive faces of Nancy Peabody and Jack over the bleeding body of her lover.

"Is he dead?" Jack asked, and Sally trembled at the deadly calmness of his tone.

"He soon will be," replied Nancy Peabody, raising the gun again. "In fact, they both soon will be."

Sally stared straight up the barrel of the shotgun, cradling Reuben's head in her lap, arching her body over his in a futile attempt to shield him.

"Bridget!"

A voice, clear and defiant, rang out from the other side of the barrier. A woman, little more than a girl really, with long, silvery white hair gleaming in the moonlight. Her slender body was draped in a gown of lichen green, and her large dark eyes were fixed upon Nancy Peabody and Jack.

Nancy raised the shotgun. "Sylvie!" she spat furiously.

Once more, the gun yelped in the darkness. The girl leapt into the air, before Sally's stunned and disbelieving eyes, turned mid jump into the White Hind and bounded away into the trees.

Howling with rage, Jack shoved Nancy Peabody towards the barrier. "Go after her!" he ordered. "Do not rest until she is finished, once and for all..."

"But I cannot harm another within the Forest," whined Nancy, and Sally's scrambled brain stored the nugget of information away. "You know the Forest will not allow bloodshed of another within its heart."

"Not directly no," agreed Jack, a smile, terrible and cold, spreading across his face. "There are other ways," he said. "Summon the hunters, it shall be as before. Hunt her down until her heart pounds fit to burst and terror turns her soul to ice. Call up the hounds of malevolence and greed and spite. Set them upon her scent. They will not stop until she is dead, and they are feasting on her bones. Go!"

"It shall be done," promised Nancy Peabody, almost licking her lips in anticipation. She glanced at Sally and Reuben disdainfully. "What about them?"

"Leave them to me," Jack's lip curled sardonically as he took the shotgun back, Sally shivering at the dark hatred in his eyes. "Now, go," he commanded again. With a last sneer at Sally, Nancy Peabody picked her way delicately to the barrier and pressed upon its shimmering surface, staggering as if walking against the wind, she finally reached the other side and vanished amongst the trees.

"Sally..." at the hoarse whisper Sally looked into Reuben's pain-racked eyes. "I'm sorry..." he gasped, voice faltering on a groan of agony.

"Don't be," she cried. "I love you. If this is all the time we were destined to have together, so be it..."

"How touching," sneered Jack, gesturing towards Sally with the shotgun. "But let's make it a little more sporting, shall we? Go on, make a dash for it. I'll even give you a head start, to make it fair. You never know, you may even make it. Then again, you probably won't," he laughed.

Sally's hackles rose, slowly, with quiet dignity and fluidic grace, she stood and stepped towards him.

"No," she stated calmly, experiencing a flicker of satisfaction at the momentary surprise in Jack's eyes. "I won't run from you, Jack."

The creature shrugged with irritation. "Jack is gone," it insisted. "He no longer exists except as something twisted to my will. Do not think to appeal to him, because, even if he could hear you, he is powerless to help, nor would he want to. You rejected him. All he asked for was your love, but you discarded him, casting him off like an old shoe. For that, and that alone, you deserve to die."

"No, you're wrong," replied Sally, heart pounding at the note of hurt which crept into the creature's voice. "I never stopped loving you, Jack. You are my kin, my cousin. You've been my best friend all my life, my soul mate, my other half. You alone shared my cot and my childhood toys. You knew all my secrets, my dreams, my fears. We have so much history, you and I, Jack, I hardly know where to begin remembering it all. You were and are, everything to me, and I love you."

"Yet not as you love him!" spat the creature, gesturing angrily to where Reuben lay grey faced with pain, hands clutching feebly at his blood-soaked side, eyelids flickering as he tried desperately to hang on to consciousness.

"No," agreed Sally, as calmly as she could. "Not as I love Reuben. But, the love I feel for you is not diminished by that which I feel for him. You're still all, and everything, that you ever were to me."

"But he wanted more," howled the creature, "So much more. He wanted you to be his wife, but you chose the other one. You always choose the other one."

"I'm sorry you were hurt by that, Jack," continued Sally. "I couldn't help falling in love with Reuben. He is the man I choose to be my husband. You will always be the man I choose to be my friend."

"Friend!" spat the creature. "What use is that to a man who longs to be your lover? It is not enough!"

"It has to be," stated Sally. "The heart cannot help where it loves. Killing Reuben or killing me, will not alter that fact."

"You let him touch you," cried the creature, Sally caught an echo of Jack and hope flared in her heart. "I heard you, in the hayloft, you and him. How could you Sally? And then you both laughed at me, I know, the other one told me. She heard you."

"She lied," declared Sally firmly. "Who would you believe, Jack? A woman you've despised all your life? A woman now so enthralled by evil she'll say and do anything it orders? Or someone you've known and trusted since you were a babe? Someone who loves you with all her heart. Wants only to take you home, for us all to go home. Back to our families and people who love us…"

As soon as the words left her mouth, Sally knew she'd made a fatal error. The spark that was almost Jack vanished from his face, and the entity was back, the gun gripped firmly in its hands.

"Family?" it howled angrily. "Poor Jack had no family. No one who loved him. You were his last hope of that, but you turned him away. When you did, you destroyed any chance he had…"

"Jack, I'm sorry..." began Sally desperately.

"Enough," snapped the creature curtly. "It's too late!" He raised the shotgun. Sally dropped to her knees in despair, gathering up Reuben in her arms, determined to spend her last moments alive in the arms of the man she loved.

"I love you," his words were faint, edged with pain.

Sally buried her head in his shoulder. "I love you," she whispered, closing her eyes, hearing the click as Jack pulled back the trigger, her scalding tears dropping onto Reuben's face.

"Jack, no!"

"Stop, Jack, oh please, please stop!"

Startled, Sally looked up, Miss Violet and John Blacksmith were standing at the edge of the clearing, faces drawn with horror. Her gaze flew to Jack, and the creature he contained. Slowly, Jack's head turned, and Miss Violet gasped to be confronted by those pitiless black eyes, the malevolence of his face, and the stark fact of the shotgun pointing straight at his best friends.

"Jack," pleaded Miss Violet again. "Please, don't do it."

"Put the gun down, son," John Blacksmith's voice was calm, yet the anxiety lay taut beneath his words.

"Son?" Jack smirked cruelly, the creature's voice ripe with disdainful amusement. "You now call him son? Where were you, father dear, these past twenty years when your son needed you? Where were you? Lost in your own selfish grief, never noticing how badly Jack craved your love and attention. Well, it's too late now, Jack has come back to his true family, to the ones who really love and care for him."

"Family?" John Blacksmith asked incredulously. "What do you mean? You are no family of my son. You are evil incarnate and have possessed him."

"Possessed him?" mocked the creature. "Well, and if I have," it mused thoughtfully. "It was no more than he wanted. All his life, Jack has ached to have a family and now he does. He has returned home where he belongs."

"He does not belong to you!" snapped John Blacksmith.

Shockingly, the creature relinquished its control and Jack looked at them.

"But I do," he stated flatly. "She is my mother."

Sally and Miss Violet gaped at each other in shocked disbelief.

John Blacksmith stepped forward, shaking his head in abject denial, uncaring of the gun still clasped tightly in Jack's hands. "No," he declared firmly. "It's not your mother, Jack. I know how badly you long for it to be true, but it's lying to you. Using your vulnerability to trap you…"

"But it's true," insisted Jack. Sally's heart ached to hear his voice, so alone and afraid, sounding as if it were coming from a hundred miles away, struggling through layers of controlling malevolence. "I don't know how it's possible," Jack continued. "But the blood connection is there. I feel it, know it to be the truth. She is my mother."

"Your mother was Rosie Cairn from West Farm," insisted John Blacksmith. "She was the prettiest, sweetest, most loving woman in the world. When I lost her my heart was ripped from my body and thrown into the grave with her. I didn't know how to live without her, so for over twenty years I haven't. And I see now how wrong that was. I've neglected you Jack, and I'm so sorry. But whatever this creature has told you, listen to me now. Your mother loved you…"

"She didn't have a chance to love me!" cried Jack.

"But she did," insisted his father. "For nine long months she carried you beneath her heart and she loved you. I'd hear her singing, such sweet, loving songs. She'd make them up and sing them to you, hands clasped around you within her, eyes so full of love that tears would spill down her cheeks from the joy of waiting for you to arrive."

"I-I didn't know that," Jack stuttered.

"I should've told you," John Blacksmith shook his head in self-disgust. "If I'd only stopped to think. She commanded me to love you, to raise you in the light, and I failed her. The last words she spoke were of you. In my blind, selfish misery, I forgot them."

"She spoke of me? What… what did she say?" Sally heard the desperate eagerness in Jack's voice, her own tears falling like raindrops on her cheeks.

"When you lay on her breast and the doctor was trying to stop the bleeding, she knew… she knew she was going to have to leave us… She told me to lie beside her, and I did. I held you both in my arms and cried out in anger. But she silenced my rage with the sweetest of kisses, told me not to stain our last moments together with bitterness. She showed me the perfection of our baby, kissing your tiny feet and hands, begging me to love you until my last breath. To protect you. Raise you to be a good and honest man," John Blacksmith paused and swallowed, long denied emotions choking the words in his throat.

"She made me promise, and I did. But I failed her. I failed my Rosie. I failed you, and I beg your pardon Jack, I'm so sorry." Then this silent giant of a man, who'd probably just spoken more words than he had in twenty years, fell to his knees before Jack, large frame shuddering with the strength of his feelings.

For a long terrible moment there was silence within the clearing.

Jack stumbled forward, eyes fixed on the bent dark head of his father. "Tell me..." he murmured, John looked up at the naked plea in his son's voice. "Tell me about her," Jack finished.

"She had a dozen different smiles," John allowed a glow of remembrance to light up his face, "and any one of them would warm you from within." He hesitated, unsure how to convey the essence of a mother long gone, to a son so gripped in the claws of malignant possession, the slightest misstep could lose him forever.

"She was always happy, always singing, a typical Cairn. You know, always so bloody cheerful sometimes you want to shout at them..."

John paused as Jack smiled, a fleetingly brief smile that shot hope through Sally's wildly beating heart. "I know that feeling," Jack murmured, dashing a sideways glance at Sally.

"She had such a tender heart," John continued, his own tears flowing unnoticed and unchecked, as if by finally speaking of his wife he was lancing that which had been allowed to fester for so many years.

"She couldn't bear to see anything suffer. I remember once," he paused, dashing a hand furiously at his eyes. Jack made a tiny telling step towards him, large dark eyes fixed hungrily and unwaveringly on his father's face.

"A baby bird fell from a nest in the garden. Nothing else would do, but I climb up a ladder and put it back." He gave a small rueful laugh, lost in the memory. "I remember, as I was coming back down, I slipped and fell the last two rungs. She rushed over, scared I'd hurt myself, and I played up a bit, enjoying having her fuss over me."

"Tell me more..." Jack begged. Miss Violet and Sally exchanged fleeting glances of hope, and Sally refolded the blood-soaked cloth, attempting to staunch the steady flow of blood from Reuben's side, noticing with alarm the greyness of his face and the glassy, fixed set of his eyes.

"She had the most beautiful eyes I'd ever seen on a woman," John continued, looking at Jack. "You have her eyes," he remarked candidly. "And it fair near tore me apart every time you looked at me with them. I kept seeing her, hating the fact she was gone."

"You hated me for killing her, I know," commented Jack bleakly. Sally flinched from the edge which had crept back into his voice.

"What?" John looked shocked, then horrified, "No, Jack, never! Is that what you've believed all these years?" At Jack's stillness of assent, he spoke hurriedly, words tumbling over themselves in his urgency to convince his son of their validity.

"I never hated you, Jack! Never! And I certainly never blamed you for your mother's death! You were a babe. How could it possibly have been your fault? No, it was a tragic twist of fate. If anyone should be blamed, it should be me. I let my grief weigh me down, when I should have been caring for you, my son, her son. I let you down Jack, and I'm so sorry. I never told you how much I love you. How much you mean to me. Please, Jack, come back to us, please…"

"But he can't!" the shutters crashed down. Once again, the creature was in control, and Sally's heart dropped like a stone as Jack turned to face her, cruelly mocking smile back on his face, every trace of Jack eradicated.

"How vastly entertaining that was," mused the creature. "But, for all the impassioned pleas of a penitent father, it cannot change the fact that the woman he loves has rejected him. Chosen another. Given her heart…" it sneered nastily in Sally's direction, "And her body to another. So, you tell me. What's in this life for Jack? Nothing but loneliness and despair, that's all…"

"No!" insisted Sally hotly. "Jack will never be alone, he has me. I'll always be his true friend."

"He has me," stated John Blacksmith, rising to his feet, reaching out to the shell of his son with hands that pleaded and implored.

"And he has me," Miss Violet spoke up, stepping forward to range herself, shoulder to shoulder, with John Blacksmith, face glowing with devotion for the boy she loved.

"Jack…" at the feeble whisper, Sally helped Reuben pull himself up, his breath catching when the movement caused the wound to gush afresh. He looked upon his best friend, his gaze firm and steady. "Jack, you will always be my friend. I need you to promise you'll take care of Sally for me... I can't hold on much longer, I need to know..."

"Reuben..." Sally sobbed, heart breaking at his words.

"I need to know," Reuben continued as if she hadn't spoken, "that Sally will be safe and protected. Will you promise me that, Jack?"

There was a long, still silence in the clearing. One by one, the faces of those who loved Jack most, turned to see what effect, if any, the passionate plea of his dying best friend would have upon him.

"No," drawled the creature sarcastically, and brought up the gun. Sally cowered over Reuben as Jack's finger squeezed on the trigger.

"Jack, no, don't!"

Dimly Sally heard the cries of Miss Violet and John Blacksmith as they moved towards Jack, knew they wouldn't be able to stop it. A curious calmness descended upon her. Strangely unafraid, she knelt in the mud and looked death in the face, her blue eyes still and serious as they locked with the blankly dark orbs of the creature.

"I trust you, Jack," she heard in a dream her own voice, low and steady. "I love you. I believe in you."

Jack's whole body twitched, muscles standing out on his forearm. Deliberately, slowly, he forced his finger off the trigger. They watched in frozen fascination as his face jerked and rippled like he was having some kind of seizure, sweat beading on his forehead.

"Do not fight me!" roared the creature. Jack staggered, and once again the gun swung upwards to aim unsteadily at Sally. But Jack fought back. The agonising strain forcing veins to rise on his temples. Lips drawn back in a gruesome grimace, he battled against the enemy within.

"Nagggghhh!" screamed Jack. With a mighty, final thrust, he ripped the shotgun from his hands, tossed it towards his father who deftly caught it, jumping back out of range as the creature momentarily seemed to gain the upper hand and made a grab to snatch it back.

Falling to his knees, Jack fought the entity within. First Jack seemed to gain the advantage, then the creature, all the while fearsome shrieks and groans were rent from Jack's soul as if he battled the very devil himself.

Holding onto Reuben's icy cold hand, Sally cried out in encouragement, her shouts echoed by those of John Blacksmith and Miss Violet. Suddenly, shockingly, Jack fell silent, head hanging, his wheezing breath hoarse and ragged in the still night air.

He threw his head back. Screamed. A great, dense cloud poured from his mouth, spiralling upwards into the trees. On and on, he spewed up the foulness which had invaded his soul. Not stopping until every last speck was purged from his being, then he collapsed, drained and exhausted, onto the frozen Forest floor.

The cloud hung for a brief second above him, then plunged itself at the barrier. Sally saw it burst through and coalesce on the other side, before disappearing away into the blackness between the trees.

Quickly, John Blacksmith strode forward, ripping off his coat and wrapping it around Jack's shuddering form, hugging his son firmly to his chest, trembling with the strength of his own emotions.

"You did it, lad," he mumbled. "You did it, you beat it. I'm so proud of you. You did it."

Jack nodded, raising his head to look at them, and Sally marvelled at the difference on his face. It was as if all the bitterness and jealousy had been wiped from his soul. He was her Jack again. Not as she remembered him, but a new Jack. Spotless. As if he'd never had an envious or dark thought in his life.

"Reuben?" Jack staggered to his feet and hurried to where his best friend lay, dropping beside him, eyes flashing horror towards Sally's at the blood, so much blood, and the shadow of death which lay heavily over Reuben's brow.

"He needs a doctor," cried Miss Violet anxiously, pulling her scarf from her shoulders and handing it to Sally, who folded it into a thick pad and pressed it fruitlessly to Reuben's side.

"There's no time," stated John Blacksmith bluntly. "Nearest doctor's miles away. He'd bleed to death long before we could get him there."

"We must do something," Jack insisted, guilt nagging his words.

"I know," said Sally slowly. "We'll take him to Granny Mole's."

"The witch?" cried Jack. "Are you mad? What could she…"

"She knows about herbs and ancient medicines," interrupted Sally desperately. "She could help, I know she could."

"Maybe," John Blacksmith agreed slowly. "I've heard rumours she knows of such things."

Sally glanced about, dragging together her scattered wits, attempting to get her bearings. "Her cottage isn't far away," she cried. "We must take him there."

"Sally are you sure?" asked Miss Violet. "I still think a doctor…"

"We've no other choice," insisted Sally, voice shrill with concern, nodding at John Blacksmith who knelt, gathering up Reuben in his arms as if he weighed nothing. Reuben groaned at the movement, eyes rolling up into his head. Still he fought against the shadow and reached out a hand to Sally.

"Sally?"

"It's alright," Sally caught at his hand. "I'm here. We'll get you to Granny Mole's. She can help, I know she can. I promise I won't leave you…"

"No," he moaned. "Think I'm done for, but there's something important you must do for me."

"Yes, anything…" sobbed Sally. "Anything at all. What is it?"

"Sylvie," he exhaled on a sigh of pain. "Alone in the Forest, being hunted like before. Help her Sally, she's a friend. I love you, yet Sylvie is important. Know you understand. She's to me what Jack is to you. Can't bear to think of her being hunted to her death. Even though, I know it's already happened. But perhaps, this time, it could be different…"

"But… but Reuben," stammered Sally in shock. "Go into the Forest? I can't… I mean how can I get through the barrier, what about the creature?"

"Know you can do it…" he swallowed, managed a smile. "Have faith in you, Sal… love you, please, promise me you'll try …"

"I promise…" Sally faltered, a dry sob escaping from a throat constricting with the knowledge that this was probably the last time she'd see him alive. "I don't want to leave you," she whispered miserably.

"I know," Reuben nodded, eyes intense on hers, then he glanced at Jack, the plea still unanswered.

Jack moved to stand beside Sally. "I promise," he assured.

Reuben closed his eyes in satisfaction, head lolling back against John Blacksmith's chest. Miss Violet moved to stand beside them, face tight with worry, but the hand that held the torch to light their way steady. The thought flew unbidden through Jack's mind, dishevelled as she was, he'd never seen the spinster shopkeeper look so beautiful.

The trees closed behind them and they were alone. Jack shrugged into his father's jacket, looking at Sally expectantly, as if she somehow knew what happened next.

"I don't know what to do," she admitted, face crumpling. "Oh Jack," she whispered. "I'll never see him again, will I? He's going to die. Nothing can save him, and it's all my fault, it's all my..."

"Hush that," exclaimed Jack, cupping her face tenderly in his hands, his eyes warm with love. Sally felt her eyelids droop, exhaustion threatening to drag her under, and for a moment allowed herself to lean into his strength, drawing courage from his love. Then she opened her eyes and flashed him a watery smile.

"I suppose we'd better get on with it," she murmured.

"That's my girl," Jack remarked approvingly, pressing a firm, though chaste, kiss to her forehead, before releasing her and stepping back. "Reuben will make it," he reassured her. "He's tough, it'll take more than a bullet to stop him."

Gratefully, Sally nodded at his comforting lie, went to the barrier face stilling with concern, and placing her palms on its invisible but tactile surface, she sensed the power coursing under her touch. Ancient energy which had existed since the dawn of time, and would continue to be, long after man had destroyed himself.

She sighed, bending until her forehead touched its warmth, waiting for the rejection, the nausea, the gut-wrenching push she'd experienced before.

It didn't come. Sally frowned, wondering, and gathering her thoughts attempted to send them into the Forest, to the power within.

Why? A moment... a silence... a sigh... a whisper... a reply.

You know why. Confused, Sally glanced at Jack, who frowned.

"What is it?" he whispered, overawed by the solemnity he perceived the occasion warranted.

"I'm not sure," murmured Sally, voice as hushed as his. She paused, a wild and unexpected thought darting through her mind. "Oh," she murmured. "That would explain it."

Without a word of warning to Jack, she grasped his hand and stepped lightly forward, pulling him smoothly through the barrier to emerge, shaken and surprised, on the other side.

Jack reeled back in shock, eyes wide and disbelieving. "We're through!" he gulped. "But… but that's impossible. How did you do it?"

"Who are allowed to enter the forest?" Sally asked.

"The Marchmant family and the forester," he replied, clearly baffled.

"And who else?" she pressed.

"No one else," Jack shrugged in exasperation.

"No," Sally shook her head. "Think Jack, who else is allowed in? How did we cross before?"

"Well, Reuben brought us through…"

"And how was he able to do that?" Sally insisted.

"Because, he's the offspring of the forester."

"Exactly," announced Sally, patiently.

Jack's eyes widened with comprehension, flew to her stomach, bitter jealousy twisting his features. Instinctively, Sally's hands rested protectively over the spark of new life she now knew she carried.

Jack turned away, thumped the bark of a nearby tree, struggling to compose himself. "He will marry you," he finally snapped, voice thick with barely concealed emotion.

"That's the plan," Sally agreed mildly, wrapping friendly arms about his stiff back, as he shook with the effort of coming to terms with the revelation. "I'm sorry," she softly whispered.

A deep sigh was ripped from the very core of Jack, as he returned her hug, resting his chin on her head, holding her so tightly Sally could hear his wildly beating heart.

"Oh Sal," he murmured at last. "I wish it could have been me."

"I know," she replied softly. "I'm sorry."

They held one another for what seemed an eternity but was probably only mere moments, before Jack pulled away and smiled, shrugging off his disappointment. And although she knew it was still there, would always be there buried deep within his soul, Sally understood he'd not let it fester and consume him.

Jack had faced the demon within. Faced it and won. It would never control him again.

"Hey," he said, touching her nose in an old, familiar gesture of affection. "Don't look so guilty, Uncle Jack's pretty good… I mean, that's something special, right?"

"Of course," she agreed, shaky with relief. "Not just Uncle, but Godfather Jack."

"Godfather huh?" Jack thought for a moment, grinned. "I'd like that." He looked around the Forest apprehensively. "What now, do you think?"

Sally shivered, gazing around at the silently looming trees, conscious of the quietness buzzing in her eardrums, and that not an animal stirred, not a leaf moved in the still, night air. The silence was total. Complete.

"I don't know," she murmured. "I don't know what to do... I suppose, we try to find Sylvie. Although what we can do to help her, I don't know."

"So, who is this Sylvie person then?" he asked.

"Oh, of course," Sally started in surprise. "I forgot, you don't know anything about her, do you?"

Jack considered. "No, although her name seems familiar. When that... thing... was inside me, I could feel its hatred of her. So much rage and jealousy and hatred, thick, all-consuming hatred. But I don't know why, or what Sylvie had done to warrant it."

"She's a woman who lived long ago," explained Sally. "Somehow, Reuben has been meeting her in the Forest for years, since they were children."

"Has he indeed?" drawled Jack dryly. "The sly old dog," he chuckled. At Sally's expression, he hurriedly composed his face into neutrality.

"They're friends," Sally replied primly. "Like you and me."

"Of course," agreed Jack blandly. "Like you and me. So go on, where does she fit in?"

"I'm not sure," mused Sally. "But somehow she's at the very heart of it. You saw, she turned into the White Hind. She is the White Hind. I believe she's the Lady of all the tales we were told. And did you hear what she called you?"

"Bridget," agreed Jack thoughtfully. "That name was in the tales too."

Sally nodded slowly, stiffening as a sound, unexpected and shocking, shattered the silence. As one they turned towards it, exchanging glances of fear when the noise grew louder, and both recognised it for what it was. The baying of hounds.

Molly Mole stoked up the fire, urgency apparent in every thrust of the long, iron poker and the trembling of her gnarled fingers, deep crevasses of concern etched sharply into her lined face. The fire blazing to her satisfaction, she swung the large, copper kettle back over it, paused, head cocked to one side considering, her whole demeanour stiff with the intensity of listening.

It came, the sound she'd been waiting for. A thud of feet, urgent pounding on the door. Quickly, she opened it, wordlessly gesturing towards the table already cleared, as John Blacksmith staggered into the room carrying Reuben, closely followed by Miss Violet. Her startled eyes flicked around the room, taking in at a glance the neat rows of bottles, the warmth of the roaring fire, the singing kettle, and the ancient crone who bent over Reuben.

"He's been shot," began John Blacksmith, and the old woman raised a hand.

"I know," she stated flatly. "I felt the disturbance and the Forest warned me. Now, you," she snapped at him, "expose the wound. Let's see what we have."

Mouth gaping with surprise, John Blacksmith hastened to obey. Gripping the blood drenched fabric in his strong hands, he ripped it apart, and Miss Violet's stomach heaved at the sight of the raw, mangled flesh beneath, her breath catching on a sob.

Surely, they were too late. No power on earth could save the young man who lay so still and pale.

Chapter Sixteen
~ Pages from the Past ~

Hurry, pounded Sally's heart. Hurry, screamed the blood thumping through her veins. Legs trembling, a stitch throbbing in her side, she ran with Jack, his hand clasping hers firmly, his longer stride dragging her almost off her feet, as they raced towards that awful, chill noise of hounds in pursuit of prey.

Further and deeper into the Forest they went, much deeper than they'd gone with Reuben, Sally's confused vision barely had time to notice ancient, imposing trees towering above them, and lush clearings of exquisite wild flowers, in full bloom despite the time of year. She noticed how warm it was, as if autumn had been left far behind at the Forest's perimeters.

Jack skidded to a halt, head snapping this way and that, trying to locate the sound which had abruptly, shockingly, been cut off in mid bay.

"W-where?" he pleaded, breathing ragged and noisy in the almost painful silence of the Forest.

"Why can't we hear them anymore?" Sally cried in surprise as daylight, gently pervasive, began to wash steadily through the trees, and above them a bird sang a trill tribute to the morning.

"It can't be dawn," Jack frowned. "Not yet. It can't be much beyond two."

Sally looked around wildly as light deepened into the rosy, lilac glow of a perfect summer sunrise, absentmindedly unbuttoning her coat, having unexpectedly become too warm.

"It's so hot," she began, as Jack gripped her arm and pulled her behind a tree, flinching when his hand, warm and strong, silenced her words.

Urgently, he nodded through the trees. A girl, petite and reed slender, her long silvery white hair lifting slightly in the gentle breeze, stepped from behind an oak. Hands clasped nervously at the fine wool of her long, green gown, her eyes scanned the Forest with an expectation that turned into joy, her whole face ablaze with happiness when the shrubs parted and a young man, sturdy and handsome, joined her beneath the tree.

"Sylvie," he said.

"You came." She turned her beautiful eyes up to his, allowing him to take her hand. In their hiding place, Jack and Sally exchanged glances of shocked confusion. It was Reuben. Yet at the same time, it wasn't...

The couple walked arm in arm, while at a distance Jack and Sally followed, seeing from their intimacy that a long acquaintance existed between the pair. Sally wondered if they were lovers, something telling her they were not. Finally, the man bid Sylvie farewell, his long legs carrying him easily through the trees and Sally saw his face as he passed by, mere inches away, apparently unable to see them. The easiness in his expression wasn't one of a man parting from his love, but one of friendship and a deep regard.

Sally then looked at Sylvie, knew by the intense yearning in her eyes, the sadness of her expression, that this woman loved him utterly, wholeheartedly. Looking at Jack, she saw that he'd seen and understood...

Again the light changed. It became stark and cold, their feet crunching through snow underfoot, and Sally shivered, pulling back on her coat, her breath chilling in her lungs. They heard voices raised in argument ahead, instinctively slowed, easing through the trees until a clearing was revealed. The quarrelling couple was Sylvie, and the man who looked so like Reuben as to be his twin. Both looked older, more mature, as if years had elapsed since their last meeting witnessed mere moments before.

"You cannot marry him, Sylvie."

"I must, I have to. We are betrothed, I am promised to him."

"I do not care. He is twenty years older than you."

"He is our Lord."

"You do not know him, you cannot love him."

"I must do my duty," Sylvie paused, touching a hand gently to his flushed, angry face. "I have no choice," she murmured.

"Come away with me," he pleaded desperately, clasping her hand. "I will protect you."

"I cannot," Sylvie shook her head in despair. "I cannot dishonour my family in such a way. Nor will I expose you and your family to the danger such a rash action would cause. I will marry him when he returns in the Spring, I must."

He gazed at her for a long, still moment, anguish clearly written on his features. In an instant, Sally realised he now loved her every bit as passionately and intensely as she loved him. The steadiness of his personality, and the duty ingrained within his soul, not letting him take that single step necessary to admit it, cast aside doubt, and claim her, damning all consequences.

For a second, he trembled on the brink. Sally held her breath, aware of the enormity of the moment, realising an entire future could be re-written and remoulded into a very different shape if he'd only... he could not. He turned on his heel, left, and Sylvie sank onto the Forest floor.

Sally turned away, tender heart aching to hear Sylvie's pitiful sobs as she wept for love denied, love lost, love never even given a chance to begin. Around them, the Forest changed again...

A woman entered the clearing; a dark elderly woman, eyes flashing with a cunning and intelligence which belied her humble appearance. Sally inhaled sharply. It was Molly Mole. Not as she'd last seen her, gnarled and decrepit, but strong and powerful.

Molly's eyes flickered at Sally's cry, and for a moment Sally thought she could see them, but the old woman only frowned, eyes scanning the undergrowth without resting on them. Eventually she shrugged, seeming to dismiss the notion from her mind, turning to face the young, dark girl who followed; a girl who appeared familiar, Sally puzzled at the thought as the girl flounced after Molly, a sulky pout marring her petulant beauty.

"Oh, do stop sulking, Bridget," snapped Molly. Sally and Jack's eyes flew, wide and shocked, to each other. So this was the Bridget of the stories. The one who'd committed an act so heinous, so vile, she'd been condemned to eternal malevolence within the Forest, crouching at its heart like an evil, black widow spider.

"I have already told you," continued Molly fervently, "I do not know any dark arts. I am wise enough to leave it well enough alone, it can only ever end in misery and destruction. So cease your pestering child. My mind is quite made up. Should you wish me to instruct you in the various medicinal uses of herbs and the suchlike, now that, I am quite agreeable to. Nothing else."

"But, mother," the girl's voice was whiney with disappointment. Recognition stabbed at Sally, and she glanced at Jack. Nancy, he mouthed silently, and she nodded in agreement.

"Don't you, 'but mother', me," snapped Molly waspishly. "I am returning to the Hall to supervise my Lady's supper. You gather the flowers she desires, and make sure you get enough. I expect to see her chamber fair blooming."

Bridget shrugged, pulled a face at her mother's retreating back, and half-heartedly began yanking flowers up from the ground, head snapping up at the sound of approaching voices. She stepped nimbly behind a tree, concealing herself as a young couple burst into the clearing.

Again, Sally felt herself recoil as they looked upon themselves. Only again, not quite. There was something about the cast of their faces, the way they moved, which was so alike, but at the same time so very different, from the Jack and Sally who watched in shocked confusion.

"Sunniva!" The young man who looked like Jack caught up with the laughing, glowing version of Sally, who turned to face him, panting from exertion, eyes sparkling in merriment as he tenderly clasped her by the shoulder, gently shaking her in tolerant exasperation.

"Well this is a merry dance you have led me, my lady," he cried. She laughed her happiness at being with him, and something shifted in Sally's heart, a dim, far away memory of that love.

"And if I did?" Sunniva retorted. "It was a dance you were only too happy to follow."

"Tis true," he murmured in reply. Stepping closer, he crushed her to his chest, engulfing her in a kiss of such passionate intensity, Sally felt her face flame with embarrassment, unable to look at Jack.

She watched as the girl, herself, Sunniva, wrapped her arms fiercely around the young man with Jack's face and returned his kiss, sunlight dappling through the trees to bathe the young lovers with gently warming caresses as around them the Forest sighed its approval.

The young man groaned with pleasure, hands moving lightly over the laces at the front of the young girl's gown. She pulled away, lips swollen from his kisses, face flushed, a dazed, blinded look in her love stormed eyes. Contritely, he held his hands wide, and she dimpled her displeasure.

"Sunniva," he began, tone pleading.

"No," resolutely she shook her head. "I've told you, not until we're wed..."

"It wants but three weeks to our wedding day." Beside her, Sally felt Jack's shocked intake of breath.

"I know, and I will come to you a maid," Sunniva insisted. The young man's face softened. Stepping forward, he placed a chaste kiss on her freckled, upturned nose.

"Do you know how much I love you?" he murmured.

Her expression softly serious, Sunniva gently lifted a hand to his face, her touch tender and loving.

"If it is only half as much as I love you, then I indeed count myself blessed," she replied.

Again the lovers kissed, their embrace strong and unbreakable, Sally blinking back tears as they wandered away into the trees, arms around one another's others waist, heads bent in softly whispered confidences.

The undergrowth rustled as Molly Mole's petulant, spiteful daughter stepped from the bushes, her expression set with chilly malevolence, and Sally felt a shiver of unease move through her body, wishing for some way to warn the young couple to take care.

Jack pulled her away into the trees, his flushed face and gleaming eyes, telling Sally the scene had affected him as much, if not more, than it had her.

"We were married," he murmured, voice hoarse with joyous disbelief. "You saw, Sal. We were in love. You loved me. We were in love."

"No," she cried, gripping his arm in her intense desire to convince. "They were, not us, them... This all took place hundreds of years ago, Jack, it's not us. They're not us, whoever they may look like. She is not me and he is not you."

"I know," he bit his lip. "I know Sal, it's just…"

"What's happening?" she cried. "Why are we being shown this? How does seeing all this help us to help Sylvie?"

"Perhaps we're being shown the truth in order to understand," Jack replied soberly. "Maybe, only by knowing what happened, really happened, will we be able to stop all this."

"Maybe," agreed Sally. Around them, the light in the Forest abruptly shifted and changed and they looked up in expectation, wondering what new moment from the past they were about to witness…

The trees parted and Sylvie appeared, face set and pale, passing by them so closely the hem of her cloak swept over Sally's foot. She felt an icy chill as her skin passed through the fabric as if it were not there.

Wringing her hands in anguish, Sylvie turned at the sound of pursuit, body relaxing as Molly Mole pushed through the trees, face drawn tightly with anxious concern, arms held. Sylvie gave a strangled sob, and rushed into her embrace where she cried bitter tears of misery. Molly petted and shushed her, rocking her in a fond embrace, as though Sylvie were a mere child, and she her doting mother.

"There, there, my little lambkin," she murmured. "It won't be so bad, you'll see. Old Molly's got something for you, something to make it all better."

"What… what do you mean?" sniffed Sylvie, holding a beautifully embroidered handkerchief to her eyes. "How can it possibly be made better? I am to be married tonight to a man twice my age. A man I do not know, cannot ever love. And my heart…"

"Hush," cautioned Molly, glanced fearfully around the silent Forest. "Do not give voice to matters which I must not be aware of. Oh, my child," she continued, seeing Sylvie's crestfallen features. "Did you think I did not know? I have been your nurse and closest companion since your dear father placed you in my arms, still bloody from your poor little dead mother's womb. I took you to my heart as his tears anointed you. Trembling he bade me care for you, be your mother, and haven't I always done that? Loved and cared for my little lambkin?"

"But what shall I do?" cried Sylvie in heartfelt anguish. "How shall I bear it?"

"With the aid of this," replied Molly. She took from under her cloak a small corked bottle which Sylvie gazed at curiously.

"What is it?" she asked.

"This be a special potion I have brewed for you," Molly smiled knowingly. "A potion that'll cause its drinker to fall in love so passionately, they'll be lost to any other but the object of their adoration. Now," she went on, as Sylvie opened her mouth in shocked protest.

"How you use it is up to you. Give two drops of the potion to your lord and not take any yourself, and then he will be your loyal and devoted slave and will do whatsoever you bid. Or, take two drops yourself and become so enamoured with your new lord, your eyes will be blind to all his flaws and faults so intensely will you love. Or, and this is what I suggest, you both take of the potion. Then the love and passion will be mutual, and you will be assured of a happy life as you will love and in turn be loved with a desperate intensity."

"But Molly," Sylvie began in shocked dismay, "I cannot drug my lord, you surely cannot expect me to do such a thing? Why, it would not be right, it..."

"And where's the hurt in it?" demanded Molly almost peevishly. "It does no man any harm to be in love with his wife, for then he is more inclined to treat her gently. As for you, my lambkin, will it not be a blessing to surrender your maidenhood to your lord willingly and with loving eagerness?"

"I... I do not know, I suppose..." stammered Sylvie, a frown creasing the milky white skin of her brow. "It seems somehow dishonest."

"Nonsense," insisted Molly, as she pressed the phial into Sylvie's hand, closing her unwilling fingers tightly around its smooth green surface. "I will leave you to think on it," she said, rising creakily to her feet.

"But remember, no more than two drops. It be powerful stuff, I do not care to think what any more would do to a body. Now, I must be off. There's aplenty to do before the wedding this evening. Do not tarry too long," she cautioned. "It will soon be time to prepare you to be married. Should you decide to take the potion, then pour it into the wedding cup from which none but you and your lord will drink. I promise you, my child, by the time you reach the wedding chamber, it will be your heart's desire you will be fulfilling."

She hobbled away amongst the trees, and Sylvie sank upon a fallen tree, gazing in trepidation at the potion clasped in her slim white fingers. Time went, and still Sylvie mused.

"It would be dishonest and cowardly," she declared aloud, rising to her feet, voice firm with conviction. "And it would feel a true betrayal of my unspoken love. If I must marry from duty to my family and my future lord, then I will perform that duty as honourably and honestly as I can. Not with magic and trickery."

Almost scornfully she tossed the bottle into the undergrowth, stalking from the clearing with such a bearing of regal authority, Sally felt a lump rise in her throat, and almost applauded, admiring beyond words the other girl's courage and integrity.

Moments passed... The bushes parted, revealing Bridget's cunning, foxy face, as she peered suspiciously around the clearing, expression alive with malicious glee. Carefully, she knelt and felt amongst the undergrowth where Sylvie had thrown the bottle, body tensing with excitement as she held aloft the intact phial.

Sally felt her unease grow as pure evil flared in the girl's face. She tucked the phial into her bodice and raced away into the trees, a burst of breathless, delighted laughter drifting back to them, before being abruptly cut off, as once again, time shifted, and they found themselves in another place and another time...

A man, tall, regal and handsome, although slightly grizzled as from the ravages of war, stepped lightly through the trees, pausing to offer his hand to aid Sylvie. Hair flowing silkily over her shoulders, she smiled her gratitude at his aid, lifting her foot nimbly over the half-concealed root buried in the undergrowth.

Sally stared curiously at the man, instinctively flinching as his gaze, piercing in its blue intensity, swept unseeingly over them. She guessed from his face, and the colour of his eyes, that he was a Marchmant; the ancestral Lord who'd been Sylvie's husband.

Behind the noble couple paced Sunniva and her betrothed, a sedate distance between them. Sally saw their eyes meet and mingle, the secret, private message communicated in the way only lovers can, and the guilty start they gave as their Lord addressed them.

"Here will be a fine spot," he ordered. The young man who looked like Jack hastened forward, placing a richly woven cloth carefully on the ground, and Sunniva knelt, pulling out a flagon of wine and packages of what Sally assumed to contain food, from the rush basket she held over one arm. Tenderly, reverently, the lord helped Sylvie to sit, then glanced up at their waiting servants.

"You may leave us now," he ordered. "Come back in an hour."

"Yes, my Lord," they chorused, bowing and curtseying, left the clearing, hands softly reaching for one another as Sylvie and her lord exchanged indulgent glances.

"Ah, to be so young and so in love," sighed the Lord.

"You are not old, my lord," Sylvie replied softly, the kindly look she gave her husband implying her marriage was not the torture she'd feared it would be.

"It pleases me you do not find me so," he murmured, tenderly stroking a long tress of shimmering, silvery hair from her face. "Still, I would wish to be younger in years and firmer of body, to please my new wife who so delights me."

"Your body is firm enough, my Lord," assured Sylvie. She realised the double meaning in her words, face flaming, as her husband threw back his head, his loud roar of delighted laughter echoing through the trees.

"I thank you for the compliment, my lady," he finally replied, expression oddly wistful as he stared after the young couple. "I believe they wed tomorrow?" he asked, and Sylvie nodded.

"Yes, my Lord, they do, and I must confess I do not know whom to be the more nervous, my maid or your man-at-arms. I am pleased Sunniva has found such a true and steady mate, for she is a dear girl whom I love very much."

"Then I shall order a cask of finest ale to celebrate the occasion," decided the Lord abruptly.

"My Lord, that is so generous" Sylvie beamed with pleasure. "I know Sunniva will be honoured."

"And whilst we drink to their long life and happiness, I shall drink a private toast to my new bride of two weeks, whom I find to be all I could ever desire." He raised Sylvie's hand to his mouth, his eyes never leaving her beautiful blushing face. As he reached for her, the Forest spun dizzily around them...

Once again, Sally felt time slip. She saw the same clearing, but deserted this time, remains of the alfresco meal scattered over the cloth. She saw Sunniva kneeling, hastily loading it back into the basket, whilst her young man kissed the back of her neck and tickled her cheek with a feather.

"You are not helping," she cried, half laughing, half annoyed, as she pushed him away. He sidled closer, trying to pull her into his arms.

"Tomorrow, my love," he murmured, and Sunniva melted into his embrace, face blissfully happy. "Only think, by this time tomorrow you and I shall be wed. Then I will be your lord and master and you shall have to do as I command you."

"Oh, is that right?" mocked Sunniva. "And what would you command me do?"

"Love me," he replied earnestly. "Promise to love me and only me forever."

"Why, that is the easiest command in the world to follow," she whispered, face suddenly serious. Gently, he eased her down onto the rug, his mouth searching greedily for hers, hands roaming her body as the lovers entwined, their breathing when their mouths finally separated, hoarse and ragged with desire.

"Oh, my Sunniva, my sunny girl. Let me love you, here, now," he begged, but Sunniva pulled away.

"One more day, my love," she promised. "One more day. Then I will come to you and in our own marriage bed I shall be a maid no longer. Instead, I shall be a wife, your wife, and it will be all I shall ever want for the rest of my life, my lord," she added, with a dimpled smile to soften the sting of rejection.

"You are a hard mistress," grumbled her betrothed, but rose to his feet, helping her up with good grace. "Though I do love you to distraction," he continued. "And, to prove it, I will clear this up and allow you to go, for I know your mistress will have need of your assistance."

"Best of lovers," she cried, pressing a quick, firm kiss to his mouth, before gathering up her skirts and hurrying from the clearing. Sighing, the young man busied himself with packing all neatly into the basket, picking up the flagon and shaking it.

"A pity to waste it," he murmured, and tipped the dregs of ruby red wine into a tumbler, raising it to his lips. He paused, head cocked in enquiry as a sound, as if of a stone striking a tree trunk, rang through the still air. Putting the tumbler down, he moved to the edge of the clearing and peered into the undergrowth.

"Is anyone there?" he asked. "Sunniva, is that you?" He listened intently, and Sally's attention was drawn by Jack, back to the tumbler as a hand appeared from behind the tree, a slim white hand which clasped the phial of love potion. The bottle was carefully tipped, half its contents swirled into the wine and the hand slyly vanished once more into hiding.

The young man strode back to the picnic. With a rising sense of panic, Sally realised what was about to happen. "No," she cried, jumping forward. "Don't drink it." He walked straight by, his gaze passing through her as if she was as insubstantial as air.

"Don't!" yelled Jack, stepping into the pathway of the man who wore his face, but he didn't falter. To Sally's disbelief, he walked straight through Jack, who cried out and clutched his chest, skin turned to goose-flesh. The young man stopped and shivered, a frown on his handsome face, as he peered curiously over his shoulder.

"Strange," he muttered, reaching for the tumbler. Sally and Jack clasped hands in helpless horror as he raised it to his lips and drained it dry, the tumbler falling from suddenly nerveless fingers. He staggered, clutching at the trunk of a tree for support.

"What ails me…?" he panted, wiping a hand over a face suddenly ashen, a brow suddenly clammy.

The undergrowth parted and there she stood, dark eyes watching, malicious with amusement and expectation. He straightened, gazing at her, the madness of obsession filling his eyes as he reached for her. The Forest tilted around them and they felt its displeasure. The last thing Sally saw was the sly malevolence in the girl's eyes, as she raised her mouth to the passionate kiss of Sunniva's betrothed…

They blinked, and were again somewhere, sometime else. The Forest was silent and still, except for the sound of bitter, heartbroken sobbing. They wandered, still holding hands, shaken by the events they'd witnessed. Rounding a vast oak tree, they found curled up at its roots, a young woman, body heaving with the depths of her despair. It was Sunniva.

Sally felt a lump rise in her throat as she guessed what must have happened, understanding this sunny, happy child, so much in love, so loved in return, had been disappointed in the most cruelly vile way. Desperately she reached for her, wanting to comfort, but her hand passed straight through the girl's shoulder.

With a little cry of despair, she turned to Jack, whose pale set face reflected the power of his own emotions, then heard another's approach through the Forest.

It was he who looked like Reuben. At the sight of Sunniva and her abject misery, he stopped, the whistle faltering on his lips, compassionate understanding on his face. He quietly knelt, handing her a square of linen, which Sunniva gratefully took and wiped at a face ravaged with anguish.

"I... I suppose you know," she finally murmured.

"Aye," he admitted, "I heard..."

"Today," she sobbed, tears flowing afresh. "Today was meant to be our wedding day, looked forward to for so long. I love him so much and I thought he loved me. Then today, in front of all those people... in front of my family, the Lord and my lady, he told me he loved another. He loves her!" Sunniva spat the word out in a passionate frenzy, her normally placid face twisting into lines of hatred.

"Tis almost beyond belief," he murmured. "I know he loved you, only you. I cannot believe him so lost to reason. I am sure you will find it all some mistake, some jest gone seriously wrong perhaps..."

"No, no!" she interrupted him almost violently, "He has married her. That is no jest. Even if it were, there is no power on earth or beyond would make me trust him now! He is lost to me. I shall never forgive him. Never! No, not if I live for a thousand years more, and he came to me on his knees and begged me to love him. I swear on my eternal soul, I will never trust him again!"

A cold sweat drenched Sally at the young girl's impassioned words, the trees slipped in and out of focus, and she clutched at Jack's hand to steady herself. Never love him again! Never trust him again!

The words hammered at her brain in an incessant, pounding rhythm, Sally finally understanding what had prevented her from returning Jack's love. The sting of utter betrayal which had echoed down the centuries stopping her heart from trusting, believing in him and his avowed passion for her.

"Sunniva," gently the young forester helped her to her feet and led her to a fallen tree trunk, settling her carefully as if she were made of glass. "Such a pretty, old-fashioned name," he mused. "How came you by it?"

"My family have always dwelt on the downs," she replied, a ghost of a smile whispering through tears. "We love the sun and the wide-open spaces. It has long been tradition that daughters within my family bear the name Sunniva, which means child of the sun."

"These are dark times for us, child of the sun," he said seating himself beside her, and taking one small trembling hand into his large, work roughened grasp.

"Yes," she agreed, bottom lip trembling.

For a while they sat in companionable silence.

"What will you do now?" he finally asked.

"I do not know," Sunniva shrugged in despair. "I was supposed to be a wife now. My lord and lady had been so kind to us, given us a set of rooms which were to be ours… But, she is to live there now, all the pretty things I had made for them will go to nought." She paused, eyes flashing, moving beyond misery into anger.

"He has made such a fool of me," she snapped.

"Nay," denied the forester, shaking his head vehemently. "He has made a fool of himself. Will you go back to your family, or continue to live in the castle?"

"I cannot go back to my family," stated Sunniva flatly. "Not now, I simply cannot. Besides, I could not leave my lady. Since she first came to our land from so far away across the sea, I have been her maid. She has become very dear to me. Her kindly ways and gentleness make her a very easy lady to love."

"Aye, they do," remarked the forester flatly. Sunniva studied him in silent sympathy, before laying a hand gently on his arm.

"You are right," she whispered. "These are dark times for us. As for what I should do next, I confess to be at a loss. I refuse to go back to my family as if I am the one in disgrace. If I continue to dwell within the castle, then I must see them every day, and have it continually pressed upon me what has occurred."

"There is another choice," he began hesitantly.

"What other choice?" She looked at him curiously.

"You could marry me." Sunniva's mouth gaped, eyes rounding at his statement and he hurried on, words tumbling over themselves in his zeal to convince her of their veracity. "Think on it," he urged. "I have my own cottage. 'Tis small, but you could do with it what you like and be mistress of your own home. Tis close enough to the castle you could still attend your lady, yet far enough away to be private. As for me? Well, I know I am far from what could be considered perfect husband material, but, I would do my best, and I promise would never treat you with anything other than the utmost respect and courtesy."

Sunniva gazed at him in silence. Mortified, his honest open face flushed with discomfort and his eyes dropped to his clumsy boots. Sunniva's expression softened, once again laying a hand gently on his arm.

"I would like children," she murmured.

"I would like that too," he looked at her with relief. "A family," he paused, a smile spreading slowly across his face. "Yes," he said. "That would please me very much." They grinned at one another, then he slipped onto one knee and took her hand.

"Sunniva," he began, face solemn. "Will you marry me?"

"Yes," she agreed instantly. "I will. Thank you, thank you for restoring my dignity."

Sally wiped at tears she found on her cheek, risking a glance at Jack who turned to her, face thunderstruck with shock.

"I never stood a chance," he muttered. "I never stood a bloody chance. It was always going to be Reuben, every time…" Not knowing what to say, Sally bent her head to his shoulder…

Again, the Forest twisted sickeningly. The light sharpened. The air chilled, and Sally wondered what new coil in this tale of dark deeds and denied love was about to be revealed. Bridget stalked angrily into the clearing, belly swollen with hugely advanced pregnancy, her husband trailing miserably after like a whipped puppy dog.

"But, my love, be reasonable…" he whined.

"Be reasonable?" angrily she turned on him. "How am I supposed to bear it? She has a whole cottage to herself which our lady has insisted on completely re-fitting for her. Whilst I must live like some kind of animal cooped up in those poky rooms. It has been a year since our wedding, still no one can bring themselves to say a civil word to me. They all blame me, I know they do, yet if you recall, it was you who begged me to marry you, who threatened to throw yourself onto your sword if I did not become your wife."

"Yes," he interrupted eagerly. "I did, and I would, oh my love." He threw himself at her feet, clutching with hungry, desperate hands at her gown.

Bridget's lip curled into an unattractive sneer and she gazed at him with open contempt. "Oh, get up," she ordered scornfully. "You disgust me." She shook him free from her skirts, striding away into the trees, her husband scrambling hurriedly to his feet and hurtling after her…

The light changed, heaps of coppery leaves drifted… Bridget immediately re-entered the clearing from the other side, her stomach flat and her waist trim.

"Bridget!"

She paused, eyes rolling heavenwards as Molly struggled into the clearing behind her, a fretful, dark eyed babe on each hip. "Precisely where do you think you're going to missy?" demanded her mother.

"Out for some air," Bridget retorted with barely concealed exasperation. "I cannot bear to be stuck indoors with those mewling brats a minute longer."

"Those mewling brats, as you call them, are your children," Molly snapped peevishly. "And as your children are your responsibility, not mine, certainly not any of the other maids you foist them onto."

"Well, go and find that useless husband of mine," ordered Bridget airily. "They're his spawn; let him take care of them."

"He has accompanied our Lord on a hunt, as well you know," replied Molly. "I am uncomfortable being so long gone from our lady, what with her nearing her time and being so out of sorts. I worry about her."

"Yes, far more than you do your own daughter," snarled Bridget.

"That is not true, and you know it," stated Molly evenly. "My lady is unwell. She is not strong like you, and this pregnancy has been hard on her. I promised my Lord I would care for her, and that is what I intend to do. So, come back to the castle and look after your own children, I have not the time to do so."

"It is so unfair," sulked Bridget. "Just because she is a lady and has the love of a lord, she does not have to lift a finger to do anything. When her brat is born, none will think any the less of her for having a nursemaid. Why if I were a lady…"

She stopped, turned abruptly away, gazing straight through Sally and Jack, a look, breathtaking in its cunning malevolence, passing across her features. Sally groped for Jack's hand, suddenly afraid.

"You are absolutely right, mother," she murmured, turning back to her mother, eyes downcast, her expression wiped clean of any emotion. "I will take the children back to the castle and feed them. Then, maybe our lady would like me to accompany her on a gentle walk to take the air. I know she misses Sunniva now she too approaches her time. Perhaps she would care for some company."

"Perhaps," agreed her mother, casting a shrewd glance at her daughter. "What new game are you about now?" she demanded.

"Nothing," Bridget turned an affronted gaze upon her. "I have merely seen the error of my ways."

"Humph," grunted her mother sourly. "That I would like to see, but by all means take the twins, they are hungry and need changing, and maybe my lady would be appreciative of some company." She stomped from the clearing, followed by Bridget, a tiny triumphant smile playing about her mouth.

"We have to stop her," Sally turned to Jack in despair, "She's going to do something awful, I know it."

"Yes," agreed Jack, "but what can we do, Sal? They can't see or hear us. We can't touch anything in their time. So what can we do?"

"I don't know," Sally cried in anguish, "but we have to try. That awful woman. How much more misery is she going to cause?" Jack shook his head, as the Forest moved familiarly around them…

Sunniva slowly and carefully entered the clearing carrying a basket half full of hazelnuts, vastly extended belly impeding her progress, as she picked a handful of juicy blackberries, eating them with pleasure. Sensing movement at the edge of the clearing, she looked up, expression darkening as her former lover, Bridget's husband, entered, handsome mouth twisting into a sneer when he saw her.

"Well, well," he began. "What do we have here? The forester's little wife. How quaint and thrifty, gathering the fruits of the forest. At least my wife does not soil her hands performing such lowly tasks."

"A task is only lowly if you believe it to be so," replied Sunniva, her tone placid. Sally sensed a new contentment, a new maturity about the other girl, as if a year of marriage and impending motherhood had tamed the savage disappointment, leaving Sunniva calmer, more accepting.

"My husband will enjoy the nuts I have gathered, is appreciative of the pies and preserves I make from the berries. In his pleasure, will I find happiness, thus the task is elevated from lowly to joyful."

"What a comfort you must be to your husband. How thankful he must be for my cast offs," he sneered sarcastically. "For how else would a slow-witted woodsman ever have achieved such a prize as you?"

"Do not speak of my husband in that way." Sunniva snapped, eyes blazing.

"I wonder, Sunniva. Do you lie beside him at night and think on what you lost? Do you compare that lumbering oaf you married to me? Do you think of what might have been?"

"Indeed, I do," she replied steadily, and his brows rose in surprised satisfaction. "I often think on it," she continued quietly, "and reflect on what a lucky escape I had. And when I compare us to you and your wife," her voice steeled on the last word, finishing wryly, "I think I made the better bargain."

She smiled a thin, mirthless smile of triumph, as he spluttered with outrage, for once speechless, aware that her calm, reasonable reply had made his outburst appear small and petty. For a second he glared at her, then, face tight with fury, turned on his heel and left.

Sunniva sighed, her face sad, and ate more berries, rubbing with an absent-minded frown at her stomach, her contemplative expression lightening into a smile when her husband appeared.

"There you are," he exclaimed. "I worried when you were not home. You should not wander so far in your condition."

"I am well and healthy," she protested, but Sally knew her husband's loving concern pleased her. "Not like my lady…" her face fell, and she seemed barely aware of her husband taking the basket, gently slipping a hand under her arm.

"Come," he said. "Let me take you home." She nodded and stopped, a strange look gripping her face, hands flying in wild confusion to her stomach, as she cried aloud.

"What is it?" cried her husband, and she turned eyes huge with fear onto him, wordlessly holding out her skirts. Sally saw the spreading stain, knew Sunniva's waters had broken and she was going into labour.

"Oh my," drawled her husband wryly. "Never let it be said, my pet, you did not have a remarkable sense of timing. Come, best we take you home." He swept her up into his strong, confident grasp.

Trustingly, she placed her arms about his neck, laying her cheek against his with a sigh. "I did make the better bargain," she murmured.

He looked at her in confusion. "I mean," she continued slowly, "if I had the chance to choose again, I would always choose you. A thousand times over, it would always be you. This past year has been a time of great contentment for me. I did not feel my heart could ever learn to trust or love again but I was wrong. It could. It does."

"What... what are you saying, Sunniva?" he asked. Slowly, she ran her fingers through his hair, her eyes never leaving his, her expression solemn, and Sally thought how small she appeared, despite her stomach, clasped in her strong and handsome husband's arms.

"I am saying I love you," she finally whispered.

Sally heard the answering echo in her own heart, the sense of absolute trust she felt in Reuben's arms, the knowledge he would never hurt her. That loving Reuben was the right path, the safe path to take.

"Oh, Sunniva," he breathed. Their lips met in a tender, passionate kiss, Sunniva groaning with joy and pain as a contraction gripped. He laughed happily, eyes alight with a promise to be fulfilled later.

"Come, my wife," he cried. "Let me take you home and get this baby birthed."

"I can see why," Jack muttered bitterly beside her. "I know why. I can even understand why. But it's so bloody unfair, Sal."

"I know," she murmured, as the Forest shifted and changed around them...

The fallen leaves remained. It was still autumn though the shadows were longer, the air chillier. Instinctively Sally knew it was late afternoon, but whether it was late afternoon on the same October day was anyone's guess.

A hunting party moved through the Forest, and Sally flinched in fear from the slobbering jaws of the great hounds held tightly on the leads of burly-armed men. Hackles raised, the dogs sniffed around their feet and stared through them, low savage snarls rumbling deep within their throats, until, confused, the men hauled them away with angry expletives.

"What ails the hounds?" cried the Lord.

"I know not, my Lord," the head huntsman shook his head. "They act as if something were there as you can see, but if there is, it is merely some will-o'-the-wisp."

"Take them further in," commanded the Lord. "Perhaps they will pick up some other trail and lead us to better sport than shadows and spectres."

"Yes, my Lord." To Sally and Jack's vast relief, the dogs were pulled back, whimpering and snapping their annoyed reluctance.

"Drink, my Lord," murmured Bridget silkily, appearing unobtrusively at his elbow, dark eyes deep with fathomless expectation as she handed the lord a goblet of wine. He tossed it back in one swallow before Sally and Jack could even think of attempting to stop him.

Chapter Seventeen
~ Innocent Blood ~

Horrified, they saw him stagger, sweat pooling on his brow, eyes glazing over, as Bridget watched, lips twitching into a smile. He straightened, a familiar look of obsessive desire leaping hotly into his eyes. He advanced on her, willingly following as she led him away amongst the trees, stumbling over roots, gaze blindly fixed upon her trim body until, at last, she let him catch her. He grabbed her, hands roaming desperately over her breasts, breathing hoarse and noisy in the suddenly still Forest.

Angrily, he ripped at her laces, exposing lush, creamy breasts, ripe from childbirth, greedily suckling at them. Bridget's head tipped back, her triumphant laugh catching at the frigid air, momentarily succumbing, before pulling away, ignoring his moan of despair as she covered herself.

"My Lord," she chided, tone one of utter teasing. "We cannot. I am a married woman. My husband is one of your men-at-arms. I am not free to be your lover," her fingers played with the severed laces, teasing him with a tantalising glimpse of the heaving flesh beneath.

"And if you were free?" he growled, hands rough on her arms, biting savagely at her neck.

"Why then, my Lord..." She pulled his ear to her lips, and whispered something which had his head snapping back and his eyes widening, Sally and Jack stared at each other in dismay as the Forest once again moved...

The Lord strode into a clearing where Bridget's husband stood alone. "My Lord," the young man with Jack's face began, "we have been looking for you. The hounds have picked up a new scent."

"Tell me," ordered his Lord abruptly. "Your wife, how deep is your affection for her? Could you ever conceive of parting from her?"

"Parting from her?" exclaimed the young man, shocked. "Why no, my Lord, never. Not under any circumstances. She is like a fever in my blood, a delirium in my soul. She has possessed me. Nothing would induce me to let her go."

"As I feared," stated the Lord bluntly, drawing his sword and running it through the young man's stomach.

Screaming in horror, Sally started forward, barely noticing that Jack was no longer by her side. Her attention solely on the awfulness taking place in front of her eyes, watching Jack, her Jack, being murdered.

Bridget's husband cried out in surprised pain and clasped his Lord's arms, blood welling from his mouth, staring at his killer with shocked eyes.

"Why?" he managed to gasp. His Lord held him almost tenderly, slid the sword from his body and eased him to the ground.

"Because now she has possessed me, I would commit any deed, no matter how foul, to have her."

He wiped his sword on a nearby pile of leaves and rose, thrusting it back into its hilt, turning eagerly as Bridget stepped lightly into the clearing, ignoring the still twitching body of her husband.

"My lady," growled the Lord as he strode to her, forcefully grasping her. For one appalling moment, Sally thought he intended to take her there and then, by the body of her murdered husband.

"Now you are free," he growled, hands fumbling eagerly at her skirts.

"Yes, my Lord, I am," she agreed, stepping easily away from his grasp.

"You promised," he cried, face darkening with angry frustration.

"I am free, my Lord, tis true," she murmured smoothly. "But, you are not."

"Bitch!" he cried, "Whore! I have killed your husband for you! What more do you want?"

"I want to be your wife," she replied coolly, placing a coldly calculating hand on his groin. "Give me that," she hissed, "and I will give you everything."

He hesitated, and Sally felt a wild hope he would refuse, but madness gleamed in his eyes and he nodded. "It shall be done," he vowed.

Bridget glowed with triumph, and led her frantic lover from the clearing.

Left alone, Sally knelt beside the body of the man who bore Jack's face, helplessly clasped his hand, tears starting into her eyes. His fluttered open, focusing on her face.

"Sunniva?" he murmured, and Sally realised he could see her, the maniacal glint gone, his gaze steady and lucid. It seemed this close to death, the potion was no longer effective.

"Sunniva?" he asked again.

Sally nodded, tasting the salt of her sorrow. "Yes," she said. "It's me, I'm here."

"My sunny girl," he mumbled. "I'm so sorry, I do not know… It is like I have been under a spell. How can you ever forgive what I did to you? Although, I know not why I did it. I do not love Bridget. I have never loved anyone but you."

"I know," she murmured reassuringly, wiping at the blood on his lips with the sleeve of her coat. "She drugged you with a love potion. It wasn't your fault. You couldn't help it. It was all Bridget's fault."

"Oh Sunniva," the name drawn out on a long breath of pain. "My darling girl, your forgiveness is all I crave now…"

"You have it," Sally cried, hot tears splashing onto his face.

"Love you," he murmured brokenly, and Sally pressed a kiss to his cold cheek.

"I love you too," she sobbed, saw by the stillness in his eyes he was gone, and she didn't know whether he'd heard. At the thought of him going alone into the darkness, she broke down and wept, for he was so like Jack… so like Jack.

"Sally?" Jack, her Jack, was there, arms warm and strong as he gently lifted her off the body. She buried herself in him, sobbing wildly. Jack stared at the body of himself, breath catching at the sight of the sword wound and the blood, so much blood, staining the Forest floor.

All around the Forest groaned in rage at the violation of its domain. Hastily, Jack helped Sally scramble to her feet, holding her tightly as the trees swirled and the wind howled out its wrath.

"What happened?" he shouted above the roar.

"The Lord murdered you," Sally cried, too tired and confused to understand her words. "He killed you on her orders, and now goes to kill Sylvie so he can marry Bridget. We have to stop them, Jack."

"How?" he yelled in despair, "How?"

"I don't know," she sobbed, as the Forest fumed and stormed. The floor heaved beneath their feet, and above them thunder rumbled. It was angry, Sally thought, angry at what had happened...

Reality bent around them. Sylvie was there, pale and ill, stomach protruding obscenely as she clutched at a tree for support, turning gratefully to Molly who rushed upon her, taking her by the arm.

"You should not be here, my lady," she chided.

"What's happening?" Sylvie raised terrified eyes as a fork of lightning cracked the sky, and thunder banged on the roof of the world.

"Something has upset the Forest," Molly shook her head. "Some dark, unnatural deed has disturbed the balance of things and now the Forest makes known its disapproval."

"You speak as if it were alive," commented Sylvie, her tone fearful.

"Why, and so it is, my lady," replied Molly. "The Forest is an ancient and wise power. It has existed since the dawn of time, guiding and controlling the lives of those within its domain. Indeed, it was one of the reasons I urged your father to accept the Lord's offer, because he is Lord of the Forest, this Forest, and I believed nothing but good would come of such an association. But now, we must away home, the storm is increasing, and you should not be out in your condition."

Sylvie nodded, allowing Molly to lead her to the edge of the clearing, crying out in abrupt fear as a sudden crack of lightning lit up the dark, unsmiling figure of her Lord.

Relieved, she held out her hand. "My Lord, are you come to escort me home?"

"Nay, my lady," he replied, eyes blank discs in his still, pale face. "I have come to dispatch you to the afterlife." He drew his sword, and Sylvie staggered back, a shocked cry erupting from her lips.

"What madness is this?" yelled Molly, desperately pulling Sylvie away.

"No madness," he said, advancing remorselessly upon them, his blade flashing in the gloom. "You stand between me and my happiness with another, my lady," he informed her with shocking calm. "So now, you must die."

"Desist!" ordered Molly, flinging a handful of dust from her pocket into his eyes, muttering twisted words of ancient power under her breath. The Lord froze, expression twitching with displeasure as he found himself unable to move.

"Release me, you foul hag!" he screamed, the veins in his temple standing proud as he struggled against his invisible bounds.

"My Lord," sobbed Sylvie, clutching at her stomach as Molly tried to pull her back. "What have I done to deserve such treatment? How can you serve me thus?"

"You must die," he raged, "Both you and your servant, whom I now see to be a witch, it is my duty to rid the world of you both."

"No," cried Sylvie, "I do not understand, I believed myself loved by you, my Lord? I cannot have been so mistaken."

"Well, you were," he spat furiously. "I do not love you."

"Come, my lady," urged Molly. "We must away and seek sanctuary elsewhere."

"I will find you!" the Lord screamed, as Molly led the sobbing Sylvie from the clearing. "I will hunt you down like a common criminal, madam, and that spawn of the devil you carry!"

Sally and Jack hurried after the fleeing women, the frenzied roaring of the trapped Lord grow fainter as Molly led Sylvie deeper and deeper into the Forest.

"Oh, Molly," groaned Sylvie, stumbling and almost falling. "Where can we go? What can we do? My strength is almost extinguished, I cannot go on."

"You must, my lambkin," urged Molly, stiffening as the sound of baying hounds erupted behind them. "The spell has worn off," she muttered, and Sylvie cried out in alarm, "He has set the dogs on us."

Staggering through the trees, Jack and Sally followed helplessly until they reached the edge of the stream, its normally placid temperament whipped into a frenzy of churning white water and gushing, bubbling sound. Molly lifted Sylvie in her arms and stumbled into the icy waters, carrying her precious burden safely to the other side, leading her to where a pair of trees, entwined as close as any lovers, formed a snug bower in their heart.

"Wait here," she ordered. "I will go and lay a false trail for the hounds, then come back for you."

"Do not leave me," pleaded Sylvie, clutching at the older woman's sleeve. "Please, Molly, I am so afraid. Please, do not leave me alone in this terrible place."

"I must," Molly insisted. "You will be safe here. I shall lay such a trail the hounds will not be able to resist following. Then I will return, I promise."

"Be careful, Molly, if they should catch you…"

"I pity the beast, be it man or hound, that catches me," replied Molly with a grim smile. "Stay out of sight, my lady, I shall return as quickly as I can." Sally and Jack hesitated, torn between following Molly or staying with Sylvie. Abruptly Sally knelt beside the shivering, terrified woman, gently holding a hand to her brow.

"We can't leave her, Jack," she murmured. "I know she can't see, hear or feel us, but I promised Reuben I'd look after her. I can't leave her so alone and scared." Softly, Sally stroked the shimmering mass of silver hair, even though she felt nothing beneath her hand, and poured her soul into comforting thoughts and images of strength. Sylvie looked up, dark eyes puzzled, reminding Sally of someone. Then the memory, if that's what it was, vanished, and Sylvie murmured words into the storm-tossed Forest.

"I feel you spirits of the Forest. I sense your presence and believe you mean me no harm. Oh spirits I pray, if you have any powers at all, help me and my faithful servant, for we have been cruelly abandoned this night."

"I can't help you," whispered Sally sadly. "I wish I could, but I can't, I have no powers. I can't even touch you." Time passed, and still Sally crouched beside Sylvie, softly stroking her hair and crooning reassuring words, and even though the other girl could not hear her, in some strange way, Sally believed she was aware of her presence, and was comforted by it.

Suddenly, Sylvie lifted her head sharply, her whole posture one of intense concentration. Then Sally and Jack heard it too; the baying of hounds plainly getting closer. They looked at one another in dismay.

Stumbling to her feet, choking back a sob of fear, Sylvie looking wildly around, as if hoping to see Molly's reassuring figure appearing through the trees.

"What shall I do?" she murmured anxiously. "What shall I do? Molly…?"

The savage sounds increased, and with a frantic sob, Sylvie lifted her skirts and stumbled through the trees. The storm, which had been all sound and fury up to this point, finally broke, a downpour of monumental force crashing upon them. Sylvie sank to her knees, crushed by the oppressive weight of the rain.

"I thought the Forest would help," screamed Sally, "Why is it letting this happen to her?"

"It is trying to help," called back Jack. "The dogs will find it harder to follow her scent in this rain."

Sylvie staggered back to her feet, bent double, clutching at her stomach, moaning in pain and terror. Sally's heart throbbed in impotent despair. We can do nothing to help her, she thought desperately. They could catch her, rip her to shreds in front of us, and there'll be nothing we can do to stop them.

A stream lay before them. Whether a loop of the one they'd previously crossed or another, Sally couldn't tell. With a wild sob, Sylvie slipped down the muddy bank into the frothing waters, floundering waist deep until she reached the other side, painfully dragging her aching, swollen body up the bank to collapse in the undergrowth.

Her beautiful gown was soaked, begrimed with mud and debris from the Forest floor, silvery white hair plastered sleekly round her small, neat head, giving her the look of a seal. Sally wondered how much more she could bear. Surely she must be at the limits of her endurance? Sylvie rolled to her side, slowly clambering back to her feet, some internal courage forcing her on.

Slipping down the bank, Sally and Jack waded through the stream, its chill not touching them, so when Jack pulled them both safely up the other side they were still dry. Looking up into the canopy, Sally realised that although she could feel the rain smashing against her face, it didn't wet her, instead it seemed to almost float through her to patter against the ground below.

The trees shifted, blurred. Sally realised with a sinking heart that the Forest was moving them away from this time and place.

"No!" she cried. "We can't leave her. Please don't take us!"

But, it was too late, everything changed...

They blinked stupidly at each other in a dry and quiet place. They were inside, the continuing storm now muted by stout walls of wattle and daub. A warm and attractive cottage with a table laid for tea before a roaring, welcoming fire, a basket of sewing things set beside a rocking chair, a simple carved cupboard holding a variety of plain but honest homewares. Sally looked around, understanding this was Reuben's home as it was in the beginning,

A cry, hoarse and guttural, almost that of an animal in pain, rang out above their heads. Quietly, Jack took Sally's hand and led her to the stairs, no need to question whether they should ascend or not, knowing this was what the Forest wished them to witness next.

Upstairs into a large room as pleasant and homey as downstairs but a scene of battle and struggle. Sally caught her breath at the sight of Sunniva, face pale and glistening with the sweat of long toil, twisting and writhing in anguish upon the bed. Crouched between her straining, blood streaked thighs, was her husband, sleeves rolled up to his elbows. As they watched, he gave a cry of triumph.

"Almost there, my love, I can see the head. One more push!"

Gripping the wooden bars of the bed, Sunniva's body lifted, surged with intense, primeval strength. With a gush of dark blood, the baby's body slithered out onto the bed into the capable hands of its father whose cry of joy turned into a moan of despair. Craning to see over his shoulder, they saw the baby, a daughter, face purple, eyes bulging over a thick fibrous cord cruelly encircling her tiny throat.

"No, no!" he begged, hands busy with his knife to release the babe too late. The child was dead.

"What is it?" Sunniva pleaded in alarm, struggling to pull her battered and blood-soaked body up. "Where's my baby?" she demanded. Tenderly, he moved to cup his wife's face in his hand. As time once more shifted around them, Sally heard her wild scream of denial, then they'd moved on...

To the same cottage, downstairs again. Sunniva, cleaned and clothed, seated in the rocking chair before the fire, held the swaddled body of her poor dead child. Her husband knelt on the floor beside her, head bent with misery into her lap, one large hand cupping the tiny, still body of their baby, the other clasping his wife's knees, his large frame shaking with the tears he was openly shedding.

Turning away, Sally and Jack looked helplessly at one another. This was too much to bear. Too much to witness. They had no place here; they should leave. A sound, tiny but persistent, came at the door and they glanced at the grieving couple, wondering if they'd heard, if that small disturbance could possibly find a way through such a barrier of mourning.

It came again. Sunniva looked at the door, a frown pulling at the frozen whiteness of her face, she gently shook her husband, and at his look of enquiry, nodded towards the door. "Something is there," she murmured, voice hoarse and choked from a surfeit of tears.

Wiping a hand over his face he rose awkwardly to his feet and crossed to the door. Pulling it open, he instinctively caught the frail, drenched figure of Sylvie as she toppled inwards. Sunniva cried out in alarm, jumping to her feet and moving to her lady's side, kneeling beside her as her husband slammed the door, shutting out the wildness of the night.

"My lady!" she cried. "Whatever is this? Why are you here in such weather, in your condition?"

All in the room realised in the same instant the liquid staining Sylvie's long silken gown was not merely mud and rain. It was blood. Deep and red, it left a long smear on the wooden floor. The forester pulled his childhood sweetheart into his arms, shocked gaze meeting that of his wife over the prone body of their lady.

"It's her time," he cried.

"Get her upstairs!" Sunniva clutched at his arm, placing the body of her dead child tenderly into a wooden cradle by the table, before swiftly hurrying to attend to the needs of the living...

Time tilted. Sally and Jack were upstairs again. Dumb witnesses, as Sylvie struggled against all odds to bring her child into the world. All night Sunniva and her husband battled to save their lady. Finally, as thin tendrils of dawn slid through the tiny cottage windows, the child crept from her womb, cried lustily its outrage at being forced to quit such a warm and cosy bed.

It was a boy, strong and sturdy, and Sally wondered at the incongruity of the apparently healthy Sunniva producing a tiny dead girl, whilst Sylvie, the frailer of the two, gave birth to a strong and fair-sized son.

It was the quiet at the very end.

Sylvie lay still and exhausted, too feeble to even hold her own son. Her eyes, huge and shadowed with pain, gazed hungrily as Sunniva sat beside her, showing her his perfection.

"I did not think to enquire," she whispered. "Your own babe, Sunniva, what did you have?"

"A little girl, my lady," murmured Sunniva, downcast eyes fixed upon the warm and living body which fretted and squirmed in her arms. "She... she did not survive the birth."

Sylvie's eyes grew wider and she laid a sympathetic hand on Sunniva's arm. "I am so sorry," she whispered. "So very sorry for you both."

Her regard lingered regretfully on the forester, silent and unobtrusive in the corner, his soul reeling from the drama of life and death he'd born witness to that night.

A cry, weak and unsubstantial at first, quickly growing in strength and insistence, issued from the untried lungs of Sylvie's son. Sunniva felt the primitive response of her body, pressing a hand to breasts aching to undertake the task for which they had been created, helplessly looked at Sylvie, who slowly nodded her assent.

"Please," was all she said, "for I cannot."

Clumsy with unfamiliarity, Sunniva unlaced her gown, and held the baby to her breast. Instinctively, he nuzzled at a nipple already dripping with life giving liquid, hungrily and eagerly latching on, greedily beginning to suckle, his cries abating. Sunniva's eyes met those of her mistress in a mutual moment of satisfaction.

"So very hungry..." observed Sylvie softly.

"He's a fine, strapping lad," said Sunniva, as satisfied as if she'd birthed him herself.

"Can you tell us why you're here, my lady?" enquired the forester.

Sylvie turned large, soulful eyes upon him. "My husband, my Lord, has... turned against me," she began slowly. "I do not know why. This morning he was as solicitous of me as ever. Concerned and loving, worrying about my health and that of the baby. Mere hours later, he attempted to kill me. Were it not for Molly, he would have succeeded. In terror of our lives, we fled into the Forest. When we heard the hounds baying, realising he was hunting us, Molly bade me conceal myself, said she would draw them away, but, she did not come back. I stumbled alone and afraid through the Forest for many hours."

She paused and looked steadily at them.

"Then I realised my time had come. For my child's sake, if not my own, I had to find somewhere to birth him safely. I knew of no other place but here. I am truly grateful for the aid and sanctuary you have given us, but am afraid it will not be long before my Lord thinks to come here. It is probably only the storm which has delayed his arrival long since. That is why I must leave, or risk bringing down his wrath upon you both..."

"You cannot leave," stated the forester flatly. "You are in no condition to even quit that bed, let alone set off, destitute and friendless, into the wilds of the Forest."

"And you are certainly not taking this young 'un away," put in Sunniva firmly. "He would die from exposure, that's if the dogs did not get him first."

"But he will come here," insisted Sylvie desperately. "I fear for the lives of us all if he finds you have sheltered me. No, I must leave."

She struggled to drag herself into a sitting position, even that small movement leaving her breathless and ashen faced, leaning helplessly against Sunniva's supporting arm.

"I am so sorry," she whispered. "I should never have come. It would have been better if we'd perished in the Forest. Oh, my poor baby, what is to become of you?"

"We will think of something," the forester assured, crossing to stand at the foot of the bed.

Sylvie stared at him, her eyes dark and solemn. "Promise me you will not let him get my son?"

The forester and his wife exchanged a quick glance of determined agreement. "I promise to keep your son safe," he vowed.

"None that intend him any harm shall ever come near him," Sunniva promised. Sylvie smiled in satisfaction, then her eyes shifted and locked with Sally's.

"Promise me," she whispered, voice faint and ethereal as her soul shifted uneasily within its wearied frame.

"My lady?" the forester asked, glancing nervously over his shoulder, gaze passing through Jack and Sally in the manner to which they'd become accustomed. But Sylvie's eyes, grown larger in a face bleached of natural colour, did not move from their steadfast contemplation of Sally.

"Promise me," she demanded again.

"Yes." Sally stepped forward. "Anything, anything…"

"Please, try to protect them," begged Sylvie.

"I will try," promised Sally. "But I really don't know what I…"

"Try…" murmured Sylvie urgently, and Sally nodded.

"I will," she vowed.

Satisfied, Sylvie fell back onto her pillow. The confused faces of Sunniva and her husband changed to alarm as blood, vivid and shocking, suddenly gushed, Sylvie's eyes went still, and the room began to fade, as Sunniva cried out her lady's name and her son began to cry…

They were outside the cottage. All around the storm lashed, ripping at the trees, which swayed and creaked in resistance to the brute strength of the gale as it snatched and tore at their leaves, scattering them wilfully to the ground like a child grown bored with its toys.

"She saw us." Jack cried over the roar of the storm.

"Yes, and so did you, just before you died. It's as though being close to death gives them the power to see us," replied Sally, hair lashing over her shoulders in the face of such elemental force.

"Listen," cried Jack. They both stilled as the sound of hounds, faint and distant but rapidly growing in intensity, rose above the storm.

"They must've picked up her trail," shouted Sally. "We have to stop them."

"Before, they could smell us" said Jack. "Perhaps we could make them track us instead, lead them well away from here."

"Do you think we could?" asked Sally a wave of tiredness sweeping over her body. They'd seen so much, witnessed so much betrayal and death and life, she felt weepy and exhausted, longing for her room, her bed, the comforting glow of her night light. Most of all, she longed for Reuben. For his strength, and the comfort his presence always brought. She wondered how he was, if Molly Mole had been able to save him, or if maybe he was already...

She stopped abruptly, swallowing down the panic in fierce denial. She could not think along such lines, not here, and certainly not now. No, now she needed to focus on the task at hand, her obligation to fulfil a promise given a dying woman.

Resolutely, Sally squared her shoulders. Drawing in a deep breath, gathering up her scattered courage, she turned to face Jack, eyes shining with renewed determination. He gazed back in stunned admiration, thinking he'd never seen her so beautiful.

Before he could think of stopping himself, he'd gathered her to him and kissed her shocked lips. For a single, glorious moment he vowed to live on for the rest of his life, she allowed him, then pulled away, face saddened with regret.

"I'm sorry, Jack," she said.

"I know," he shrugged with resignation, silently offering her his hand which she took. They set off through the Forest, towards the demented barking and howling which set Sally's teeth on edge, scraped icy nails of fear down her spine.

The dogs were alarmingly much closer than they'd thought. It seemed no time before they were in their midst, Sally gripping Jack's hand in apprehension at the sea of brindle and black snarling bodies surrounding them, sniffing furiously over and through them, shouts of the huntsmen echoing through the trees as they called to the dogs to hold the prey.

"Come on," called Jack, pulling her after him. "Let's take them on a hunt they'll never forget."

It could almost have been fun. Once Sally's instinctive terror of the hounds faded and she realised they truly could not hurt them, she could almost have enjoyed the merry dance they led them, were it not for the severity of the consequences should they fail.

Over fallen trunks and under low hanging branches, they took the pack, through the thickest of brambles, which Jack discovered to his glee they could pass through unscathed. Round and round large clumps of trees, so the lead dog nosed the tail of the last, always the confused curses and cries of the huntsmen echoing through the Forest behind them.

On and on they went. Hours passed. The sun rose, still the storm continued unabated, the melee of wildly tossing branches, madly falling leaves and ear-splitting winds generally adding to the confusion, almost as if the Forest aided and abetted them in their plans.

Finally, they were lost, far away from the forester's cottage. Jack and Sally paused for breath, daring to hope they'd succeeded, and that Sunniva, her husband, and Sylvie's child were now safe.

"Are you alright?" Jack asked. Sally nodded, panting, side throbbing with a stitch of exertion. "I mean, in your condition," he finished solicitously. Sally started, hands flying wildly to her stomach.

"I… I suppose so," she stammered. "I hadn't thought… I'd forgotten…"

Jack turned away, surveying the hounds which milled about in confused disarray, slobbering jaws dropping foam onto the undergrowth, legs lifting on trees as their dishevelled and disgruntled handlers arrived, gasping and exhausted, staring around the apparently empty clearing with exclamations of annoyed disbelief.

"Another phantom prey?" snapped one, tone ripe with irritation.

"What ails these hounds?" enquired another, his fresh face and slight frame marking him out as the youngest of the hunters. The oldest man present, a well-seasoned and weather-beaten veteran of many a hunt, spat disdainfully onto the ground, gingery whiskers screwing up into an expression of distaste.

"The Forest be in a fury about something," he declared bluntly. "Taint no use trying to pick up scents if the Forest don't allow it."

"Get away," sneered the young man. "You don't believe such stuff, do you?"

"Aye, I do," answered his elder sourly, fixing a baleful glare on the younger fellow. "And if you had any sense, boy, so would you," he paused, glancing up at the scraps of storm-tossed sky visible through the canopy. "And if truth be known," he continued slowly. "I have no stomach for our task. Hunting animals, that's one thing, but hunting women, well, I don't know about that."

"But you heard the Lord," insisted the young man. "He said they were witches."

"Aye, I heard him," stated the other man flatly. "But I find it hard to believe such a sweet and gentle lady could be wicked. Don't seem right to be hunting her down, especially not in her condition…"

Several of the other men murmured agreements under their breath, shifting uneasily at the rebellious thoughts he was voicing. "But, what about the other one, the old servant?" insisted the youth.

"Molly? Well, all I know about Molly is she's always been a help to folks with potions and possets to cure and ease their aches and pains. If it weren't for her tonic for the rheumatics, I'd be seized up solid all winter," he paused, gaze resting thoughtfully on a nearby clump of wild garlic.

"Winter be nearly upon us again," he remarked mildly. "T'would be a shame if Molly's not around to cure all the coughs and colds that are bound to occur. As for that ale she brews, well, mealtimes would be mighty dry without it."

"So, what are you saying?" demanded another huntsman, exchanging a quick glance with the darkly silent, hulking men beside him, their features so alike it declared them brothers. "Are you saying we should let them go? Because that kind of talk will get us all hanging from a gibbet before nightfall."

"Me?" enquired the other, eyes rounding innocently, one gnarled hand scratching thoughtfully at his straggly ginger beard. "I'm not saying anything..."

His voice trailed away. He stared meaningfully at each one of the hunters, and Sally felt the collective decision pass through them, excitedly turning to Jack.

"They don't want to hunt them," she whispered. "They're going to tell him they couldn't find them."

Jack nodded, eyes shining with relief. Suddenly, the lead hound which had been nosing around a nearby patch of undergrowth, threw back his head and sounded, a mournfully chilling howl which had Sally grabbing Jack's hand.

"What is it? What's happened?" she cried in alarm, as one by one the other dogs took up the refrain, streaming from the clearing, following the frantically plunging body of the lead hound.

"Damn and blast it!" exclaimed Molly's defender. The men rushed from the clearing following the excited anticipation of the hounds as they tore through the undergrowth, their eager yaps and whimpers leading the hunters further into the Forest. Jack and Sally exchanged dismayed looks, wondering what the dogs were tracking, praying it was merely a woodland animal

"We'd better follow," stated Jack. "Maybe we can distract them."

The Forest had other ideas. Once again, the trees moved, and they found themselves elsewhere. Another clearing, although from the light and the storm which still raged, it seemed they were in the same time...

Bridget entered the clearing, a crying baby on each hip, impatiently shaking them to be quiet. When their cries only increased, she angrily dropped them to the ground and knelt beside them.

"Soon," she exclaimed. "Soon I shall be married to the Lord and he will do my bidding. Then the power I have so longed for will be within my grasp and there will be no place for the miserable get of another man. Infatuated as he is, even my Lord will not stand for that."

She gazed unemotionally at the twins who kicked and thrashed their annoyance at being so cold and exposed, their little legs gleaming whitely in the pale morning light.

"I am sorry for it," she told them. "But I have no other choice..." Her hands pinched lightly over their mouths and noses, and Sally dashed forward, pounding impotently on the woman's back.

"Stop it!" she cried. "You can't do this!"

Bridget startled, hands flying free of the twin's mouths who bawled their displeasure. It was not Sally's attempts which had detracted her, but the arrival of the Lord as he stalked into the clearing, mouth set in a grim line, eyes firm with hot resolve.

"The dogs hunt my wife," he stated flatly. "She shall be dead by nightfall and we shall wed. I have done as you requested. I'm now come to claim my prize."

"But my Lord," began Bridget, rising to her feet and moving away from her crying children, "it would not be right, not until we are married. Propriety does not..."

"Damn propriety," he snarled, ripping her bodice down the front, "I shall take what is mine. You will submit to my desire, willingly or unwillingly. The choice is yours, madam."

"No," she cried, struggling in his grip. "This is not the way it should be. My husband would never..."

"Your husband was a boy," he scoffed. "I am a man, with a man's needs and wants, which you, my lady, will now fulfil," He bore her to the ground, ignoring her shocked gasp of pain. Hungrily, he savagely feasted upon her heaving breasts and Bridget gasped again, this time with surprised delight.

"Yes," she growled, hands fumbling at his clothes. "Take me, hurt me, I want, need you to be rough." Growling with lust, the Lord rolled onto her, his mouth fastening onto hers. Bridget raked her nails through his hair and down his throat, body arching into his, their breathing hot and impatient.

Stunned and speechless, Jack and Sally exchanged mortified looks, wondering what reason the Forest could have for showing them this.

Struggling, screaming, the nature of Bridget's cries had changed as she fought to free herself from his weight pinning her, spread eagled, to the ground. Molly rushed forward, heavy branch in hand, which she used with devastating effect across the back of the lust distracted Lord's head.

He slumped to the ground, blood welling from a jagged gash at the base of his skull, and Molly pulled her wildly sobbing daughter into her arms, Sally understanding it was all an act. Bridget must have spied her mother, instantly changing from willing lover to victim.

"Mother, oh mother," cried Bridget. Molly rocked her child in her arms, soothing and shushing, as Bridget held the tattered shreds of her gown together.

"What happened?" asked Molly, when her daughter's sobs had grown less wild.

"I brought the twins to the Forest to search for you," explained Bridget, face a study of innocence. "I heard they hunted you and our lady, was afraid for you both and for us. I determined to find you. He came, the Lord. Attacked me. Would have succeeded in his foul intent if you had not come along."

Once again, she broke into a fresh torrent of sobbing, but Sally saw the coldly calculating glint in the other girl's eyes over the supportive shoulder of her mother, marvelling that Molly could be so easily fooled.

"It's alright," reassured her mother. "He will not hurt you again..."

"But what about when you are no longer here?" interrupted Bridget desperately. "How shall I protect myself and my children from the vile cruelties of men?"

"Your husband..." began Molly.

"My husband is dead!" screamed Bridget. "Murdered by him! He boasted of it before he... he..." She burst into a fresh paroxysm of wails and sobs so compelling, had Sally not witnessed the real turn of events, she'd have been convinced.

"Sweet lady!" exclaimed Molly in horror. "How is the man so lost to all reason? I thought him a good man, a man fit for my lady. Is it possible I could have been so badly mistaken?"

"You were, mother," wept Bridget. "See my marks on his throat where I fought to defend my honour and the lives of my children, whom he threatened to kill. He was too strong. If you had not happened along, he would have succeeded in his foul intent, for I am only a weak and feeble woman, unable to protect myself or my children. Oh, what is to become of us?" She burst into fresh sobs, gathering up the twins, rocking them in her arms.

"You shall not be without power," promised Molly fervently, "for I shall give you all the power you will ever need, so you may never be vulnerable again. For the sake of my poor abandoned child and my grandchildren, I will pass on that which has run through the veins of the women in our family since time began. An ancient and mystical power which men cannot understand and so fear, calling us witches, killing those they suspect to possess it."

"You would do this for me?" asked Bridget, fighting to keep the glee from her face. "Oh, my mother, to be safe, forever safe..."

"You shall be safe," promised Molly, and power crackled and danced around her body. Her eyes flashed fire. Her face turned proud and strong, filled with a wild, deadly beauty.

Frenzied barking sounded. Startled, Molly turned as hounds poured into the clearing, followed by the huntsmen, surprise and dismay evident on their faces at the sight of Molly, quickly turning into concern when they saw the body of their Lord.

"She's killed him," cried one in horror.

Molly cast him a scornful glance, and with a wave of her hand checked their impetuous rush towards her. "He is not dead," she exclaimed, "Merely stunned, although death be too good a reward for this day's work. Is this our mighty and just Lord? What, pray, has he become? Murderer of innocent men? Despoiler of women? Even now, our poor sweet lady flees through the Forest, lost and alone, so close to her time. I fear for her life and that of her unborn child."

The hunters shuffled uneasily, exchanging looks. The grizzled older one nodded his head in agreement. "What do you suggest, Molly?" he asked slowly, and Molly flashed him a look of gratitude.

"This cannot be allowed to continue..." she began, but was interrupted by a wave of excitement amongst the dogs, as more hounds exploded into the clearing, barking and snarling their frenzied enthusiasm.

"They've found something," cried one. "Look, there's blood on their jaws."

Panting with importance, the two lead dogs sat before their handlers, and dropped a pair of small, almost insignificant, objects from their foaming, slobbering mouths. One was a lady's slipper so begrimed with mud and rusty stains of blood, the delicacy of its original state was almost completely disguised.

"That is my lady's shoe," cried Molly.

The whole clearing grew terribly still and silent as the second dog also dropped a mauled trophy at the foot of its handler. At first, Sally couldn't understand what she was looking at, until suddenly, horribly, it clicked in her mind, and she recognised it for what it was.

The severed arm of a baby.

Chapter Eighteen
~ Curses and Consequences ~

The Forest imploded with the force of Molly's wrath. All staggered and fell to their knees, as power, raw and primal, ripped through the trees, their sturdy trunks bowing under the pressure. Squinting against the glare, Sally turned terrified eyes upon Molly as light, glorious and deadly, exploded from her fingertips, scorching those nearest who cried out in pain and fear, shielding their eyes from her brightness.

"Hear me, oh spirits of the Forest!" she bellowed, face transformed. No longer a mild and harmless elderly woman, she was ageless and eternal, features suffused with a fierce, wild beauty, her body strong and powerful.

"Innocent blood has been spilled. Innocent blood! Hear me and comply, ancient and wondrous spirits. I call upon you as my kinsfolk, remembering how in millennia past we were one, the land and the trees and the people who roamed free and true. We believed in the unity of our spirits, understood and venerated your power. But others came. Others who did not believe. They destroyed the land. Chopped down the sacred woodlands. Persecuted your people until we were virtually extinct, living a shadowed existence, hiding our true nature for fear of torture and death. I now invoke those ancient ties of kinship. Call upon you to witness, make come to pass the curses I lay upon those who would murder innocence. Help me, oh spirits! I know such powerful magic cannot help but come at a great cost. But know this, whatever price you demand for such assistance, I will gladly pay and entreat you to hear my plea!"

All around, a great gale swirled and raged, whipping up fallen leaves into a frenzy of crazily dancing shapes, and a figure formed from the flying russet and green coloured foliage.

A giant, vaguely human shape, it arose from the forest floor, its face as old as time, oak leaves and acorns entwined through the roots it bore in place of hair and beard. It looked at them, with amber eyes that glowed fiercely with the wisdom of ages past, looked right through them, into their very souls, its gaze sweeping dismissively over all, bowing to Molly in regal, unmistakable agreement.

"Grant my lady, Sylvie, wherever she may be, the power to flee her enemies, to be free of their grasp. Grant the soul of her poor nameless child eternal contentment. I further command, within this Forest no more innocent blood may be spilled. I pass to my daughter, Bridget, the boundless power I possess, that she may be free of the vile intentions of man, may protect herself and her children from any that would do harm!"

Behind Molly's back, Bridget straightened, head flung back in glorious triumph, eyes glowing red as power streamed from her mother into her, mouth agape in a shout of shocked wonder.

"I further call upon you, oh wise and powerful spirits," Molly continued, blind to events occurring around her, "to hear and implement this curse upon those who have carried out this heinous act upon a good and sweet lady. To the one responsible, I order eternal damnation. I command them be trapped, vilified and alone, forever tormented by the pain of evil corruption, a prisoner of their own malicious intent..."

Unseen by Molly, Bridget's triumphant expression snapped into a snarl of fear. Leafy tendrils were reaching for her, gripping and wrapping unrelenting fingers around her body, thrusting down her throat. She gagged and twisted in their grasp.

Sally cried out in disgust, as the other girl's body bucked and warped in silent agony, her eyes bulging wetly. The tendril withdrew, dragging in its wake a long, black, perverted rope of soul. It struggled in its grasp, and Sally recognised the oily mass as the entity which had pursued her through the Forest.

Once Bridget's body was vacated, it crashed to the Forest floor. Leaves swirled over it, absorbing and crushing, until all that could be seen was a vague outline in the undergrowth. A sharp wind, bitter and forceful, swept through the clearing, and the mortal remains of Bridget were gone.

Bridget's soul, that dark, eternally damned wisp, struggled and writhed in the Forest's grip, and two small sparks of black spat from its mass, landing on the screaming twins.

Sally watched in wonder as the brands lay for a moment on their foreheads, before sinking through their skin to be seen no more. The tendril gave another determined yank, and the black mass was ripped away through the trees.

"Upon the accursed Lord's family, I wish them the pain of loss," ranted Molly, unaware of the fate of her daughter. "Of having their heart taken from them. I command that as the heavens move, so shall the son and heir be taken by the Forest, taken and punished according to the crimes of this, their most evil of ancestors," she gestured disdainfully towards the still prone figure of the Lord.

"That this shall stand until a Marchmant values the life of my lady, or one of her kin, more highly than his own. Only thus shall the curse be broken."

Molly's gaze raked scornfully over the shivering, grovelling huntsmen, who trembled under her accusing stare.

"And upon everyone who has played a part, no matter how small, in the foul work carried out this day, I wish perpetual discontent and reflection upon their crime, to be inherited by their children and their children's children, throughout the generations, for all eternity."

Molly paused, face wet with tears. "And I further curse myself never to know the gentle sleep of death, the glory of the hereafter, until I have saved my sweet lady, my little lambkin, or until I kneel by her grave and know her to be at peace." She gathered her breath and threw up her arms in an impassioned plea.

"As I speak it, so must it be!"

Light exploded through the trees, billowing outwards in a blast of power, searing to the soul.

In a noiseless discharge of energy, Sally and Jack were thrown, hurtling, twisting through time to arrive... shocked... breathless... tossed onto the Forest floor, knowing they were back in their own era...

"Sally?" Jack rolled to her side, eyes concerned. Gathering her up in his arms she gaped with disbelief and bemusement, staring around at the darkness, realising that events spanning the whole night had taken but a few moments.

"Where are we?" she breathed, struggling to sit, body aching from the force with which it'd been thrown to the hard ground.

"Exactly where we were, I think," Jack replied, cocking his head to the demonic howls of not so distant dogs. "They're hunting Sylvie. Come on, there's still time. We have to stop them."

Shakily, Sally accepted his help to stand, brushing leaf mould and dirt from her clothes, recovering her torch from where it had fallen. Taking his hand followed him through the trees as he homed in on the frenzied, savage snarls and yelps, heart hammering with fear and apprehension.

Movement in the bushes ahead. A flash of milk white. The White Hind leapt from the undergrowth, dark liquid eyes alive with the panic of the hunt, sides heaving with ragged, frenzied pants, the silvery sheen of her hide glistening with the terrified sweat of adrenalin.

She swerved to avoid them. A hound streaked from the undergrowth, savage and wolf-like, but Sally knew this was no ordinary dog. Created from the store of negative and hostile emotions Bridget had drained from her victims over the years, these beasts were not made of flesh and blood, but of lust and envy, greed, jealousy and spite; hatred formed their hearts and black malice pumped through their veins.

Snarling, foam daubing its gaping red maw, the hound leapt, great savage jaws fastening onto the White Hind's flank, and she screamed with pain, crashing down into the undergrowth.

Jack snatched up a nearby fallen branch, yelling with hoarse, primal rage he charged at the beast, striking it across the back and head, until it turned on him, blood dripping from its mouth, dark eyes glinting with malevolence.

Sally screamed in terror as it leapt at Jack, snapping at the branch and Jack staggered back, bravely lashing out at the beast, drawing it away from the White Hind.

Sally rushed to her side, falling to her knees beside the beautiful beast, gathering her up in her arms. Sylvie turned her glorious head, fixed pain-filled eyes upon her, and Sally realised anew how fragile and vulnerable she was. Her tiny body, now clothed in human form, appeared to weigh nothing in Sally's arms, and she winced away from the jagged bleeding gash in Sylvie's hip.

"Thank you," murmured the woman, her beautiful eyes locking with Sally's. Once again that odd feeling of familiarity flickered across Sally's consciousness, the sensation that someone else had looked at her recently, with the same shaped eyes, their features stamped with the mark of Sylvie's.

"You kept your promise," continued the woman. "You protected them, for that I thank you…"

Blood gushed, and Sally desperately pulled her coat off, oblivious to the cold, pressing it firmly to the wound, and Sylvie clutched at her with fingers that felt like the touch of winter.

"I will not forget," she promised, eyes glazing over, breath catching on a gasp of anguished pain.

"Jack," cried Sally as Jack advanced on the dog, breathing heavy with exertion. The hound snarled and growled. Teeth bared, it eyed the branch with caution, circling the boy, looking for an opening.

"Jack, she's hurt, she needs help."

"Don't we all," muttered Jack, gaze never leaving the evil beast, his grip firm on the branch, wondering how long he could hold it off. The dog growled again, answering howls erupting through the trees and Jack's heart sank. He quickly sprang forward taking the dog by surprise, striking it soundly round the head, observing with satisfaction as it crumpled silently to the ground.

Striding to Sally's side, he thrust the branch in her hands and lifted Sylvie in his arms, barely registering the slightness of her weight, looking at Sally in despair. "We need to move. The others will be here in a moment."

Swallowing down her fear, Sally nodded, following as he ran through the trees. Behind them, a howl sounded, keening and triumphant. The others had picked up their scent and were in pursuit.

"We're not going to make it," screamed Sally.

Jack flicked her a concerned glance over the barely conscious body of the woman from the past.

"Whatever happened to no innocent blood shall be spilled in the Forest?" he asked.

"Maybe Bridget's power has increased over the years," Sally shook her head in bewilderment. "Or perhaps, after so long, the curse is beginning to break down."

They stumbled into a large clearing, heard the frantic rustling of the undergrowth and the frenzied baying of the hounds, knowing them to be on their heels. Desperately, Jack thrust Sylvie back into Sally's arms, grabbing the branch to defend them as the hounds poured into view. Dozens of them.

Sally knew it was hopeless, Jack couldn't fight so many. It was only a matter of moments before they were torn to pieces, all of them, and she bent her body over Sylvie's to protect the other woman from the fate that awaited them all.

Two hounds leapt from the trees. Jack braced himself, knowing it was hopeless. Death was mere seconds away...

Thwack, thwack! A pair of arrows sang overhead, and the beasts fell dead at his feet.

Startled, he looked round. Men, armed with swords and bows, poured from the trees, all with the piercing blue eyes and familiar features of the Marchmant lords, and there was their leader, strong and sturdy, muscles bunching as he calmly pulled back his bow and loosed another arrow into a hound, its howl transforming into a whimper of pain as it died.

"Lucian?" screamed Sally in disbelief, daring to recognise him from Reuben's description and her earlier, fleetingly brief glimpse, when he'd saved her from the entity.

Lucian bowed, eyes flashing with dry humour. "My lady," he confirmed, turned to Jack as around him his men drew their swords and fell upon the ravening pack of frenzied, snarling brutes.

"Well done, lad," he cried, spitting a hound on the end of his sword. "You held them off long enough for us to reach you. Let us deal with them now. You protect the womenfolk, get them to safety. Her ladyship means much to us... There is not a man amongst us would not die to protect her."

Dazed, Jack dropped the branch and staggered back to Sally. Lifting Sylvie once more into his arms, he cast a disbelieving glance back as Lucian and his men fought, relishing a chance to finally strike back at the evil which had denied them their lives, snatching them from their families and loved ones, exiling them to a half-life; a twilight existence within the Forest.

"Come on," urged Sally, and Jack followed, crashing through the Forest in her wake, until the savage sounds of battle faded behind them.

They ran, not knowing which way they were going. In Jack's arms, Sylvie stirred and moaned, face pale in the moonlight glinting through the canopy above, long silvery hair flowing like quicksilver over Jack's arms. He'd never seen anything so breathtakingly beautiful in all his life.

"Wait Sally," he cried. Sally paused, breathing painfully loud in the stillness of the night, eyes wide and unseeing. Carefully, Jack lowered Sylvie to the ground and knelt beside her, noticing with concern the waxen quality of her skin, her shallow breathing, and the fluttering of her eyelids.

"She's going into shock," he cried. "We're losing her."

"What can we do?" Sally demanded, stroking a long silvery tress off the other woman's face. "Jack, what can we do?"

"I don't know," Jack shrugged in impotent helplessness. "This is a woman who should've died hundreds of years ago. I don't know, I mean, is there anything we can do?"

"We can't watch her die," sobbed Sally. "I promised Reuben I'd look after her. There must be something we can do!"

"Unfortunately, not," mused a horrifyingly familiar voice. Sally and Jack started in terror. Nancy Peabody was there, not a gleaming dark hair out of place, the cloud of blackness swirling and coalescing around her, crackling and snapping with energy.

"Thank you," oozed Nancy, eyes bright with malicious glee. "Thank you for bringing her to me. At last she is weak enough for me to complete what I started so many years ago. She is to blame for my long incarceration. She is the one responsible for my predicament. For centuries I have barely existed, trapped in this accursed Forest like a fly caught in a spider's web."

"It was your own fault," screamed Sally. "You poisoned her husband against her, made him set the hounds on her."

For a moment, Nancy Peabody looked taken aback, then grinned evilly. "So, you have been shown the past have you? Well, what of it. She did not love him; it was only fair I took him off her."

"She honoured and respected him," retorted Sally. "She was making a success of her marriage. You had a husband. You'd taken away Sunniva's love. Then, when you thought you could do better, you had him murdered."

"He was in my way," Nancy Peabody dismissed her former husband with a casual shrug. "What else was I supposed to do?"

Pushing Sally behind him, Jack again transferred the slight weight of Sylvie into her arms, facing the darkness alone. "You want her, you go through me first," he bravely declared.

Nancy Peabody chuckled indulgently. "Silly boy," she mused, almost fondly. "Do you really think you're any match for me? Jack, oh Jack, join us again. Be as one with your family, your real family. Join with your mother and sister again. Feel the power flow through your veins. Remember how it felt, to be invincible, inviolate in your supremacy."

She paused, smile spreading as she took in his unyielding stance, hands bunched into tight fists, prepared to fight until his last breath to defend the two women huddled on the ground behind him.

"Come now," she crooned. "What allegiance can you possibly owe to Sylvie? She died centuries before you were born. She means nothing to you. As for the other, what is she? A lost love, a forgotten love. Nothing to you but the sweetness of nostalgia, and, let's not forget she betrayed you, gave herself to another, to that simple oaf of a woodsman. You owe her nothing, least of all your life," she smiled serenely, her words rich with promise.

"Why if she means that much to you, I will spare her life, and you can take her, over and over, losing yourself in her body. It would be amusing to see my enemy so humbled and despoiled."

"Never," growled Jack. "I would never do that to Sally," he swallowed bravely, chin raised in bold defiance. "You want them," he declared again. "Then you have to go through me to get them!"

"If that's the way you want it," shrugged Nancy, carelessly.

"And if you do manage to get through him," drawled a familiar voice, "you'll then have me to contend with."

Nancy Peabody's head lashed up, seeking the source of the mocking words, and Jack and Sally exchanged swift shocked glances as the trees at the edge of the clearing moved and Lord Jolyon stepped forward, his stance casual, gaze firm and steady, eyes glittering with resolve.

"A Marchmant," spat Nancy Peabody. "You shall make easy meat."

"Not that easy," Lord Gilliard stepped up to his brother's shoulder.

"And if you manage to get through their lordships, which I doubt," came another voice, "then I reckon you'll have to deal with me," Daniel Forrester stood at Lord Jolyon's other shoulder, shotgun in hand, his usually placid face firm and intractable.

"And me." The voice was rich with familiar country burr, and Sally stared as her father stepped forward. "And me, and me…" Voices rang out as all around the perimeter of the clearing the night parted, and the village men were there, flanked by the women.

The kindly benevolent face of Reverend Arnold beamed at Sally. "I told you I'd bring reinforcements, my dear," he chortled.

Sally looked at her father in confusion. "I don't understand," she cried. "How did you get through the barrier?"

"It suddenly fell about half an hour ago," he explained. Sally realised once again the Forest was trying to help them, lowering its defences to allow this little army of villagers to penetrate its hitherto forbidden heart.

"Pitiful fools!" mocked Nancy Peabody. "You cannot possibly hope to defeat me."

"I reckon we can have a damn good try," replied Daniel Forrester. There was a murmur of assent from the others.

"Why, Daniel Forrester," cooed Nancy Peabody, "surely you wouldn't hurt me? Could you really bring yourself to shoot an innocent, defenceless woman? Why, I'm one of you…"

"Don't listen to her," screamed Sally. "She shot Reuben."

"Did she now?" Daniel Forrester's jaw tightened. "Well, I reckon I owe her one then," he stated, snapping the shotgun shut and raising it to his shoulder.

"You think to stop me with that pathetic toy?" scoffed Nancy Peabody, black tendrils spinning from the massed entity and snatching the shotgun from Daniel Forrester's suddenly numb fingers. Before the disbelieving eyes of the villagers, it spun the weapon into the air, twisting and snapping the metal, releasing it to fall with a thud, a misshapen hunk of scrap, onto the Forest floor.

A current of trepidation rippled through the villagers, Sally saw some edge away from the eddying, swirling cloud of blackness, fear evident on their familiar, homely faces.

"Don't be afraid," she cried, leaping to her feet. "She can be defeated."

"How, Sally?" asked her father, eyeing the entity with concern. "Tell us how?"

"Faith," she replied simply. "Faith in something or someone, it doesn't matter what, but it has to be something you believe in with your whole heart. She can't understand such emotions. All she knows is hatred and jealousy, envy, greed and spite. Good, honest feelings such as love, commitment, and trust, are poison to her."

She turned to Jack and held out her hand. Slowly, deliberately, he reached out and took it. Looking into his eyes, she smiled and nodded, seeing he understood. Together, they turned to face Nancy Peabody, and the bilious mass encircling her.

No words needed to be spoken. Sally opened her heart to the lifelong love and fidelity she knew Jack bore her, reaching deep into her soul for memories of childhood; a childhood in which not a single day had passed that did not contain him.

She remembered - shared triumphs and calamities, laughter and woes, days when they'd quarrelled bitterly, and still, somehow, through it all, she'd remained rock solid in her absolute conviction he would always be a part of her life.

Warmth, energising and inspiring, heated their clasped palms. Hearing awed gasps and exclamations from the assembled army of villagers, Sally opened her eyes and gazed without fear at the aura of light surrounding Jack, knowing without even needing to look, that such an aura also cloaked her own form.

She raised her free hand, tracing a finger wonderingly over the angled planes of his dearly beloved face, feeling the love and dependency well in her own eyes, and seeing the answering echo in his.

"What are you doing?" screamed Nancy Peabody. With the knowledge the Forest had shown them, they recognised the voice that spoke from her as Bridget's and Sally felt anger, hot and white, growl within her stomach at the wrongs committed by this woman.

They turned as one element, hands and hearts united by pure blinding energy. Light arced from their bodies towards the entity, scorching where it touched, The Forest rent with its agonised scream as it twisted and wrenched itself free.

"No mercy!" howled Nancy Peabody. "You shall be shown no mercy!" She spread her arms, the creature within flowing free, merging with that which had occupied Jack. It reared up, sizzling and crackling with frenzied, demented malevolence. Again, light streamed from the union that was Jack and Sally. Again, the creature screamed its torment.

The villagers cheered, but their glee was short lived. The creature unexpectedly fragmented itself into a myriad of deformed vile beings, monsters from the realm of nightmare which whooped and shrieked before hurling themselves onto the villagers.

The clearing was suddenly the scene of a pitched battle. Sally had a brief glimpse of her father's face, calm and unafraid, before he was engulfed by a sea of blackness. She felt a frisson of fear until he emerged from amongst them, sturdy honest face glowing with the light of triumph as the foul beasts of darkness fell from his touch, his own aura of faith illuminating the gloom within the trees.

All around, the villagers fought. Some with a steady glowing light which highlighted their outlines in sharp, bright relief. Some had but the merest glimmer about them, and it was these the beasts targeted. Their neighbours, recognising the strategy, came to their aid, lending the strength of their own faith.

As she and Jack aimed blast after blast at the misshapen creations, Sally was afforded brief snatches of vision. She saw Jolyon and Gilliard fighting back to back, their auras strong and true. Saw Daniel Forrester steadily battling his way towards Nancy Peabody at the epicentre of the conflict, her head thrown back in maniacal laughter

She saw elderly Wally Twitchett swiping at the gibbering, writhing forms with a strength and passion which belied his apparent frailty, noticing with incredulity, the bulky form of Dorcas Blunt at his side. She saw their hands join in a sudden blaze of light and had time to wonder, before she and Jack were once more themselves faced with scores of clawing, ravening monsters.

Daniel Forrester reached Nancy Peabody, his expression tight and certain.

"You hurt my son," he declared evenly.

"What if I did?" she laughed in his face. "What are you going to do about it, woodsman?"

In one swift, abrupt movement, Daniel grabbed her shoulder and dragged her close. Sally saw the face of Nancy Peabody change, an expression of incredulous disbelief sweeping over it. She staggered back, staring in stunned outrage at the blade of Daniel Forrester's gutting knife glinting scarlet in his hand, then at the livid slit in her stomach through which entrails and blood seeped.

"You cannot kill me!" she shrieked, blood spurting between fingers splayed over the rapidly spreading crimson flow, trying to hold her lifeblood back.

"Reckon I just did," announced Daniel Forrester calmly, pushing her back to collapse, screaming with agonised rage, at his feet.

"Mother!" howled Nancy. The black entity rushed to her side, but Daniel held fast, joined by his wife and others, forming a phalanx around the dying girl, preventing the darkness from re-entering and halting her death, their auras strong and true, steadfast against the frenzied raging of the creature.

Then Sally saw Sylvie. She'd dragged herself to the edge of the clearing, face drawn and pale from the effort, the ravaged flesh of her wound releasing a steady flow of fresh blood. Leaning weakly against a tree, she watched the battle, expression taut with concern.

Sally saw the entity abandon its attempt to reach its dying child, its new intention clear, and she raced to intercept its deadly, headlong rush.

She screamed for Jack. They'd become separated moments before when he'd rushed one way to go to the aid of Winston Blunt, thrust to the ground by a splinter of darkness, and Sally had gone to help her mother destroy a small pack of them a few yards away.

Now, he turned at her scream, trying to reach her, but she was too far away. There were too many creatures between them. When Sally reached Sylvie, she was completely alone, turned to face the evilness unaided.

For a single exhausted moment, her faith faltered, her aura extinguished, and with a howl of gleeful triumph, the thing gathered itself and leapt to consume her.

"Sally!"

With a bellow of rage, Lord Jolyon threw himself in the creature's path, receiving the full force of its death blow into his body. He staggered, falling, the creature also reeling back howling with sickly pain, its sides shrivelling inwards on itself.

Sally saw relief on Jack's face that she still lived. Regained her faith, she blasted bolts of pure love and trust into its rapidly shrinking mass.

Sylvie crawled to Jolyon, cradled his head in her lap, as he looked at her with startled eyes.

"My lady," a glimpse of his old, womanising ways creeping onto his face. "You are so beautiful," he murmured, coughing harshly, face creasing with pain. "Am I dying?" he enquired curiously, his voice mild as if asking if it were time for tea.

"I am so sorry, my lord," she murmured, attempting to pull him into a more comfortable position. He groaned in agony, blood seeping from the corner of his mouth.

"It was... worth it," he muttered, eyes resting upon the triumphant figure of Sally as she drove back the entity with bolt after bolt, until it snapped away from her.

Howling in rage, it fled to the far side of the clearing, drawing all its misshapen creatures of destruction to its side, amalgamating and assimilating, growing in size and strength as it engulfed into itself all its separate factions.

Sally saw Jolyon lying on the ground, the stricken look on Sylvie's face, and fled to his side, dropping to her knees, grasping his hand and crying desperately. "My Lord? Jolyon!"

His eyes flickered open, focused on her face, and he smiled that devastatingly male grin that had vanquished many a young woman's heart, his piercing blue eyes softening with love.

"Sally," he murmured, raising a hand and gently stroked the hair flowing freely over her shoulders. "All hail the Forest Queen," he whispered, fighting the shadows as they crept ever closer, straining for one last look from his love.

Comprehension, knowledge, and understanding exploded in Sally's brain, and she dropped his hand, scrambling frantically to her feet.

"Of course!" she shouted. "How stupid I've been. The answer was there all the time..."

"Sally?" began Sylvie. "What do you mean?"

"Look after him," ordered Sally.

Sylvie nodded, "I will, but what do you intend to do?"

"Finish this!" declared Sally firmly. "Finish this, once and for all. Jolyon... my lord," his eyes opened to look at her, standing so strong and brave in the fierce moonlight, and his lips quirked in a salute to her glory. "Don't you dare die," she commanded, and the quirk became a sardonic grin.

"I will endeavour to obey, oh my queen," he drawled.

Sally dashed back to the clearing, reaching Jack and gripping his hand tightly. "We must form a circle," she cried, flinging out her other hand to grasp her father's.

"Hold hands," she ordered. "Form a circle around the being."

"But Sally," began her father, "what good will that do?"

"Do it!" she screamed, turning to Jack as word spread and the villagers hurried to obey. She saw the apprehension on his face and hurried to explain. "Think Jack," she urged. "Remember the old folk legend, Mad Meg? Remember it's supposedly her exact words we recite at every Festival?"

"Yes, but I don't see…" he began.

"Yes, you do," she urged. "Think about what she claimed she saw in the Forest."

"A man made from leaves," he replied, and his face cleared. "Of course," he breathed. "The spirit of the Forest. She saw it. The words were a message from the Forest, but why…"

"The Forest was trying to help," cried Sally. "But Meg's mind was so fragile, what she saw, what she experienced. It drove her mad, killed her. But she did manage to achieve what the Forest intended, she brought back the words, she passed them on to the village, for us to use…"

"But Sally," interrupted Jack desperately, "I don't understand. What are the words?"

"A weapon," snapped Sally, seeing all had now joined the circle, linking hands, forming a never-ending ring around the black entity. It hesitated, swaying backwards and forwards, as it surveyed the waiting villagers, their faces turned as one towards Sally.

"The Forest Queen is chosen," she began, her young voice ringing out, clear and strong.

"All hail and praise the Queen." Jack's voice chimed in.

"May her power be unchallenged, the Forest ever green."

Sally's father's rich country burr rumbled over the old, familiar words. Gradually, the other villagers joined in, voices strident, impassioned and the clearing rang with the centuries old rhyme.

"We join together gladly, our hearts and minds as one,
We stand beneath the moonlight, and warm, life-giving sun.
Wykenwode, Wykenwode,
Defender of the innocent! Protector of the good!"

Their auras, already warm and true, blazed into increased life as Sally tasted the ancient words of power on her tongue. Saw them join, merge, link, until the circle was an unbroken ring of fire, solid and indestructible.

"Wykenwode, Wykenwode,
Defender of the innocent! Protector of the good!"

The creature screamed with rage and anguish, hurling itself against the circle of joined villagers, but it could not break through. Time and time again it tried and was thrown back, repelled by the white hot light as the individual outlines of the villagers blurred, flowed, became fluidic.

"In the face of mortal danger, of evilness and sin,
We stand against the darkness and know that we will win."

Sally became as one with her neighbours and friends… was aware of their emotions and thoughts, the beating of dozens of hearts.

"Against the crimes of passion, of jealously and greed,
United we must face them, for our inner strength be freed.
Wykenwode, Wykenwode.
Defender of the innocent! Protector of the good!"

The ancient, immortal power, placed into them by the Forest centuries ago moved through them all, finally released, its trigger words of command given, yet not understood, to a simple child of the village.

*"Wykenwode, Wykenwode,
Defender of the innocent! Protector of the good!"*

Long centuries had slipped by, the rhyme had passed into folklore and tradition, dismissed, but not forgotten. Until now, when another child of the village, this one strong and clever, realised and understood their importance. Finally, finally, the words were used as the Forest had always intended.

*"Link hands with your neighbour, join forces with your friend,
Face the foe united, the oldest crimes to mend.
Let the circle come together, the light of faith shine out,
Our voices sound as one, oh hear our battle shout.
Wykenwode! Wykenwode!
Defender of the innocent! Protector of the good!"*

Lightning crackled over their joining, eyeballs burnt as an explosion of pure, white brilliance exploded upwards in the night sky, a mushroom cloud of power which incinerated all in its path.

*"Wykenwode! Wykenwode!
Defender of the innocent! Protector of the good!"*

The creature howled with deadly pain, melting in the blast. The fireball fell back down to earth, billowing outwards, washing over and through the circle of villagers, engulfing Sylvie and the fallen Lord Marchmant where they lay. Renewing, restoring, healing, until suddenly, it was gone.

The villagers were left, unharmed, retinas imprinted with the force of the blast, staring at one another across the now empty clearing, blinking watering eyes, and struggling to adjust to the darkness. Auras fading, legs crumpling, they collapsed panting and spent, onto the welcoming cool of the Forest floor.

Sylvie looked down as Lord Jolyon's eyes opened, clear and painless, blinking in surprise.

"What happened?" he asked. "Am I still dying?"

"No, my lord, not yet," she said, voice low and joyful. "By your actions, you have broken the curse laid upon your family so long ago. Never again will any of your kin be taken by the Forest."

"Curse?" he asked, struggling to sit, rubbing the tender spot on his chest where the force of the creature's thrust had felled him. "I don't understand. What curse?"

"It is not for me to explain," she replied, stroking a lock of hair tenderly off his forehead. "You are so much like my Lord," she murmured, glancing up as the villagers let out a ragged cheer realising the battle was over. They'd won. The creature was no more.

Sally staggered to her feet, her father's strong arms encircling and protecting, and Lord Jolyon's face fell into lines of admiration and anguished hope.

"I know what it is your heart longs for, my lord," Sylvie began, his piercing blue eyes flicked to her enquiringly.

"And will I get it?" he asked, his manner casual, but the yearning could be heard.

"Eventually," Sylvie promised, helping him to a sitting position. "But it will not take the form you expect," she cautioned.

"I don't care how long I have to wait," he said, eyes locking fervently with Sylvie's calm perusal, "so long as I can hope…"

"There is always hope," she promised, and smiled.

The fight was done. In the quiet stillness, the villagers gazed at each other, breathing heavily, hardly daring to believe it was over and they'd won.

But victory had not been achieved without casualties.

Many of the villagers were injured, and others went to their aid. Lying in crumpled, undignified heaps were the bodies of Miss Iris Peabody, Thomas Dodd, and Joseph Hunter. The creatures had proven too powerful for them, or perhaps their faith had simply not been strong enough.

Farmer Cairn and his wife were embracing Sally, enclosing her within a loving circle of relieved fear. Her two brothers, flushed and excited from the fight, also joined the family circle, admiration of their elder sister in their excited voices, as they clamoured for her to tell them all her adventures.

She turned finally from her family and Jack was there, bruised and breathless. Wordlessly, she fell into his arms, feeling his strength and warmth, their embrace one of relief and comfort.

"We did it," she murmured, and he grinned at her.

"No," he amended. "You did it."

"I can't believe it," Lord Gilliard surveyed the clearing, the shocked expressions of the survivors, hardened warriors all, pride in themselves dawning on faces still coming to terms with what had occurred. "It's over," he finished with satisfaction.

Sally looked round wildly, realising someone was missing. "Where's Sylvie?" she asked, and Lord Jolyon was there, taking her hand, gently pulling her from Jack's grasp.

"She went," he replied, ignoring the furiously dark scowl Jack shot him, "but left you a message. She said you know all now, that she owes you a debt beyond measure which she will repay."

"What?" murmured Sally, confused, "What debt? I don't understand." As she spoke, she became aware of the tug of war occurring between Jack and Lord Jolyon, her hands held prisoner by each as they gently, persistently, attempted to pull her to their side.

"Oh, for heaven's sake," she exclaimed crossly, wrenching herself free of them both. Then she saw Daniel Forrester and his wife picking their way across the churned-up floor of the clearing, faces stiff with purpose, and realisation drenched her with icy memory.

"Reuben!" she gasped, and turned and bolted from the clearing.

The Forest

~ a tale of old magic ~

~PART FIVE~

There is no real ending. It's just the place where you stop the story

~ Frank Herbert ~

Truth is stranger than Fiction, but it is because Fiction is obliged to stick to possibilities; Truth isn't.

~ Mark Twain, Following the Equator, A Journey Around the World ~

Chapter Nineteen
~ Sally's Tale ~

How long, Miss Violet thought despairingly. How long could this night possibly last? Existence had narrowed to this one point in time, the gloomy cottage, the fire crackling in the hearth, the vague meanderings of Molly Mole as she worked to save Reuben's life.

Miss Violet found it hard to conceive that somewhere out there in the dark, life continued. That Sally and Jack were even now trying to save a woman who was already dead, facing untold dangers, could even have been killed themselves. Miss Violet was concerned and deeply afraid for them, yet at the same time, struggled to grasp the importance of anything beyond this moment and the young man stretched out on the table, so pale and still.

Finally, Molly stepped back, shaking her head. "I've done as much as I can," she announced, placing a gnarled hand gently on Reuben's feverish brow. "It's out of my hands," she continued. "It's up to the spirits, and the lad himself, whether he lives or dies. Either way, the decision will be made by dawn."

"What do we do now?" demanded John Blacksmith. Miss Violet knew he longed to be active, that the hours of sitting and watching had gnawed at his soul until he was like a caged tiger, stress emanating from his agitated body, stiff with tension.

"Now?" said Molly, and grinned, a toothless smirk in a sea of wrinkles. "Now, we wait…"

Sunlight, he could feel sunlight gently playing over his tightly clenched eyelids, hear softly evocative cooing of wood-pigeons, smell the fresh, green scent of trees and other living things, feel the breath of gentle breezes wafting gently over his face.

Cautiously, Reuben opened his eyes and the pain was gone. He gazed in wonder at the lushly vibrant woodland, knowing he was in the Forest, unsure of which part. It seemed altered, changed. Always beautiful, now the Forest glowed with the rosy, golden hue of perpetual summer, the dappled patches of light and shade sprinkling the Forest floor performing a glorious dance of coquettishness.

He stood gingerly, expecting pain, not remembering why. There was none. His body felt renewed, energised, and he stretched towards the sun coyly peeping through the rustling, verdant canopy. He felt good, better than good, alive with joyful purpose, a sensation of blissful vigour flooding his body until each nerve ending tingled with the promise of extreme awareness.

Not knowing why he was there, not even sure of who or when he was, Reuben wandered through this paradise of abundance, smiling at a squirrel which darted around a tree trunk, pausing to throw him a quizzical look as if it also wondered at his presence. A flash of vivid blue, a gurgle of water, and Reuben was beside a stream. A kingfisher soared heavenward with its morning catch clasped firmly in its beak, and he knelt, scooping the freshly invigorating water into his mouth.

It tasted good, beyond mere water. As it flowed through his body with the clarity of finest champagne, Reuben threw back his head and laughed, almost drunk with the simple joy of being alive in such a place as this. He walked further in, watching the creatures of the Forest bound about their busy lives, as if he was seeing it all for the first time, and his honest, handsome face glowed with the thrill of discovery.

He entered a clearing and felt a dart of recognition. He'd been here before, knowing with a dim, distant echo of memory it was important to him, that here events of great importance had been played out.

She sat in the clearing's heart on a fallen tree trunk, long silvery hair spread over her shoulders like a shimmering sheet of water, darkly gentle eyes watching him approach. Her beautiful face alight with pleasure at seeing him, those temptingly soft lips parting in a smile of greeting.

He saw her and stopped. He knew her. Her name came easily.

"Sylvie," he said, remembering her and the love he bore her, eagerly going to her and lifting her gently to her feet. Their lips met, and it was as it should be.

The kiss lasted an eternity whilst the sun blushingly hid its face behind a pillow of cloud, and all around the Forest sighed with approval. He held her in his arms, marvelled that she fitted so completely, as if each had been created for the other.

"I love you," for the first time ever he spoke the words. Her face shone with happiness, yet her eyes remained clouded with sorrow. He frowned at it, could not bear to see her so saddened.

"What is it?" he asked.

She sighed, shaking her head, and would have drawn away from him but he pulled her closer, the wild beating of his heart in her ear as she tremblingly laid her head upon his broad chest.

"I love you," she murmured. "It is a love that was always meant to be, but, you cannot stay."

"But I want to," he insisted hotly, fear clutching his heart at the thought she meant to send him away. "Why can't I?"

"Oh, my love," she whispered, placing small hands on either side of his face, gazing lovingly into his eyes. "Once, we were parted by the constraints of duty and obligation. Even though they no longer keep us apart, still, we cannot be together."

"Why not?" He demanded.

"Because there is a debt I must repay. A promise, yet unspoken, binding, which must be honoured. Even though it tears my heart apart to do so, I must send you back to another."

"Who?" he cried, face creasing into lines of incomprehension, "I love none but you," he insisted, "It has always been you, there is no other…"

Even as he spoke, a voice, low but persistent, echoed in his ear, calling his name. Memory stirred sluggishly, but still he clung to Sylvie.

"I refuse to go," he cried. She pulled him to her for a final kiss of goodbye, wild and sweet, it touched his soul and he cradled her in his arms.

"You must," she whispered sadly. "Even so, it will be as you desire. She will give you a strong son," her brow rose with amusement, "and even stronger daughters."

The other voice called his name again and Reuben started, feeling the conflicting tug of emotion. He looked at Sylvie, but already she was fading from his vision. He struggled to hold on to what she was to him, but the pull of the voice was too strong. He turned to it, not seeing the ravaged look of pain on Sylvie's face as she stepped away, letting him go, even though it killed her to do so.

"Reuben!" Sally's voice called his name, sharp and insistent. It reached into the Forest of his dreams, dragging him back. He exhaled, and opened his eyes to find Sally's face, wet with tears, eyes pleading, lips forming his name.

The other woman, that other place, retreated to the private and secret realm of half-forgotten dreams, never to be recalled except in that hazy twilight world between sleeping and waking.

Reuben opened his eyes and blinked at her, the clouds of fever gone from his gaze, his regard steady and lucid. Sally sighed with relief, clutched at his large, warm hand, and he smiled at her, grey eyes creasing at the corners.

The final piece of the puzzle clicked into place and at last she knew and understood all.

It was later, and Molly's cottage was crowded. The Forresters, closely followed by the Cairns and the Lords Jolyon and Gilliard, had hurried after Sally's headlong desperate flight from the scene of the battle, Jack hastily explaining Reuben's wounding and the events leading up to it, voice faltering at the telling of his own part.

Daniel Forrester had merely clamped a strong, steady hand onto his shoulder. "Well done, lad," he'd simply said. "Well done for fighting it off," and Farmer Cairn nodded in agreement, ruddy honest face sobered by the things he'd witnessed that night.

Of Sally and Reuben's newly found intimacy, and the fact that Sally now carried his child, Jack stayed silent, not feeling this part of the tale was his to tell. But when they crowded into the cottage and Sally's mother saw her daughter caught up in the strong arms of Reuben Forrester, noting the dazed, loving look in Sally's eyes, she surmised it wouldn't be long before she was planning a wedding, her mother's heart thrilling at the thought.

Lord Jolyon, with a pang of regret, realised the struggle for supremacy of Sally's heart seemed to be over. The burly, blond son of the forester had won, and he sighed to himself with pained disappointment. Yet Sylvie's words still inspired hope, so when his brother glanced at him sympathetically, guessing a little at what his younger brother was feeling, he was able to shrug and grimace wryly at his own, apparently shattered dreams.

Now they all sat, fortified with draughts of some treacly, dark liquor Molly had poured from a thick corked bottle, throats gasping with raw shock as it burnt its fiery way down.

"Sally," began Lord Gilliard, "you seem to be in possession of all the facts. Please, tell us what has occurred this night?"

"Well," Sally looked for support to Reuben. He smiled, squeezed her hand encouragingly, then glanced at Jack. Warmed by his nod of agreement she be the one to tell it, she settled herself comfortably on her stool and began.

"It all started hundreds of years ago, I'm not sure exactly when, certainly long before the Norman Conquest. The then lord of the Forest, one of the early Marchmants, although understanding it was a special and magical place, probably didn't realise how powerful and ancient it was. Anyway, some years earlier according to custom, he'd entered into agreement with a rich and noble family across the Channel that he'd marry their daughter. She was sent to him, along with her servant, an elderly woman who'd cared for her since birth when her own mother had unfortunately died. Isn't that right, Molly?"

All eyes turned to the ancient crone in wonder, and she nodded, chuckling. "Aye, that's right, my lady Sylvie was but fourteen years old when we crossed the sea and came to this place. The lord was away, fighting by the king's side, and did not return home till she was seventeen, not knowing during those long years of absence, that she had met and fallen in love with the forester's son. But, because of the honour of both their souls, neither ever betrayed by look, touch or deed, that they loved with a depth and passion unrivalled by any."

"With Sylvie and her serving woman also came another," continued Sally, "the serving woman's daughter, Bridget." She paused, looking sympathetically at Molly. "I'm so sorry," she said.

"Sorry, little maid?" Molly looked at her curiously. "Sorry for what?"

"What happened to your daughter Molly? What happened to Bridget?"

"She were taken from me," Molly Mole's face creased in an agony of remembrance, all the centuries that lay between then and now as nothing in the face of a mother's grief. "And it were my fault. I knew all magic came with a price, a price I promised to pay. I just didn't know the price would be her. But why do you ask?"

"There are things you must hear, things you must know," replied Sally. "Things it will pain you to learn of," she took a deep breath. "I swear they are the truth. Last night, the Forest took Jack and I back, and showed us what really happened. Nothing was as it seemed, you had no idea…"

She paused, shook her head sadly, took a deep breath and glanced around at the circle of expectant, spellbound faces. "Anyway," Sally continued, "to cut a long story short, Sylvie knew she had to marry the lord and was afraid. He was much older than her and she was deeply in love with another. But, duty compelled her to honour the betrothal, so she knew her love could never be. You went to her, Molly, gave her a love potion, advising her to pour two drops of it into the wedding cup so she'd fall deeply in love with the lord and he with her. She couldn't do it, felt it would be a dishonourable act and threw the bottle away."

"Is that what she did with it?" mused Molly, "I did wonder. The lord seemed so enamoured of her I believed she had given it only to him."

"No," Sally shook her head. "The lord fell genuinely in love with his wife, with her sweetness and youth. Left alone it would have been a good marriage. He had strong feelings for her and Sylvie was grateful for his kindness. Given time they would have made a go of things. They were not allowed that time; fate, or rather, your daughter Bridget, intervened."

"Hey what?" Molly turned startled eyes upon Sally. "What's that you say?"

"Do you remember Sylvie's maid, Sunniva?" pressed Sally. Molly nodded, puzzled, her cloudy eye never leaving Sally's serious expression.

"Aye, I do," she agreed. "She was the dead spit of you, such a cheerful and sunny little soul, none could help but love her. She was to be married to a young man-at-arms who had found much favour with the lord."

Molly paused, gaze flicking disdainfully to Jack. "But he betrayed her," she snapped, disgust tainting her voice. "Like most men, proved fickle and untrue. He abandoned her on their wedding day."

"No," stated Sally, "that's not true. That's not how it happened. Your daughter, Bridget, spied on your conversation with Sylvie. She found the bottle of love potion, gave half of it to Sunniva's betrothed and took him for herself, breaking Sunniva's heart and trapping that poor man in an obsessive love not of his choosing." Molly groaned, hands clutching at her chest. Sally continued relentlessly.

"The forester found Sunniva humiliated and heartbroken in the Forest. Suffering from disappointed love himself, he sympathised and offered her marriage. It meant family and companionship for both. For Sunniva it was a means of restoring her lost pride, but this marriage of convenience became so much more, as both came to appreciate and cherish the qualities of the other. Gradually, their wounded hearts fell in love."

"Tis true," Molly nodded. "He was a good lad," she cast a fond look at Reuben. "A fine, honest man. He and Sunniva seemed happy together. She was expecting her first child at the same time as my lady, I would hear them laughing and chattering together, excited about their approaching motherhood," she paused, a reflective look settling on her face.

"It troubled me that my Bridget did not enjoy the same intimacy with my lady. Oh, I could understand she was blamed by many for stealing Sunniva's man, and, tis true her tongue could be abrupt and harsh. I did think though, after the twins were born, that my lady would be friendlier with her, but it did not happen."

"Of course not," agreed Sally. "How could it? Sylvie loved Sunniva, she'd seen how devastated Sunniva had been, and even though her marriage to the forester turned out better than any could have expected, still Sylvie was loyal to her friend. Also, there was something about Bridget she didn't trust. How right she was, for it was Bridget who would lead to her downfall and the end of everything."

She stopped and looked directly at Molly. "I'm sorry," she said again.

Molly's jaw firmed. "Whatever it is," she stated flatly, "best you say it, for I reckon 'tis things I need to know. Things I perhaps should have known long since."

"Bridget's ambition was to be lady of the manor," Sally continued. "To achieve that goal, she gave Sylvie's husband the rest of the love potion. Under her influence, he murdered her husband, and set his huntsman to track down his heavily pregnant wife, claiming she and her serving woman, you Molly, were witches. Shocked and unhappy about the orders, but afraid to disobey, the hunters set the dogs loose."

Molly sat heavily in a chair, ancient face collapsing into fathomless crevasses of extreme shock.

"After you left her in the Forest, Molly, Sylvie went into labour, perhaps from trauma or perhaps it was her natural time, we'll never know, and realised she had to find shelter, somewhere to give birth. There was only one place she knew would take her in, so she went to the cottage of the forester, arriving not long after Sunniva herself had given birth."

Sally paused, clutching at Reuben's hand, the power of the memory enough to make her shiver, then looked straight into the old woman's eyes. "Sylvie died of natural causes, Molly. She haemorrhaged after giving birth to her child, and there was nothing either Sunniva or her husband could do to save her."

"The dogs hunted my lady and her child to death!" protested Molly. "I saw the child's arm, my lady's shoe and forced the hunters to retrace the dog's tracks. On the edge of a bottomless pool deep within the Forest, we found my lady's trail leading straight to the water, her cloak all torn and blood stained by its side. Her other shoe, ripped to shreds, was floating on the surface with the ribbon I had myself tied in her pretty hair only that morning, and under a bush, so small and pitiful, the remains of her baby, that poor little soul! It almost killed me, my lady's dear, wee daughter, still and cold, mutilated by those savage brutes. They murdered her. They hunted her down like an animal, killed her and her poor defenceless babe."

"No," interrupted Sally firmly. "That's not what happened. Sylvie gave birth to a son, a perfect healthy boy. He lived Molly. He was strong, a fighter, and he lived!"

"But... but I saw," stuttered Molly.

All eyes turned avidly to Sally as she sat so calmly. Keeper of secrets. Teller of the tale.

"The child you saw was Sunniva's stillborn daughter. She and her husband loved Sylvie so much they'd have done anything to keep her and her child safe. They promised to protect her child and that is what they did. The forester took her cloak, the clothing you found and the precious body of their daughter, knowing what fate awaited it, realising it was the only way. He laid a trail of blood through the Forest to the pool for the hounds to follow, scattered about the clothes, placing the body of his baby amongst them. We can only imagine what he must have felt. He then went home to his wife and they raised Sylvie's child as their own. Don't you see? It was the perfect plan, no one would ever suspect. Sunniva's child had been born the same night, and no one would look closely at the child of a forester."

"They did have a son," muttered Molly, tears streaming down her face. "A fine lad, their only child. The apple of his father's eye, he became forester in turn. All that time, my lady's son was right before my eyes and I never knew, never suspected... I believed her child dead, and I hated. Blamed with a passion."

"Yes," agreed Sally, her eyes gentle. "And that leads us to the curses and the consequences that came about because of them. You longed passionately for Sylvie to still live, begged the Forest to give her the power to always flee her enemies. But, she was already dead, so the Forest did the best it could. It trapped her soul and gave her the form of the White Hind. You condemned her to eternal misery, Molly, unable to move on Sylvie was a prisoner within the Forest, forced to watch as again and again the tragedy of the past was replayed."

"My poor lady," wailed Molly. "I did not know, did not realise..."

"Sylvie's child, whom you believed to be dead, did indeed know contentment all its life. Down through the generations, the foresters have always been known for being happy with their lot in life." Sally paused, her smile taking in both Reuben and his father as they grinned ruefully at one another.

"You passed on your power to your daughter, believing her to be an innocent victim, but in the very next breath commanded the one guilty of committing the crime against Sylvie be punished, trapped within the Forest. It was a complete contradiction of terms. You were unknowingly both granting power to, and punishing, the same person. Bridget inherited your power, there was nothing the Forest could do to stop that, so it did the only thing it could: it erected a barrier and trapped her. If none could get in, none could be injured by her. The only exception was the Marchmant family, and these the Forest protected, knowing them to be innocent victims."

Sally looked at the Lords Gilliard and Jolyon, a faint blush warming her cheeks when she met the piercing blue regard of her would be lover.

"So that thing in the Forest, that dark and twisted creature…?"

"Was your daughter, Bridget, yes," Sally tried to soften the blow of her words, but there was no softening, no lessening the impact and Molly reeled back upon her stool, hand to her mouth, tears brimming out of eyes that had seen too much to forget or forgive.

"But what was the price then?" she finally wailed. "If not Bridget, then what?"

"Oh Molly," the skin was gnarled into leathery knots under Sally's touch as she took one of the old lady's hands in her own. "You've been alone for so long, so many years, eaten alive by hatred and bitterness and regret… you've seen so many young lives destroyed because of you, because of your curses. You must have wondered if it was all worth it, if revenge was really worth the price it extracted from the innocent. So, don't you think you've paid enough?"

Overwhelmed, Molly wiped her hands over her wet face and silently nodded.

"You also cursed the Marchmants, Molly," Sally continued. "Commanding that a son and heir were to occasionally be taken. The Forest obeyed you and took the lords but would allow no injury to come to them, instead they continued to live within the Forest. A drawn out half-life it's true, but they were alive and unharmed. The only others allowed through the barrier were the forester and his offspring. It's always been assumed the Forest allowed this merely because the forester was essential to maintain it and maybe that was one reason, but of course, there was another far more valid one. The foresters were direct descendants of the son of Sylvie and her lord; they were Marchmants, entitled to enter the Forest whenever they wished."

Lord Jolyon whistled, low and surprised. "So, the forester has more claim to the title than we do?" he remarked dryly to his brother.

"Have no fear, my lords," Daniel Forrester hurried to reassure, "As far as I'm concerned, nothing has changed in that respect."

"You also decreed any who'd played a part, no matter how small, in the tragedy, were to be forever discontented. As the huntsmen looked to me to be made up of Hunters, Dodds and Blunts, I'd say that part of the curse was carried out to the letter," Sally paused as the others exchanged wry smiles, for it was true those particular families were notorious for their perpetual dissatisfaction.

"What happened to the twins, Molly? Bridget's children, what happened to them?" Molly looked up at Sally's question, face numb from the shock of revelation.

"They were given to foster families," she replied quietly. "The little lass went to a merchant family in the village. The boy, well, the blacksmith and his wife were without child, so he went to them, and became blacksmith thereafter."

"When Bridget was taken by the Forest," continued Sally, "she placed a part of her soul into each child. Through the generations, that seed of evil has waited, biding its time, until all the pieces fell into place and Nancy and Jack were born. Without her whole essence, you see, there was no way Bridget could ever escape the Forest. With the strength of her children there was a chance she could."

"And she very nearly did," Jack commented bitterly.

Sally's face softened. "Don't blame yourself," she ordered gently. "You managed to fight her off, that's what's important."

John Blacksmith laid a hand on his son's shoulder and the bitterness eased from Jack's face. Miss Violet stood beside them and Sally thought how like a family they looked, united and unbreakable.

"But what about all those countless tragic triangles which have occurred throughout the centuries," Miss Violet enquired, "All those murders and suicides every time the White Hind was sighted?"

"Bridget would wait, biding her time, gathering her power," Sally explained. "Then she would try to escape, reaching out to any whose soul was in torment, to those who were unhappy or frustrated in love. She'd lure them to the Forest, drawing strength from their negative emotions. Sylvie would desperately try to warn the village, but being unable to approach them her presence was misconstrued as an evil omen. Gradually, over the centuries, Bridget harvested such a store of power from these poor unfortunate souls, she hoped to be able to finally break free from her prison. When Reuben took me and Jack through the barrier, it triggered an inevitable chain of events. Bridget felt Jack's essence, recognising at last her son had come back to her, and through him, she was able to reach Nancy Peabody. A lonely, spiteful child, she succumbed gladly to the lure of the creature, but Jack was not so easy to coerce. He was unloved at home, that was true…"

John Blacksmith had the grace to look ashamed. Unthinkingly, Miss Violet slipped her hand into his, offering comfort and sympathy.

"Yet Jack had family and friends who loved him," continued Sally, "and being a stronger character than Nancy, resisted Bridget. She knew events would have to be manipulated to gain control over him."

Sally paused, took a deep breath, cheeks flushing rosily at the next part of the tale she must tell. Reuben's grip on her hand tightened, guessing at her discomfort, but he didn't know the half of it, Sally thought desperately, wishing there was a way to avoid what must now be said.

"Bridget, through Nancy Peabody, used Jack's jealousy to gain control over him. She knew he was in love with me, and when she found out Reuben and I were in love, realised she had the perfect weapon."

"And like the blind fool I was, I fell for it," muttered Jack. "I allowed her to take control of me, and Reuben very nearly died because of it."

"Don't be so hard on yourself," comforted Reuben. "I'm alright, it would take more than a bullet to stop me. But there's one thing I don't understand," he said, turning back to Sally. "How did you get through the barrier this time without me?"

"Oh, well, erm…" began Sally.

"I think the Forest realised how important it was we got through," Jack leapt to her rescue, warmed by the grateful look Sally threw him.

"Yes, the Forest," said Lord Gilliard. "Tell me Sally, do you think the barrier will remain down? Or will the Forest forbid all but the family to enter again?"

"I don't know," replied Sally. "I suppose we'll have to wait and see."

"Sylvie talked of a curse," Lord Jolyon exclaimed. "She said when I saved Sally's life, I'd broken the curse placed upon my family..."

"That be right," interjected Molly. "My curse was a powerful one, could only be broken should a Marchmant value the life of one of my lady's descendants more highly than his own. I thought it impossible such a thing could ever come to pass, me believing my lady's child to be dead."

Sally saw the puzzled faces and knew it wouldn't be long before the truth occurred.

"But I'm the one descended from Sylvie's child," murmured Reuben, "not Sally. So the only way the curse could be broken, would be if..." Comprehension dawned, his face flushed beetroot red to the roots of his thick blond hair and he gaped at Sally, a look of wonder creeping into his eyes, clutching her hand even tighter, and whispered, "is it true?"

Sally rested her forehead on his shoulder. "Yes," she confided, feeling his warmth and strength on her skin, drawing comfort from it, not wanting to turn and face the others.

"I don't understand," Farmer Cairn's voice was plaintive in his confusion. "What does it mean...?"

"It means," interrupted his wife dryly, "we'd better start planning a wedding pretty sharpish. That's what it means."

When Sally finally dared to lift her gaze to meet that of her parents, she found no blame or disapproval there. Tempered perhaps by the events of the night, relief they'd all survived, their expressions were of acceptance, maybe even understanding.

Reuben felt Jack's eyes upon him. He saw and understood the message they contained. Do right by her, they demanded. Do the right thing, or else answer to me. He hastily glanced away from the condemnation in Jack's stare, gripping Sally's hand, seeking for a diversion.

"How was the creature destroyed?" he asked, and Sally smiled.

"The Forest felt responsible for what had occurred, for the many deaths caused by Bridget through the centuries so it created a spell of power and tried to pass it on to the villagers, so that they may unite and rid themselves of the evilness of her presence."

"A spell?" Reuben enquired.

"The Festival rhyme," Sally replied. "But, it miscalculated. It chose a young sensitive girl, perhaps because she was in tune with forces beyond normal nature. But her mind couldn't cope. It destroyed her. Only the rhyme was passed on, the rest, the instructions on how to use it, were lost forever, until…"

"Until a certain clever young lady, figured it all out," interjected Lord Gilliard, and Sally blushed with modest pleasure at the admiration she saw on their faces.

"And is it really dead?" demanded Eliza Cairn fearfully. "Has it really gone for good?"

"Oh yes," reassured Sally, softly. "It can never come back now."

"But what happened to my lady?" Molly pawed at Lord Gilliard's arm. "Where is my lambkin buried? Did the forester throw her body into the pool? How can we find where my Sylvie's bones lay?"

"I'm afraid I don't know," he replied. "There can be no way of…"

"I know where she is," Sally said slowly. "In a way, I think I've always known."

The sun had already lifted itself above the crest of the downs when Sally led the small group carefully up the steep incline. The going was slow, John Blacksmith and Farmer Cairn held tightly to each of Molly's arms, practically carrying her every step of the way, and Sally thought how ancient she looked, as if the revelations of the night had descended heavily upon her frail and twisted body.

Lord Gilliard walked beside Jack eagerly questioning him about his experiences in the Forest, Lord Jolyon behind them. Sally felt his gaze upon her. It confused and alarmed her, her spine stiffening in response to the heat it generated within her body. Suddenly, he was beside her, long legs overtaking the others. Sally glanced at his thoughtful face, his eyes more intensely blue than ever.

"Sally, he began, voice pitched low so the others wouldn't hear.

"Yes, my lord," she replied, heart pounding in a frenzied rhythm of excited anticipation.

"You do realise I'm in love with you."

"My… my lord," she faltered, uncertainly.

"You're carrying his child. I understand you feel this obligates you to marry him, but there are other choices. I would hate you to be trapped, Sally, because of an indiscretion."

"W-what are you saying, my lord?"

"I'm saying, should you feel the same way about me, I would be prepared, more than prepared, to accept the child. I would never reproach you about it; nor would anyone else. You'd be Lady Marchmant, and although the child could not inherit, it would not be treated any differently from our other children."

"You'd do that?" Sally exclaimed, turning to face him with a frown.

"There's nothing I wouldn't do for you, Sally, nothing," he replied earnestly, raising her hand, and pressing a firm, hot kiss to her palm. "Don't answer me now," he said hastily, stopping the words which trembled on her lips. "Promise you'll think about it. I love you. If you feel the same way, then anything is possible."

He gave her a slight bow, expression serious, eyes glittering with an intensity of emotion, before walking away to join his brother. Jack hurried over, face creasing into a darkly furious scowl of jealousy

"What did he want?" he muttered. Sally shook her head, not wanting to stoke the flames of Jack's frustrated passions any further. "Sally," Jack pleaded, and Sally raised weary eyes to his.

"I love you," he whispered. "After last night, I think you realise we were meant to be together. If it hadn't been for… well, you know… then we'd have been married all those centuries ago, would have been so happy. None of this would've happened. Maybe, who knows, maybe you wouldn't be afraid to love me now… I understand you've chosen Reuben, because, well because he's the safe path, because you feel you can trust him and even because of what he did, all that time ago," he paused, swallowing hard.

Sally stared down the hill to where the others steadily climbed, watching as Reuben was helped by his parents, slowly and painfully struggling after them.

"But he will never love you the way I do, Sal!" Jack whispered urgently, gripping her wrist. "And I will wait for you, forever if I have too, but I will wait for you."

"Jack, I…" she began, stopped, unable to speak, the constraints of the past crumbling in the light of all she'd learnt, all she now knew.

"I love you," his voice was low and insistent. Still she could not speak. Then Molly and the others reached them.

"Where is she?" demanded Molly, close to tears. "Where is my lady?"

"Up here," replied Sally, leading her to the toper-most point on the farm, that curious, oddly shaped grass mound where Sally had spent so much of her childhood lying in silent contemplation, gazing up at the sky in strange contentment.

"Well, I never," exclaimed Farmer Cairn in surprise. "There? That's nothing but a mound of earth."

"No, it's not," replied Sally, digging at its sides, tearing her flesh on the tough stalks of moorland grass. Daniel Forrester stepped forward, and with the same knife he'd used to kill Nancy Peabody cut away at the turf, exposing tightly packed stones underneath.

"What is it?" asked Miss Violet curiously.

"It's a cairn," explained Sally. "The forester and his wife brought Sylvie's body back to the farm where Sunniva's family lived, trusting them not to ask any questions. They buried her here, high up, where she could feel the sun and wind move over her. They guarded her body throughout the centuries until eventually all memory of her faded, and only their name remained as a clue, Cairn."

"My lady," sobbed Molly, clawing blindly at Sally with one withered paw. "Help me to her," she begged. Gently, Sally placed an arm around the ancient woman, and half led, half carried her to Sylvie's final resting place.

"Thank you," Molly muttered, placing a hand on Sally's head. "Your heart be true," she declared, a knowing look sliding into her eyes. "You have a decision to make, my child," she whispered. "Make sure it be the right one."

"I know," Sally replied. "But, I'm not sure..."

"Yes, you are," answered the other woman wisely. "You know which path you have to take. You always have known, deep down inside, which way is right for you." Gently, she turned Sally to look down the slope at the others.

To the right stood Lord Jolyon, tall and handsome, confident in his status and position, his brother standing firmly at his shoulder. Sally knew that way lay material wealth and position, should she wish it, and neither she nor her children would ever know want. As Lord Jolyon's eyes met hers, she felt a shiver of remembered desire.

To the left stood Jack with his family, John Blacksmith and Miss Violet. Sally momentarily marvelled at how completely they all seemed to fit as a unit. Jack met her gaze with an intense stare, his expression serious and Sally's heart thudded at the memory of a passion so strong, echoes of it had lingered through centuries.

In the centre stood her parents, their eyes warm and encouraging, Sally knew that whatever decision she made, even if she chose to stand alone, they would support her, and the knowledge warmed her heart.

Then, pale and trembling slightly but determinedly there, stood Reuben, who smiled when he felt her eyes upon him. Sally knew that way lay the safe path. Reuben was reliable and steadfast, had proven himself in the past, and she had no doubt her heart would always be protected in his keeping.

Confused, she turned back to Molly, seeking her advice. Molly had gone. The last piece of the puzzle complete, kneeling by the side of her lady's grave, knowing her soul to finally be at peace, Molly's spirit had departed leaving her brittle, ancient shell to crumble and disperse on the brisk winds which rushed over the hillside, blowing away all before it.

Sally was left, facing her choices, alone…

Chapter Twenty
~ Completions and Connections ~

Sunlight, moving gently across his face disturbed him, and Reuben awoke in his chair, realising ruefully he'd slipped easily into a light doze, wondering how long he'd slept, cocking his head to hear any sounds of the family returning from church. Normally he'd have accompanied them, but an inexplicable bout of tiredness had struck, and Sally had perched on the bed, face crinkling into lines of concern as she'd felt his brow.

After twenty-five years of marriage Reuben thought them beyond romance, but as he'd grabbed her hand and unexpectedly kissed it, Sally had blushed like a young girl, pressing a quick kiss to his lips. How beautiful she was, he thought, her face as fresh and unlined as it'd always been, the ravages of time and life which confronted him every day in the mirror seeming to have barely touched her.

His Sally, his wife. The quarter of a century which had passed in a heartbeat was as nothing, and he felt an exhilarating rush of passion. "I love you," he'd said, voice rich with desire. Somehow, it seemed vitally important he tell her before she left, even though he knew it a mere few hours before she'd be back, bringing all the family with her for the traditional Forresters Sunday lunch.

"Later," she'd murmured in his ear, "Later, after lunch, when they've all gone home." He'd run a hand through her gleaming, shoulder-length hair, regretting the loss of the long braids, sacrificed many years ago to the more pressing demands on her time of a home and an ever-growing family.

The family, Reuben's lips moved into a smile of affection as his mind touched briefly on each member. Their eldest daughter, Jacqueline, born a scant eight months from their wedding day a mere four weeks after that eventful night in the Forest.

Possessing her mother's good looks and her father's height, Jackie Forrester was the jewel of the village. Strong, independent and frighteningly intelligent, Jackie had quickly outpaced the teachers at the local school, and for the first time, with the help and encouragement of her parents, a child left the village and went away to university. She returned with a degree in business studies, three languages under her belt and a clear idea, even at barely twenty-two, of exactly where she was going in life.

Lord Gilliard, impressed by her achievements, offered her a position working for the family. When Jolyon, who shortly after Sally's marriage had moved abroad to further the family's interests in Asia, telephoned his brother, disillusioned and frustrated, he had made a spontaneous decision which would change everything.

The deal was on the verge of collapsing, Jolyon complained to his sympathetic brother, the translator had been taken ill, and the company they were interested in acquiring had suddenly developed cold feet. Nothing was going to plan, and he was rapidly losing patience with the brick walls he seemed to continually run up against. In short, he needed help.

No problem, his brother had reassured him, I'll send you Jackie Forrester. She's smart, intuitive and quick witted, plus she speaks the language fluently. She had also studied the deal intricately. If anyone could help get things back on track, it was her. Grudgingly, Jolyon agreed, not sure what a child barely out of her teens could accomplish, but intrigued by his brother's glowing report of the daughter of his former love.

That evening, returning to his hotel, thoughts of Sally intruded into Jolyon's rigidly ordered life. For the first time in years he allowed himself the luxury of regret, lying awake long into the night, missing her, thinking about what might have been.

Unmarried, much to his mother's regret, at forty-seven still a strikingly handsome and youthful looking man, Jolyon had never quite got over losing Sally. The decision to move abroad being the desperate action of a man, forced to witness the woman he loved happily married to another.

Next morning, gritty-eyed and short-tempered through lack of sleep, Jolyon returned to the conference room to find a message awaiting him. Miss Forrester's flight had been delayed. She was travelling straight from the airport to the office and would arrive as quickly as possible.

That moment. That moment when the doors opened, and she strode confidently in, Jolyon finally realised what it was he'd been waiting for all those years, why he'd resisted the charms of various eminently suitable women, and the subtle and not so subtle hints of his mother. It was because his soul had been suspended in limbo, waiting for this moment, this woman.

Her eyes, cool and collected, the same deep grey as her father's, locked with his in an intensely expressive gaze in which so much was said and implied. Her lips parted on a small oh of surprise, twin spots of colour flushed her cheeks. And he'd known she'd realised it too.

Thirty-six hours of extensive negotiating later, Jackie had achieved everything the family wanted, and more. Silent with admiration, head so full of her there was no room for anything else, Jolyon took her back to their hotel. Heart hammering, for once his smooth and witty repertoire deserting him, they rode the elevator up to their rooms in silence.

At the door to her suite they'd turned to one another, the decision already made, as if forces set in motion centuries before were finally reaching completion. That night he'd stayed with her. They'd not been parted since, shocking their families when they'd contacted them from Singapore two weeks later, to present them with the fait accompli of their marriage.

Alarmed and vaguely perturbed, after all he was old enough to be her father, and if she'd chosen differently, Sally couldn't help but reflect wryly, he would've been, she awaited her daughter's return. Saying nothing of her concerns to Reuben and unsure of her own feelings, she needed to talk to her daughter, to look into her eyes before she could pass judgement.

The newlyweds returned a few weeks later. At the first glimpse of her beautiful and unique daughter, hand in hand with her tall, handsome and utterly besotted husband, Sally relaxed. They fitted, completely and absolutely, and she swallowed down the last fleeting wisps of regret and reflection, realising life had indeed come full circle.

Silently witnessing her daughter's supreme satisfaction with her husband, her marriage, her career and exciting life that took her to the furthest reaches of the world, Sally was happy for her headstrong and passionate daughter. Happy, and if she were to be completely honest with herself, a little envious that life had dealt Jackie such a diverse and rich hand.

Upon hearing the news of his goddaughter's surprise marriage, Jack had been silent for a long moment before remarking mildly on the coincidence of the identical age gap between Jackie and Jolyon and that of Sylvie and her lord, further strengthening Sally's conviction this union was meant to be.

Jack, Reuben's grin stretched even wider as he reflected on the surprising twist of events in Jack's life. He knew that losing Sally had been hard for Jack. Reuben remembered that fateful morning up on the downs, standing by Sylvie's grave, sober reflection in Sally's eyes as her gaze swept over them all.

He felt again the pained jolt his heart had given, sudden realisation dawning that after all Jack and Sally had been through together, the suppressed flame of their passion may have been re-ignited, the breath catching in his chest at the thought of losing her.

For a moment she'd hesitated, Reuben fancied he'd seen a yearning, a softening towards Jack, then she'd seemed to draw herself together, stepped to his side slipping her arm around his waist, letting him lean weakly upon her, offering him her strength and courage. The bleakness upon Jack's face, the barely veiled disappointment on Lord Jolyon's; those he could still recall, as well as the rush of triumph. Finally, at the end, Sally had chosen him.

The years had been good to them, despite concerns over his health. Never fully recovering from the wounds inflicted upon him by Nancy Peabody, Reuben's existence, by necessity, had to be a staid and steady one. Time had flowed gently over them, a still, barely moving backwater.

At times, he'd fretted that maybe Sally longed for more, chafed at the restraints of the insular narrowness of their lives. But on the few occasions he'd anxiously questioned her, her eyes had gone soft with love, her avowals of perfect contentment ringing true. Still, sometimes he wondered.

Two other children had followed Jackie, born in rapid succession, and the small cottage had continually rung with the voices of children. Next to be born had been their son, Luke, tall and strong, a carbon copy of the blond huskiness of his father. Lacking the fire and ambition of his sister, Luke had barely scraped through school, having no interest in book learning, preferring to escape into the Forest.

As a child, he'd talk often about the imaginary friends he had there, Sally and Reuben exchanging glances and wondering. For the barrier, which had fallen to allow the villagers entry during the Forest's hour of darkest need, had quickly re-established itself, and once again only Marchmants and Forresters were allowed passage.

It was the way it'd always been. Given the fast-developing nature of the world, Reuben understood the Forest's need to protect itself.

A few years previously, Luke had become forester alongside his father, and Reuben rejoiced that the family tradition was being upheld. Once established with a wage and cottage of his own, Luke had calmly announced his plans to marry even though barely twenty-two, his childhood sweetheart, Molly Blacksmith, only nineteen.

It was a good marriage, solid and enduring, Luke's bride having the dark fiery temperament of her father, tempered by the uncomplicated sweetness of her mother. Already, a wee black-eyed babe had arrived, and Reuben's heart lifted at the thought of seeing his grandson that afternoon.

Also coming for lunch were Molly's parents, and the table had been extended to fit everyone around it. Sniffing appreciatively, Reuben smelt the tempting aroma of beef wafting out into the garden, remembering Sally's firm instructions to turn the oven down in an hour's time.

Reuben shifted into a more comfortable position in his chair, feeling a twinge of cramp, thinking about his daughter-in-law's parents. Still hale and hearty even in his seventies, John Blacksmith had much to be grateful for, his second marriage to Miss Violet Peabody having been an unmitigated success, despite the cynical predictions of the village when they'd announced their engagement at Sally and Reuben's wedding.

That fateful night in the Forest had opened John Blacksmith's eyes to a lot of things: the mutual need he and Jack had for one another, the love he bore his son, and that life could and did exist beyond the death of his wife.

In the aftermath, as the village struggled to come to terms with what had happened, burying its dead and attempting to pick up the reins of normal life, John Blacksmith found his feet straying often to the village shop. Attempting to create a normal home life for his sullen and heartbroken son, John went originally to buy food and ask advice of its kindly, quietly beautiful proprietor.

As the weeks slipped by and the whole village got caught up in preparations for Sally and Reuben's wedding, another love affair blossomed. Unseen and unremarked upon, none were aware of the intensity of the romance being played out right under their noses, until the wedding, when John Blacksmith and a delightedly blushing Miss Violet, had announced their commitment to the world.

They'd had two children, of which Molly was the youngest. The oldest child, Joe, was also related as he'd married Reuben's youngest daughter, Sylvia. As proud of his oldest daughter as he was, Reuben secretly admitted to a fond preference for his youngest child. Shy, dreamy and kind, Sylvia had floated through childhood, drifted through school and dreamt her way through young adulthood.

A pretty, serious child with big dark eyes, Reuben often fancied he caught a glimpse of Sylvie in her expression and his mind would return to those almost forgotten, far off days, a small nagging regret wrinkling at his heart. For a moment, he'd feel there was something he needed to remember, something important, but whatever it was, it eluded him.

On her eighteenth birthday, Sylvia married Joe, her companion since birth, closest friend and confidante. It'd been no surprise to anyone, neither set of parents raising any objections. Joe was already established running his father's garage and upon their marriage, John Blacksmith and Miss Violet moved back to the little cottage next to the shop now jointly run by her daughter Molly and her daughter-in-law Sylvia.

What an incestuous clan we are, Reuben thought with a chuckle, looking forward to the day, reflecting with pleasure it was to be by way of a reunion. Not only were Sylvia and Joe, Luke, Molly and their baby son coming to lunch, along with Molly and Joe's parents, the Blacksmiths, last night Jackie had phoned. They were back in the country, she and Jolyon, along with their little daughter, Sarah, and would be with them by evening.

Reuben longed to see his daughter again. It'd been many months since they'd last returned home, and he had a need to see her and his granddaughter. They grow so quickly at that age, he thought fondly, in the three months since their last visit, Reuben knew Sarah would've changed from baby to toddler. He ached to see her.

To Reuben's delight, Jack was also home, and it really had been too long since they'd seen him. Frowning, Reuben added up the weeks and the months, shocked to realise it'd been two long years since Luke and Molly's wedding, the last time Jack had been home.

Jack. How eventful his life had been, and how proud the village was of its successful and wealthy son.

For a while, Reuben had worried desperately about Jack. During the months following his wedding to Sally, especially after the birth of Jackie to whom Jack was godfather, Reuben had silently and helplessly watched as Jack slipped further and further into a decline.

Unable to remedy the problem, understanding by marrying Sally he'd effectively broken Jack's heart, Reuben experienced many pangs of guilt for his closest friend.

Briefly rallying after his father's marriage to Miss Violet, genuinely delighted with his new stepmother, Jack seemed to be recovering, but the daily torture of seeing Sally, contentedly cocooned in a blissful state of marriage and impending motherhood, had proved too much. Increasingly, Jack's thoughts turned to escape, where and how eluding him.

Then, one day, a visitor came to Marchmant Hall. A close friend of Lord Jolyon, Rowland Sims was a race car driver of no small talent, and even the village, insular though it was, knew and admired him. Recovering at the Hall from a fractured leg sustained in an accident, Sims had needed a chauffeur. Lord Jolyon offered the temporary position to Jack, who'd jumped at the chance of a diversion from the unremitting misery of his life.

Impressed by the skilful, competent driving skills of the young silent lad with the darkly brooding good looks, Sims had been further intrigued by the extent of Jack's knowledge of cars. When he'd finally left the Hall to return to the glamorous and exciting world of motor car racing, he'd taken Jack with him.

It'd been the saving of Jack. His father and stepmother observed with mingled emotions of relief and fear, his rapid, obsessive rise up the ladder to success. Beginning as a valued member of the pit team, Jack was unaware of Sims continued interest in him, until the afternoon he'd asked Jack to 'try out a new car for him'.

Racing into a bend, heart thrumming with exhilaration, Jack found the memory of Sally temporarily buried beneath a sea of adrenalin, the clean simple connection of man and machine freeing him from the morass of misery and regret weighing down his soul. Watching the young, obviously troubled man race, Sims realised he was a natural. After that, Jack never looked back.

Two minor smashes failing to slow him down; now, twenty-five years later, Jack was a celebrity. His dangerously handsome looks and taciturn nature making an enigmatic icon of him. Aging had also seemed to bypass him, and Reuben would sometimes wonder... wonder about that night he and Sally had spent spiralling through the past within the Forest. Wonder if some residual after effect had left them both immune to the harshness of time.

Often, Sally would turn the page of some newspaper or magazine to find her childhood friend and suitor staring moodily back at her, usually at some elite party or other, surrounded by the very beautiful and the very rich, yet still seeming apart from them. Looking closely at his eyes, she would fancy she could see his loneliness, and would quickly would turn the page, brow creasing into a frown of confused emotion.

Despite the social circles Jack moved in, he'd never married. On the few occasions he returned home, Reuben would watch him, wondering if his heart still ached for Sally, but never, by word or deed or look, did Jack ever indicate his regard for Sally was now anything other than that of devoted friend and family member.

Reuben shifted in his chair again, wondering if it was time to go and check the joint, but feeling so settled that the mere thought of moving exhausted him. His gaze wandered around the garden. He'd lived in this house all his life, save for the first five years of his marriage, when he and Sally had rented the tiny cottage Wally Twitchett had formerly lived in.

At the memory, Reuben's eyebrows twitched with amusement, another topic of fervent and excited gossip amongst the villagers, when Wally Twitchett and Dorcas Blunt, a mere three months after the funeral of her husband Amos, shocked the village to the core by openly setting up house together.

To help Dorcas run the pub, was the official reason why Wally had given up the tenancy of his cottage and moved into The White Hind. But, it soon became common knowledge he shared her bed, and, for a few weeks, tongues wagged fast and furious.

Undaunted, Wally and Dorcas held their heads high, openly meeting the eyes of their most vocal detractors. Gradually, the gossip died down, until the couple became accepted and when Wally finally died last year at the ripe old age of ninety, all had mourned with Dorcas, none being surprised a mere two weeks later when she sat down in her chair one day and never got up again. Aneurysm said the doctor. Broken heart, declared the village. Reuben, having witnessed the love shining between the pair, was forced to agree.

He and Sally lived happily in the tiny cottage until more babies began arriving and conditions quickly became extremely cramped. Finally, his parents stated their intention of moving into the village, offering them the larger, more comfortable cottage traditionally afforded to the forester and his family.

Reuben sighed and stretched, feeling once more a twinge of cramp, rubbing at his chest, and wondering if he should take something for indigestion before lunch. His eyes threatened to close again, and crossly he pulled himself upright. It wouldn't do to doze off and let the meat burn, Sally would never forgive him.

"Reuben," the soft sigh of his name from the direction of the Forest had him opening his eyes, peering curiously into its bewitchingly dark and leafy realms.

"Who's there?" he called. There was no reply, only a long drawn out sigh which could have been a sudden, gentle breeze, but it wafted a perfume, subtle and achingly familiar to his nose, and the memory he'd groped after for so many years was suddenly close.

Slowly, Reuben climbed to his feet, noticing with a tinge of surprise that the perpetual stiffness and pain he'd carried around for years was gone. For the first time since he'd been shot, he remembered what it felt like to be young and supple, to be able to move easily and quickly, with no fear of painful reprisals.

"Hello?" He let himself through the gate, stepping amongst the trees and feeling the temperature drop, relishing its cool shadiness after the direct heat of the garden.

She stood before him, long silvery hair rippling over her shoulders like quicksilver. Memory came flooding back, and his heart bounded with joy.

"Sylvie?" he could barely contain his disbelief and elation. "I remember you." he exclaimed. "How could I have forgotten you?"

"It was as it was meant to be," she replied, her voice light and gentle, laying a tiny hand on his cheek. "But it has felt so long," she sighed. "Oh my love, so long, my heart trembles to be with you."

"Can I come with you this time?" he asked anxiously, smiling with relief when she nodded, her beautiful eyes filled with love and passion for him.

"Yes, it is time, I have fulfilled my promise. The timelines have been repaired. All that should have been has now come to pass. Now, finally, it is our turn."

"What about them?" he asked, gesturing vaguely towards the cottage, dimly aware that back there, lay love, family, duty and commitment.

"They will do very well," she reassured him. "They are bound tightly with chains of love and loyalty. The wheel has come full circle. This time, all shall be as it should have been. As it was always meant to have been, all those centuries ago."

"What about that?"

Reuben looked curiously at himself lying slumped in the garden chair, hand clenched into a fist on his chest, face stiffly frozen into an expression of incredulous surprise.

"You will not need that any more, my love," Sylvie promised, dismissing his discarded body with an airy wave of her hand. "Come," she commanded, and held out her hand.

Hesitating only a moment, Reuben took it. Gently, she led him away deep into the Forest, the trees closed behind them, and all was still and silent again...

Should she really feel life was done with her, Sally thought dejectedly. Was this small mundane existence really all she could look forward to? Fiercely resisting attempts by her family and the village to banish her into the realms of elderly widow, I'm only forty-six she'd crossly object, Sally wished desperately for something to happen, unsure exactly what form that something should take.

She'd been happy with her lot, contented with the quiet, simple routine she and Reuben had fallen into. If perhaps sometimes she'd longed for a little more excitement in her life, she'd quickly snapped herself out of such silliness by close involvement with her children's lives, in the chaotic whirlwind weddings and the birth of children inevitably caused.

Now, exactly one year after Reuben's death, Sally found herself in a rut, not knowing what she wanted from life. Merely knowing she wanted more.

Reuben. Sally shifted uncomfortably on the firm, wooden bench the family had placed at the edge of the graveyard, eyes boring into the clean, white surface of the erect headstone, reading abstractedly the names and dates engraved in black upon its surface.

What a shock it'd been, that blazing hot Sunday last year, when they'd returned home to discover the beef smoking in the oven; Jackie's scream of disbelief when she'd run out to surprise her father with her early arrival and discovered Reuben's body slumped in a chair in the garden.

Sally remembered being engulfed in a waxy numbness which gripped her through the necessary awfulness which follows a death, and the busyness of the funeral, until it'd released her the night she was first left alone in their bed, in the home they'd shared for twenty years. The house in which their children had been raised and married from, leaving the nest with confident steps and barely a backwards glance, knowing behind them lay a permanently open door and open hearts. Finally, Sally realised her utter and complete aloneness, grief striking with a hammer like blow.

Forty-six. It was no age to die. Cardiac arrest, the doctor had said, caused by the failure of a heart already weakened so many years previously. It was also no age to be left, bereft and alone, unsure what to do with her life.

Sally had mourned Reuben. All through the long, bitterly cold winter which followed, she'd felt her own heart lay encased under deposits of thick ice. Then Spring had arrived, and with it the first tentative buds of recovery.

Now, she sat alone by his grave as she did every Sunday after church, taking a few moments to visit with him, strangely comforted by the rustling presence of the Forest behind her, that sensation she was being watched from its mysterious depths by benign eyes.

"Oh, Reuben," she whispered sadly. "I need your advice. What shall I do now? I'm not old, but feel my life is over, and know that I face the very real danger of slipping into old age, of allowing years to wash over me until suddenly I'll wake up, realising I'm old and that I've wasted my life. Tell me, my darling, what shall I do?"

She closed her eyes and felt his presence. It was no surprise. Many times over the past year, Sally had imagined his comforting warmth, heard his breathing and seen his shadow, knowing it to be a mere fancy of her mind, yet still being comforted by it. But this… this bulk by her shoulder, this touch on her hand, this sense he was sitting there beside her was different, was alarmingly real. She opened her eyes, gazed into his loving, grey regard.

"Hello, Sally…"

"Reuben?" she blinked, aware she was dreaming, had to be, had perhaps slipped into a drowsy state, lulled by the warmth of the sun and the melancholy tilt of her thoughts.

"It's time to move on, Sally," he said.

"I don't understand," she shook her head in confusion. "I don't know what you mean…"

"You will," he promised, and smiled his habitual, slow, gentle smile which she'd missed so much. "Open your heart, Sally," he ordered. "Open your heart to what can be…"

A rook flew from a nearby tree, squawking indignation to the sky. Startled, Sally looked, automatically tracking its progress, and when she turned back, he'd gone.

A long shadow fell over the gravestone.

Sally jumped in anticipation, almost expecting to see him again, shading her eyes as she turned to look directly into the sun at the looming, black figure which had appeared silently behind her.

"Jack," she exclaimed, almost in disappointment, heart still skipping with shock. "You startled me. Where did you come from?"

"I went to the cottage," he explained, sitting carefully beside her. "Sylvia said you'd be here. She also said to remind you, lunch in thirty minutes."

Sally nodded, struggling to regain her scattered wits, strangely shy and tongue tied with the man who, apart from Reuben, knew her better than any other. Perhaps it was because she'd not seen him for almost a year, not since Reuben's funeral, when he'd helped carry his best friend's coffin to this very grave, had stood staring at it through the interment, face bleak and shuttered, before throwing her the briefest of farewells and walking abruptly away. Away from the grave, the churchyard and the village. Away from her.

"How long are you here for?" she asked, hating the banality of small talk as it slipped past her lips. Beside her, Jack shifted almost irritably on the bench.

"The weekend," he replied. She nodded. A silence, stiff and awkward, fell upon them. Sally despaired that they'd been reduced to this. Two strangers with nothing left to say to one another.

"Do you still miss him?" Jack asked unexpectedly. For a moment, so scattered and random were Sally's thoughts, she didn't understand his meaning.

"Reuben? Yes, of course I miss him, very much. He's always been a part of my life, as you have. When he died…"

"Have I waited long enough?" Jack's impassioned interruption stopped Sally in her tracks.

"Waited? I don't… what do you mean, Jack?"

"Oh, Sally," Jack grasped her hand, face set with such an intensity of spirit, Sally bit her lip in sudden, agonised realisation. "Don't you know?" he implored. "How could you not know?"

"Know? Know what?" Sally faltered, a tiny, quiet voice insisting, yes, she did know.

"How much I love you. How much I've always loved you. All these years, there's not been anyone else for me. I waited. For you, Sally. I waited for you. But, I loved Reuben too, couldn't wish him any unhappiness, certainly didn't want him to die. Last year at his funeral, I was so angry and disgusted with myself. Because the whole time, even though I was missing him, mourning him… he was my best friend… when he died, it was… awful. But at the same time, I couldn't stop thinking about you, Sally."

He dropped her hand, half turned away, rubbing a shaking palm over his still handsome face, the fleeting, desperate thought occurring to Sally how attractive he still was, the Jack of her memories. Only here now.

"You stood there, so pale and solemn dressed in black. I wanted you so badly. Wanted to carry you away with me. Take you and show you the world! There's so much world out there, Sal. So much you've never seen or even dreamt of. I wanted to give it all to you. But I couldn't. I knew it was too soon. So I left. I would've stayed away longer, but last week I had the most curious dream. I saw Reuben. I swear to you Sally, it felt as real as my talking to you now does. I saw him. He spoke to me. He told me to come home. Told me to come to you. So I did. Mad isn't it, to act on a dream? But, I did. Here I am. And, oh... what I need to know, Sally, is... have I waited long enough?"

For a long moment, Sally was silent, thoughts in a whirl, the encounter with Reuben fresh and green in her mind. She thought about the Forest, about its strange powers and wondered. All through the long years, her marriage to Reuben, their children, their lives so inexplicably tangled up together, had Sally ever allowed the smallest tinge of regret at her decision to creep into her heart?

No, she decided firmly. She'd loved Reuben. It'd been the right choice, the safe path. Since the marriages of her children, Jackie to Jolyon, Luke and Sylvia to Molly and Joe Blacksmith; Sally had seen so many circles completed, had sensed the natural order of things being righted. She'd come to believe she could've chosen none other than Reuben. That forces other than herself had played a hand in turning her heart towards him, eschewing the passion given by Jack, the love offered by Jolyon.

Although, hadn't some secret and forbidden part of her wondered? Hadn't events witnessed in the Forest that long ago, never forgotten night, returned to her in dreams? Hadn't her body warmed to the memory of Jack, the passion of his touch?

Sally turned to him, her answer in her eyes, and saw his face break with relief, the dazed wonder reflected in his look. Cautiously, fearfully, he reached for her, half afraid, the enforced disguising of his true feelings a hard habit to break after a quarter of a century.

Laughter bubbled in Sally's throat, finally she was free to touch him, to love him. He laughed with her as she pulled his lips to hers, and suddenly life was spread out before her like a sumptuous feast, full of fascinating and exciting possibilities. She felt young and carefree again.

They stood, no words being needed. He offered her his hand, and without hesitation she took it, at last the final circle was complete.

Within the Forest, the watchers moved away, content.

The End...

~ About the Author ~

Julia Blake lives in the beautiful historical town of Bury St. Edmunds, deep in the heart of the county of Suffolk in the UK, with her daughter, one crazy cat and a succession of even crazier lodgers.

Julia leads a busy life, juggling working and family commitments with her writing, and has a strong internet presence, loving the close-knit and supportive community of fellow authors she has found on social media and promises there are plenty more books in the pipeline.

She's been writing all her life, but only recently took herself seriously enough to consider being published. Her first novel, The Book of Eve, has met with worldwide critical acclaim, and since then, Julia has released the epic novel, Becoming Lili, a coming of age, ugly duckling tale. Eclairs for Tea and other stories, a delightful collection of short stories, flash fiction and quirky poems. Lost & Found, a punchy, fast-paced, romantic suspense. Fixtures & Fittings, its exciting and heart-warming sequel, and Erinsmore, a fantasy novel of dragons and quests in the style of Narnia. Her ecological sci-fi novella, Lifesong, is also causing a stir with its powerful, environmental message.

Julia says: "I write the kind of books I like to read myself, warm and engaging novels, with strong, three dimensional characters you can really connect with."

~ A Note from Julia ~

If you have enjoyed this book, why not take a few moments to leave a review on Amazon or Goodreads?

It needn't be much, just a few lines saying you liked the book and why, yet it can make a world of difference.

Reviews are the readers way of letting the author know they enjoyed their book, and of letting other readers know the book is an enjoyable read and why. It also informs Amazon that this is a book worth promoting, and the more reviews a book receives, the more Amazon will recommend it to other readers.

I would really be very grateful and would like to say thank you for reading my book and if you spare a few minutes of your time to review it, I do see, read and appreciate every single review left for me.

Best Regards

Julia Blake